Dream into Amethyst

By M. De Armas

Copyright ©2024 Line By Lion Publications
www.pixelandpen.studio
ISBN 978-1948807784
Cover Design by Thomas Lamkin Jr.
Editing by Dani J. Caile

LINE BY LION
PUBLICATIONS

For papi.
Your passing awakened the writer in me and created the sanctuary where this story was born.

GEMMA

MOUNTAINS
OF ALEXANDRTIE

OPAL DESERT

Chapter One

The trouble with dreams, for many, is the way the outside world always bleeds into them, diluting the magic with the mundane. But since this school year began, Melissa has had the opposite problem.

The extraordinary and outlandish world she dreaded and longed for interrupted the routine of her life: dreams of a magical world her abuelito told her about before bedtime. She was already a heavy daydreamer, but these recurring dreams filled her with endless wonder.

In her dreams, she could feel the warmth of the bright sun as it shone on a field of colorful sunflowers. She could hear the far-off calls of winged horses gliding through a periwinkle sky, and she felt a shiver of fear at the thought of sea serpents breaching in an ocean as blue as a sapphire stone.

The sweet smell of rain filled Melissa, and she hummed a 'mhm' sound. Her hands searched for soft sheets but grasped onto something else. She peeked an eye open to find herself lying in a bed of tall grass surrounded by emerald sunflowers.

She jerked upward, her heart pulsing with excitement. The light breeze danced through her dark-ash hair, tickling her cheeks; she looked up and blinked against the periwinkle sky.

Another gust of wind blew, and all at once, the sunflowers' colors rippled from indigo to crimson, then emerald, and settled in sapphire. She stretched her neck and sniffed one flower nearby; the whiff of ocean breeze washed away the smell of petrichor.

She sprang up and staggered, eager to seek Alisha, the supposed messenger who appears midway through her dreams. The tall grass caused her to walk with a wobble on the rolling hills, her fingers caressing the petals with every step.

Images flooded Melissa's memories: she was a child, sprinting away from something while holding a ruby sunflower. *Is this a memory?* she pondered, but the voice of her cynic best friend, Emmy, lingered. "You're missing Pipo's stories," Melissa shook her head.

But then the past words of Alisha, "worlds away," echoed in her mind, and a bit of hope glimmered inside her. *Have I been there before?* she thought, biting her lower lip. *Or is this really just a reimagining of Pipo's storytelling?*

A herd of ivory-white and midnight-black horses sprinted in front of Melissa, startling her so much that she lost her footing and toppled on her behind. When she stood back up, her lips curled into a half-smile. She marveled at the herd as they galloped with grace and beauty.

The horses had a silver spiraling horn attached to their head, and she exclaimed, "Unicorns!" She had seen winged horses soar before but never unicorns. Rooted where she stood, she observed them graze on the grass and felt tempted to approach them.

Just as she moved towards the creatures, an arrow pierced through the neck of a unicorn, and it bellowed in pain. Blood gushed, spraying the grass in crimson red, and Melissa shrieked, "No!"

The other unicorns whinnied before sprinting away and leaving their wounded mate on the ground. She dashed towards the wounded animal, and her eyes searched for the direction the arrow had come from.

Her eyes caught a hooded figure wearing a black velvet cloak. It pulled out another arrow, and just as its fingers released their grip, Melissa pounced in front of the injured unicorn to shield it. She flung her arms over her head to cover it and was ready to receive the arrow that would penetrate her chest.

But the arrow passed through her body like she was mist and struck the unicorn whose wails echoed in the meadow, piercing Melissa's ears. Shocked, she slipped to her knees and watched the magical animal take its final breath.

She croaked, "No," her tears threatening to spill, "I'm so sorry. I-I... I don't even know how that was possible?" Blood soaked the unicorn's silky coat, and her heart ached for the dying unicorn.

She closed her eyes and whimpered as droplets of tears rolled down her cheeks. When she opened her eyes, she was kneeling in the field again, and the unicorn was grazing on the grass as if nothing had happened.

"You risked your life for the unicorn," a voice drifted in the air like a melody, "like a true dragon rider would do."

Melissa scrambled off the ground and found herself face-to-face with stormy gray eyes staring directly into Melissa's own: red, puffy and coffee-brown. She stepped back from the woman in a white lace dress; her silky blond hair reached her chest, and her pale-white skin glowed.

"Alisha!" Melissa hiccupped, "What just happened?"

"I allowed you to witness an exiled being attacking the animals belonging to the Kingdom of Amethyst."

"Why? Why would they want to hurt that poor unicorn?"

"Because they are vile beings. It is in their nature to commit cruel acts. It is your job as a dragon rider to protect the Kingdom from them." Alisha responded with such simplicity that Melissa was unsure if she should take her seriously. "You see," Alisha gestured for Melissa to sit with her in the meadow, "because you are not here, the enemies are taking bolder steps, coming into the Kingdom and attacking. It is time for you to come home. If you are not here, I fear there may be a war."

"War?! I don't want that to happen! And you keep saying it as if it's my fault bad guys are raiding. I want to be here, and I wanna be able to torch problems. I don't know how to come here, and I'm not even sure this world exists!"

"You do not remember your dragon, do you?" Melissa knitted her brow, shaking her head.

"You used to come to Gemma, and you and your dragon were inseparable."

Melissa scoffed, "I'm sure I would've remembered I had a dragon."

"Not if your memories were affected after that mysterious illness you had when you were three." Alisha's smile wavered.

"How do you know that?" Melissa muttered.

Alisha inhaled and elevated her pointy chin, responding, "The danger is very real, and if we cannot bring you here soon, the enemies will surge the Kingdom of Amethyst. You must find the boy who lives worlds away. He is the key for you to enter Gemma." Melissa pressed her lips and let Alisha's words sink in. Her eyes caught the pointy end of Alisha's ears, and she tilted her head.

"You're... an elf?" Alisha curled her lips into a sly smile, and Melissa opened her mouth to speak, but instead of words flowing from her lips, she mimicked her alarm clock. Her head bounced back until she realized she was waking up.

*   *   *

She tossed and turned in the bed, trying to immerse in the magical world again, but returning to her dream was impossible. She stumbled towards her computer desk and slumped on her swivel chair.

On her desk was a round dragon pendant, a list with the words scribbled, "Clothes to buy for the Boone trip," a jar labeled 'fairy dust,' and a book titled 'Monsterology.' She rummaged through it until she found her journal.

The journal appeared to be a regular composition notebook, but inside, it contained all the details of her recurring dreams so reminiscent of her abuelo's storytelling.

She snatched a pencil nearby and wrote on a new sheet: October 12, 2006.

It happened again. I've been dreaming about my abuelo's made-up world for two months. First, I was lying in the meadow, admiring the red petals that turned green, then blue on the sunflowers and the periwinkle sky. Then BOOM! For the first time, I saw someone kill a unicorn! Then Alisha appeared right after! Whenever I saw her, I wondered how someone could be so flawless? And that's when I noticed the sharp, pointy end of her ears. She's a friggin' elf! But before I could process this new revelation, I woke up... she repeated the same thing as the last few encounters. It's always, "Come home,

dragon rider. Without your presence, your Kingdom is vulnerable. Your dragon misses you dearly. You have been gone far too long."
And now she mentioned a war! Maybe I'm investing in these dreams too much.

It'd be dope if I had a dragon. I'd scorch all the problems I have in my life. And all my homework too... She keeps saying I need to find the boy who lives 'worlds away.' Whatever that means... It'd be nice if my abuelo's world were real. Everything he described about Gemma, a realm hidden on Earth where mythological beasts exist, sounds amazing. I wonder if that's how he envisioned it when he told me the stories.

Whenever I wake up from my dreams, I remember the emptiness I felt after his disappearance. I miss his stories. His lullaby. His voice. Gosh, I remember he used to tell me I'd one day grow to be a dragon rider meant to fight evil ogres and goblins in Gemma. If this world was real, the empty void in my heart may finally disappear.

She felt tears clinging to the corner of her eyes like she did every time she wrote about her abuelito. So she dropped her pen, shut her journal, and hid it in a false bottom drawer. A wave of sorrow washed over her, leading her to open another drawer for a photo.

Her breath hitched once she found it. There was a heaviness in her heart contrasted by a smile when she gazed at the black-and-white photo featuring her abuelo, Pipo, his two older brothers, Pablo and Patricio, and Paloma, her abuela, whom she never got to meet.

She observed Pipo: he was in his mid-thirties, but despite the hunger and poverty he fought against in Cuba, his body was lean and muscular. In the background was a rickety raft-like boat, and based on the sunken look on their faces and dark circles beneath their eyes, they had just arrived in Florida after their harrowing escape from Cuba.

Memories of Pipo retelling the story of his journey from Cuba to Florida brought a smile to Melissa's face because he swore he fought a Kraken along the way.

First, he'd described the unforgivable waves and how they easily tossed the raft. Then, he'd explain how a giant tentacle breached the water to grasp their rickety vessel. This story resonated with Melissa. Ever since she could remember, Pipo told her tales of dragons and beasts living in the magical world of Gemma.

Pipo always told her he, too, was a dragon rider and that Melissa was next in line to ride a dragon; it's how her love of lore and magic came to be. When her mother opened her desk drawers, she found them loaded with mythological studies and beasts. But her favorite were the mythical creatures of the air: griffins, hippogriffs, and winged horses.

But dragons captivated her heart. She would often imagine herself riding a fire-breathing dragon. This fascination was so intense that she had even created an imaginary friend named Jake, a vibrant red dragon with a spirited personality. They would play together in her yard, bringing her fantasies to life.

Pipo used to take her horseback riding down in the south of Florida, encouraging her to believe she was riding a dragon. There was no doubt Melissa was a hardcore dreamer and a believer in magic, but even she felt Pipo took it too far with the horses.

It didn't matter, though, because she went with it anyway.

Her finger traced her abuelito, and as she did, the corner

of her lip curled, and her eyes brimmed with tears. She pressed
them shut, wiped the tears before they could fall, and took a
deep breath before getting up and slouching her way to the
bathroom.

Her mind still dawdling on Alisha's words, "Come
home. Your Kingdom is vulnerable." She couldn't wrap her
mind around the idea someone, much less an entire kingdom,
needed her. The images of the unicorn dying before she
flickered, and her heart sank. She shook her head and splashed
her face with warm water; she combed her unkempt dark-ash
hair and put it up in a tight ponytail that revealed her diamond-
shaped face.

Bah, she thought, inspecting her face in the mirror. *My
chin is sooo pointy.* She refused to continue to watch her
reflection and headed to the closet to change into her school
uniform: khaki pants and a navy blue collar shirt neatly tucked
under her black belt. Her uniform was only complete once she
added her worn-out faux leather combat boots.

Just as she was about to leave her room, she looked at
herself one last time in the mirror. She surveyed her bony body
and pinched her arms, attempting to find some fat. The
nagging, negative voice in her head reminded her she was too
skinny.

"I need to get active again," she mumbled. She often
yearned to leave the same four walls she caged herself in most
of the time, but she had no energy to do so and no one to
encourage her to venture out of the house.

When Pipo was around, he placed her in mixed martial
arts and occasionally took her abuelo horseback riding. He was
involved with wrestling in Havana, Cuba, and was a well-

known fighter in his village. According to Melissa's mother, it's how he met Paloma, the beginning of an epic love story.

He had Melissa join MMA; like him, she fell in love with the sport. She loved boxing, kickboxing, judo, and jiu-jitsu. Melissa felt better about herself when she was active in MMA. Now, she has struggled to find herself since the disappearance of Pipo.

Like her abuelo, Melissa was a natural-born prodigy in the martial arts. Her veins surged with adrenaline in the ring, and her coach, who was none other than Pipo, would cheer her on as she fought round after round.

She missed those simple times.

The warm, nutty aroma of coffee filled her nose, causing her stomach to growl. She darted out of her room and into the kitchen, where Melissa's mother prepared a breakfast of sunny-side-up eggs and oatmeal. A headband pulled back her shoulder-length hair, and she wore royal blue scrubs.

"Buenos dias," her mother sang.

"Good morning, Mami," Melissa replied as she pulled out a chair to sit.

"Here's your favorite." Her mother handed her a mug filled with cafe con leche: warm milk blended with espresso and two spoons of sugar.

The rich scent of coffee caused her stomach to rumble again, and she blew on it before sipping its sugary sweetness. Her stomach craved the cafe con leche, but eating actual food was dreadful. Her longing for Pipo brought sadness and anxiety, and it would ruin her appetite.

"Did you wake up hungry today?" her mother asked when she sat down across from her. She sipped on her cafe con leche.

M . D e A r m a s | 11

"Um, yeah," Melissa shrugged her shoulders.

Hungry? Nah, more like empty, she thought as she forced herself to eat the eggs, *but how can I ever tell my mom how I feel? How do I tell her I'm not really hungry? Or that I don't have energy and that I just want to escape into my dreams and never wake up?* Her mother had endured so much already. Three years after they presumed her abuelo dead, Melissa's mother worked double shifts at the cleaning company to afford the roof over their heads. Her mother carried the weight of all the financial burdens in the house, reflecting her physical appearance.

Her once soft hands were now coarse and rough. Her hazel eyes had dark circles beneath them that only seemed darker as time passed.

Melissa couldn't prevent her mind from spiraling into a darkness of her own fears. *If Pipo were still here, maybe she wouldn't be working as hard as she is now. What if something happens to her?* The mere thought of losing her mother caused her heart to pound against her chest. The familiar feeling of panic was creeping into her mind and taking control.

"Hey, what are you thinking about?" her mother asked and waved a hand over Melissa's dazed look.

"Nothing," Melissa's voice squeaked. It always did that when she lied, and her mother knew it. She cleared her throat before responding, "I am thinking of our trip to Boone. We have to buy gloves and scarves."

At the mention of Boone, a pained look crossed her mother's face, and Melissa felt her stomach drop.

What was that look? Whatever appetite she had vanished at that moment. Her mother had promised to take Melissa to Boone this winter break to visit her family, whom she hadn't seen for so long. When Melissa was six, Pipo's brother, Pablo, moved his entire family to Boone.

"We're still going, right?!" she asked, crippled with anxiety.

Her mother sighed, "Well, I wanted to talk to you this morning about that." But Melissa shook, and she spoke before letting her mother continue.

"I get it, Mami. I know we can't go."

This trip would have cost us an arm and a leg. I knew better than to hope for a trip like this.

But a smile that seemed to start in her mother's squinty, hazel eyes crept over her before she said, "Actually, I'm not going... but you still are."

"Wait, what?" Melissa's head bounced back.

"Yeah, your sister doesn't want to go since she wants to stay here with her boyfriend, and Uncle Rudy and Aunt Nina are still going, so they offered to take you. You can go with them as long as you promise me you'll improve your grades and do your chores."

A wave of relief washed over Melissa; she yearned to escape the city of Miami and the same four walls of her room that held so much sadness.

"I hate I won't be going," her mother continued, and Melissa worked up a weak smile, "but since you will not have a quince, it's the least I can do."

In reality, Melissa cared little for a 'quinces,' or Quinceanera, the Latin celebration of a young girl transitioning into a young lady. Melissa's classmates were talking about all the ideas for pictures and parties.

Even her own best friend was boasting about her quince. But Melissa was content not having a quince because she despised being the center of attention—a side effect of her withdrawal from social situations.

Her mother said, "I want you to have some adventure too and see the family." Her mother giggled to herself, and Melissa tilted her head, "Do you remember Pipo used to say they moved worlds away? Pfft, your abuelo was something else."

Mid-bite, Melissa's thoughts drifted to Alisha's repeated insistence on finding a boy worlds away. *Impossible! That can't be a coincidence! What if... the dreams were more than fantasies?* Her mother's voice pierced through, jolting her back to reality.

"You know, I want you to go too because I don't want to be the reason you don't have fun. It's that..." Melissa's mother hesitated before saying, "I almost lost you once."

Ohhhhhh, my goodness, Melissa thought and muted her mother's voice. *Here we go again. She never lets me forget.*

"You got that nasty virus and were in a coma for two days!" Her mother winced, retelling the story. "You were only three. Pipo and I have never been so scared. We thought you were going to die. The doctors couldn't figure out what was wrong."

How many times do I have to hear this story? Melissa pondered. *Wait a minute, Alisha said an illness affected my memories... what if?*

"Mami," she interrupted her mother who looked up puzzled, "Pardon for interrupting you. But did I lose any memories or anything like that after I woke up from the coma?"

Her mother pondered for a moment, and a flicker of realization flashed in her eyes. "You did, actually. You couldn't remember certain things." Her mother continued recalling the incident while Melissa's mind spiraled.

Whoa, Gemma is real! That means I need to get it together and save the Kingdom of Amethyst! Realizing Alisha knew about her illness and her potential memory loss, a surge of energy fueled her.

As her mind continued spiraling, she felt the usual slap on the back of her head and her sister's familiar annoying, shrill voice shouting, "Buenos dias!" to mask Melissa's painful grunt. Victoria served herself a shot of espresso and chugged it before mocking her little sister, "Awe, the baby is drinking her leche."

"Nice to see you in high spirits," Melissa remarked.

Victoria glared at her and scorned, "Well, someone has to remind you to toughen up. Mom is already babying you by reminding the world you almost died one time."

"I am so glad you're not going to Boone with me," Melissa mumbled.

"Excuse me-" Victoria said, but their mother interfered.

"Victoria! Melissa!" she barked. "Basta! Can you girls please try to get along for once?" she muttered in Spanish.

Melissa clearly heard her, though, and understood what she said: they'd disappoint Pipo if he saw them arguing like now. They bickered before, but it's only gotten worse, and it only added shame to the anxiety she was already feeling.

For a moment, she imagined Pipo sitting at the dinner table reading the Miami Herald while chugging a shot of espresso. Her mother then interrupted her thoughts to ask if she was ready for school.

"Yeah," she responded dully. She stood up and slung her busted Jansport backpack that weighed her down, making her feel like a horse wearing a harness.

Ugh, she briefly thought, *it's no wonder people have back pains nowadays.* "Victoria," her mother said. "I'm giving you some cash so you can pass by the market and pick up some food." Victoria grunted, and Melissa couldn't help but snicker. Her sister shot her a glare and hissed, "What? You got something to say, Casper?" *What a low blow!*

Victoria knew Melissa was sensitive about her appearance. Melissa sullenly looked at her pale white hands. Compared to her sister's and mother's honey-colored skin, she was the whitest of her family.

Do I even belong to this family? Melissa bit her lower lip. *Well, Mom said Dad was white like me.* She caught herself imagining scenarios of what her life could have been like if her father never died in a car accident on the day of her birth.

Maybe she wouldn't have low self-esteem like she does now, and maybe her mother wouldn't have aged so fast. Maybe her family may have been in a better financial state. Perhaps even Victoria wouldn't have been as cruel as she is now. She wondered if Pipo would have been as involved in her life. Since her dad's passing, Pipo was the one who raised her, cared for her, and disciplined her. Would she be different if her father had been in the picture?

The only thing she knew of her biological father was, like Pipo, he was from Havana, Cuba. But unlike Pipo who escaped in a raft, he was exiled to America due to a political arrest for sabotaging a factory, thus going against the Cuban government.

Her father was lucky enough to be deported to the United States. He never returned, as do most Cubans in similar situations, since he was afraid of being entrapped on the island again.

Even though based on her mother's stories, he missed his native land dearly. All his family was still there since he was the only one who came to America. Melissa and Victoria had never met them physically, but their mother often sent photos of the girls to his family, and they sent photos as well.

To Melissa, her father was Pipo, but not to Victoria. Her sister had a different dad. Her sister never touched the subject of their father. She'd shut down the conversation or make a snarky remark.

Victoria pushed back her long, curly, raven hair, and Melissa scanned her features: yes, she had honey-colored skin like her mother, but where did her oval brown eyes, round-dimpled face, and button nose come from? Even Victoria's plump lips made Melissa feel paper-thin.

Examining Victoria's beauty heightened Melissa's insecurities. That was the cherry on top of her anxiety. *She's the one who doesn't look like she belongs in this family*, Melissa scoffed. There was no doubt Victoria was beautiful, and she wielded her beauty like a weapon.

"Alright, Victoria, please don't forget the food. By the way, don't you have a big midterm you need to study for?" her mother nagged, and Victoria rolled her eyes. "Mh-hmm, remember our deal? You don't pay bills here because you go to school, don't slip."

Melissa let out the same mm-hmm sound she made, but her mother glared at her next, "And you, if I get one more call that you're distracted in class, I will ground you. C'mon, let's go, or you'll be late for school."

Her mother gestured for her to hurry to the car, and they drove off in a red Toyota Camry whose engine made a funny noise and carried scars from an accident. Melissa placed a hand under a chin and watched outside the window as they drove off from their mustard-color, one-story house. Their house was dirt-speckled, discarded car parts -relics from Pipo- strewn around the porch, and a tree that had dispersed rotten mangoes throughout the lawn.

Melissa looked away with disgust, embarrassed to call this place her home. *Maybe this weekend I'll clean it up*, Melissa thought. *Why can't there be a magic wand so I could abracadabra it and make it brand new?*

She wanted to help, but whenever the weekend came, she trapped herself in her room and listened to music, read books on legends and myths, or journaled her thoughts. Her mother used to have this house spotless when Pipo was around, and she used to garden so much.

Maybe I can convince Victoria to build a garden for her. Ugh, but what's the point? She's going to shut the idea down like she always does. Her mind wandered off again while her eyes became lost in the clouds. One cloud reminded her of a frog, and she fantasized about turning Victoria into a toad.

As she gazed out the window and watched the bustling street of her city, Melissa pondered on Alisha's words. She wondered if the coma had any link to Gemma.

The idea of having a dragon fueled her desire to escape Miami and enter Gemma. She longed for adventure and purpose.

They pulled up to the high school only ten blocks from her home. Melissa jumped at a sudden knock on her mother's window. A short, plump Afro-Cuban girl greeted her mother with a traditional Hispanic cheek-kiss.

She had frizzy brunette hair, and her excited smile showed off her braces. Melissa's mood brightened at seeing her best friend.

Melissa hopped out of the car, and Emmy flung an arm

around her neck. "Hey, girl!" Emmy squealed.

"Hey!" Melissa hesitated to fling her arms in return. Any physical affection made her feel instantly awkward. Her sister, as had their mother, had always been cold with her, but Pipo was the only one who showed physical affection.

She awkwardly wrapped an arm around Emmy's neck and left a chunk of space between her arm and neck.

Emmy then handed her a white paper bag; inside it was a Cuban dessert delight: pastelito de guayaba y queso. It was an iconic puff pastry filled with guava and cream cheese. Melissa's mouth watered when the fruity scent filled her nostrils.

"You are the best!" Melissa squealed.

"I know," Emmy winked. She waved hello to Melissa's mother and added, "Hey! So, my mom is doing a double shift, and I was wondering if I could come to your house today?"

"Emmy, you're always welcome to the house. Maybe you can get Melissa to do her homework early."

"Ugh," Melissa groaned.

"Will do! Thanks!" Emmy raised a thumb. The girls turned around and walked towards the school's double doors.

Teenagers crowded the hallway and chit-chatted by their navy-blue lockers about homework, exams, or their raging hormones. Melissa did not want to get dragged into any of those conversations. The effort of faking interest in the latest gossip seemed exhausting.

Her high school was a moderately sized public school that looked rustic and needed renovation. There were a few rust spots on the door hinges, dents in the lockers, and the desks suffered cracks and chips from teenage boys' horseplay. Yet, the school had decent ratings, overzealous teachers, and a plethora of clubs and sports available.

Her sister boasted about being a cheerleader in high school and being one of the popular kids. Being popular was the last thing on her mind. With time, her insecurities overpowered her like a strong current.

It affected the way she acted in front of people. She lacked confidence and over-analyzed conversations. Sometimes she hated herself for it. She remembered feeling her veins pump when she had to fight in the ring. The cheers from people fed her adrenaline. She was powerful and confident, but that was a different Melissa.

"Guy," Emmy bugged, "I was worrying you would be late even though I reminded you several times we would host the TV news today!" A few of their friends from TV production greeted them here and there as they made their way through the crowded hallway.

"Oh yeah, I am so stoked," Melissa remarked while stuffing her face with the pastry.

"Melissa, c'mon, this class is important to me. You know my dream to be a TV reporter… Plus, you love journaling. Maybe this class will motivate you to consider journalism as a career."

"Emmy," Melissa sighed. "We're in our freshman year. I'll think about my 'career' when I'm a senior." Melissa quoted career with her fingers, and Emmy rolled her eyes.

After eating her pastelito, Melissa pulled out a thin leather book titled 'Mythical Creatures' to continue her studies of the distinction between mermaids and sirens. "More dragons? Seriously?" Emmy scoffed, and Melissa cracked open the slim book.

"No," Melissa shouted defensively, then muttered, "it's

about mermaids."

"BAH! You and your fantasies. Still using that journal I suggested?" Emmy raised a brow.

"Yup!"

"You see? Future journalist in the making. I'm sure if a career in dragonology existed you wouldn't stop talking about it." Emmy remarked.

"Actually... There is a career called cryptozoology, which studies animals rumored to exist. Kinda like the group of people from that show trying to find Bigfoot!" Emmy's mouth hung low at that comment, but Melissa chuckled, "If a career in dragonology existed, then you already know what major I'd do, hahaha. By the way, last night I dreamt about Gemma again, and I learned Alisha is a friggin elf! If this world is real, I am definitely going to be the one to find them."

"Dude, you are really investing in these dreams, and as your best friend, it is my duty to remind you that these are dreams. You're just a lucid dreamer, that's all."

"Emmy, c'mon, let a girl dream-"

"No-" Emmy snapped and furrowed her brows at Melissa. "There are no dragons, and Pipo definitely did not fight a kraken on his way to Florida." Emmy stumbled upon her words. "You're probably missing Pipo's fun storytelling, and that's why you're having these recurring dreams."

"Maybe not, just maybe his stories of Gemma are real." Melissa retorted to placate Emmy.

"What do you mean 'maybe'? Gosh, you're a hopeless dreamer."

"Better to be a dreamer than a cynic," Melissa attempted to quip back.

"I'm not a 'cynic,'" Emmy looked at her firmly. "I'm a

realist."

Emmy's natural intellect gave her the edge of every discussion between them. Melissa knew better than to push Emmy's buttons. This short friend of hers had a large temper. After all, it was Emmy's intellect that had kept Melissa from failing her classes.

Melissa clicked her tongue and said, "Emmy, don't you remember when we were in third grade and Pipo used to take us to the park? We'd pretend to be princesses in a land of magic-"

"Uh, wait a minute," Emmy interjected, "I'd pretend I was a princess; you were some warrior trying to kill a make-believe ogre, heheh."

"Haha, you're right!" Melissa giggled. ""One time, we even made flower crowns."

"Oh my gosh, that's right! Your mom wanted to kill us because those flowers were from a bouquet of lilies, lavender, and- what was the other flower?"

"White jasmines," Melissa said.

"Yes, those! Pipo got her that mix," the best friends shared a giggle.

"I think my mom threw a chancla at me that day!" Melissa winced, remembering the flying sandal whacking her in the head. "It took Pipo forever to find a flower shop that made the combination."

"Does your mom love all those flowers?" Emmy asked.

"No, she loves lavender, I love lilies, and Victoria loves white jasmine."

"That explains why we only clipped the lilies," Emmy remarked, "but that's sweet of Pipo."

"I know," Melissa murmured, her heart ached thinking

of the small gestures he'd done for his family. A part of her wanted to share this thought with Emmy, but she didn't. Not because she didn't trust her but because it was too painful to admit how deeply she wished he was still around. Opening up to anyone was difficult because she could never find the words to express the empty void inside her.

She'd tried a couple of times to talk to her sister, but her sister shut the conversation down quickly. She'd imagine her saying, "Toughen up big baby, and get over it." *I should get over it,* she thought.

"How old were we?" Emmy asked, snapping Melissa from her thinking.

"Um, eight? I know we'd just became friends 'cause it was third grade,'" Melissa said, scanning Emmy before fixating on a single thin, black thread with an evil eye on it. Melissa arched a brow before exclaiming, "Hey! You wore that bracelet the day we met."

At first, Emmy looked at her bracelet perplexed. But then a cheeky grin crept on her face and she responded, "Oh yeaaaaah, you're right. You have a good memory! That day, you stood up for me in class 'cause everyone laughed when I tried talking in English."

"Ohhhhh, yeah! I hate it when people laugh at English Language Learners. I guess some people think they're entitled since they learn English quickly. Entitled and annoying if you ask me."

When Emmy first arrived from Cuba, Melissa took it upon herself to teach Emmy English, and Emmy picked up the language rather quickly considering its difficulty.

When Emmy first started helping Melissa with her homework, Melissa worried it was out of some misplaced sense of duty to repay her for her help.

But she soon learned that the straight-laced and straight-faced was just Emmy's default setting, and she couldn't help but butt in on Melissa's lackadaisical attitude toward school and everything else for that matter.

Thus making them the perfect complement to each other, even though they had quite opposite personalities. Where Melissa was a carefree, head-in-the-clouds kind of girl, there was Emmy to bring her back to reality. And when Emmy became hopeless with the realities of life, Melissa was the voice to remind her to believe in hope.

Hope is what Melissa often clung to. She hoped her mother didn't have to work as hard. She hoped her sister would one day treat her better. And most of all, she hoped to find the answers to her abuelo's disappearance. But, hoping seemed pointless now.

Her abuelito had been gone for three years now—three long and painful years. Not having the answers felt so unfair and frustrating. She didn't even bother to believe if her dreams were real or not. She didn't want to disappoint herself further. Even though deep down she wondered if they were.

"Hey, you alright?" Emmy asked. Melissa didn't notice how heavy her breathing became.

"Yeah," her voice squeaked. "Um, just thinking about my project with Mia."

"Ugh," Emmy pretended to gag at the sound of Mia. "Don't do the homework for her."

"I know."

The bell rang, and the girls split off to their homerooms and classes.

Chapter Two

If someone were to ask Melissa how her classes had gone today, as usual, she would have nothing of value to say.

She spent most of her time in class lost in her thoughts and doodling a dragon on her papers instead of paying attention to her teacher's notes. She imagined what her dragon would look like and how big it could be if she had one.

As a child, she envisioned her dragon being blood-red and standing on four legs. She wondered if she would have a Chinese dragon or a Wyvern. *Nah, Wyverns have two legs,* her mind wandered.

Her favorite type of dragon was the European dragon because they were typically massive, fire-breathing, scaly, horned lizard-like beasts with bat-like wings, four legs, and a tail. *There we go.* She added a horn to her doodle at the tip of each wing.

She created a bubble thought by the dragons that read "worlds away." Since her mother brought the memory up, she's been reminiscing the times her abuelo would say it. She wanted to be home to search through her journal and reread all the times Alisha mentioned that phrase.

Not only did the phrase haunt her, but so did her memory loss. She wanted more than anything for the dreams to be real. For her abuelo's world to be real. Now, it was becoming too real, and Melissa felt compelled to take action herself.

"Psst." Melissa ignored the call, but her head felt a thump caused by a paper ball. Annoyed, she snapped her head back at the girl and gestured, 'What.'

The girl's skin was fair complexioned, and she had wavy, honey-brown hair with blonde highlights. She whispered, "Have you gotten started on our project?"

"No, Mia," Melissa hissed, "you promised to help."

"Oh, c'mon, Melissa. I have dance practice, and I don't have the time."

NO! Melissa wanted to say but replied, "Fine." She immediately felt weak for giving in so easily.

"Melissa!" The teacher called her attention, and Melissa turned around quickly, "Next time you're distracted, you'll get detention." Melissa sighed; her head hung low as a few classmates snickered.

If I don't focus on this stupid lecture, my mom will take away my trip. Melissa placed the pencil down and placed her hand under her chin to focus. *Why do I need to know the square root of 9? I need to know how to figure out if Gemma is real. And if it is, I'll have my dragon burn any possible math book that exists.*

When the last bell rang for the students to go home, Melissa strolled to the school's patio to meet with Emmy. They socialized with Melissa's TV production classmates for a while. The whole time, Melissa appeared interested.

Right before leaving, Melissa felt a hard tap on her right shoulder; she swirled around to find Mia arching a brow at her. She scowled at Melissa, "You better get started on that project. I don't want to fail."

"I'll get it done," Melissa quipped at the Puerto Rican-American teen. The sound of a deep rumble from an exhaust startled Melissa and Emmy.

Mia snickered, watching them, "That must be my boyfriend picking me up."

"I thought you had dance practice?" Melissa remarked.

"Uh-um, I- do," Mia stumbled on her words. "He's going to watch me practice."

"Um," Emmy interjected, "is that Josh?" Melissa looked over to see a popular senior, Josh, drive up in a red sports car. "Mia, isn't he much older than you? He's like a senior! We're freshmen!"

"And?" Mia responded hastily. "First of all, it's none of your business. Second, who's gonna tell me who to date?" Melissa and Emmy exchanged annoyed looks. "Get it done, Melissa." Mia glanced down at her boots. "Wow, those kicks look used... then again, so do you. Later." Mia hopped in the car and drove off with her boyfriend.

"I'll give you a nice kick," Emmy muttered.

"Just ignore her, Emmy," Melissa said.

"Dude, how are you letting her make you do the project? She clearly doesn't have dance practice and is totally going to take the credit like she normally does. Hello, she's using you!"

"It's not a big deal." Emmy scoffed at the comment. "It's true, she's not gonna do the project, anyway. I enjoy doing nice things for people."

"Melissa, no, you're being used by her c'mon, stop dreaming."

"No." Melissa frowned.

"What do you mean no!?" Emmy spat.

"Maybe one day she'll see how nice I am to her, and she'll be nice to us. Maybe even invite us to one of the senior parties!" She doubted this but refused to give in to Emmy.

Emmy rolled her eyes and facepalmed herself before speaking. "She'll never acknowledge you as a nice person. You gotta learn to stand up for yourself. You did it for me in third grade. Why can't you do it for yourself?"

That last comment stung Melissa. "If I were you, I wouldn't do it all. If you both fail, she'll get in trouble with the dance coach, and you'll get grounded for a few days."

"Emmy, I can't get a bad grade. Otherwise, my mom will cancel my Boone trip." Melissa recapped the Boone trip deal she made with her mother. "I haven't seen my family in such a long time... Pipo used to say they live worlds away-" Melissa paused, realizing her dreams were more than just her imagination running wild at night.

There it is again. I'm hearing it everywhere now.

"Um... Earth to Melissa?" Emmy waved her hand over a dazed Melissa.

"Emmy, I have something crazy to tell you." Melissa's heart pounded against her chest. "So Alisha told me I used to come to Gemma until I was three, but then my memories got affected by an illness! Remember, I was in a coma when I was three?" Emmy nodded, her eyes full of skepticism.

"So, I asked my mom, and she told me I actually forgot a lot of things when I woke up from my coma. That can't be coincidence!"

"Dude," Emmy rolled her eyes. "No way. No one remembers things at three years old."

"Um, yeah they can, I have a superb memory, you said so yourself."

"Then why can't you remember algebraic questions?"

"Because I hate math! Ugh! And anyway, that's not the point. Look, in my past dreams, Alisha has told me I'm supposed to meet a boy worlds away, right? My mom reminded me how Pipo used to say that same thing when my family moved to Boone. I know these dreams are real! And that's my first quest, I *have* to find that boy in Boone!"

"Wow, you're a dreamer." Emmy scoffed at Melissa's epiphany, but Melissa had muted Emmy as her mind raced with hope and excitement.

I need to dream again tonight. I need answers! Melissa swung her book bag over her shoulder, and the girls walked home. When they walked into Melissa's home, the girls gasped with enthusiasm. Sitting down at the kitchen table drinking a shot of colada was one of the most charismatic men they'd ever met.

Jacob came into the Paz-Guerra's lives about a year ago. He began pursuing Victoria after they met at their gym. Jacob swears it was love at first sight, but Victoria admits it took her a while to let him break down her guarded walls. Victoria built walls up after losing her dad, but they only got taller after Pipo's disappearance.

When Melissa first met him, she didn't take long to accept him. The way he spoke confidently and interlocked his eyes with hers in a conversation made her feel comfortable. Even Melissa's mother quickly fell in love with the idea of Jacob being her son-in-law.

Jacob often assisted the family without having to be asked. It came from the good of his heart to buy the family pastelitos or mow the lawn. He listened to Melissa and was attentive in ways Victoria wasn't. Even as simple as asking how her first day of school was. "Jacob!" Melissa exclaimed.

"Hey!" Jacob embraced Melissa with a bear-like hug.

"I want a colada!" Emmy said, hugging Jacob right after.

The Cuban-style espresso with sugary foam was iconic in South Florida. College students were prone to drinking it excessively to help keep them awake during study sessions. Yet, for some Cubans like Victoria, it had no effect on her. It was as if the espresso coursed through her veins.

"Snow White came back!" Victoria exited the bathroom and stood beside Jacob. "And she brought back a dwarf."

"What dwarf do you think she brought back?" Jacob followed along innocently, "Happy?"

"Nah, Smelly."

"There's not a dwarf named Smelly," Emmy said shyly and lowly.

"You're right, you'll be Dopey then," Victoria remarked. "Actually, you'll be Snow White, and Melissa should be Dopey." Jacob shot a glare at Victoria. He came to Melissa's defense whenever he felt Victoria crossing the line.

"Babe, be nice."

"It's a joke." Victoria rolled her eyes.

"Well, stop," he said, his voice gentle. "How was school?" he asked the teens.

"Booooooring!" Melissa barfed out. "But... Emmy and I gave the school news today."

"Oh, you must've loved that spotlight." he joked, and Melissa shook her head. She loved that he knew the spotlight was a dreaded place for her. He listened to her, unlike Victoria.

"No, I dreaded it, but," Melissa looked back at Emmy and smirked. "It's Emmy's dream to be a reporter... so I do it for her." Emmy grinned.

"Nice," Jacob high-fived the girls. "I don't know why you hate the spotlight so much."

"I just don't like the attention," Melissa admitted.

"Sure," Victoria scoffed. "When Pipo had you in MMA, you loved the attention when you had to perform."

Those were old times. Melissa gritted her teeth. *It doesn't matter anymore.* "Well," Jacob cleared his throat. "Sometimes we grow out of old habits. But it's nice to see you guys involved in school."

Victoria and Jacob began dating when Victoria was nineteen, and Melissa was nine. Through Melissa's eyes, Victoria hit the jackpot.

Not only was he a loving, brotherly figure, but he was also attractive: short, chocolate petite and pointy nose, broad cheekbones aligned perfectly with his rigid jawline, and crystal blue eyes that felt like they were piercing your soul.

Melissa then heard a stomach grumbling for food and asked Emmy, "You hungry?"

"Ummm, duh!" Emmy responded, and Melissa turned to Victoria to ask, "Did you go to the market?" Her older sister shook her head. "Why not?"

"Because I'll go later."

"But we're hungry," Melissa stated.

"You're literally always hungry after school."

"That's because I don't like cafeteria food. It's disgusting!"

"That's your problem then. Why should I care?"

She didn't care to eat but didn't want her friend to starve.

"And what? You're gonna tell mom? Huh? You're

gonna tattle tale like the big baby you are? Maybe you should be a dwarf called Baby."

Melissa's face twitched with a grimace, and Emmy glanced at Melissa's balled-up hand. Her friend grabbed Melissa's arm and forced her to walk silently to Melissa's room. It wasn't the first time Emmy had to de-escalate a situation between the feuding sisters.

They heard Jacob whisper in an assertive tone to Victoria. Possibly warning her to be nicer, or Melissa really would tattletale.

But it wasn't like Melissa would have. She had given up trying to expose her sister's mistreatment a long time ago since it was always a failed attempt.

"She's the dopey one!" Emmy said in a half-shout, half-whisper kind of voice, the one where it's clear you're angry but do not want the person you're mad at to hear. "I mean, there are only seven dwarves. She is terrible at remembering their names."

Melissa released a glum sigh and quickly glimpsed at her palms with the nail marks carved in them, a habit she did when upset.

Her abuelo always warned her she had the Guerra's rage: an impulsive type of anger that led to actions that would soon prove to be regretful. He'd jokingly say it was because the Guerra's carry the dragon's wrath.

Melissa assumed that's why Pipo put her in MMA. To learn to control that rage they shared. But now, without MMA, she has found different ways to release her wrath—much unhealthier coping mechanisms.

"You okay, dude? Wanna talk about it?" Emmy offered.

"Nah, I'm okay." She hid her hand. "I've accepted

Victoria will never stop being mean to me."

"But why is she so mean?" Melissa shrugged her shoulders.

"She wasn't always this cruel. I mean, she gave me this room," Melissa gestured to her bathroom. Her bedroom was the master room that once belonged to Pipo.

"You have the best room in the house," Emmy curled a smile. "That was nice of her."

"I think it's the only nice thing Victoria did for me... and even then, it's probably because my mom convinced her to give it to me since Pipo was closest to me. Victoria doesn't really care about me..." Melissa switched the subject before Emmy opened her mouth to protest. "C'mon, let's do girly stuff! Like maybe you can finally let me fix that mane of yours."

Melissa remained hopeful in the two seconds it took to register that the look on Emmy's face clearly read, 'Really, bro?'

"Fine! I'll get myself all educated and start on my homework." Melissa whined.

"Ya' know, a good feeling comes from doing good work and earning your own grades. Ya know you're smarter than you think- you just use your brains for myths rather than academics."

"Mhhh. Ya know you're right. But I'm generously trying to let you feel that 'good' feeling for helping me with my project since, ya know, I have to do double the work cause of Mia. So, you should be thanking me."

"Oh, yeah," Emmy replied sarcastically. "I'll be sure to do that just as soon as your dragons show up." Melissa scoffed playfully but giggled alongside Emmy.

Melissa was quite clever, but she dreaded math problems and essays. She often implemented her ideas in academics, such as, "How deep can a mermaid swim beneath ocean waters?" Or "If dragons breathe fire, what chemicals do they use?"

Just as the girls finished their homework, a male voice yelled, "Emmyliana!"

Emmy instantly grunted, "Ughhhh, I hate my name." Melissa snickered. Emmy dragged her feet across the floor in Melissa's room and out the door toward the living room with Melissa following.

As expected, Emmy's parents were chatting with Melissa's mother in the living room. Emmy took after her mother, Emilia. They had the same short, plump body and frizzy hair. However, Emmy's owlish hazel eyes hiding behind squared glasses and wide cheek-to-cheek smile were like her father's, Alvaro.

Melissa wondered if she would have the same courage as Emmy's parents if she lived in a communist country. Would she have taken the bold risk of traveling the ocean on a rickety homemade boat for a chance at a better life for their family?

Emmy rarely talked about the five days and four nights she spent in the middle of the ocean. It was the only thing Melissa knew about it. She had asked once what it was like when Emmy first arrived.

Emmy remained silent. It was unlike her to not be outspoken. Whatever she had endured, it seemed to have traumatized her. Pipo was so open about his experience, and it perplexed her how Emmy wasn't.

But Pipo scolded Melissa for probing Emmy about her experience. He explained to Melissa that everyone handles trauma differently. Melissa never understood what he meant until he went missing, and she had to deal with trauma of her own.

Emmy left with her parents, and Melissa took a much-needed shower before changing into her pajamas. She grabbed her dream journal and skimmed through it. There was a light knock at the door, and her mother let herself in. "Hey honey." Her voice trailed off, and Melissa quickly closed her dream journal.

"Ohh, is that a diary?" her mother joked.

"No, it's some notes for math..." she deepened her voice to prevent the squeak.

"Well, at least you're studying," her mother mused. "So, um, how's school?"

Melissa arched a brow at her mom. *She never asked me about school. Did my teacher call her?* She cleared her throat before saying, "Yeah, it's fine."

"¿Estás segura?" Her mother asked. "You're not distracted or anything?" Melissa shook her head.

At that moment, Melissa felt her heart hang low like the moon on the horizon; she yearned to tell her mother how her soul felt like an empty void and wished she had the energy to leave her room.

Instead, her sister's voice echoed in her head, and her tongue became thick and dry. *Get over it.*

And that is exactly what she did. Either way, she immersed herself in her dreams of Gemma and temporarily escaped the darkness that followed her day after day. "I'm fine, just a little overwhelmed with homework and everything happening in freshman year," she finally said.

"Well, I know high school is never easy. But if you want to join a sport or after-school activity, you can. I mean, your sister was-"

"The cheerleading captain, I know," Melissa finished for

her with a roll of her eyes. It wasn't about the actual sport; it was about the cost. If Pipo were around, then her mother could afford it.

But he's not, so Melissa responded, "Mami, it's okay. Cheerleading isn't my thing. The one thing I love is martial arts, and it's so expensive. All the sports are. Anyway, I'm in TV production with Emmy. I'm also in Dance. I'm okay with that." Her mother sighed before responding.

"Those are your electives. It's not a club or after-school activity. I know cheerleading isn't your thing, but the high school has no martial arts besides the boy's wrestling team. Don't worry about the cost, I'll manage it. So, think of something in the school you might want to do. Maybe you and Emmy can do it together? That way, you're out of the house more and having fun." Melissa remained quiet, but she nodded.

Her mother sighed, pressed her lips against her forehead, and wished her goodnight before closing the door to continue watching her telenovela. Melissa wondered why her mother loved those Spanish soap operas. Then again, she often sat with her mother on the sofa and watched them alongside her.

Melissa waited a few seconds after she left before she got up and wrote in her journal. *Pfft, cheerleading. I don't want to join sports. TV production is good enough. Even my stupid dance class is fine. Ugh, I just hate that Mia is in that class, too, & I hate it when the teacher annoys me about joining the after-school dance club. If only she knew I couldn't afford it. Mami acts like she can manage, but I know it'll be hard on her, which is unfair. Anyway, what I want is some adventure! Something fun! Something like riding a dragon in a periwinkle sky... Worlds away. Man, Gemma is real. I know it is! Tonight, I'm gonna get my answers.*

Melissa closed her journal and put it away. She snuggled in her soft sheets and closed her eyes, allowing her dreams to sweep her away from reality.

Chapter Three

The wind tickled Melissa's warm cheeks. She took a deep breath, filling her lungs with the fresh scent of grass. The sun's rays radiated her skin, but it felt nice to feel the warmth. She fluttered her eyes open and set them on a ruby sunflower.

She searched the sky painted in a soft periwinkle. The hope of seeing a dragon soar made her heart race. There was a familiarity with being in the meadow, surrounded by the colorful sunflower and purple sky, that tugged at her heart.

"Hello," Alisha's voice sang, and Melissa scrambled off the ground.

"You have to stop doing that!" Melissa hissed.

"My apologies," Alisha giggled. The elf parted her lips to speak, but Melissa stopped her.

"Look, I believe Gemma is real, and that the Kingdom of Amethyst needs me, so what do I need to do? You said it starts with a boy who lives worlds away-" her breath hitched. "Wait! Alisha! Oh my gosh, I think I know where I'll meet the boy."

She swore she saw the elf's pointy ears twitch, "How so?"

Melissa explained to the elf how when her family moved to Boone, her abuelo would comfort her by saying her family moved worlds away and that she'd see them one day. Alisha's eyes widened, and her mouth hung slightly ajar. She had never seen the elf so intrigued before.

Alisha then muttered, "Henry... you clever old man."

"Henry?" Melissa's head bounced back. "How do you know Pipo's name?"

"Pipo... Oh my," Alisha's eyes twinkled. "It has been ten years since I have heard the name Pipo." Alisha's lips tugged into a smile.

She talked about Pipo with so much familiarity- it could only mean-

"Whoa! Wait! You knew Pipo!?" she blurted out before she could organize her thoughts. "Ten years?!" she squealed in her petite voice. "Waddaya mean it's been ten years?!" Melissa stammered as she wrapped her mind around the notion of Pipo entangled in this world.

The elf knew of her abuelito, which only emboldened her belief that Gemma was real.

"You are correct. My oh my, have so many seasons breezed by since I last saw you?" Alisha questioned herself.

"How'd you know Pipo?" she asked the elf. This time, Melissa's eyes glistened with hope.

"Your grandfather was," Alisha's gray eyes wandered as if finding the right words, "was an important figure here."

"Wait, so this is not really his magical world Gemma? Is this Cuba?! Why would Pipo leave this paradise for a dump like Miami?" Alisha giggled wholeheartedly. "No, dear, this is not Cuba. This is Gemma."

"I don't understand," Melissa groaned. "All this is just a dream. Right?"

"It is not a mere dream, dragon rider. Look here," Alisha pulled out a necklace with a shimmering white, oval-like stone. "This is a moonstone enchanted to allow me to visit one's dreams. I can use dreams as a form of message. Gemma is real; you have been here long ago by your young human standards. You have grown so much since then."

"Human standards?" Melissa mumbled. *Whatever that meant,* she shook the thought, "Whoa, wait... whaddaya mean I've grown so much?" Melissa furrowed her brow at the elf's statement. "You said I've been here before, but why can't I remember? My mom said after I woke up from my coma, I forgot a lot of things."

"Follow me," Alisha's voice sang.

They strolled through the open field, descending several rolling hills. Behind them, Melissa took notice of an evergreen forest just beyond the sunflowers. Ahead, the sun was cresting the horizon, the pastel yellow and fiery orange mesmerizing Melissa.

Melissa took great care to avoid stepping on the sunflowers while Alisha effortlessly stepped through them unimpeded without even looking. Just ahead, Melissa took notice of a willow tree, the only tree standing alone in the meadow, next to a small log cabin.

The cabin appeared to be a tiny house made of hazelnut-colored logs stacked one on top of the other, with moss filling the gaps. Freshly polished wood covered the log.

It was one story, and it appeared small enough only to have one bedroom and one bathroom. It reminded Melissa of a small shed house.

Once they reached it, Melissa's eyes studied the tree whose branches drooped down, almost touching the ground and swaying from just one soft gust of the wind. Its canopy of spiny leaves dancing back and forth.

Melissa's fingers traced one of the few shallow grooves in the tree's bark as she strolled around it, wonder-struck by its deceiving appearance of normalcy. She felt connected to it somehow.

"This tree..." a memory struck her of a little girl swinging on the branch and Pipo yelling for her to be careful in a hoarse tone. "I know this tree! The memories are faint, but I know it's there. Pipo always spoke about it too, during storytelling."

Melissa recalled one of Pipo's lines and said it aloud for Alisha to hear. "The willow tree holds a rare magic." She continued to observe the soft glow of the bare trunk, and Alisha continued to speak.

"Henry is from Gemma, Melissa, and he was born in the Kingdom of Amethyst. He was more than he led on, dragon rider. Why do you think he shared so many magical stories with you? Those stories he told, he lived through them."

Melissa snapped her neck at Alisha and scoffed; she crossed her arms and spoke. "So you're telling me that my Abuelo actually traveled through the Atlantic Ocean and fought a Kraken to come to Florida?"

The mere thought of her fighting a ferocious squid-like beast bewildered her. Her abuelo wasn't being imaginative and feeding into Melissa's love of lore. All this time, he was recounting tales of his past. This realization shot adrenaline through her veins.

Alisha chuckled before saying, "Yes, dear, he indeed fought a Kraken." She gave Melissa a moment to process the information. "You see, landmasses, islands, and different geographical parts that once belonged to Earth are now in this realm, and many species of beings and animals have stayed behind. Elves, dwarves, fairies, and many more are inhabitants here. This tree," The elf paused as Melissa walked around the trunk, her hand feeling its smooth bark as more memories of her playing around this tree rushed in, "is an entrance to Gemma. Your grandfather accidentally landed in Cuba through what you humans call the Bermuda Triangle, and when he returned to Gemma, he asked the fairies to create an entrance with it, an entrance that connects to a tree near your home. Per your grandmother's wish, he married her and wanted to build a family away from Gemma."

"But... he still came and visited the kingdom?"

"Not often enough," Alisha admitted. "But when the last dragon egg hatched for you, he made an effort to come in more."

"What?"

"When you were born, the last dragon egg in the Kingdom hatched. A dragon hatches for a human whose heart is pure, and the last dragon chose you."

"He chose me?" Melissa gasped, overwhelmed that a magical beast chose her to be a protector of a magical realm.

"Indeed, and in doing so... the prophecy has come true."

"Prophecy?" A brow raised on Melissa's face. "What prophecy?" Alisha inhaled a breath before speaking it.

"Upon the day the last pearl breaks," Melissa suddenly felt her stomach become queasy as Alisha continued, "and the aid of a Tungsten ring, it shall be then the final war wakes-" Melissa interrupted by finishing the line.

"And the Ruby shall confront the false king."

"You recall?" Alisha gasped, seemingly amused. Melissa knew the line.

"Pipo... he told me once or twice..." Melissa avoided the elf's gaze and swallowed the lump in her throat. She glared into Alisha's eyes and asked, "This is real, isn't it?" The elf bobbed her head. "Well then, when can I come and see my dragon?"

"I am afraid," Alisha looked away, "you will be unable to enter."

"Huh?" Melissa's head bounced back, and she glared at the elf quizzically. "Why not?"

"The boy from worlds away..." Alisha's voice trailed off.

"What about him? What does the boy have to do with anything?"

"As the prophecy states, without the aid of a tungsten strength, there will always be war in our Kingdom. Your grandfather was terrified of the prophecy and did everything he could to protect you from it, including making you drink a powerful potion that wiped your memory of this world. He made every effort to keep you safe from the prophecy. However, I am afraid he has done more harm than good. Your grandfather brewed a concoction that forbids you from entering this realm without the Tungsten. The boy is not of Gemma; he is a human from Earth. Tungsten is a metal that pertains to Earth only. You will not find it here in Gemma. Your grandfather wanted you to find the Tungsten. What he did not anticipate is that the enemy would steal the Diamond of Dragons. We need you here more than ever, but you cannot come without the Tungsten, he is the key for you to come home."

"Wait, let's back it up- how will I know he's the 'tungsten'?"

"You will fall in love with him." Melissa's lips hung low,

and she knitted her brows.

"How can you know that?"

"Because the ring in the prophecy refers to marriage. I will offer you this assistance: his name is Chad."

Melissa stared at her, blinking several times, then cackled, "Yeah, okay! Now I know the dreams aren't real. HAH!" Melissa let out a disgruntled 'pfft'. "Of all names! Chad?! Emmy is going to shred me with this one! How do you know I'm going to fall in love with him? Geez- as if it wasn't hard enough to get a guy in the ninth grade."

Alisha raised her hand and prepared to answer before Melissa rambled, "Alisha, this is insaneeeeee! His name had to be Chad. I might as well give up on these dreams. And anyway, just because it says 'ring' doesn't mean I will marry the guy!" she frowned. "Well? Are you gonna say something?" Melissa prompted as Alisha seemed to wait in amused silence.

"Is it my turn to speak then?" Melissa rolled her eyes at the comment. "All I can say with certainty, young dragon rider, is that fate has a way of making things happen. When exactly will you be traveling to this 'worlds away?'"

"Umm, for Winter Break, which is December 22." Alisha remained poised, possibly processing the information. Her silence, however, had Melissa riddled with anxiety. "Melissa," the elf finally said, "now that I know you may meet the Tungsten, you will not see me for some time. I have to begin making preparations."

"Wait! Why?" Melissa blurted.

"Rider, I have faith you will meet Chad. Before we part ways, you shall receive a gift soon from me."

"A gift?" Melissa asked.

"Yes."

"What gift?" Melissa pried.

"I am giving you a gift that will protect you if harm ever came your way, dragon rider. You have enemies, and I fear they may find you, eventually. He will do more than protect you, dragon rider. He will comfort your human emotional needs since your dragon cannot."

"Emotional needs?" Melissa scoffed, "First of all, I'm not emotional," her voice squeaked, and she cleared her throat. "If I really have a dragon, then why haven't I seen *him* in my dreams?"

Pfft, maybe my best friend is right… These dreams aren't real.

"Dragon rider," Alisha giggled, "we shall see each other soon." With a snap of her fingers, Melissa's body dissolved into a mist, vanishing along with the realm.

* * *

Melissa awoke in the middle of the night. She scrambled out of her bed, stumbled in the darkness, found her desk, and pulled out her dream journal from her false bottom drawer. In it, she scribbled her fresh dream on a new sheet. She felt as if she was recalling actual events that happened rather than a sleep-induced adventure.

After she closed her journal, she tip-toed to her window spot, grabbed a walkie-talkie she had hidden under the mattress, and called out to her best friend. "Emmy, it's Melissa. Are you awake?"

There was a moment of silence, but then static played, and a raspy voice responded, "Dude, it is three in the morning. What can you possibly call me about?"

Melissa gave her the dream recap, and after a long

silence, Emmy said, "You wake me up from my dreams to tell me that an elf told you that the love of your life is a dude named Chad? There is no Chad-" Emmy stumbled on her words. "I mean, there are guys named Chad. Pretty sure there's a country in Africa named Chad, but there's not one specific Chad waiting for you. Which, by the way, of all the names there can possibly be, why Chad? Such a douchey name, bro."

"Yeah, I know, I thought the same," Melissa assured her. "Do you think Alisha meant what she said? No more dreams?"

"Dude, these dreams aren't real. They're a reflection of your memories." Emmy sighed. "I'm going to bed. We'll talk more about this tomorrow. Goodnight. Emmy over and out." The static in the walkie-talkie muted.

Melissa placed it back under her bed, quickly snatched her dream journal, and sat back down in her window spot. This spot of hers carried an immense amount of grief and tears.

When her abuelo was first declared missing, Melissa isolated herself in her room and cried for many nights in that same spot. She'd looked for shooting stars to wish for his reappearance. Sometimes, the window spot wasn't enough. She'd open it and escape, which her frustrating conversation with Emmy urged her to do now.

She knew the consequences if her mother found out she snuck out at night to sit in front of a small lake: she'd risk spending time with her best friend on school days and weekends. She'd have to do double the chores she already had to do.

But Melissa took the risk anyway. The calm waters soothed her whenever her anxiety was crippling her. But it wasn't just the lake that grounded her.

Something inside the woods by the lake drew Melissa.

She never went in because her abuelo told her 'El Coco' dwelled there: a Cuban version of the boogeyman. Because of that, she never dared to go in. But the shadowy groves called to her.

She wanted to go, but it was close to morning. Instead, her eyes searched the night sky, which carried very few stars because of the light pollution in Miami. There was a myriad of colorful buildings, luxury shopping centers, and stunning Art Deco architecture in her city.

But for Melissa, what truly made Miami the Magic City was its pristine beaches, tropical weather, and Latin influences. The thought of entering a state with mountains and an actual cold winter pumped her.

What excited her even more was the thought of meeting 'Chad,' the Tungsten from the prophecy. The prophecy replayed in her head several times, and she longed to know the truth.

She wrote again:

He is not from Cuba! He's really from a magical world. Why would he leave Gemma for Cuba? From all the stories Pipo told me about Cuba, why would you leave a magical realm and settle on an island with a horrible leader? And why is he protecting me from that prophecy? This prophecy is real, and I will fulfill it and protect my Kingdom. I have to make my preparations. I need to find Chad in North Carolina.

Melissa closed her journal, inhaled a deep, determined breath, and returned to sleep. Images of dragons, elves, and a massive Kraken filled her dreams.

The following morning, she felt a tap on her shoulder. She groaned and pulled the sheets over her head. Her mother said, "Melissa, look what showed up at our doorstep." Melissa clicked her tongue and pulled the sheets off, and through her blurred vision was a ghostly white chihuahua snuggling between the arms of Melissa's mother.

She pressed her eyes hard and gasped. "Where did you find it!?"

"It was sleeping right outside the door mat! It doesn't have a collar. It reminds me of Pipo's two chihuahuas that looked just like this little one, but they ran away. He always said chihuahuas were the best dog breeds."

"Haha, yeah, he did," Melissa recalled.

The pup squirmed out of her mother's arms and waddled towards Melissa. "Wow." Her mother watched how the pup wagged its tail vigorously at Melissa. "Seems to like you."

"Awe, Mami, can we keep-" She lifted the puppy and checked. "Him?"

"Well, we have to check if he belongs to anyone... he just magically appeared at the door."

The word magically echoed in her head.

Is this the gift Alisha told me about? she thought, her eyes fixated on the chihuahua's beady black eyes. *Why would she give me a dog? I mean, I'm not complaining about it, but a chihuahua... I can't picture a chihuahua living in a world of magic.*

"Well, if no one claims him... can we keep him?" Melissa asked hesitantly. She knew pets could be financially draining.

But her mother smiled and nodded, responding, "I don't see why not... he'll be a good companion for you, but just as long as you're responsible and train him."

"I promise!" Melissa responded.

"Welcome home, little guy," Melissa's mother scratched

the pup's head. "Looks like we'll have to give you a name. Unless you're already thinking of one, aren't you?"

"Ehhhh," Melissa bit her lower lip. "well, he appeared 'magically', maybe Magic should be his name." Her mother giggled.

"You know, typically, I'd tell you to get your head out of your magical world, but I think Magic is the perfect name for your puppy." Melissa chuckled, and her mother stepped out of the room. She felt a sense of calmness wash over her. Magic felt like a connection to Pipo, him being Pipo's favorite breed and all.

She knew once Victoria saw the pup, she would say something negative. No doubt, upon seeing Magic, she quipped, "Should've named him Tragic."

But Magic wasn1t all too positive about Victoria either.

Victoria reached out to pet the Magic, but he evaded her hand with a swift head movement. Unfazed, he leaped into Melissa's waiting arms, snuggling against her.

"He's fitting right in," Melissa's mother commented.

"I know, right?" Melissa hugged Magic's neck and gave him a smooch on his head. Melissa loved her new pup, and it's all she thought about in school. So much so that she received detention for not answering a question her teacher asked.

But it didn't matter to Melissa. She was too ecstatic to go home and greet Magic by scooping him up into her arms. She had even asked Emmy to come over and meet him. Surely, Emmy poked fun at the name she chose for him.

On their walk home, they briefly talked about Melissa's dream, and Emmy rolled her eyes, responding with, "Let me get this straight: an elf got you a chihuahua?"

"Okay, it sounds unbelievable when you say it like that."

"It doesn't matter how I say it! Gemma is not real, neither is this 'Kingdom.'" Emmy air quoted and mumbled to herself.

"Dude, I had my doubts, but after she shared that prophecy, it was like Pipo..." her words could not flow, so instead, she said, "...I know Gemma is out there," Melissa emphasized. "Look, when I leave for Boone, I will search for Chad. And when I find him, will you believe the dreams then?" The previous night's dream had Melissa dead set on getting her best friend to believe what she knew to be true because she no longer wanted to be alone in her beliefs.

"Pfft, sure," Emmy responded with sarcasm.

When the girls got home, Emmy fell in love with Magic, and he liked her back. They played with Magic and tried teaching him a couple of tricks. He proved to be a quick learner.

That night, Melissa placed a pillow on the floor for Magic. Almost immediately, the pup started whimpering, and Melissa sighed because she knew she would pick him up and let him sleep with her.

"Goodnight, Magic. I'll be sure to thank Alisha for bringing you into my life." But when Melissa awoke the following morning, she couldn't remember having any dreams. She wondered if they would ever return, but they did not.

She knew the Kingdom of Amethyst needed her and felt determined to find the boy who lives worlds away; the Tungsten of the prophecy: Chad.

Chapter Four

A bump caused Melissa to snap out of her deep thinking of the prophecy.

"You alright, kiddo?" her Uncle Rudy asked while he looked at her through the rearview mirror.

"Just a little bump."

His wife, Nina, looked back at a dazed Melissa. "Just a few more hours, and we shall arrive at our destination," she said, amused.

Nina was a thin woman with narrow green eyes and a brown pixie cut; she was a few inches taller than Uncle Rudy. If she wore heels, she'd tower over her husband which is probably why she never wore them. Her joyous persona lit up any room she was in and she always had a joke up her sleeve.

Melissa appreciated it; Nina was often a light in the Paz-Guerra family. But Melissa's heart ached for them because she had once overheard her mother and Victoria discuss her inability to get pregnant.

I wish they could become parents, Melissa often thought. Her Uncle Rudy and Nina often took it upon themselves to take Melissa to the beach or park. Deep inside, Melissa knew they would be great parents.

Melissa's mother and Uncle Rudy were twins and almost identical to one another. Uncle Rudy had a pointier nose and thinner lips, and his eyes were a darker shade of hazel. He often mocked his twin by calling her by her full name, Janessy, rather than Jane.

Before she embarked on her journey or rather quest, her mother shed a few tears. Melissa knew it was hard for her to let her go. But she promised her mother that even though it would be hundreds of miles away, she'd call daily and keep her updated with her adventures.

Melissa even promised her mother she'd try to continue watching telenovelas in Boone so they could discuss the drama and chisme – gossip - occurring in the Spanish soap operas when she returned.

Emmy wasn't too happy that she and her best friend wouldn't spend Christmas together. But Melissa was going to miss her all the same. She had come to the inevitable conclusion that Emmy was her only friend, and she was okay with that. Emmy was more than enough.

She made that conclusion one afternoon when she had to stay behind for detention after failing to answer a question her teacher called her out on. Teachers often picked on Melissa because of her lack of effort to participate or engage with her academics. She overheard Mia gossiping about her after failing to answer the teacher's question.

Mia had no idea Melissa was behind her; she sat on Josh's lap and said, "Melissa didn't even do the project. She's too dumb to do it herself. I always gotta clean up after her mess. We *always* get partnered."

We always get partnered because you want to be my partner… because you know I'd do both of our work.

"Oh, that weird girl?" Josh asked, and it stung Melissa that a cute boy would say that.

"Pfft, weird and dumb," Mia cackled.

Melissa clenched her jaw and balled her fist, digging her fingernails into her palms. She felt the urge to yell at her. But she bit her tongue instead, inhaled, collected her thoughts, and approached Mia.

Mia had to double-take when Melissa stood before her, and her eyes gaped; Melissa simply pursed her lips and raised a brow. "Melissa- I- I-" Mia stammered.

"No worries," Melissa pulled out a piece of homework. "Here's my part of the assignment. I'm not doing yours. If we fail, that's on you."

While Melissa may not have stood up for herself in the way she hoped, she did manage to walk away with pride. The right thing would have been to confide in her mother about Mia, yet she chose not to burden her with school bullies and girl drama, knowing that her mother already had a lot on her plate.

Emmy was proud of Melissa for standing up for herself. Still, Melissa was internally freaking out because she didn't want to fail or earn a bad grade. After all, then that meant no more Boone.

But Emmy assured her Mia would do her part. Otherwise, Mia wouldn't be able to dance. And, like always, Emmy was right. Mia did her part, and neither girl was penalized. Reinforcing Melissa's trust in Emmy.

Magic was curled up in a tiny ball on Melissa's lap as they rode along in the car. The little pup had grown several inches since he was 'magically' found in October. It amazed Melissa how a little animal brought so much love to her life.

Before the ride, Uncle Rudy placed absorbent white pee pads stacked three deep across the back seat area at Melissa's feet. "Not one drop of puppy puddle in the carpet of this Escalade... you'll be scrubbing this car," he warned her.

Melissa made the mistake of calling the Escalade a minivan only to hear Uncle Rudy drone on for hours about how the Escalade was more than a car, more than a minivan. She almost thought he was trying to sell her the vehicle the way he boasted about it.

But Magic was no trouble; they only made two stops so far.

During most nights after the dreams disappeared Melissa's loneliness amplified. She often sat at her window spot and felt her mind spiraling into a dark void.

She missed her dreams of Gemma. She missed the mysterious elf. But most of all, she missed feeling connected to Pipo.

Magic must've felt the darkness that Melissa endured because he'd hop next to her and nudge her hand with his paw to remind her that she wasn't alone.

What is she up to? Alisha had told Melissa had to make preparations. *What kind of preparations?* But it didn't matter too much because Melissa had a quest of her own. She had to find Chad, the tungsten ring from the prophecy. It excited her to be working towards fulfilling the prophecy. It was a glimmer of hope in her new, dreamless reality.

Her mind then drifted to Chad. *How will I fall in love with a guy I don't even know? How can I even love if I don't know what love is... at least not in a romantic way...* Melissa watched couples at school. They held hands and swung or hid in a corner and kissed.

A part of her craved to have a boy's attention, but she felt it was useless since young love rarely lasted long. Either way, nothing in her life seemed to last long. Melissa didn't want to get hurt, especially not by a boy. She had a few classmates ask her out before, but she declined them all. Emmy would pester her about it too. No boys ever approached Melissa because she was the 'hard-to-get' kind of girl. But it only fueled her insecurities: was she being too picky? Was she not good enough? Would she ever find a boyfriend? It also didn't help that Josh gossiped with classmates and spread a rumor that Melissa was weird after confronting Mia the way she did.

She shook the thought off and continued looking out the window. It felt like an eternity since leaving Florida, and the thought of still driving through South Carolina was dreadful for her. She glanced again at Magic, who was snoozing away in his dreams.

I'm so glad Magic came, Melissa's mind drifted. *Victoria wouldn't have taken care of him the way I did. She'd probably shave his hair and chain him outside.* The mere thought of Magic chained made Melissa cringe.

She laid her head down on her arm and dozed off.

Chapter Five

A hand lightly shook Melissa; she was buried deep in her dreams. "Huh?" she groaned. "Rise and shine, we made it!" Uncle Rudy exclaimed.

A jolt of excitement caused her to spring out of the car. But almost instantly, her teeth clattered; her nose and fingertips felt numb from the chilly wind. The thin black-sleeve shirt and worn-out boots she wore barely kept her warm.

Uncle Rudy had parked his car in front of a red-brick, two-story house decorated with colorful Christmas lights and a pathway with candy canes that followed along the trail to the door. From above, droplets of white powder fell, and Melissa took an overdramatic gasp: *snow!*

She crouched, letting her palm feel the wet snow, and then glanced at Rudy, puzzled. He said, "It's not what you thought it'd be, huh?" Melissa shook her head, feeling dumbfounded. *It doesn't feel fluffy or light… It's cold and wet, yuck. I'm still doing snow angels and snowball fights.*

Magic whimpered, possibly annoyed his owner left him behind. He pounced out of the car and sprinted to Melissa, leaving tiny paw prints along the way, his color blending with the snow. His entire body trembled, and when Melissa snatched him up, he curled into a little ball in her arms for warmth.

"Can we go inside?" Melissa asked, trying not to whine even though goosebumps rose all over her body, "I'm freezing."

As if on cue, a tall, slender man with long raven hair streaked with silvery white and olive-colored skin like Pipo stepped out and declared, "Mi familia!" My family!

Uncle Ozzy embraced Uncle Rudy with a warm, welcoming hug. They held the embrace for a while. Melissa swore she saw tears well up in their eyes. *It's really been such a long time.* Then Uncle Ozzy gave Nina a hug.

"Oye, estás gordo!" Uncle Ozzy sneered at Uncle Rudy, who pouted at him.

"Thanks," Uncle Rudy muttered and glanced at his beer belly. "Honey, I think after New Year's, I'm starting that diet tly again."

Melissa stifled a chuckle from his comment, and Uncle Ozzy spun around, looking for the source of the noise. "I'd know that familiar laugh anywhere!" Melissa giggled even more. "C'mere!" He pulled her into a bear-like hug, and Melissa gave him an awkward, friendly tap.

"What kind of hug is that?" Uncle Ozzy scoffed. "Con gana!" Melissa wrapped her arms around him and squeeze him tightly.

"There you go! Wow, Melissa, you look so grown." He looked at her long, and Melissa put on her trademark half-smile. "Oh, that smirk of yours hasn't changed a bit. Wait till the girls know you're here. I didn't tell them you were coming."

Uncle Ozzy lent a hand to the family with the suitcases, and they followed him into his home. Magic snuggled into a ball in Melissa's arms. Uncle Ozzy hadn't noticed her dog until he placed the suitcases down. He asked, "Whoa! Who's that pupper?"

"This is Magic," Melissa introduced the chihuahua.

"Wait until your little guy meets Toby. He's a pure-bred Siberian Husky. Cost me like three grand!" Melissa's eyes gaped, her lips parting at the mere thought of paying an insane amount for a dog.

Ummm… There are lots of dogs in need of adoption. Melissa wanted to remark but bit her tongue instead.

Inside Uncle Ozzy's home, warmth enveloped the space, and the delightful aroma of cinnamon and apples wafted into Melissa's nostrils. The pale, yellow walls were adorned with picture frames capturing moments of Uncle Ozzy and his family. Among them was a collection of photos showcasing Melissa and her cousins.

One photo stood out: she was six years old and had one arm wrapped around a boy's neck with an appearance and a smirk like hers.

"Ethan," Uncle Ozzy commented. "That was right before he left for Minnesota. He was supposed to fly down and join the family. But they couldn't make it."

I would have loved to have seen Ethan, Melissa sighed glumly. *We had so much fun playing hide-and-seek.*

They walked past the hallway, and Melissa's eyes widened at the immense size of the living room and kitchen.

Woooooow. This kitchen is the size of my frigging living room!

In the corner by the television was a giant Christmas tree decorated with red and green lights spiraling the pine tree. The sweet, sappy aroma filled Melissa's nose; the Santa-inspired ornaments brought out the classic Christmas spirit.

Melissa took in the smell of pines and hummed. *I wish*

we could get a real tree. It definitely beats the fake tree. Melissa's mother would set up a dusty, worn-out artificial Christmas tree every year. She could never complain about this to her mother, though, because despite the financial struggles and trauma the family had endured, her mother still made an effort to put up a Christmas tree.

It pained Melissa momentarily as she thought about how she wouldn't keep the tradition of decorating the tree with her mother this year. Melissa usually decorated it alongside her mother and made the most out of the artificial tree. Victoria used to join them, but she became less involved as the years went by.

Two young girls were sitting on the couch, watching a cooking channel with a look of immense boredom. Both girls had golden bouncy hair, slim features, round, sky-blue eyes, and a body similar to Melissa's, except the younger sibling's body was scrawnier. The hair of the oldest reached her waist, while the hair of the youngest was cut to her shoulders and was highly frizzy.

Uncle Ozzy's cheerful whistle caught the attention of the girls, and in an instant, their faces lit up with joy. Springing off the couch, they rushed toward Melissa, enveloping her in a whirlwind of hugs and excited squeals.

"I can't believe you're here!" exclaimed Rose, the eldest among the siblings, her enthusiasm echoing through the room.

"No one told us anything!" Lily added. Rose was two years older than Melissa, and Lily was two years younger.

"Seriously, we would have cleaned our room," Rose murmured so no one could hear. However, a sharp feminine voice followed.

"That means you should *always* clean your room so that

when unexpected guests arrive, they don't have to witness your monstrous room." Cynthia scolded her daughter as she walked downstairs.

Rose and Lily bore a striking resemblance to their American mom, the only notable difference being that their mother had a heavier build.

Cynthia spoke again, her blue eyes gazing at Melissa. "Melissa, it's great to see ya again." She hugged Melissa with one arm. "You have gotten so beautiful! It's been three years since I last saw you." She last saw them at Pipo's and Patricio's funeral.

Melissa heard heavy paws from upstairs. A wolf-like dog came dashing from upstairs to greet Melissa. It pounced on her, causing her to topple on her behind. The men roared with laughter, and Cynthia and Nina rushed to help Melissa return to her feet.

Magic jumped from Melissa's arms and bared his tiny teeth at the wolf, "Magic!" Melissa gasped.

"That's Toby," Uncle Ozzy restrained Toby. "He's just *really* hyper. He won't bite Magic... but I think Magic might bite him."

Hair rose on Magic, and he continued to growl. "He's protecting me." Melissa explained. It wasn't the first time Magic had done so. Magic often bared his small teeth at Victoria whenever she mocked Melissa. It was as though he knew when Victoria was being cruel. "It's okay, Magic, he's a friendly dog."

It was as if Magic understood her words. He approached Toby slowly, sniffed him, and his ears perked up. Both dogs wagged their tails and played instantly. Melissa was still worried, though. Magic was tough, but he was tiny compared to the massive wolf.

The girls took Melissa on a house tour and then to their rooms, where she would sleep. Their room was monstrous: the two twin-sized beds with a mountain of clothes covering it, and papers and books scattered the floor.

But the room was lovely: the walls were peachy, and the closet had vibrant clothes and an abundance of shoes. Even though the sisters shared the room, Melissa could tell the girls had their own style.

Rose had boy band posters, while Lily still had Disney Princess posters on her side. Rose's bed was pastel pink and carried so much simplicity. Lily had funky orange and purple colors all over her side.

Victoria and I could never, Melissa thought. *She'd decorate her way, and her way only.* Rose gestured for Melissa to sit. "Your hair is long! Let me do a French braid." Rose parted Melissa's hair and built a braid. They briefly spoke about the family and school. Rose was dating her 17-year-old neighbor who lived in the house across the way; she was in cheerleading and was running for junior class president.

Lily was heavily involved with the theater program at her middle school; she was learning to play the guitar and earned decent grades.

Melissa felt embarrassed that she had nothing to share except that she was in TV production with her best friend. But the sisters paid no mind to that; instead, they wanted deets on Melissa's duties.

Melissa felt like she barely had a social life or any fun hobby. When the girls asked if she was still in MMA, it pained Melissa to admit she wasn't. After chatting for a while, the girls helped set up an air mattress and layered it with blankets to keep her warm throughout the chilly night.

Ugh, I'm gonna miss Florida weather this weekend, Melissa thought as she readied herself to take a quick shower. *Well, a few cold nights away from home is worth it. I hope I meet Chad soon.*

Before lying in bed, she had asked her Uncle Rudy for his cell. He handed her his Blackberry, and it took Melissa a while to figure out how to use its complex keyboard and weird layout.

When her mother answered, she peppered Melissa with all the motherly love questions in the world, like "How was the arrival? How's the family? Is it cold? Are you making sure you're staying warm?"

"How's Victoria and Jacob?" Melissa asked. She hoped they missed her even though it had been one day.

"They're here now. Let me put you on speaker so you can talk to them."

"Hey guys!" Melissa said.

"Hey, Melissa!" Jacob called out, and it was like music to her ears.

"How was the long trip?"

"It was tiring. I slept like a baby on the way here."

"Well, you are a big baby," Victoria remarked. "But I'm glad you're safe." That but most likely came from a nudge Jacob gave her or possibly a glare from her mother, maybe even both.

Not wanting to keep talking to someone who didn't want to talk to her, Melissa said, "I'll talk to y'all later. Love you guys. Bye, Mami, I'll call tomorrow."

"Te amo, mi niña." They hung up.

When she lay in the uncomfortable bed, she continued fantasizing about Chad. She hoped their soon-to-be encounter would be magical and imagined falling in love at first sight.

Her mind lingered on the thought of him while she snuggled herself into the blankets, flopped onto her pillow, and shut her eyes.

Chapter Six

The morning sun filtered through the window, casting a warm glow on Melissa's face. She groaned in protest, not quite ready to wake up. Reluctantly, she emerged from beneath the covers, only to shiver as the chill of the room hit her exposed skin.

She reached for her softest, coziest blanket and wrapped it around her shoulders, seeking warmth and comfort. As she wiggled her numb toes, she blinked away the last remnants of sleep. When she finally sat up, a sharp pain pierced her lower back.

First, the cold… now the bed- but two weeks of backache is a pretty fair deal in exchange for the time away from home, especially from Victoria, Melissa pondered. She tossed and turned to find comfort until she lay on her back, facing the ceiling and wondering if she'd get any sleep at all this Winter Break.

The smell of pancakes reached upstairs, and Melissa's stomach growled, a rare thing since she often had no appetite. But the scent of rich buttermilk took her back to when Pipo would take her to eat pancakes.

He'd tell her stories of how pancakes weren't typical in Cuba and then lectured her about being thankful for the small things.

At that moment, she was grateful for pancakes. *Wow, I haven't had pancakes in forever.* Melissa's mouth watered, and she jerked up. She noticed the sisters weren't in bed, and she stood up.

She slipped her combat boots over her fuzzy red PJs and a shirt that read, "Sleep Queen." She placed a black leather jacket over it for extra warmth. She let Rose's braid go, and her hair, usually straight, kept some curls.

I like this. Melissa turned her head to watch her hair swish and then tottered down the steps. Her entire family was eating scrambled eggs and pancakes and drinking either cafe con leche or straight-up espresso.

"The beast has awoken!" Uncle Rudy roared in a joking manner to embarrass her, just like the rest of her family typically did. But Melissa let out her best bear growl and held her fingers to bare her freshly painted nails.

Thus, she did not allow Uncle Rudy to humiliate her. The room rippled with laughter. "What are you in the mood for?" Cynthia asked. "Pancakes, eggs? Both?"

"Pancakes and some cafe con leche, puh-lease!"

"Sure thing, 'Sleep Queen.'" Cynthia taunted her wholeheartedly, and Melissa half smiled.

Cynthia served her a stack of pancakes, and Melissa drenched it with syrup and allowed the butter to seep through the fluffy cakes. She devoured them entirely and chugged her cafe con leche. It felt good to have an appetite and actually enjoy her food.

"Hey, do we have any plans today?" Melissa asked, her eyes twinkling. She hoped they did so that she might run into someone named Chad who fit the bill of 'soulmate.'

"Not sure about today," Cynthia admitted. "Tomorrow,

we're definitely going to Grandfather Mountains. Your Uncle Ozzy made an itinerary, so I'd ask him."

Just as Melissa stood to ask, Magic greeted Melissa with a lick, and she carried him, rubbing his face on her cheek. "Mornin' lil guy, let's go take you out to pee." She placed him back down, and Toby came along and sat in front of Melissa, waiting to be petted by her. When she did, he pounced on her to cover her in licks.

"Hey, if you're taking Magic out, can you take Toby too?" Uncle Ozzy asked, and Melissa nodded. *I'll ask him when I return inside- I can't leave Boone without meeting Chad.*

The dogs dashed to the door, and when Melissa opened it, a cold shock went through her thin pajamas; she felt the chill go down her spine- literally. To Melissa's annoyance, the dogs sprinted around, searching for a tree to urinate on.

Magic left little paw prints that were eventually turned into massive paw prints by Toby. Despite the cold, the sun was beaming down, and for a moment, Melissa missed sun-soaked Florida. She was thankful it wasn't snowing.

I didn't think I'd miss home. Melissa thought of Miami and looked at all the different trees in the neighborhood. *I even miss the palm trees.*

A loud bark startled her, and she glanced up to see Toby chasing after Magic, who had sprinted across the street towards a boy wearing a dark beanie and shoveling snow. "Hey!" Melissa yelled. "Come back!" She bolted after the dogs.

The boy crouched down to greet the dogs; his chuckles filled the air. Melissa approached him, and his earthy-brown, almond-shaped eyes stayed locked with hers when he glanced at her. He stood up and was slightly taller than Melissa, but he had the same fair skin as her that would easily sunburn in

Miami.

"Hi." His voice was boyish. "Is this lil guy yours?"

"Um." Melissa observed his slightly crooked jaw and thin lips; he had a narrow, crooked scar right above his left eyebrow. "Yeah."

Her hands became clammy despite the cold weather, and her tongue felt dry. *I guess this is Rose's boyfriend. No kidding, he is super cute.*

She was blissfully unaware that in the long time she'd been gazing at him, Toby had charged straight for her to play, and her inattention let him bowl her straight to the ground.

The boy suddenly laughed that a more decent person might have contained, but he offered her his gloved hand- "You alright there, kid?"

Kid!? Oh, hell nooooo. Even if he is 17, I am no kid!

She batted his hand away spitefully, stood up on her own, and put all of her effort into keeping her voice from squeaking. "I'm perfectly fine, thank you very much." She failed utterly.

"Nice PJs, Sleep Queen." Any other voice might have sounded sincere, but this felt rude, especially after the 'kid' put-down.

She stood up, patting the white powder off of her clothing. "Magic, c'mere. Leave the mean old man alone."

Turnabout, she decided it was only fair play.

"Old!? I'm only 15!" he said defensively.

"So? I'll be 15 in a few months. Where did you get off calling me a kid?!"

"I mean," he rubbed the back of his neck almost as if it embarrassed him she caught in a false assumption. You are younger than me, so technically…"

"So technically, you're an old man," she finished for him, aiming to win this awkward exchange with the admittedly handsome douchebag.

"I, uh…" He seemed to look for a comeback. "Wow, I've never been bested by a chick before."

A sudden explosion of snow erupted behind his head. He spun around, and Melissa saw a slightly older-looking boy over his shoulder.

"Oh, you are so dead!" the younger boy shouted and seemed to prepare to chase after the other.

Melissa saw her chance, and she took it. She hooked his ankle with her foot, sending him toppling into the snow. But just as she was about to make a snarky remark, something along the lines of "Have a nice trip" or "Oh snow, you didn't!" Toby tackled her again, sending her lying flat across the body of the obnoxious teenager.

"Hey, Chad! Looks like all the girls are 'falling' for you today!" The snowball assailant teased from a safe distance.

"Chad?" The name rang in her ears, and her eyes gaped. "Your name is Chad?" She locked her eyes with his. She could hear Alisha's voice saying Chad echoing in her mind. Her palms instantly became sweaty, and she felt her throat tighten. A myriad of emotions overwhelmed her: ecstatic because the prophecy was real, angry because this "Chad" was a douche, confused because she liked him but didn't want to like him, and then anxious because she didn't know how to process this revelation.

"Yeah," the boy broke eye contact and sat on his elbows. "Chadwick Lovette. I'd say it was a pleasure to make your acquaintance, but everything about the last five minutes has been a total nightmare, and it would just be... super if you could remove your elbow from my ribcage."

Nightmare doesn't even begin to describe it. Melissa panicked as she stood up and helped Chadwick up. *This guy cannot be my soulmate. He might have the correct name and the right location, but I am not soulmates with some douchebag!*

"Well," she spat, "you're no dream either. Seems like the reputation of 'Chad' follows you," she remarked. Chadwick's lips parted, and he frowned his eyebrows at her, shocked at Melissa's spice. "Oh, now you don't have something to say?" she prompted.

He could not respond, so she snatched Toby by the collar and whistled to Magic while storming back toward the house.

"You're not even gonna give me your name, at least?" Chad, who was clearly not the one from the dreams, shouted in mild sarcasm. Melissa liked to think it took him a minute to grow a pair and finally ask her after her comeback.

"It's Melissa." She opened the front, guided the misbehaved dogs inside, and looked back at Chad, her eyes glaring into his. "And I'm not a kid!" In a huff, she stomped to the dining area where Uncle Rudy was still eating.

"Dios mio! Mija, que te paso? You look like the Abominable snowman's disaffected niece."

She had almost forgotten how covered in cold, wet snow she was and thought she was mad enough to melt it off of herself.

"I fell in some snow," she rolled her eyes. "Do you think I could use your phone again?"

"As long as you put on some real clothes." He handed his Blackberry over to her. She went upstairs, tripping because

of her focus on the prophecy and not her motor functions.
Finally, in the bathroom, she attempted to dial Emmy's number
on the phone.

Time seemed to pass rapidly as she paced across the
bathroom floor, waiting for Emmy to pick up the phone.

"Buen Dia," Emmy's mother answered.

"Hiya, Miss Emilia, may I speak to Emmy? It's urgent!"
She stuck her thumbnail in her mouth and chewed it lightly.

"Hey, dudette, miss me already?" Emmy teased.

"Emmy! I'm dying!" Melissa's tone shouted while she
kept her actual volume low enough to be contained in the small
bathroom.

"What?! What happened? Do you want me to call your
mom?!"

"No..." Melissa whimpered. "Not that kind of dying...
I'm just dyiiiiiing."

"Oh- you miss me that much, huh?" Emmy had never
had a strong concept of when not to joke.

"You're not gonna believe it, but I met a guy named
Chad... And-"

"And he turned out to be a douchebag." Emmy guessed
accurately. "Did I not warn you that all Chads are douchebags?
That African country I told you about? Their chief export is
bagged douche."

"Emmy, this is serious. He's a guy around my age, he's
worlds away, and his name is Chad... I don't wanna have a
soulmate that's a douchebag! At first, I thought he was super
cute, but then he called me a kid and got snarky with me,
UGH." Emmy let out a snorting laugh at the thought.

"Don't laugh at me!" Melissa demanded. "Surely there's
got to be other Chads out there my age that are equally

handsome and not cocky jerks, right?"

"Girl, for starters, let me say that I don't believe in soulmates, but if I did, I'd say that the guy who has the name of your dream soulmate, who you bumped into on your first trip out of Florida ever, who you just described as 'handsome' is probably the guy."

"Noooo." Melissa pressed her back to the door and sank to the floor. "Don't say that! Maybe it doesn't count. His name is technically Chadwick!" she pitched.

"Quit trying to let yourself off on a technicality." Emmy jokingly said. "Don't get me wrong, I would love it if you'd take your head out of the clouds and believe me about Chad not being your soulmate and dragons not being real, buuuut we both know you're not gonna do that. You should talk to this guy if you think your dreams are real. Watch, you're gonna call me back in a day or two talking about how he's not so bad, and you think he might be the one, and maybe you two will have a future together. Blah blah blah... Classic dreamer crap."

"Not this time, Emmy," Melissa insisted. "If I never speak to that stupid boy again, it'll be too soon."

"Well, gracias a Dios para un pequeños milagros." Emmy thanked heaven for little miracles.

She stood up, pinning the phone to her ear with her shoulder and resting her hands on the sink. "Okay. I'm gonna go, I'm never gonna talk to that boy again, and I'm gonna enjoy the rest of this trip." She spoke into the mirror as much to herself as to Emmy. She hung up the phone.

She peeked outside to see if the coast was clear of Chadwicks. To her abject horror, Chadwick, as she was determined to call him to distance him from the name of her soulmate, and the other boy, who she assumed was Rose's boyfriend, Alex, was out in the street talking to Rose and Lily.

She also assumed Alex was Chad's older brother; they resembled each other, only Alex's jaw was not crooked, his eyes were rounder, and he had patches of hair around his cheekbones.

Ew, is he trying to grow a beard? Melissa thought and shifted her gaze back to Chadwick. His name is Chad, well Chadwick... she pondered deeply, horrified this might be her soulmate. Is he really THE Chad? He's cute and all, but gosh, his cockiness is so annoying, and he is so arrogant; I don't want a guy like that to be my soulmate. Then again, I'm Melissa Paz-Guerra. I should have known not to expect more.

A portion of Melissa's dreams may have come true right in front of her eyes, but it *is all real.* Not that she doubted the dreams before, but now she really worried how true the 'soulmate' part was. *Maybe Alisha was wrong, and a ring doesn't mean marriage? Ugh, no, I can't be with a guy like him. The important part is that I found him... it is all real. Now I can enter Gemma!*

The thought of being a part of a world where all magical beings exist sent sparks of adrenaline through her. She felt an inkling of joy she hadn't felt for some time pumping through her heart.

Ugh, my dragon better not be a douche too! What a nightmare. Has he dreamt of me? I haven't even thought about that. How do I tell a guy, 'Hey, according to my dreams, you're my soulmate'? She groaned.

"Pull yourself together, girl! This guy is not your soulmate." She spoke her thoughts aloud and mustered up the courage to stand up. "I will prove he's not the Chad from the prophecy. No way is this douche the tungsten." She changed into regular clothes, skinny jeans, and a plaid shirt and walked back outside to join the others.

"Finally, you took forever!" Rose exclaimed.

"Well, yeah-" Melissa stumbled on her words. "I had to change. My pajamas were wet and cold because of *him*." She hissed at Chadwick, whose face hardened. "I was freezing."

"Me?!" he scoffed. "You tripped me! Not my fault Toby pushed you." Before Melissa could speak, Rose spoke.

"This year, the cold ain't so bad. You'll get used to it."

"I hope so." Melissa put on her half smile and noticed Chadwick's cheek turning rosy red again; he looked down at his shuffling feet.

"Are you blushing?" Melissa called him out, raising a brow, and Chadwick stared at her blankly.

"Uh, um..." he stammered. "Pretty sure it's just this chill in the air."

Melissa noticed Alex gathering another baseball-sized snowball and aimed it straight at Chadwick's head. As she watched the snowball rocketing towards Chadwick, Melissa shoved him out of the way and allowed the ball to hit her instead.

The boy shouted, "I am so sorry!" and then said, "Damn it, you're lucky that chick saved you, Chad!" He had almost certainly gotten more snow on him because of falling than he would have if he'd been hit by a snowball.

"Wow, you have fast reflexes," Chadwick complimented, trying to get back up.

"Thanks," Melissa muttered, shaking off the snowball that hit her chest.

"I'd help but, ya know..." he explained, pointing at her chest, and Melissa smirked.

"Do you always do that cute smile?" The word cute caught her off-guard, and she didn't like it. But at the same time, her heart skipped a beat.

"Yes, I do," she responded with spice.

"And do you normally blush too?" he remarked.

"Uh," she stammered and then quipped back with sarcasm. "It's just the chill in the air."

"You've got a mouth on you, huh?" he winked, and Melissa scoffed.

"And you're full of yourself, aren't ya?" Chadwick's eyes widened in disbelief.

The boy approached the group and said, "So, who's the new dog walker my brother's blushing for?"

Chadwick glared at his older brother, and Rose introduced Melissa to Alex.

"Nice to meet you, Melissa." He shook her hand. "You like it here so far?"

"I mean, I haven't seen much, honestly... So far, I don't like this weather, and the locals have been none too friendly." She glared at Chadwick; his eyes locked on her with an unblinking gaze.

"I can imagine. Florida is always hot, isn't it?" Alex pressed a smile.

"It can be super-hot at times. I mean, that's why our basketball team is called Miami Heat," Melissa joked, and Alex chuckled at her witty response.

"Wait, you're from Miami?" Chadwick's eyes gaped at her.

"Yeah." Melissa shrugged her shoulders, unfazed by his obvious excitement she was from South Florida.

"Ohh man, my brother is really gonna like that about

you," Alex taunted. "He loves anything to do with the ocean, and Miami has some of the best beaches. But anyway, we should all go out tonight," Alex suggested. "That way, Chad- I mean, *we* can get to know you," Alex joked, and Chadwick's pink cheeks had now turned crimson.

"Well, Dad was taking everyone to Grandfather Mountain tomorrow..." Lily mumbled.

"Nice!" Alex exclaimed.

"Why don't you guys come?" Rose asked. "It'll be fun, Alex."

Without hesitating, Alex scoffed and replied, "Of course, I'll go, babe. Anything to be with you, yes. Chad, are you down to go?" Alex replied, turning to face Chadwick.

"Definitely!" He flicked his eyes at Melissa, and she awkwardly looked down at her shuffling feet.

"Let's make sure Melissa has a good time." She looked back up, and he locked his eyes with hers in an unnerving gaze; she noticed how his eyes twinkled, and then the tug of his mouth crept into a shy smile.

"I appreciate it," Melissa stammered to him. The boys bid farewell and promised to meet them around seven.

Melissa followed the girls rushing upstairs and squealed as soon as the door closed.

"Melissa!" Rose squealed as only a teenage girl can. "I have never seen Chad act like that! I go to school with this kid, and all the girls drool for this guy, literally! I know he likes you, Melissa!"

Melissa glanced at Rose with her eyebrows frowning. "I don't care if he does, he's kind of a douchebag."

"Noooo, he's actually a sweetheart! I saw how he got nervous for ya; he likes ya." Rose continued to squeal. "The

Lovette boys are cocky, but they're each one of a kind, and they're charming. Ya know... our grandpa was the one who helped his parents buy a home here."

"What?" Melissa couldn't imagine Pipo's brother Pablo in real estate. But then it clicked for her, *oh my gosh... Pipo must've found Chad! But how?! How did he know he was the boy from the prophecy? How did he know it was him!?* Melissa felt her heart drop a bit; the dreams were becoming all too real, but so many questions were rushing inside her mind.

She didn't realize Rose continued to rant about Chadwick. "Oh c'mon Melissa, get to know him! Let's get you all dolled up for tomorrow."

"For what?" Melissa rolled her eyes and snapped out of her thoughts. "I don't even like him. I don't care to impress him. It's not like he gave a good first impression, anyway." Melissa gave a "pfft," at the end.

"Ugh! First impressions aren't everything! I'm telling you, Chad likes you!" Rose ranted on.

"Um, no, I'm good. But I love makeovers. Can you do my eyebrows? My mom is not gonna be happy about it, but I figure it'll be okay since I'm not even doing quince photos."

"You're not? How come?" Rose asked, but Lily interrupted.

"Neither am I! I'm having a sweet sixteen instead."

"Yeah, but I'm not having one 'cause we can't afford it..."

"Oh," Lily sighed.

"That sucks!" Rose added.

"It's okay, guys. Since I'm not having one, maybe doing my eyebrows won't make my mom too mad."

"Alright, let's get this makeover started!" Rose squealed.

"Yes!" Melissa exclaimed. "But," she emphasized, "I'm not trying to impress Chadwick!"

"Alex outgrew most of that bull-headed crap a couple years ago, but Chad's gonna need some work before he's any kind of a catch," Rose mocked. "C'mon, let's get started!"

Lily dashed to the closet and scavenged through it. Pulling out shirts and dresses, she said, "Wow, Alex and Chad like Latinas."

"Haha, you're right. Sucks for Miss Diana," Rose commented. "So much for trying to get her boys an all-American girl. They both like Latinas."

"Who's Diana?" Melissa asked, puzzled.

"Their mom," Rose explained. "She hates Hispanics, she always refers to us as 'the Mexican family.'"

"That's rude..." Melissa commented.

"Yup. When Alex's mom found out we were dating, she almost had a heart attack... I mean, either way, I am half-American, so she sorta approved of me."

"Why doesn't she like Hispanics?" Melissa asked, and Rose shrugged her shoulders.

"I don't know and neither do they. We just know she hates them. Whenever Alex invites her to eat with our family, she refuses. I can only imagine how bad Chad's gonna get it when she finds out you're full-on Hispanic, knowing Spanish and all."

"Whoa, I was born here, and so was my mom... maybe not my dad, but I am an American with Cuban roots." Melissa was processing the information. "Anyway, I don't like him, so why should I care what his mom thinks? Plus, even if I did like him, he lives hundreds of miles away. I doubt this will be anything more than a winter fling, and I don't want that. If I'm going to look cute, it's because I want to, not because I have to for some dude I don't even like, ugh."

But in Melissa's mind, she thought differently. *I need to get to know him. I have to prove he's not the Chad from the prophecy. Oh my gosh, what if he really is the Chad?* She pushed the thoughts aside to enjoy the evening.

Melissa and the girls rummaged through the closet to find outfits and mixed-and-matched styles for tomorrow. It made Melissa happy she could share this with her cousins. At home, Emmy always whined whenever Melissa attempted to do girl stuff, and her sister always refused, which strained their relationship.

Melissa felt like Rose's personal Barbie doll. She plucked Melissa's eyebrows, waxed the thin hairs on her upper lip, and suggested different outfits. There were breaks in between where the girls would pause and enjoy a movie, play with the dogs, and gossip about school, boys, and family.

Rose built a tight French braid on Melissa and said, "We're officially done! You look hot, girl!"

"Yes, she does!" Lily exclaimed. "Can we please watch Titanic tonight?"

"A chick flick?" Melissa blurted but quickly said, "I mean, I am so down!" she squeaked. "I'll meet you guys downstairs." The sisters nodded, and they rushed downstairs to prepare the VHS.

Melissa watched Rose place the videocassette inside the video home system and rewind the movie to the beginning. Melissa felt her VHS was a barely functioning antique compared to their state-of-the-art home entertainment system.

Melissa changed into her PJs: fuzzy black pants, a white

long-sleeve, and fuzzy black socks. She snatched her blanket, and before she went downstairs, she looked out the window to peek at Chadwick's house.

"Could you really be the 'Chad?'" Melissa mumbled, closing her eyes and releasing a sigh.

There was a static-like noise, and Melissa lowered her eyebrows. "What the..." She searched for her walkie-talkie and said, "Emmy?"

Static continued to buzz. "Emmy? I thought she said it wouldn't work so far away." She tried hitting the walkie-talkie to get it to work.

"Really, dude? A snowball?" a voice responded.

"Yeah, dude," a familiar voice responded. "Yes! She took a snowball for me; it was pretty badass."

Melissa gasped and exclaimed, "It's Chad! Oh my gosh, it picked up his channel!"

"You hear that noise?" his voice said, and Melissa covered her mouth. "Never mind, but yeah, the girl is my brother's girlfriend's cousin. She hates my guts. She's got a mouth on her, dude!"

Pfft, Melissa rolled her eyes.

"But she's beautiful." The comment caught Melissa by surprise.

Unwillingly, a smile crept onto her face, and her cheeks grew warm. "And she's pretty funny. And calls me out on my stuff! Dude, I never had a girl do that to me before. She makes me feel... I can't even explain it- I like her. We'll see how it goes tomorrow, later," Chad ended.

Melissa glimpsed at the mirror and noticed her face burned red at Chad's comment. She shook her head to shake the color away from her cheeks. *Stop blushing...* she told herself. She stared at her own reflection and thought, *the douche thinks I'm beautiful. Ugh, that doesn't matter because he's not the Chad.*

At that, Melissa joined the girls downstairs and put herself through torture by watching the third chick flick of the day with the girls. She thought, *Where is the horror, man!* She felt miserable while watching the romance of Jack and Rose; *it would be nice, though... to have a love like that.*

And for a moment, Melissa felt special. Sure, she didn't like Chadwick, but he favored her. He was undoubtedly handsome, even though she dreaded admitting it.

Chapter Seven

A soft tap on Melissa's shoulder woke her from her slumber. "Stop..." she groaned and rolled over on her side.

"Um, you're on the couch, and I'd like to sit," Chadwick's voice spoke. Melissa lifted her head and struggled to open her eyes; through her blurred vision, she saw Chadwick dressed in hiking gear: blue jeans, a gray sweatshirt, boots, and a coat that hung open.

He then mocked, "Good morning, Sleep Queen."

"Ugh," Melissa scoffed; she didn't care that he saw her in her PJs and snoozed away on the couch. "What time is it?" she asked.

"It's six in the morning," Chadwick explained. "Looks like someone fell asleep on the couch."

"Can you blame me," Melissa rubbed her eyes with her knuckles. "Pfft, Rose and Lily played chick flicks all night."

"Wait, you're a girl, and you don't like chick flicks?"

"So, what? You assume because I'm a girl, I enjoy chick flicks?" Melissa stood up, yanking the blanket up with her.

"No! I mean- I-uh, I think it's a little odd... never met a girl who doesn't like chick flicks."

"Well," Melissa clicked her tongue. "I'm Melissa. Nice to meet ya." She stretched out her hand, smirking. Chadwick chuckled nervously at her witty comment, turning pink in the cheeks as he reached out to shake it.

He didn't let go, but neither did she. Melissa noticed Chadwick couldn't find the words to break the silence.

"Uh-" he stumbled. "Um." His eyes locked onto hers and they twinkled. Melissa felt anxiety stir inside her, or was that how butterflies felt? She didn't want to feel butterflies for the douche. Still, they stormed inside her stomach, especially after last night's comment about her beauty.

That fueled her anxiety, so she broke contact and yanked her hand back. "Um, I'm going to get dressed."

"Sure! Yeah- um, see you in a bit."

She ambled upstairs and dressed in her leg warmers underneath dark blue jeans, a long-sleeved scarlet shirt, combat boots, black gloves, and a beanie; her beanie had a tiny unicorn on it.

Lily walked in just as Melissa slipped on her black leather jacket. "You're really going for that… uh…tomboy-type look, huh? It's super cute!" The "S" in 'super' sounded off as the young girl's tongue pressed against her teeth, giving her a slight lisp.

"Thanks!" Melissa appreciated the comment. "It's nice to hear someone appreciate the tomboy style!" She referred to her mother and sister's opinions about her fashion choice. "Don't get me wrong, I like good fashion, but how fashionable can you go hiking?" Melissa asked as Rose strolled into the room, wearing a complete pink camouflage hiking outfit with two French braids. "I take that back," Melissa mumbled.

The girls went downstairs to meet with the Lovette boys

and the rest of the family.

The brothers were sitting together on the couch, chatting and chuckling. Melissa noticed how Alex nudged Chadwick at Melissa's sight. Chadwick glanced at her, and again, his eyes twinkled; *why do his eyes shine every time he sees me?* Melissa felt her cheeks grow warm. *Stop blushing for him, Melissa! Coño!*

"Is everyone ready?" Uncle Ozzy asked, and everyone nodded.

Uncle Rudy approached Melissa and squinted his eyes. "Wow, you look nice for hiking!" He looked back and noticed Chadwick and spoke in Spanish. "Oh, when a cute boy comes around, then you're the beauty, but when it's just us lowly uncles, you're the beast?"

"Grrrrr!" She winked at her uncle, and they laughed as Chadwick watched them in amusement. She then told him in Spanish, "I look cute for me, Uncle Rudy; I'll never dress to impress a boy, much less a douche."

All the minors were told to ride with Uncle Rudy and Nina in his Escalade. Alex held Rose's hand and hurriedly pulled her to the back seat. Rose called out to Lily. "Lily! Sit next to me, hurry!" she hissed at her little sister.

It took Melissa a while to interpret their lopsided smiles; they tried forcing her and Chadwick to sit together in the second row. Chadwick was oblivious, or at least pretended to be since he just sat in the back and gestured for her to climb in.

Melissa climbed in but sat on the far right while he was on the far left. She glanced at him: he sat straight, but she noticed how he fidgeted his fingers. *Can this kid really be the love of my life?* Melissa bounced a leg, *and if he is, how can I ever tell him about my dreams? According to an elf, you're the love of my life because a prophecy says so. No pressure! UGH! Emmy is right. I gotta*

get my head out of the clouds… but I met a Chad… worlds away.
Melissa released a heavy sigh.

"Hey, are you okay?" Chadwick asked.

"Huh?" Melissa snapped out of her thoughts.

"Are you nervous to hike?" he asked.

"No! My bad, it's just cold."

"Oh, would you like my jacket?" Before Melissa could say no, he was already taking it off and handing it to her.

"Oh, thank you." Melissa took it and placed it over her shoulders. She wasn't freezing, but she felt terrible declining his kind gesture. *Maybe he's not so much of a douche…*Rose, Alex, and Lily talked in the back while Melissa and Chadwick remained quiet.

"So Mel," the way Chadwick said, Mel shook her. "Are you missing home yet?"

No one has ever called me Mel before…

"I do," she responded. "I didn't think I would, but I miss the humidity. I'm not used to this cold, and snow is not what I thought it'd be."

"That tends to happen," Chadwick explained. "People think snow is light and fluffy."

"That's what I thought!" Melissa admitted.

"Is this your first time out of state?" Melissa nodded. "What?! That's crazy. I've been to New York, Maryland, D.C., and Pennsylvania," he bragged. It reminded Melissa how dull her life was.

It's because he's a privileged white boy. Of course, you've traveled a lot and need to brag about it to a girl who's never left Miami. "I really want to visit Miami," Chad added after boasting about his past trips. Melissa remained quiet, but when he sighed, she glanced over. He fidgeted his fingers some more and bit his lower lip. Guilt instantly washed over her like a heavy rainfall.

C'mon Melissa, that's not fair, she felt her conscience speak to her. *Stop feeling sorry for yourself. Make an effort to talk. He gave you his jacket to keep you warm. He may not really be a Chad- an egocentric, lazy, privileged white boy.*

"Your brother mentioned you love Miami... how come?" Melissa asked, and Chadwick looked at her, gleaming at her question.

"I love the ocean," he admitted. "My dad takes me surfing sometimes in the Outer Banks during the summer."

"Oh nice, I'd love to surf, but Miami isn't a great place to surf. But I love the ocean, too. I feel like water grounds me. Uncle Rudy takes me to Miami Beach sometimes with my best friend."

"I'd love to see the beaches in Miami. They say they're some of the best in the country. I'm obsessed with marine animals. I saw this episode on Animal Planet about whales, and it's so dope the way they jump out of the water and call one another with their calls."

I wonder what your thoughts on mermaids and Kraken are? Melissa pondered and felt tempted to ask but said, "I like birds more, like eagles."

"Nice," his eyes fixated on her lips, and Melissa arched a brow.

"Why are you staring at my mouth?" she asked, and his face flushed red as if embarrassed she pointed that out.

"'Cause..." Chadwick stumbled on his words and suddenly blurted, "You have an interesting accent."

"I have an accent?" Melissa responded, puzzled.

"Oh, yeah!" Alex joined in. "Can't you tell?"

"Not really," Melissa scratched her head. "I thought you

guys were the ones with an accent."

Chadwick chortled at her comment and gave her an explanation. "In all honesty, I think we all have accents. Your uncle and aunt have the same accent as you. I guess it's a Miami accent?"

"I guess," Melissa shrugged her shoulders.

"I noticed you know how to speak Spanish when talking to your uncle at the house."

"Si." Melissa gave her usual smirk. "Tu eres un bobito." Her Uncle Rudy and Nina both burst into laughter.

"Whoa, what did you just say?!" Chadwick asked, excited for her to translate. "It means 'nice to see you.' Uncle Rudy explained, and Melissa muffled a laugh.

While on their way to Grandfather Mountain, Uncle Rudy stopped at the local fast-food spot to grab a quick bite for the hungry teens. Melissa and Chadwick continued their small chit-chat about Miami, Boone, and anything else between those cities.

When they finally arrived at Grandfather Mountain, Melissa returned Chadwick his jacket, but only for him to refuse. Instead, he just stuck by Melissa throughout their walks, explaining the history of Grandfather Mountain.

They walked through the steep, rocky paths amid evergreen trees, and saw bulging rocks peering over the cliff edges. Melissa had never seen such rock formations since Florida was a flat state.

Despite the chill in the air, the sun was relentless as they walked, but it was worth it when she reached the top. At the peak of their hike, she gazed upon the vast blue sky, which stretched as far as the mountains.

"Ya know, you!re currently standing on a long history of rock formation," Chad boasted and explained the formation of rocks and its Cherokee name, 'Tanawha.'

"You really know your geography," Melissa commented. "Or is that what you tell all your girlfriends?" she remarked.

"Um, I don't have a girlfriend, but- I've never told a girl about rock formations or how I love the ocean. I guess you can say I like nature, but you're the first person I've ever opened up to about that." It seemed it perplexed Chadwick to admit such minor details of his life, but Melissa found it amusing.

Should I believe him? She doubted him, but whenever his eyes looked into hers, they would twinkle again, and Melissa felt the butterflies again.

She gulped and shifted her thoughts to Gemma. *If he loves geography that much… I wonder what he'll think of Gemma. No, Melissa. He would think nothing of it because I still think he's not the 'Chad.' Ugh, but whenever he gives me that look, I can't help but feel nervous. His eyes are pretty dreamy.*

A part of her was stubborn- she had this initial thought of him being a douchebag, but he was so kind and made small gestures that would catch her off-guard. He'd offered his hand to help her climb up to the rocks, and he refused to take his jacket back even though she was perfectly warm.

She continued to gaze at the evergreen forest. Melissa's lips stretched wider into a gaping grin, and her eyebrows arched for the sky. Chadwick giggled as he watched her embrace the scenery.

"It's so beautiful," Melissa said under her breath after taking in a deep breath. "If only I was in Gemma."

"Gemma?" Chadwick responded, and Melissa didn't realize she had thought out loud.

"Um, er-" Melissa stumbled. "I said, epa, haha, it means wow in Spanish!"

"Oh," Chad shrugged. "I thought you said Gemma. It would be cool if you had the game."

"Wait, what!?" Melissa exclaimed. She thought she must have misheard him.

"Yeah," she startled him. "POG? Power Over Gemma? If I'm not mistaken, Rose and Lily's grandfather created it with his brothers."

It was as if a bucket of ice-cold water washed over Melissa. She turned paler than a ghost, and Chadwick must've noticed because he asked, "Are you alright?"

"POG? Is there a kingdom called Amethyst?"

"Yeah! So, you do know about it?"

Is everything based on a silly game? Melissa's mind spiraled into a panic; *no, it can't be! Because otherwise, why would I have dreams? No... it has to be real! I mean, I met a 'Chad' worlds away... and Great Uncle Pablo helped to move Chad.... So they must've known about Chad being the tungsten ring. No, no... this is real. Don't doubt your dreams now, Melissa.*

"Um, can you tell me more about the game?" Melissa prompted, and Chadwick did. As he did, they both walked closely together while they hiked.

With her mind clustered, Melissa tripped over a rock, and Chadwick caught her arm in the crook of his arm, saving her from the fall.

"Thanks," Melissa muttered. Part of her didn't want to release her arm from being crossed with his, so she stayed that way, and they continued to hike.

"The game is a lot like WOW." Melissa knew exactly what he was talking about. She had always yearned to play World of WarCraft, not just because of the game's magical elements and world-building but because most of her friends from the TV crew played it. But alas, she didn't want to pester her mother into spending money on a fantasy game.

Chad continued to explain POG to her. "Supposedly, the girl's grandfather, Pablo, created it because he and his brothers loved magic and fantasy. I thought they would launch the game but didn't want to. It was just more of a hobby, I guess. But it's a super fun game because you can be a human, an elf, a dwarf, or a centaur. Your role is to protect the land from dark creatures from the Dark Forest of Garnet."

Melissa quickly recalled the hooded figure that murdered the unicorn in cold blood. She shuddered. "But Gemma is fun. There's a meadow with-"

"Colorful sunflowers?" Melissa finished for him.

"Yeah, so you *do* know about Gemma?"

"Well… my abuelo, Pablo's brother, told me stories of Gemma growing up. He always said I was a dragon rider meant to fulfill some prophecy… I don't know, I've kinda held onto that." Melissa gulped, hoping this admission didn't scare him off.

"Well, it seems like your family has a great imagination. The world is so detailed, and sometimes even I think a world like that could be real."

"What if it is?" Melissa asked, and Chadwick gave her a sidelong glance.

"Um," his eyes searched up as if finding the right words. "I mean, it'd be nice, but… we both know it's not."

"But-" Melissa wanted to tell Chadwick about the dreams, the prophecy, and how he might be her soulmate. But she swallowed her words instead, and they continued walking.

In front of them were Alex and Rose, holding hands and swinging them like little children. Melissa noticed Rose's eyes would meet with Alex, her cheeks flourished with color, and her nose crinkled. It was clear her heart longed for his.

Alex's heart longed for her, too. His smile never faded when Rose was around, and Melissa noticed how Chadwick would do the same with her.

Wow, maybe this douche really does like me, Melissa thought, feeling her hardened emotional shell cracking ever so slightly.

Lily skipped past Chadwick and Melissa and towards Rose and Alex, her voice singing with optimism. "Can we go to the Mile-High Swinging Bridge?"

"What's that?" Melissa asked Chadwick.

"It's a bridge that's a mile above sea level. You can see all the forest. It's an awesome view, look!" Chadwick pointed his finger to the bridge.

"No way! I am *so* down!" Melissa squealed.

"You're not afraid of heights?" Chadwick probed.

"Nah," she whispered. "I'm a dragon rider, remember?" She winked at him, and Chadwick chuckled, amused by Melissa's daringness and fantasies.

"Ugh, that's *soooo* boring," Rose whined. "Melissa is not gonna wanna do that."

"I don't mind!" Melissa called out.

"You see! C'mon, let's go do it."

"Lily, no, " Rose bluntly told her. "We've done it *soooo* many times. The view hasn't changed."

"Melissa has never seen it," Lily pleaded. "Puh-lease."

"I said no," Rose said.

Melissa and the Lovette brothers remained silent during the awkward dispute. It reminded Melissa of the venomous quarrels she and Victoria engaged in.

"Just because you're a scaredy cat doesn't mean you should take the fun away from others. You're ruining the fun for Melissa!"

"No, I'm not ruining *anyone's* fun," Rose spat.

Melissa attempted to calm the heated discussion between sisters, but Chadwick shook his head, a gesture not to get involved.

In the spur of the moment, Lily screeched at Rose, "I HATE YOU!" and bolted off from the group, her figure quickly lost in the trees.

Melissa took the initiative and sprinted after Lily, and the group followed behind her. They all called out her name, "Lily! LILY!"

"Rose," Alex said, "we have to tell your dad."

The group rushed to Uncle Ozzy and told him about the argument between the sisters and how Lily disappeared into the forest. Melissa saw the color flush from Uncle Ozzy's face, and he instantly roared at Rose.

"What did you do!? Huh?" A grimace twisted his mouth. "You know how sensitive she can be. All she wants to do is to be with you and not feel left out! Do you know how dangerous these woods are?"

Melissa knew Rose regretted her words to Lily. Her eyes twitched wildly, her breath became shallow and heavy, and her face flushed red. Melissa was familiar with that anxiety. It was as if she was reliving the day she was told her abuelo was officially declared missing in Alaska.

Her mind became a hurricane of negative thoughts. Her own breath became shallow, and her heart hammered against her chest. She relived that moment, only now it was Lily who went missing. She couldn't control her mind from the whirling negative thoughts.

She felt her hand squeezed and glanced at Chadwick, who whispered, "We'll find her." The softness of his voice calmed her anxiety to a manageable level.

"Listen up, everyone!" Uncle Ozzy spoke. He gestured to Uncle Rudy and Nina towards them. "Let's split up now and meet back in this spot. When you look up, you can see the bridge in the perfect shot." Melissa nodded. "Good. We need to spread out and find Lily before the day gets dark."

"Melissa, follow Nina and I," Rudy told her.

"I'll come with you." Chadwick interrupted Uncle Rudy. "We can all be close but still spread enough to cover all parts."

"Okay, you guys search that way, and we'll be on the opposite side. Don't venture off too much, or you'll get lost too."

"I have an idea." Chadwick pulled his glove out and placed it by the tree. "We know to come back to this tree."

"Good idea, kiddo, now go." Uncle Rudy and Nina walked away.

Melissa and Chadwick wasted no time searching and calling her name out.

Chapter Eight

It had only been fifteen minutes since Melissa and Chadwick had been searching for Lily, but it felt like an eternity. Melissa had to take deep breaths and remind herself they would find her.

"Hey, we're gonna find her," Chadwick promised.

"You don't know that," Melissa hissed.

"No, I don't, but you have to be positive. I know it's hard, but we'll find her." He assured her, and Melissa knew he was right; she had to be positive.

"I'm sorry," she admitted. "I lost Pipo-my abuelo, when I was 11; he went missing in Alaska; I guess I'm just reliving the moment."

"I'm sorry," he said. "What was he doing in Alaska? Lily!"

"He had to do something with his brother, not Pablo, the other one, Patricio. But they never came back. LILY!" Before Chadwick could ask more questions about Pipo, she asked, "Do Rose and Lily fight often?"

"LILY!" Chadwick sighed. "Yeah, but she's a kid, ya know? She wants to hang out with her older, cool sister and my older, cool brother."

"Let me guess, you're cool too," Melissa remarked.

"Haha, maybe," he placated.

"I bet you are, Chadwick."

"Haha," he chuckled. "I thought you were starting to like me."

"Me like you? Pfft, I'm not easy to win over, ya know," she stated firmly.

"Noted, I like a challenge."

"Is that what I am to you? A challenge? Pfft." She rolled her eyes and continued. "Is that what you told your friend last night?"

"Wait- how do you know I spoke to my friend?" Chad gasped. "You're the channel that kept interfering! How much of that conversation did you hear?"

"Well…" Melissa taunted him, but a sudden fresh smell of pines consumed her senses, and Melissa said, "Wow… it smells like Christmas."

"Yeah, yeah, don't change the convo now."

"Chadwick," Melissa whirled around. She noticed the trees were luscious and vibrant green. "Was it always this green inside the forest?"

"Mhm, go ahead, change the conversation-" Chadwick stopped talking when he noticed the trees. "Wait a minute, I've never seen this side of the forest before…" he sniffed the air. "The smell of pine is pretty strong," he admitted. A flapping noise startled them, and they glared up.

Caught in a shared gaze, they locked eyes with an enormous raven. The bird, seemingly as intrigued as they were, responded with a subtle tilt of its head.

"Whoa!" Melissa exclaimed. "That thing is half the size of Toby!"

"I have never seen a raven that big," Chadwick gulped.

The raven, once more tilting its head as if deciphering the teens' conversation, held Melissa's intrigued gaze. She remained captivated by both its size and curiosity. Suddenly, the raven spread its black-purplish glossy wings and took flight, releasing a piercing cry that echoed through the forest.

"Hey Mel," Chadwick tugged on her shirt. "Are we on some type of drug? Like maybe shrooms? Because the sky is purple." His words caused Melissa to pause her breathing.

Her eyes slowly shifted to the sky, meeting its amethyst shade. At that moment, it was as if a hypodermic needle full of adrenaline jabbed her veins. Chadwick's voice muted, and she could hear her shallow breath escaping her lungs.

"Chad... where's that bridge you said that was here?" she finally spoke.

"Now she calls me Chad, " he muttered before saying, "It's-It's um, er..." His eyes frantically searched for the bridge. "Mel, I can't find it."

"Chad, I think it's because we're not on Earth."

"What?" he scoffed. "Where do you think we are? Gemma?" He scoffed again, but she waited for him to realize the only world with a purple sky was the one from his game... and her dreams.

"Oh..." he murmured, then exclaimed, "How is this possible?!"

"We're in Gemma!" Melissa wanted to jump up and down, but she remained composed. "It's all real!"

"Um.... Again, how is it possible?!" Melissa ignored him and walked around. "Um! Hello! Where are you going?" He followed her as she let her fingers caress the trees. Mel! Stop walking!"

"Why?"

"Because if this is Gemma, then we need to figure out how your family knows about this place," he muttered in disbelief, still wrapping his mind around the situation. "I can't believe this world is real!" He stumbled to find the right words, and his eyes observed the amethyst sky. "Magic is real!" A smile crept across his face, and Melissa giggled.

"My abuelo is from here," she admitted to him, and Chad's head bounced back. "It's a long story." Chad gestured for her to elaborate, and she explained everything to Chad: the dreams, the elf, the prophecy, and even worlds away. But Melissa didn't share how the tungsten ring meant marriage.

She was too afraid to tell him he may be her soulmate. What if it caused him not to like her? Or what if she was too afraid to admit that she was starting to like him?

Chadwick's eyes stared blankly into hers, and Melissa felt an inkling of anxiety swirl inside her. *Why is he staring at me like that?*

Her mind raced. "Mel, it's all true. Look." Chadwick lowered his collar and revealed a tungsten chain. "Years ago, my brother and I found it when we were metal detecting at the beach. He found this dope coin I wanted, but he promised to give me the next thing he found, which ended up being this chain, and he's been kicking himself about it ever since." Melissa's jaw dropped. "I remember that day... It's when we met Pablo... My parents were at the beach, trying to wash away their financial troubles, and minutes after I picked up the chain, Pablo had found us. He talked to my dad mostly because, well... My mom is not fond of Latin people... but Pablo helped them buy a home in Boone. Then, years later, Pablo moved into the house right across the street with Ozzy and his family."

"I didn't know you had struggled financially," Melissa felt a wave of guilt surge her. She had judged Chadwick so harshly solely based on a name. She finally addressed him as Chad.

"I've never shared that with anyone before." He grasped her hand, and Melissa looked at him and then at their hands.

"I, um..." She yanked it back and placed her hair behind her ear. "Well, what part of Gemma is this? You know more about it than I do, and that hurts to admit, given that I love magic." Chad still appeared to be making sense of his surroundings, grappling with the reality that he was no longer on earth.

"Haha, well..." They looked forward, and the forest stretched deep into the darkness. The canopies allowed a brief glimpse into the dreary sky, which made the foliage appear even darker. Melissa's spine tingled as she felt engulfed by the eerie atmosphere of the woods.

Coiling vines dangled from several trees, and an array of wildflowers flourished, brightening the otherwise somber landscape.

Various wild noises, mostly caws from ravens, brought life to the forest and harmonized with beastly noises.

"Melissa, you better hope we're not in the Dark Forest of Garnet because if it's anything like the game-"

"What about the Dark Forest of Garnet?" a voice snarled.

The teens spun around and gasped as they saw a man with scruffy, dog-like hair and thick sideburns. A black velvet cloak adorned him, making Melissa shiver as she remembered the hooded figure from her dreams.

His narrow, yellow eyes scanned them, and his button
nose crinkled when he sniffed the air. He snarled, "Who are
you?"

"We're, um, um... lost?" Melissa replied.

"Lost? In the Dark Forest of Garnet?" An eyebrow
arched, and he smacked his thin lips. "Come with me, and I will
help you find your way back." His random act of kindness took
Melissa by surprise.

"Oh, yeah, um..." Melissa was the worst liar, but Chad
jumped in, intertwining his fingers with hers.

"We're not really lost! We're just sightseeing in the Dark
Forest of Garnet. We didn't mean to disturb you, so if you don't
mind, we'll be leaving, buh-bye now."

As he attempted to walk away, pulling Melissa with
him, the man grabbed Chad and Melissa by the shirt. He said,
"That direction takes you to vampire caves, unless you want to
be dinner, be my guest." Melissa gulped, choking down her
rising fear. "I can take you to a nearby inn if you like. It's not
safe here. The Wendigos migrate here for the Winter."

"Wendigos?" By the sound of Chad's voice, he'd never
heard of Wendigos.

"Yes, man-eating creatures," the wolf-like man
explained.

"Ya know," Melissa interjected. "An inn sounds
perfect."

"Follow me," he gestured to them, and in silence, they
apprehensively followed him into the murky forest. Each
crunching sound beneath her foot made her wince.

"My name is Wesley," he continued. "Few visit the Dark
Forest of Garnet, and I have never seen humans dressed in
attires such as yours." Wesley stared at the unicorn on Melissa's
beanie, and she shrugged her shoulders.

"How'd you know we're humans, anyway?" she probed.

"I am a Lycanthrope."

The word Lycanthrope echoed in Melissa's mind. *Where have I heard that before... I know I read it somewhere.* She felt a lightbulb in her head turn on and gasped with curiosity. "You're a werewolf?"

Wesley snarled at her, pausing in his tracks, and Melissa whimpered. "A bit racist of you, huh, little girl? That is *our* word. You humans are never to use that word. Unless you are a spy from Amethyst! Only humans there call our kind werewolves."

"No!" Chad spoke up. "We are so sorry, we're not spies from Amethyst." Melissa couldn't help but feel drawn to how he spoke up.

"I'm sorry for being ignorant," Melissa added. "I'll never say it again."

Wesley eyed them but continued walking. Fear trembled through Melissa's body, and Chad gently squeezed her hand, still intertwined with his. He mouthed the word 'relax' to her.

Relax? I am very relaxed. In fact, I am so excited I'm finally in Gemma. She convinced herself, but who was she kidding?

"The inn has been empty for quite some time," Wesley broke the silence again. "The owner should be there. Maybe a few humans or vampires." The sound of vampires irked Melissa.

"Are there any elves?" Melissa asked, and Wesley stopped dead in his tracks while Chad released a disappointing sigh. Wesley slowly turned his head with a dog-like tilt; this time, his eyes narrowed, observing the teens. Melissa felt her stomach turn inside; she had made a terrible mistake asking.

"You are from Amethyst," the man stated, this time with a slight growl. "You should know the dragon rider and his band of elves banished our kind here."

"Banish!? What do you mean?" Melissa couldn't help herself, and Chad nudged her to stay quiet.

"Vampires, lycanthropes, goblins, ogres, minotaurs, and humans who dislike dragon riders' ideation are all banned from entering Amethyst simply because we once fought for the Lazarus Descendants. The food in this forest is scarce, and our people suffer. Yet, the dragon and its cowardly rider allow our suffering to continue. Victor will take back the throne one day."

"Victor?" Melissa spoke again, and Chad released a breath, frustrated at Melissa's constant questions.

"Yes, our leader, the rightful heir to the throne of Amethyst- the descendant of Lazarus."

"Oh, yes, Victor! What a nice man!" Chad interrupted Melissa, who already had her mouth mid-open. "Obviously, we've heard of Victor! We just thought some elves lived here too, ya know."

"Lies!" he snarled again, and Melissa clutched Chad's hand tightly.

"We're not lying," Chad replied. His smile remained hopeful, and Wesley's eyes glazed with malice.

He sniffed Chad, who muffled a whimper, and then sniffed Melissa. Still, the wolf's head bounced back. "One of you reeks of dragon blood." Wesley furrowed his brows. "I am taking you to Victor right this instance. Follow me, and if you attempt to run, I have no problem biting your throat." He revealed two long, sharp fangs and gulped.

Melissa shifted her worried eyes to Chad, whose face displayed paralyzing fear. Wesley seized the teens by their collars and pushed them forward, compelling them to walk ahead of him.

"You had to mention elves," Chad muttered under his breath.

"How was I supposed to know?"

"For someone who *loves* Gemma, you don't have a clue about it!" The comment stung Melissa, and Chad sighed. "I'm sorry; if you know anything about the game, you'd know how dangerous this forest is and how much they hate elves. We have to be careful, Mel."

"I see that."

The young teens remained quiet until they reached an inn-like cabin with a porch and empty swinging chairs. The lodge looked like a little, dark-wooded motel that appeared brutalized by rain. It appeared unkempt because of the high hedges surrounding it and overgrown shrubs. The property seemed to be sinister even during the day.

"Go on." Wesley pushed them to enter the inn.

Inside, there was a woman behind a wooden desk with long, raven hair and a chin so pointy that Melissa imagined her stabbing someone with it.

The wooden walls were plain, aside from a unicorn's head which hung by the stone fireplace. Melissa winced upon seeing it, and her mind replayed the horrific dream Alisha made her endure. *Now I see why Alisha wanted me to see that.*

The orange couches were old, with torn-up leather that stunk of old newspaper, and there was a long hall with wooden doors. Melissa assumed they were empty rooms. A fluffy orange and red rug was right in front of the couches.

"Wesley." The woman's voice was stern yet soothing. "I did not expect you to come by tonight."

"Nor did I." He gestured to Melissa and Chad. "I may have found two spies from Amethyst."

"Spies?" She scanned the teens. "They seem peculiar."

"They are. But one smells like-" Wesley glared at Melissa specifically but then shook his head. "Never mind. I am going to fetch Victor. I am sure he would want to meet them. Watch them in the meantime," Wesley asked the woman. "If they attempt to run, well, you have my permission to beat them, but I need them alive."

Melissa and Chad looked at each other, their eyes meeting in panicked glances.

Wesley exited the inn, and the woman glared at the teens. "Sit," she warned them.

The teens sank into the repulsive couches and glanced at the fluffy rug. The woman said,

"Do you like my rug? I crafted it from the hair of Brownies."

"Brownies? Like the chocolate confection?" Chad asked, and Melissa facepalmed and murmured to him.

"She means the small, furry creature... it's a mythological being. I thought you knew about Gemma?" Melissa jabbed at him with the comment, and Chad rolled his eyes.

"Mh, you are odd ones," the woman frowned. "Let me tell you more about brownies: they are little, fuzzy creatures used by elves and dragon riders to clean the castle and do their bidding in Amethyst. Think of them as pets, but they're more like decor for us." Melissa let out a shaky breath, and the woman cackled. "Now, you two remain quietly sitting down; I am not in the mood to torture humans today. Better yet..." The woman opened a cloth-like satchel and pulled out a small jar with black glitter. She placed some on her palm and blew on it, allowing the sprinkled dust to bathe the teens.

"Ugh!" Melissa coughed along with Chad. At first, her nose tickled, and then her eyes became heavy with sleep. She fought to keep her eyes open, but her vision blurred, and she could no longer resist the heavy slumber that took over.

Chapter Nine

Melissa woke wearing a long, ruby dress in the middle of the meadow she had missed so much over the last few months.

Realizing she was in the dream state, she instantly yelled, "Alisha!" She stood up and wobbled, trying to find balance. "ALISHA!" Her voice was screeching at this point.

"Rider, I am here!" Melissa spun around and met the stormy gray eyes of Alisha, who was wearing her classic, white-laced dress. It had been so long since she last saw the beautiful elf that Melissa forgot she wasn't human. "Your dragon sensed something was wrong; I have never seen him with such urgency about your well-being before."

"He knows I'm in trouble!" Melissa stammered, and if the circumstances were different, her heart would've fluttered with joy that a dragon knew she was in danger, but right now, her heart was hammering against her chest.

Between labored breaths, she told the elf, "Chad and I... we're stranded in the Dark Forest of Garnet, and I don't know how we even got there. " Alisha's skin turned paler than it already was. "One moment, we're walking in our world, and then we landed there."

"Melissa, who has seen you?" Alisha's voice now carried a tone of concern.

"We're in some strange inn. It looks like a cabin. Some werewolf named Wesley took Chad and me there and left to go get some guy named Victor."

"Victor..." Her gasp sounded like her lungs lost air. "You must listen to me attentively. I will notify the elves and your dragon. You must be very cautious and find a weapon to protect yourself."

"What!? Where? How?" Melissa's heart raced at the sound of the weapon.

"You are a dragon rider; it is in your blood to fight wars. Now go! We will be there shortly." With a snap of a finger, the dreams vanished.

*   *   *

Waking abruptly, Melissa shot up and let out an overdramatic gasp. She had been lying on Chad's lap, and he was still unconscious. She glanced at the desk and noticed the woman was not there. Melissa grabbed Chad's shoulders and shook, but it proved to be useless.

"Chad! Wake up!" she said in a half-whisper, half-shout. "Ugh!"

She glanced at her hand and then his cheek. She pressed her lips and scrunched her face before whispering, "I am *so* sorry."

She rubbed her hands together and slapped Chad so hard he woke up with a grunt and a fist in the air.

"What happened?" he growled.

"I am *so, so, soooo* sorry! You wouldn't wake up." She caressed his cheek, and a smile passed on Chad's face. At the sound of footsteps, Melissa said, "Shush! Pretend you're asleep."

She closed her eyes and laid her head on his chest. The sound of his heart hammering against his chest made her more nerve-wrecked than she already was. She felt the woman looming over them, and Melissa felt Alisha's words echo in her head: *It is in your blood to fight wars.*

She knew it was now or never.

Impulsively, Melissa snapped her eyes open and swung her right fist, punching the evil woman. Her memories of MMA flooded her brain, and muscle memory took over. She wrapped her arms around the woman's neck, used her foot to sweep her down, and locked her in a chokehold. There was a bit of struggle, but Melissa eventually rendered her unconscious.

"Melissa!" Chad jumped off the couch and watched Melissa tremble. "How'd you know to do that?!"

"I was in MMA for years," Melissa explained and elevated her chin. "I know a thing or two about fighting."

"You could've gotten hurt," he grasped her arm and scanned her.

"I'm fine," she assured him. "I had to do something. Alisha is on the way with the dragon, *my* dragon."

"No fair, you get to be a dragon rider, and I'm just some boy meant to assist you," he remarked, but Melissa smirked and thought, *believe me, you're more than just that.*

The woman groaned, prompting Melissa to snatch Chad's hand, and bolt out the door with a shared sense of urgency.

They sprinted towards the dense forest but in the spur of the moment, Melissa stumbled over a foot and fell flat on her face; she turned around, and Chad attempted to help her up, but the cloaked man kicked him to the ground.

The figure took a dagger out from the folds of his cloak and pointed the dagger at Melissa, and Chad yelled, "NO!"

His outcry was so loud that a flock of ravens screeched and flew away from the trees. The man raised his dagger to stab Chad, and acting on instinct, Melissa swept her foot at his legs, and the man toppled on his back and slammed his head on the ground.

Melissa scrambled up from the dirt, snatched the knife from his hand, and pointed it at him. "We're leaving, and you are not following us."

"*You* are not going anywhere." The woman from the Inn appeared. Her lip curled into a cunning sneer, and she blew a high-pitched whistle. The young teens paused for a moment and then noticed more men and women with cloaks emerging from the darkness of the forest.

Melissa sweated with fear; fighting one or even two people at a time was one thing, but there was an overflow of hooded figures. She could hear Chad's breath cutting short and took a deep breath, readying herself for the worst.

As one man attempted to grab Melissa, Chad swiftly intervened, delivering a forceful punch to his nose. The impact was so intense that Melissa swore she heard a crack. The man staggered backward, blood gushing from his nose, and cried in agony, "He broke my nose!"

The woman snarled, and when she took one step forward, Melissa held up the knife and warned her, "Don't!"

"Little girl, you do not know how to use that." Her voice dripped with malice.

"Try me," Melissa taunted her, and just as the woman was going to take a step, she paused with a gasp.

What is this crazy lady doing? Melissa gripped the dagger while the woman stood motionless.

All the humans whimpered and murmured, and Melissa heard it: a loud, flapping-like noise rushing through the forest with gusts of wind so strong that she and Chad held onto each other for balance.

A large, bat-like shadow loomed over them, and Melissa looked up, searching the skies. The shadow passed through them again; this time, its silhouette was unmistakable: bat-like wings, a slender body, and a thick, long tail. It was her dragon.

I'm a dragon rider, she wanted to say, but her thoughts wouldn't comply. She seemed to have no choice but to let the image of the dragon swooping overhead pass through her eyes, which became like dried-up sponges.

The dragon released a bellowing roar that thundered throughout every fiber of Melissa's body; some humans darted back into the forest to escape the dragon's wrath. Chad pulled on her arm, encouraging Melissa to run while they had the chance, and she managed a nod.

"SEIZE THEM!" the woman shrieked just as a sharp arrow pierced through her stomach. Melissa and Chad each released a blood-curdling screech at the sight; Melissa snatched him by the hand to sprint into the forest.

She pushed her arms back and forth, jumped over thick logs, dodged every branch, and pumped her legs as fast as she could. She could hear the sounds of running footsteps trying to keep pace from behind, and she took a sharp right turn, crisscrossing through different trees while still clutching to Chad's hand.

In the sky, they saw fireballs rain and crash into the ground near them, swallowing the cloaked figures. Melissa winced at the shrieking sounds of people being burned alive in the fiery flames that began expanding in the forest grounds.

A ball of ember ricocheted upon impact with the ground and landed on Chad's bare hand; he cried in pain.

"Chad!" Melissa shouted.

"Keep going! AHH!" He held his hand while tears rolled down his eyes.

An invisible, magnetic force lured Melissa to a fallen tree, and she noticed a den on the ground. She gestured to Chad to hide and wrapped her arms around his neck tightly as the blazes continued to scatter all around them. Chad held her, and they both shut their eyes tightly.

The sound of screeching and the crackling of the flames faded until there was complete stillness. When Melissa opened her eyes, she and Chad were back in the familiar woods of Grandfather Mountain.

Melissa and Chad glanced at each other with jaws slightly ajar and let out a breath of relief followed by a crazed laugh.

"There you are!" Uncle Rudy appeared and noticed their chalk-white, sweaty faces and eyes amplified with fear. "What are you guys doing?" Melissa relinquished her hold on Chad and stood up.

"I ummm-" Melissa couldn't find the words to lie, her veins still coursing with adrenaline.

"She fell," Chad responded. "I helped her up."

"Oh, are you okay?" Uncle Rudy seized Melissa, and she nodded. "Well, Rose and Alex found Lily. We have been calling for you guys for a while now. I was worrying we lost you guys too. What happened to meeting us back to that tree with your glove?"

"We just lost track of time, Mister Rudy," Chad explained. "I know these forests pretty well, and we got caught up. I mean, how long have we been out searching, anyway?"

"It's been about two hours."

"Two hours!?" Melissa gasped. "It felt like forever..."

"It did," Uncle Rudy agreed, and his eyes shifted to the dagger Melissa was holding. "What are you doing with that knife?"

"Oh, um, we um- found it!" Melissa squeaked.

"She found it in the ditch, which is why she fell," Chad sneered, and Melissa gave him a playful nudge.

"Oh, well, don't play with that. Put it back." Uncle Rudy turned around, and Melissa reached for Chad's hand to pester him, but he yanked it away unintentionally.

"My bad, I got badly burned," he explained, and Melissa looked at the burned flesh on his hand that was forming blisters.

"Oh, Chad... I'm so sorry!" Melissa said, inspecting the hand.

"It's alright, Mel. I'm glad you're safe." Chad stared into her eyes, and they twinkled like they always do. Melissa felt her tongue become thick. They both let the events of The Dark Forest sink in. It seemed like a nightmare, but they knew it had been real. They had gotten each other out of there safely.

"We should, um- get going," she mumbled, breaking his unnerving gaze.

"Um, yeah, sure," he sighed. "Let me grab my glove. I don't know how I can explain this to Alex, my mom...or anyone."

"Hide it with the glove," she suggested.

"Smart move!" Chad snatched the glove pinned on the tree, and Melissa offered to help. He winced in pain and shut his eyes when she put the glove on for him.

"All good," Melissa assured him. "Let's go."

They followed Uncle Rudy and Nina. Rose was clutching Lily, and Alex walked alongside Uncle Ozzy.

Uncle Ozzy remained poised, but his calmness did not fool Melissa; she knew the Guerra's wrath too well.

It was a stressful day for everyone, no matter which world it was. Melissa's mind remained fixated in the car on the Dark Forest of Garnet.

It seems like time doesn't stop when you enter Gemma... it's literally a door to another world, but how did we end up there? She gave Chad a sidelong glance and reminisced about how he protected her. *He punched someone for me...*

For the first time, she felt the urge to put her arm around a boy, and although she hesitated, she did.

He looked down at her arm and then at her; he netted his brows in confusion. Melissa's lips curled into a half-smile, and Chad pulled her closer to him, wrapping his arm around her neck. Melissa blushed, but she felt comfortable in his embrace.

There was an awkward silence in the car, except for Lily, who sniffled. Melissa twirled her hair, thinking, *I hate this silence. I can't take it anymore.*

She looked back at the girls: their heads were down, and Alex looked out the window.

"Lily, I'm glad you're okay," Melissa said, breaking the silence.

"Me too," Rose added.

"Are you really?" Lily wiped her watery nose.

"Of course!" Rose's voice croaked. "I don't know what I'd do if I'd lost you! You're my little sister. I love you more than anything."

Lily didn't believe Rose. The little sister looked out the window, her eyes hanging low, and Melissa spoke.

"My sister would never say something like that to me, Lily. I know Rose means what she says."

The words resonated with Lily. She nodded dully and turned her head to face a teary Rose; Rose opened her arms, and Lily wrapped her arms around her sister's waist and sobbed. The sisters remained in each other's embrace for the entire ride.

Once they arrived at Uncle Ozzy's house, he addressed the Lovette brothers. "Listen, boys, go home. I am grounding Rose and Lily for the rest of this week."

Alex and Chad nodded respectfully, but Chad glanced at Melissa and pouted.

Melissa looked down, exhaling a gloomy sigh, and waved goodbye to him. Her heart ached for him when he exited the house. *I will see you tonight.*

Chapter Ten

Inside Ozzy's home, Cynthia went on an angry rampage directed at Rose and Lily. Not wanting to linger around the living room where the sisters were being chewed up by their parents, Melissa tip-toed upstairs to the bedroom.

Sitting in the corner on her air mattress, she pulled the dagger from her boot and observed its dark blade with silvery double edges. Its leathery handle contained a sigil of a rooster-like dragon design, which she inspected keenly.

The door rattled with a knock, and she quickly hid the dagger underneath the piles of clothes she had taken out and prepared for when she took a shower.

"Come in!" she called out, and Uncle Rudy let himself in.

"Hey." The way his eyes avoided hers meant something was up. "Your mom is on the phone. She wants to talk to you."

"Oh…" Melissa gulped and reached for the phone. She prepped her ear for the insane amount of questions her mom was going to bombard her with. "Hola Mami." Indeed, her mom bombarded her with questions, but who could blame her? If only her mother knew Lily missing wasn't the worst part. Melissa had entered Gemma, her magical world, and escaped a fiery mess.

But she promised her mother all was well.

Melissa took a long, steamy shower. Her mind replayed everything from the moment she entered Gemma, from her dream with Alisha to their fiery escape.

I have a dragon. Melissa recalled the way the beast flew over them. *The dreams are all real... well, more like a friggin nightmare! Alisha should've had the decency to tell a girl about the cons. Then again, the unicorn dying should've been enough for me. But still... Today was horrific. I wish Pipo was here... I have so many questions. Why am I locked out of Gemma? How did you find Chad? Why did your brother create POG? What am I supposed to do?*

The droplets of water washed away Melissa's tears. She cleared her throat and forced herself to stop when she caught herself crying.

After her shower, she dressed in her fuzzy PJ pants and a thick black sweatshirt with her combat boots. Melissa used the towel and blow dryer to dry her wet hair.

Rose and Lily were quiet in the room, picking up their mountain of clothes. Melissa offered to help, but Rose responded. "No, you're not here to help us with our mess. We're sorry to put you through all this."

"Me too," Lily added. "Now we can't enjoy going out with you."

"But," Rose giggled. "You have Chad to hang out with. We saw the way he put his arm around you!" Melissa blushed and chuckled with the sisters.

"Stop," Melissa turned crimson red. "I-I don't know how I feel yet."

"Well, it looks like you do," Rose gestured at her outfit. "You look ready to go see him."

"Um… no!" Melissa's voice squeaked, and when she glanced at Rose, she wore a sneer, screaming with sarcasm. "How do I go see him? I mean… I don't want Uncle Rudy to find out…"

"Girl," Rose scoffed. "Go say you're walking the dogs and knock on his door, ask him to join you."

"I guess," Melissa began swirling her hair with her finger. "I don't know why I'm nervous… I know he likes me," she admitted.

"Because that's what it feels like to have a crush on someone." Rose winked at her and said, "Now go see him!"

Melissa nodded and dashed downstairs to take Magic and Toby out. As the dogs searched for areas to potty, she strolled her way to Chad's home.

Unlike her uncle's home, Chad's house was rather plain and dull; there were no Christmas lights, nor was it decorated for the holidays.

She nervously knocked on the door. A beautiful woman in her mid-forties opened the door. Her piercing green eyes studied Melissa, and her midnight-black hair reminded her of Emmy's hair, only much tamer, and her thick lips remained pursed.

"Hi, may I help you?" she asked.

"Hi, you must be Miss Diana," Melissa smiled weakly. "I'm Melissa." Diana raised a brow and responded.

"Oh, you must be Rose and Lily's relative. You look nothing like them." Diana added, "You look Mexican."

"You mean I look more Hispanic," Melissa corrected her.

"Excuse me?"

"I look more Hispanic, not more Mexican. I'm not from Mexico, and neither are my family. We're from an island near to Florida. It's called Cuba." Diana continued to stare at her, unamused by Melissa's witty response. "Anyway… I'm here for Chad." Melissa felt less nervous now, but standing up for her heritage had made her swell with pride.

Diana's face remained poised, her green eyes locked onto Melissa's face. "Chaddy!"

Chaddy, BAH! So, gonna make fun of him for that one. Melissa held her snicker.

Chad's footsteps ran to the door, and Melissa felt her heart quicken when she saw him run down in his sweatpants and a sweatshirt that read "wrestling" on it. When he saw her, his eyes lit up instantly.

"Hey, Chaddy!" Melissa mocked.

"No, no, you don't get to call me Chadwick, and you're definitely not calling me Chaddy."

"Well, um, I'm walking the dogs. Wanna come along?" Melissa asked, and Chad curled a cheeky smile. As he stepped out, his mother snatched him by the arm and spoke.

"Chaddy, come back as soon as you finish walking. Understand?"

"Yes, mother," Chad replied dully, and she released his arm.

"Thank you, Miss Diana," Melissa added.

"Mh." She closed the door, and the young teens walked around the neighborhood with the dogs.

At first, they walked in silence. Melissa was unsure how to talk about their insane adventure, or rather, a disastrous nightmare in Gemma. She wanted to blurt out any words, but then Chad spoke.

They exchanged an awkward "you go first" and giggled about it. He grasped her hand and said, "You go first, Dragon Rider," he mocked, and she nudged him.

"I wanted to talk about what happened today," Melissa expressed.

"Me too!" Chad spurt out.

They went over the entire day: from POG to accidentally entering Gemma, Wesley the wicked werewolf, Melissa's MMA moves, and the fire-breathing dragon.

"How's your hand?" she asked him, and Chad removed the glove, revealing his flesh, and Melissa groaned. "It's not so bad. I think it's a second-degree burn. I'll live."

"You should put antibiotics on that," Melissa warned.

"I think someone is starting to care about me. I'm guessing you don't hate my guts anymore?"

"Oh, shut up," Melissa playfully pushed him. "I still don't think you're the tungsten from the prophecy." Chad looked at her in disbelief.

"C'mon, even you know that's not true."

"I know- I'm starting to believe you really are the 'Chad.'" Melissa said it almost in a whisper.

"Why do you say that?"

"Because..." Melissa hesitated and bit her lower lip before telling him what the elf said about how he was the love of her life. When she finished, she watched Chad ponder the new information she had initially withheld.

"I'm not surprised by that," Chad finally said.

"Really?" Melissa exclaimed but cleared her throat. "I mean, really?"

"Yeah, prophecies are weird like that. I play a lot of POG, remember?" Chad reminded her, and Melissa rubbed the back of her head. "But I have never felt this way about a girl." Melissa released a sigh and stumbled to find the right words to respond, but Chad instead spoke, "You've never had a boyfriend, have you?"

"Um, no," Melissa admitted. "Technically, I'm not allowed... My abuelo had a strict rule about no dating till I was 16. But... I don't think I'd be a good girlfriend... I don't know how to be one."

"It's okay." He stopped and offered his hand to Melissa. She held it, and he nuzzled her towards him. When she looked up to his twinkling eyes, he pressed his lips on her forehead.

Melissa's cheeks turned a shade of rosy pink, and the corners of her mouth turned upward in a relaxed smile.

He said, "I love that smile."

Melissa placed her head down shyly, "Thank you."

Chapter Eleven

Melissa rolled her body over and felt a tickling sensation on her side.

"Mhh?" Melissa groaned. She felt the wind blow softly, and she opened her eyes. Above her was the purple sky, this time an amethyst shade.

She remembered the last thing she did. She had just finished her walk with Chad, wrote all the details of the Dark Forest of Garnet in her journal, and closed her eyes momentarily.

She jerked up, and her eyes met Alisha's when she turned around. Melissa yelped and scrambled back.

"My apologies," Alisha said; the elf was wearing a leather vest and skirt with a wooden bow on her back. "Dragon rider," she whispered. "How are you feeling?"

"Okay," Melissa mumbled. It took her a moment to gather her thoughts, and when she did, she peppered the elf with questions. "Why didn't you warn me about the Dark Forest of Garnet? Why did Chad and I end up there? And why do you turn your back on the species living there? Oh, and who is Victor? And who is King Lazarus?"

Alisha remained poised despite the barrage of questions; a smile crept across the elf's face, and she murmured, "In your land, some places hold magical forces. It could be possible that where you and Chad landed was once a battlefield, which explains how you landed in the Dark Forest of Garnet. Dragon riders exiled all vile creatures and beings from Amthyst. It is unfortunate you met Wesley. He is Victor's advisor and right-hand man. He is a vicious werewolf. I am... shocked he did not bite you or Chad. Victor is a vile human, a descendant of a ruthless king who lived long ago and ruled over Amethyst. Your descendants vanquished him from the Kingdom when dragon riders rose...And it is your duty to protect Amethyst from Victor and his allies as they did. Because the dragon rider has been gone for so long, that is why his people are taking bolder steps, Melissa."

Victor... The name of this evil person rang in her ears. Not to mention, he was just part of the problem. The Kingdom was in dire need of help, and most of all, it needed Melissa. She felt compelled to be there... with her dragon. She elevated her chin and felt it in her chest that she was more determined than ever to go to Gemma.

"I know you need me," Melissa said. "When can I come?"

"Without Chad, you are unable to come to Gemma," Alisha's voice lowered.

"But, technically, I entered Gemma with him already?"

"I understand your logic," Alisha responded. "Your grandfather did many things to prevent you from coming to Gemma. Wiping your memories clean was among those precautions. So was creating a concoction using yours and Chad's blood to cast a spell that forbids either of you to come without the other."

"Yeah, I found out today that Pipo and his brothers knew about Chad. How?" Melissa had been desperate to ask Alisha this.

"Your grandfather was strategic... he knew of Chad and the Council of Amethyst."

"Who is the Council of Amethyst?" Melissa gestured for her to elaborate, and she did.

"One person from each race in Amethyst, an elf, a dwarf, a fairy, and a centaur, come together to assist and provide professional advice for the dragon riders."

"So...all of you knew Chad?"

"Yes, and no. We knew of Chad, but your grandfather knew Chad. That is why he knew to leave you the clue, worlds away. Somehow, Henry took his blood... mixed it with some herbs and pixie dust, and had someone cast a spell that prevents you from entering any part of Gemma unless we break the spell by combining your blood with his in the flesh."

"Whoa..." Melissa lifted her hands. "That's gross, first of all! Second of all, there's no way around this spell?"

"Unfortunately, no," Alisha explained. "Wizards and sorceresses have been extinct for many centuries. We rely on potions and pixie dust. No one knows how Henry cast it." Melissa's eyes watered as her mind grasped so many things, such as how he knew who Chad was.

Other questions flooded Melissa's mind, like how Pipo created the spell if magic was gone? And, why? Without realizing it, a tear dripped from her cheeks. She felt betrayed by the person she looked up to most.

"Do not shed tears, Melissa. You will reunite with your dragon," Alisha encouraged her, and Melissa quickly wiped it off.

"You said before there was an entrance by my home, right? So, can Chad and I come through?" Alisha's eyes fell to the ground.

"Yes, those are the only two entrances we know of... one by your home and the Bermuda Triangle."

"How close is it to my home?" Melissa tilted her head, intrigued.

"It is the woods in front of your home." It clicked for Melissa. She never understood the magical aura the woods contained, but now she knew why she was so drawn to it. Inside the grove of trees was the entrance to the mythical realm of Gemma.

No wonder Pipo told me about 'El Coco.' He was making me avoid it.

"Okay...then, I guess I'll have to bring Chad to Miami... I can do that in the summer since we'll be on summer vacation." Alisha arched a brow, and Melissa explained the complex education system to the elf and all the breaks in between. "I hate school, though; I'd much rather be here with my dragon." Alisha laughed softly with the last comment but then sighed solemnly.

"Melissa," the elf's voice spoke in almost a whisper. "Wesley has your scent now. Do you know anything at all about Lycanthropes?"

"Werewolves?" Alisha nodded. "Ummm, they turn into a wolf on a full moon...um, something about silver hurts them?"

"Indeed, they shift unwillingly during a full moon. But make no mistake, he can shift when he pleases. Fortunately, there are several ways to protect yourself against a werewolf, and you must do so now more than ever because he has your scent. When you arrive back home, in your room, you will have a small knife made of silver laced with wolfsbane. When you find it, you should always keep it on you."

"A-a knife?" Melissa stumbled, and Alisha nodded.

"Yes. A minor cut shall do enough to hurt a werewolf." Melissa gulped as her head spun to hurt an individual, human or not. Alisha must've known, for she said, "All will be well, dragon rider. While you wait for the arrival of Chad, can you train in some ways?"

"What do you mean by train?"

"Train to fight. You should have been fighting with a sword at a young age, but your grandfather has ripped you away from that."

The way Alisha used the word "ripped" irked Melissa. It was as if the connotation showed some sort of resentment toward her. Even with the sense of betrayal, she knew there had to be a logical explanation for Pipo's actions.

"I can talk to my mom. She mentioned she wouldn't mind putting me in an activity... it's just gonna cost-" The elf gazed at her blankly, and Melissa felt it was useless to explain her financial struggle to an elf who may not know how money works on Earth.

So instead, Melissa gave a slight nod before laying back down in the tall bed of grass, closing her eyes against the amethyst sky and her mind becoming lost in her thoughts.

Chapter Twelve

The image of an arrow piercing through someone's stomach haunted Melissa's dreams since it happened. Despite the chilly nights, she'd wake up drenched in her own sweat of fears.

With Rose and Lily grounded for the first week of Melissa's vacation, it prevented them from joining the fun-filled itinerary Uncle Ozzy had created. But that didn't stop Chad from joining.

Melissa warned him about Cubans and how strict they can be. Still, Chad was bold. He'd ask Uncle Rudy permission to join them on their adventures, and he allowed him so Melissa would have company her own age.

Whenever Chad and Melissa were together, they spoke in hushed whispers about Gemma. They learned a lot about magic from each other. Chad tried his best to share his insights on POG, while Melissa did her best to retell most of Pipo's stories.

She told him about Pipo's bold risk of coming to the States and his encounter with a Kraken. But Chad posed an interesting question: why leave Gemma for Cuba? And Melissa couldn't help but think the same.

Her family's country's hunger, poverty, and suffering made her question Pipo's decision to live there. Why did her abuelo decide to live there? The more she learned about Gemma, the more questions she had about Pipo.

She told Chad about Jake, the imaginary red spunky dragon she used to play with. She rambled on about how much she loved dragons and mythical beasts of the air. Chad remarked it was clear she was meant to be a dragon rider. She had never played POG, but she knew more facts about dragons and other creatures than Chad.

One evening, while they were walking the dogs around the block, she told him about the dream with Alisha and the spell Pipo created with Chad's blood.

"So your grandfather took my blood? I never even met your grandfather!" Chad exclaimed in a half-whisper, half-shout. But then Chad gasped, blurting out, "Wait a minute... you see this scar," Chad pointed at the thin, crooked scar above his brow. "When we first moved into the house, I fell and cut myself against a marble... I bled a lot, and my parents rushed me to the hospital. I think Pablo might've gotten my blood that day."

"This is crazy!" Melissa placed her hands on her head. "Pipo must've gotten my blood. I was always falling and getting myself hurt. He also erased my memories. But why go to great lengths to protect me from this prophecy?"

"I don't know, Melissa... your grandfather knew so much...like, how did he know I was your soulmate at the time?"

"Um, I'm not sure." Melissa shrugged her shoulders, feeling nervous at Chad acknowledging himself as her soulmate. "But um, I can't go to Gemma without you coming to Miami..."

"What are you suggesting?" He arched his brow.

"Well, I was thinking, maybe you can, I don't know, possibly visit me in the summer?"

"I..." Chad hesitated, and Melissa inhaled a shaky breath. "...Would love that. But I hate to ask, do you want me to come because I'm the key for you to re-enter Gemma? Or do you want me to come because you actually want to see me?" The question surprised Melissa.

She bit her lower lip and responded, "You are the key to entering Gemma, but I would've done everything in my power to find a way to enter without you. I do like you, Chad, and I would like you to come and spend the summer with me in Miami. I'd love to show you the beaches and spend time with you. You can try pastelisto de guayaba!" As Melissa ranted, explaining what the pastelisto were, Chad worked up a smile and leaned over to kiss her, but Melissa moved her head, causing him to smooch her cheek instead.

"I ain't that easy." Melissa was too shy to admit she was nervous when he made romantic gestures, so instead, she taunted him, and Chad rolled his eyes up playfully.

In between her adventures with Chad, she spoke to her mother daily. Their conversation typically comprised her exploits and how much Melissa hated the weather. She admitted to her mother it had been impossible to watch telenovelas. Still, her mother promised they'd catch up when she returned. It was apparent her mother missed her because Victoria yelled in the background.

"Mom, give the girl her space. Wasn't that the point of it all?"

Right after talking to her mom, she'd speak with Emmy and give explicit details of her time with Chad and how, surely, she liked him more and more to the point it scared her.

"Hello, Perez's Household," A familiar voice said.

"Seriously, Emmy?" Melissa said.

"What? I can't pick up the phone and be like yooo, what's up? What if it's Cuba calling?"

"Emmy, I have so much to tell you!" Melissa completely disregarded her previous comment.

"Let me guess, I was right. You're falling for Chad."

"No, well, kinda, but it's not just about that."

"Pssshhh, I knew it," Emmy muttered.

"Whatever! Emmy, listen to me."

"Oh man, I don't need details of PDA, ya know. Keep the Public Display of Affection to yourself."

"No!" Melissa scoffed. "You're impossible, you know that?"

"Alright, alright, shoot, I'm all ears." Melissa recapped her adventure in the Dark Forest of Garnet and all her dreams to Emmy, who listened and remained quiet.

"So, wadaya ya think?" Melissa asked. There was a long silence, and Emmy cackled.

"Melissa, you deserve the Pulitzer for that one!"

"Emmy, I really wish I was lying. I even have the dagger to prove it."

"Puh-lease, you bought it as a souvenir."

"No, Emmy, I promise."

"Yeah, no… not gonna happen," Emmy stated firmly. "You can't just disappear, land in another flipping world, and then come back. It's not possible."

"Gosh, I wish you turned off your realistic approach in life sometimes and believed! UGH! Pretend, just pretend for one moment, you actually believe. What do you think of all this?"

"Well, I would say she and he ended up on the bad side of that world, and if she really is a dragon rider, then only she can defeat Victor. Victor's probably plotting something, which explains why her elf friend started reaching out."

"Well, maybe you're right," Melissa said.

"I know I am, now tell me more about Chad, is he a douche?"

"Well, I'll admit, he is a bit rough around the edges, but I kinda like it. Like, okay, the dude does have a massive ego, and he's a little cocky. But he put himself first in the forest and ensured I was safe." Melissa described his burned hand and the way he broke a human's nose in the forest.

"Well, he doesn't sound like a massive douche, still gotta meet him. And until I physically see his name on an ID, he's no name to me."

"Wow," Melissa sighed. "You are ridiculous."

"No, your dreams are."

"Well, I am starting to really like him, like a lot..."

"You just had to pick a boy hundreds of miles away. But I'm happy for you," Emmy told her and then mentioned, "So, Mia is throwing some massive party at her house, and word on the street is you and I aren't invited."

"Ugh, whatever, I'm having fun here."

"Yeah, but it's been boring without you."

"Awe, dude. I miss you too. Sorry I'm not there."

"No, dude, don't be. I'm glad you're up there. Plus, when you come back down, we'll hang and talk more crap about Mia." Melissa giggled, agreeing with her, and then hung up.

*   *   *

By Christmas Eve, Melissa and Chad's relationship had
blossomed. He and Alex joined the Guerra family on the night
of Noche Buena, Christmas Eve.

Melissa put some effort into her looks this time. She
curled her hair with a flat iron, set on some natural make-up,
wore a knee-length, long-sleeve black dress, and wore a pair of
open-toed wedges instead of her boots.

She walked downstairs, and Nina entered the living
room and immediately noticed Melissa.

"Honey, you look great! Come downstairs to take a
picture, come, come." Nina gestured to the girls to go
downstairs.

Melissa felt a tingle from her head to her toes; she was
excited to celebrate Noche Buena with her family. Every
Christmas Eve, her family gathered and roasted a full-body pig,
set up the domino table, and played salsa music.

Her Uncle Rudy typically lit a cigar, and her mother
would have a glass or two of wine. Nina approached him and
said, "Rudy, take a picture of your niece! Jane would want to
see her all dolled up." Nina tugged on his shirt.

"We haven't seen you dressed up in so long, Melissa!"
Uncle Rudy beamed at his niece. "Let me get the camera. Go
ahead, stand by the Christmas tree and pose." Melissa did as
her Uncle said, and he snapped a quick photo of her with his
digital camera.

The girls had a cutesy smile and a peace sign-up.
Afterward, she set up the red paper plates, green plastic
utensils, napkins, and white cups. She then assisted the girls
with placing the remaining presents under the Christmas tree.

When they finished, Melissa looked at the abundance of

presents surrounding the tree with their colorful wrappings and extravagant bows.

Wow, Melissa sighed gloomily. *I've never seen so many gifts before.*

Her stomach suddenly growled. The smell of cooked pork took over the classic cinnamon smell in Ozzy's home.

Everyone was doing something: Nina was preparing the salad, Cynthia was placing food on the table, Ozzy and Rudy were setting up the domino table, and the girls were admiring the Christmas tree.

She watched Uncle Ozzy and Uncle Rudy and couldn't help but have her mind linger back to the POG game. *I want to talk to them about it, but what if I'm wrong? What if they don't know about Gemma?*

"Hey," Rose approached Melissa. "So, Dad is letting me off the hook! Uncle Rudy and Aunt Nina have an appointment to go to and can't take you out."

"An appointment?" Melissa's head bounced back.

"They're going to a fertility clinic. They're trying to have a baby."

"Oh, no way..." Melissa's voice trailed off. Her mind wandered. *Geez, I hope it goes well.*

A knock on the door interrupted her wishful thinking, and the Lovettes came over. Chad took a glimpse at Melissa. A broad smile cracked, and he stumbled upon his words. "Wow... you look beautiful. I mean, you always do, but uh- yeah." He blushed a little and placed a hand behind his neck.

"Thank you," Melissa responded, looking down as she pushed her hair behind one ear. "You don't look so bad yourself." Chad was wearing dark blue jeans and a navy button-up shirt.

"Thank you, Mel," he responded. *Ugh, the way he says my name melts me.* She still couldn't believe herself, she once thought Chad was a massive douche, and now, she was getting butterflies just by the way he said her name.

The family gathered around the table and joined hands for a thoughtful prayer that Uncle Rudy gave. Uncle Rudy expressed how thankful he was for the family to be together and prayed they would do this often because it'd been so long since they had seen Uncle Ozzy and the rest of the family.

At that moment, Melissa longed for her mother, wishing she could be there with them. However, her mother found it nearly impossible to take a vacation because of the financial needs at home.

After the prayer, they ate like they had been in a long famine. Chad and Alex filled their plates with an overload of cooked pork, white rice drenched with black beans, platanito maduro (fried plantains), and yuca al mojo de ajo (cassava with garlic sauce).

"Oh man, I love Ozzy's pork." Chad moaned with every bite he took.

"I see." Melissa watched him devour the pork. *Geez, these American boys love a good pork.*

After eating, Ozzy turned up the music and danced salsa with Cynthia. After all the years Cynthia had been with Ozzy, she still danced like she had two left feet, and it puzzled Melissa.

Alex danced with Rose and wowed all the Hispanics in the room since he was an excellent salsa dancer.

Melissa was itching to dance, so she whispered in Chad's ear to dance with her. Although reluctant at first, he gave in to her pouty face. She taught him the basics of salsa:

they moved side to side, Melissa moved her hips, he then twirled her, and went back to moving side to side.

He grasped the concept, and eventually, they were both dancing salsa. Melissa's face glowed red while a smirk stained her face when she looked into Chad's twinkling eyes.

Uncle Rudy took photos of everyone and offered Melissa a photo of her and Chad by the big, beautiful Christmas tree filled with presents at the bottom. At first, she stood a couple of feet from him, but he placed his arm around her waist and pulled her towards him. Melissa responded with a nervous giggle.

"The cutest couple in Boone!" Nina declared, and the young couple looked at each other, turning crimson red and beaming.

"Hey, look below you," Chad whispered.

Melissa looked down and noticed a red box with a glittery green bow and a note that said, 'For Mel.' She gasped and grabbed the box. She looked at Chad, appalled. "Did you get me this?" He nodded, wearing a slick smile, and responded.

"I know Hispanics open gifts at midnight. We wait until morning. But I really want you to open it now."

"Chad… I don't know what to say. I didn't get you anything," she stammered.

"It's not about that, Mel. I didn't get you something, expecting something in return. I got you something because I want to see your cute smile. Plus, I wanted you to have something. At least something from me before you go home."

Melissa smiled at the comment and said, "You're so cheesy, Chad," and then thought, *he must have been rehearsing those lines all day*, and opened the box.

There was a little red stuffed toy dragon with a purple belly and beady black eyes. She giggled, "Awe Chad... he looks like-"

"Jake?"

"Yes, you remember!"

"Of course! I listen to you, Mel." Indeed he did. "I just can't believe I got my hands on it." Her eyes lit up; she felt them well up with tears, and finally, she stumbled upon her words from the shock.

"I don't know what to say." Her voice cracked. It was a small gesture, but it meant the world to her because the little red dragon reminded her of childhood and her love of lore. "Thank you," she whispered, and he pressed his warm lips on her forehead. Still, Melissa wanted to prove to him she, too, could occasionally be romantic. So she placed each hand on his cheeks and pulled his lips onto hers, kissing him tenderly, to which he responded by pulling her in by the hips.

"Wow! I've wanted to do that," he admitted.

"Guess I beat ya to it," she remarked, and then her smile faded into a frustrated frown. "It sucks so much I'll be leaving soon."

"Well, you still got a week left. Let's make it count."

"Te lo juro?" You swear? she asked.

"Tell o what?" She laughed.

"It means, do you swear? And you can never lie on 'do you swear.'"

"Well, I tell o juro," Melissa giggled at his failed attempt at Spanish.

As the festivities unfolded, the night radiated in the warm glow of laughter. Melissa witnessed the family opening gifts, capturing memories through photos, engaging in domino matches, and dancing to salsa music; creating a tapestry of moments that lingered in the air long after the last note of salsa faded away.

Chapter Thirteen

Laying upward in her bed, Melissa felt a swirl of emotions cluttering her mind. When she was with Chad, she felt pure bliss. All her insecurities and troubles floated away into an abyss. And on some nights, she'd filled the room with joyous laughter along with the sisters.

After Christmas, they were ungrounded, and Melissa got to spend quality time with them.

She grasped onto those happy moments through this trip despite the looming cloud of sadness she couldn't escape.

Then, some nights, she deeply wished that her abuelito was around to talk to him. Or she thought of her mother, who was probably working a late shift to ensure food was in the fridge while Victoria was studying in college.

Just one negative thought evolved into an avalanche of grief. The darkness inside her went beyond measure, and the immovable weight of her loneliness drained her energy. It was a certain emptiness she could not explain.

She knew loneliness didn't touch her, especially in Boone. A loving family, a potential soulmate—surrounded by them, and the reassurance that her world was real and it brought a sense of tranquility.

But an internal sadness lingered, one that she could not share.

And now Chad was on the list of names that didn't know about her ongoing depression. She could never share the empty void with him because she couldn't expect him to understand. Her thinking would just hurt him and he'd think he wasn't good enough even though he was.

She knew they loved her, but she couldn't bring herself to tell them she was in constant depression despite being showered with love.

She sighed, continuing to gaze at the ceiling as she wondered if she would always feel the same tormenting solitude at home with a new boyfriend. Chad had officially asked her to be his girlfriend yesterday on New Year's Eve.

He knew Melissa's mother wouldn't accept the official title. Still, they kept it their little secret amongst the cousins, his brother, and Emmy.

Unable to fall asleep, she sat up and pulled out her journal to transform her thoughts into writing:

I thought meeting Chad would help this empty feeling go away. Yet, I still feel just as empty as I did before. I don't wanna go home to the same crap as always. Hearing my mom stress about the bills, Victoria being a douche, and now being far away from Chad. I really like him and hope we can make it work. I just know everyone will laugh at us and say mean things. Why does the man of my dreams, and I mean literally, have to live worlds away? Couldn't Pablo have moved him to Miami? Why did Pipo and his brothers make things so complicated for me? Why is my life difficult?

Melissa shut her journal and stared blankly at it; her heart weighed heavily in her chest. She clenched her jaw and grinned her teeth. *Gosh, I wish Pipo was here,* she thought angrily.

She then curled into the fetal position, and to avoid weeping, she dug her nails into her palm.

The pain took away the tears that were forming in her eyes, and she stopped when she felt the skin tear open. She then grasped her toy dragon, clutching it as she slept.

While dreaming of sprinting away from an arrow, Melissa felt someone lightly shake her body, causing her to wake up in fright. Startled, she jerked up and raised her fists, and Nina responded by raising her hands in a surrendering gesture.

"Are you okay?" Nina asked in a voice filled with concern.

"I'm sorry," Melissa sighed in relief. "It was a bad dream."

"Honey, that was a night terror. Do you wanna talk about it?"

"No!" Melissa cleared her throat. "It's nothing."

"Okay…" Nina tone sounded unconvinced, but she shrugged her shoulders. "Well, get dressed; it's time to go home."

Home. She had finally adapted to the uncomfortable air mattress, but that wasn't the issue. She knew it'd be the last time she'd sleep in that bed because now she was returning home to her bed.

A bed steeped in a history of emotional releases, it had absorbed countless tears, preserving an intimate tapestry of her innermost struggles.

She slipped on her combat boots over the PJs and used the restroom; she put her hair in a tight bun and looked at the bags underneath her sunken eyes.

"Gosh- I barely slept," she slurred.

Still half-asleep, she dragged herself downstairs while clutching her stuffed dragon and saw Chad assisting Uncle Rudy in his PJs. Melissa approached with a grin. She tapped his shoulder and said, "Hey."

"Hey." He checked to ensure Uncle Rudy wasn't watching and pecked Melissa on the lips.

"Hehe," Melissa giggled. "I didn't think you'd wake up," she smirked.

"Pfft, what!? Of course I would," he scoffed first but then released a glum sigh. "I'm gonna miss that smirk."

Melissa pursed her lips and twirled her hair. She locked her eyes with him and cupped her hand on his cheek.

Chad brushed his finger on her face and pressed his lips on her forehead before saying, "Here's my house number and email. Will you call me when you get home?"

She nodded, and he handed her a little note. She tucked it away and said, "This is goodbye."

"No." He didn't hesitate. "Mel, this is not a goodbye. I'll see you in the summer. And when I'm there, we're gonna find Gemma." He pulled her hips towards him, wrapped his arm around her neck, and squeezed her tightly.

Melissa, too, had wrapped her arms around his torso and embraced his squeeze. She knew without a doubt Uncle Rudy and Nina were watching. After Christmas Eve, the whole family taunted Melissa's romance with Chad.

She wondered if they thought their young romance was coming to an end. But Melissa hoped this was only the beginning of a whirlwind romance.

Once she entered the Escalade, Magic hopped in and sat on her lap; her feet sank into newly refreshed pee pads. Melissa bid Cynthia and Uncle Ozzy farewell and thanked them for their hospitality.

She looked out the window and waved goodbye to Chad, whose expression was just as gloomy as hers. Uncle Rudy drove off, and Melissa kept her gaze on Chad until he became a tiny figure. Once the car turned left on the street, and Melissa could not see Chad, her heart shattered into a million pieces.

I might never see him again. She wanted to cry. But she forced herself to brush it off because she knew he'd return if Chad was who Alisha said he was. He'd come back for the summer, and they would find Gemma.

Leaving Uncle Ozzy's house and the sisters left a small hole in Melissa's heart. She loved being with her family, and she wished they lived closer.

Being with them for the last two weeks reminded her she had a family miles away who loved her; she was grateful for the time spent with them.

With Magic snuggling on her lap, she closed her eyes and took a much-needed nap after her restless night.

The sound of a car squealing woke her. Uncle Rudy had slammed the brakes of his precious vehicle.

"Whoa!" she groaned. "What happened?"

"Nothing," Uncle Rudy muttered grumpily. "We're back in Miami."

Melissa peeked out the window and knew she was on the infamous road in Dade County: 49th Street. Cars lined up, bumper to bumper, with no space for Uncle Rudy to maneuver out of there. This street to her house was constant stop-and-go traffic that was dreadful to all who called Miami their home.

Great, reality struck her at that moment. *I miss him so much already.* She was eager to call his house phone when she got home but had to play it cool. *Mami will kill me when she sees those pictures Uncle Rudy took with Chad and I. Ugh, she will ask so many questions.*

"Hey," Uncle Rudy interrupted her deep thinking. "Your mom has been calling nonstop to see how far I am from home. So, get ready for the tightest hug you'll ever receive," he warned her playfully. But Melissa knew he wasn't kidding.

Surely enough, upon arriving, she saw her mother and Emmy waiting on the front porch. When she opened the door, Magic sprinted out and watered the mango tree the only way he could.

Melissa darted to her mother, and they embraced each other. Her mother smothered her head with kisses before saying, "I am never letting you go again!"

"Mami, I can't breathe," Melissa said, barely audible, and her mother relinquished her hold.

As Melissa tightly embraced her best friend, the two couldn't help but squeal with unbridled joy at their long-awaited reunion.

Entering her home, Melissa spotted Jacob and Victoria seated at the kitchen table. Judging by the sight of Jacob assisting Victoria with what appeared to be a schedule of classes in her hand, Melissa assumed he was helping her prepare for the upcoming semester of college.

When they saw her, Jacob exclaimed, "Hey! She's finally home!"

He squeezed her with his arms, and Victoria said, "Nice to have ya back." She high-fived Melissa.

Despite her dislike for physical contact, Melissa embraced everyone in the room. When she approached Victoria, she halted her with a hand and hissed, "You just came back from a long drive. Go shower before you hug me."

Her sister's response caused a deep-seated hurt that gnawed at her, making her believe that her older sister didn't care for her as Rose did for Lily.

In the living room was Melissa's fake Christmas tree. It looked even more ancient than last year: the evergreen it once had now turned into a mold green, the lights barely functioned and flickered, and it reeked of old newspapers.

The smell reminded her of the couch in the Inn from the Dark Forest of Garnet. It sent shivers down her spine. She shut her eyes and looked below at the several gifts waiting to be torn open by her.

"Looks like you were on the nice list 'cause Santa left a few presents for the little baby of the house," Victoria mocked.

"Cool, let's see what he brought me," Melissa retaliated coolly, and Victoria's head bounced back in confusion.

Melissa's mother had gotten her a few sun dresses, new hefty combat boots, a Britney Spears perfume, and a make-up kit.

"Yes, more make-up!" Melissa squealed. "The girls taught me new eyeshadow tricks."

"Pfft, you wore make-up every day when you went out with Chad," Uncle Rudy commented, and Melissa shot a glare at him.

"Chad?" Jacob asked. "Who's that?"

"He's-um," Melissa wasn't sure how to explain who Chad was, but thankfully, she didn't have to because Nina did.

"Aw, he is such a sweet kid. He's Ozzy's neighbor. His older brother is dating Rose. He and Melisa hit it off."

"Hit it off?" her mother gasped. "You didn't tell me about him." Melissa's mother stumbled on her words, and Victoria snickered.

Emmy facepalmed herself, watching her best friend become a nervous train wreck. Melissa stopped, took a deep breath, and expressed herself.

"He's not my boyfriend, but he is a boy I like."

"What do you mean a boy you like? I don't understand."
Her mother barely let Melissa speak. "I mean- why didn't you
tell me?" Her mother glared at Uncle Rudy, who raised his
hands in defense.

"Miss Jane," Jacob interjected. "I'm sure Melissa
behaved, and Uncle Rudy and Aunt Nina were there to
supervise them. It's nice she got to make new friends."

"I supervised her!" Uncle Rudy fixed the damage he had
done. "We watched them the whole time. They would hold
hands and stuff. He was a sweet kid, Jane, you'd like him. Look
at her toy dragon! He bought it for her." He pointed at the
stuffed dragon.

All eyes fixated on the toy, causing Melissa to turn
crimson red from embarrassment. Victoria's witnessing the
discovery of a boy interested in Melissa made the situation even
worse. Melissa swore she heard Victoria and Jacob snickering
throughout the entire scenario.

"Awe, he got her a toy," Victoria sneered.

"Well, I think it's sweet he got her something," Emmy
commented. However, she added spice, "especially something
Melissa loves."

"He likes dragons?" Jacob asked, and Melissa nodded.

Her mother cleared her throat to change the
conversation, pierced her eyes into Melissa's, and pressed her
lips.

Melissa was afraid she would burst out in an angry
rampage but said coolly, "We'll talk about this later." Melissa
simply nodded.

"Here, dude!" Emmy finally spoke. "I got you
something."

Melissa opened it and was staring at a double picture frame. On the left were the girls just a few days after they met. Pipo had taken the family to the beach, and the girls had a blast.

Melissa was happy. She was smiling brightly alongside Emmy, who had darker skin then.

Must've been from all that sun during her time at sea, Melissa wondered.

On the right was a recent photo of the girls before they began high school. Both had drastic physical changes; Melissa had changed internally as well.

"I really love this Emmy," Melissa grinned at her friend.

Victoria and Jacob had gotten Melissa a new all-red backpack to replace the beaten-down Jansport. She thanked them, to which Victoria mumbled, "It was about time to get rid of your book bag."

Melissa pulled out a bag of her own. She handed out North Carolina keychains and refrigerator magnets.

It wasn't much, but she wanted to bring back something for everyone.

"Thank you, everyone for the gifts," Melissa said.

"There's another gift waiting for you in your room," her mother added.

"Another?" Melissa's eyes gaped.

"Go, run to your room, „ her mother encouraged her, and she did. Inside her room was a relatively new desktop with a green bow.

"NO WAY!" Melissa shrieked and covered her wide-open mouth with her hand.

"Well, technology is becoming a massive part of your academicism and it'll keep yourself entertained whenever you're bored at home.

Melissa later found out how much work her mom had done to make her new computer possible: it previously belonged to Uncle Ozzy. However, she paid a friend of Jacob's to bring it into this century.

"And look what I brought back from Boone," Uncle Rudy pulled out a black CD, and Melissa gasped.

"Is that what I think it is?" Melissa asked him. Her uncle had gotten his hands on POG with Chad's help.

"Yup! Chad gave me a copy," Uncle Rudy grinned. It overwhelmed Melissa with joy that so many people cared about her enough to make this work; she worried she didn't deserve all their time and help.

"I'm so going to download POG right now!"

"POG?" Jacob asked, and Melissa explained how Chad had introduced her to the fantasy game, 'Power over Gemma.'

"Your head is always in some fantasy," Victoria spat, and Melissa disregarded the comment.

Emmy assisted Melissa by downloading the game and setting up her new desktop. When her family had left the two girls in her room, Melissa took advantage and recounted everything to Emmy about her farewell to Chad.

She even pulled out the dagger to show her cynical friend what she found in Gemma.

"This is such a souvenir-looking dagger," Emmy scoffed, refusing to take another look at it.

"Seriously?" Melissa groaned.

She gave Emmy all the details of her pop kisses and all the times Chad made a romantic gesture.

"Well, look at you!" Emmy mocked.

"Stop!" Melissa giggled, playfully shoving her. "He's technically my first kiss…"

"I think it'll be nice if he comes down. I can't believe you have a boyfriend named 'Chad.' I still need to see it to believe it."

"Ugh, you're impossible."

"Why?" Emmy placated, her voice laced with frustration. "Because I refuse to believe that an elf visited you in your dreams and told you that your soulmate is a guy named Chad, and then conveniently, you happen to meet a 'Chad,' and then both of you magically end up in Gemma?"

Melissa briefly processed everything her best friend had just said but then commented, "You're impossible! Why can't you just trust me?"

"Because I don't believe in fantasies, or myths, or any of that magic mumble jumble crap."

"Whatever," Melissa shrugged her shoulders.

Afterward, the girls met up with everyone in the living room. Uncle Rudy set up his camera on the TV to show everyone all the photos.

Her mother commented on how grown and beautiful Rose and Lily had gotten. Her eyes even welled up with tears as she watched Melissa and them smiling.

I wish you had gone with us, Mami, Melissa thought. Her mother deserved a trip just as much as Melissa did.

Then images of her and Chad popped up, and she couldn't stop her lips from curling into a cheesy grin.

"Look how Melissa is blushing!" Jacob teased, and Melissa rolled her eyes.

"He's pretty cute," Victoria sneered. "He looks like a popular jock, but you look like a dork next to him. Geeze- how'd a plain-looking ghost of a boring girl like you even score that?"

"Victoria," her mother snapped. "How can you say that to your little sister? Apologize right now." Victoria muttered a forced apology, and Melissa's ears turned red hot.

More photos of the couple surfaced on the screen of them dancing and eating pork together. But it was clear Chad's presence made Melissa smile.

Emmy commented, "You guys make an adorable couple."

Her mother cleared her throat to show her dislike of the term, 'couple.'

Close to nine in the evening, Emmy's parents, thrilled to see Melissa back, picked Emmy up, and then Jacob left an hour after Emmy.

Melissa took a long, warm shower in her room and sat by the window. She reminisced about her trip. But most of all, she couldn't stop replaying the time in the Dark Forest of Garnet.

The images of fiery flames swallowing people up flickered, and she grinned her teeth. Magic snuggled by her, providing the comfort she needed.

Her mother knocked lightly and let herself in. "Hey, Mija," she muttered. Melissa continued looking out the window.

"Hi, Mami," Melissa replied dully.

"I wanted you to know I'm not upset at you about this Chad boy."

"You're not?" Melissa answered, her mouth hanging open.

"Well, I was at first, but only because you didn't tell me. Don't get me wrong, we have to discuss this because you know you're not supposed to have a boyfriend until you're 16. But that's not what I'm upset about. Why didn't you tell me?"

"I don't know," Melisa shrugged. "I was embarrassed and… I didn't think I'd like him so much."

"Well, I know what it's like being young and crushing on boys," her mother admitted, and Melissa grinned.

"Pipo would've killed Uncle Rudy for letting you be around a boy so much."

"I know, right?" Melissa giggled, imagining his angry rampage about no boys until she was 16. "I had a great time with Chad, Mami. Maybe he can come down for the summer and stay with Uncle Rudy. That way, you and Emmy can meet him, and he can have a great time in Miami with me. He loves the ocean, and I know he'd love South Beach." Melissa gave her the usual smirk, hoping it would convince her to let Chad come for the summer. "It'll be fun…" she persisted.

"So much for him being just a friend, huh?" her mother probed. "I'll have to think about it, okay?" A grin plastered on Melissa's face as hope filled her heart.

Her mother pressed her lips on her forehead, wished her goodnight, and exited her room. Instantly, Melissa pulled out the house phone she had hidden earlier to dial Chad's house.

To her delight, Alex answered the phone, not their stern mother. "Hey Alex, it's Melissa," she whispered.

"Hey! Glad you made it home safe; Chad has been waiting for your call all day." Melissa giggled, and Alex called out to Chad.

"Mel!" Chad answered the phone, his voice eager to hear hers. They spoke briefly about Melissa's road trip and all the gifts she received.

"I have some bad news," he said. "I asked my mom about visiting Miami, and she said no."

"No…" Melissa glumly sighed.

"But wait, I spoke to my dad." Hope sparked in her. "When I visit him in the summer, he's gonna let me go to Miami for two weeks, but my mom can't know."

"Oh- I don't know, Chad, that sounds so risky. Plus, you'll give up time spent with him. I wouldn't want you to do that." Melissa thought about how she'd do anything to be with Pipo again.

"I can see my dad any time of the year, but I can't see you. I want to be with you in the summer. I want to see Miami. But most of all, I want us to go to Gemma. Let's make it happen." His words resonated with her.

"Well, Alisha told me to find a trainer. I was thinking you should do the same. If you can."

"Yeah, well, wrestling season is picking up again, but I'll see if I can join a boxing gym after school." They remained quiet until Chad said, "I miss you, Mel."

"Me too," Melissa admitted.

After hanging up, she grabbed her Dream journal and scribbled a bit. She had a new quest: bring Chad to Miami and find Gemma. Now, her life was feeling more adventurous, which made her happy.

She then went to put it away in a drawer. But she had never seen a small silver knife in the drawer. It had images of four dragons embedded in the handle.

Melissa scanned the little knife and lightly bounced off of the blade. She curled one side of her lip, remembering Alisha's words: *when you return home, you will have a small knife made of silver and laced with wolfsbane. You should always have it on you.*

Melissa tucked it away in her new book bag and sat at her window to ponder her new quest.

Chapter Fourteen

That same night, Melissa dreamt of the Dark Forest of Garnet again. Only this time, when she escaped along with Chad from the enemies, an arrow pierced through Chad's guts, and his blood splattered onto her.

She looked at her hands sprinkled in red and wailed, but a swarm of cloaked humans ran towards her.

Her eyes snapped open. Drenched in cold sweat, her heart slammed against her chest, and she felt her hands trembling. She yanked the blanket off her, rolled out of bed, and stumbled towards the bathroom.

She splashed her face with cold water and took a couple of breaths to slow down the racing rhythm of her heart. Once she felt calm, she exited her room and noticed the sunshine peering through the window.

"Might as well wake up," she mumbled and went to the kitchen. She poured herself a bowl of cereal and slumped in the chair. She swirled her spoon with one hand under her chin and watched the milk form a whirlpool.

There was a knock on the door, and Melissa went to open it.

Jacob came in and sang, "Hey, kiddo!" Jacob greeted her with a cheek kiss. "You're up early."

"I couldn't sleep," Melissa responded. She slumped back on the chair and continued her gaze at the cereal. She imagined the white milk turning crimson red, and Melissa looked away, repulsing at the mere image.

"Uh-oh, what's wrong?" Jacob sat across from her.

"Nothing," her voice squeaked.

"Um, that's a lie," he pointed out. "C'mon, you know you can talk to me. What's got you down?"

Melissa glanced up, her eyes locking with Jacob's crystal blue eyes. "I had a bad dream... Well, nightmare, I guess, and I couldn't protect myself or the person I care about." She kept it brief intentionally. "It's nothing, I'll be fine. Why are you here so early?"

"I just got out of training. It's what I've been doing for a few weeks now. I lost a tournament, and now I gotta find a training partner to spar with."

"Training partner?" Melissa sat straight, intrigued by his comment. "Can I be your partner?"

"Pssh, I need a partner, Melissa. Not a trainee. I'm not a coach."

"Oh, c'mon! I was in MMA when Pipo was around and I miss it so much. Please?"

"Look," Jacob sighed. "I told your mom I wanted to help you not to be bored and cooped up in the house... but that's not the way."

"Ugh, c'mon! I need the training!" She pouted and gave him pup-like eyes. Jacob gazed at her, possibly pondering.

"Alright," he said. "How about tomorrow you meet me at the gym at 6:00 am?"

"Ew!" Melissa scoffed. "No, pass."

"Well, if you don't have the discipline to get up a little early, then you wouldn't be able to protect yourself when needed." He slipped on his training gloves, taunting her.

"Hey!" Melissa snarled. "I can do it, and I'll be there at 5:45, all warmed up."

"I'll believe it when I see it." Jacob and Melissa shook hands on it.

The following morning, Melissa woke up to an alarm she set at 5:15. Although miserable, she dragged herself out of bed and wore gym shorts, a sports bra, a muscle top, and worn-out sneakers. She left the house with a light gym bag and jogged three blocks down to the gym.

As she waited for Jacob, she stretched her arms and legs to get a head start. Jacob arrived promptly at six and beamed upon seeing Melissa stretching. "You came!" he exclaimed.

"You doubted me?" Melissa raised a brow.

"Pfft, I made a bet with your sister, and I won, haha."

He winked, but Melissa muttered. "Of course, she'd doubt me."

"Just ignore Victoria. You proved her wrong, and that's all that matters. Let's get started."

The first month of training was the most brutal, and it was clear she had been inactive for some time. Yet, despite the soreness and weariness, she remained resilient and never missed a session. Jacob even gave her the option to drop out when Melissa grew dark circles under her eyes and winced when someone would touch her arms. But she refused.

Jacob taught her how to block and strike opponents in boxing, wrestling, and Brazilian Jiu-Jitsu. Melissa knew most of the techniques and learned rather quickly, and Jacob appeared impressed by it. She felt an adrenaline rush through her veins with each training session.

On one occasion, Melissa and Jacob returned from training all sweaty. When she saw her, her sister pretended to puke. "You smell so nasty. Well, nastier than usual anyway." She chuckled at her own joke.

"Gee, thanks," muttered Melissa.

"I smell just as nasty, and you kiss me like this!" Jacob quipped to Melissa's defense.

"Ew!" Melissa laughed.

Victoria rolled her eyes and placed her hand up to ward off Jacob from enveloping her with a sweaty hug. "Don't you even dare!" she warned. "I'm studying, and I need to focus. This is my last semester before I graduate. Is Melissa giving you a hard time at the gym?"

"Not at all. C'mon Melissa, let's show Victoria some of your new tricks."

"I guess." Melissa shrugged her shoulders, and Jacob stood up and lifted his hands to fight.

"Punch me." Melissa went for a jab, and Jacob dodged it. She went for a right cross and a hook, but he slapped her hand away. When she went for another punch, he grabbed her hand and, with his foot, swept her to the ground.

Before her body slammed to the ground, Jacob quickly grabbed her; even Victoria flinched. Magic sprinted to Jacob and snarled, baring his tiny, sharp teeth.

"No, Magic, it's okay." The little chihuahua's protectiveness baffled her. "How did you do that so smoothly? You haven't taught me that!" She said.

"I know," he lifted her up. "I'll show you tomorrow."

"Melissa, get Tragic to calm down," Victoria commented. Magic was still growling, baring his teeth and drooling. Melissa snatched him up and used her voice to calm him down, but his beady eyes glared at Jacob, and he continued to rumble.

"It's Magic, not Tragic." Melissa corrected her, and Victoria rolled her eyes.

In the following sessions, he showed the sweeping kick until she got the hang of it and performed it on him.

"There you go!" he encouraged. "You're a quick learner." The sessions grew the bond between the two, and she felt she had an actual sibling through Jacob.

She often told him how much she liked Chad. Jacob listened and asked questions about Chad and the game POG, something her sister didn't do. But most of all, he helped Melissa escape her room and train. She wanted to be prepared for when she returned to Gemma.

She continued to get bruised like a peach twice a week with Jacob, but her sore arms were also causing some bruises on him. Although there were times Melissa would collapse in her bed, sore from her sessions with Jacob, she didn't stop attending, even if it meant giving up extra snooze time.

During the second and third months of training, it became smoother for Melissa. Her arms and legs didn't feel as sore, her dark circles disappeared, and her bony body finally gained some muscle mass. Her training even improved her performance at school. The early workouts kept her energized and focused.

But at night, myriad emotions would return like a wave violently rocking a ship. The thoughts of the Kingdom of Amethyst in danger irked her. She thought about her dragon, how he longed to see her, and how she longed to meet him. She also thought of her abuelo and his storytelling.

She'd often hum an iconic Cuban lullaby, 'Duérme Mi Niña,' to fall asleep. She dreaded sleeping because then the night terrors would take over. The Dark Forest imprinted on Melissa's mind and she couldn't shake it off.

Some nights, she would sneak out to the park and sit in front of the lake, grounding herself amid the chaos of her thoughts. The same enchanting aura she had felt in the nearby woods would surround her, compelling her to venture deeper into the mystical unknown. However, she resisted the urge to explore further despite the tempting allure.

This time, it wasn't 'El Coco' to blame. It was Wesley.

Despite her fears of a vicious werewolf, she refused to let it hinder her desire to be in Gemma with Chad. Her longing for her dragon grew stronger with each passing day. The image of lying down in the meadow, enveloped by the cheerful hues of the sunflowers, ignited an intense yearning within her.

Now more than ever, her heart longed to be in the magical world.

She pondered as she sat one night in the window spot. *Why did he hide me from Gemma? What were you so afraid of?* Melissa yearned to talk to Pipo, but he was gone, and she had to accept it even though her heart ached for him.

The thought of Chad coming in the summer helped her, and she longed to be held and kissed by him. She couldn't wait for summer to arrive.

Chapter Fifteen

It was finally June fifteen, the day of Chad's arrival.

A pair of hands shook Melissa, and she groaned. Emmy's voice spoke firmly. "Melissa, wake up! Your boy toy should arrive any moment now." Emmy kept shaking her.

"Chad!" Melissa exclaimed and immediately jerked up and readied herself.

The airport was a 20-minute drive from Melissa's home. Inside, loads of people were waiting around for luggage or waiting in line to board flights. Melissa had never seen so many people at once besides school.

She paced back and forth and twirled her hair, creating a thick knot. Her stomach was storming with butterflies like the day her mother spoke to Chad for the first time through the speakerphone.

That same day, her mother told Chad's father about letting him stay in Miami. Melissa's mother and Chad's father insisted they improve academically if they wanted their plans to happen. So, they buried their heads in the books to ensure they would see each other in the summer, and it paid off.

Her mother and best friend followed her every move with their head; it seemed as if Melissa's impatience was also rubbing off on them.

"Can you sit, Mija?" her mother blurted out. "Your anxiety is giving me anxiety."

"Seriously?" Melissa glared at them, and they both sullenly looked down, holding in their comments about her current anxiety. Melissa continued to pace and create more knots in her hair.

A new crowd appeared and filled the baggage claim area; Melissa tip-toed, her eyes frantically searching the crowd.

"Over there!" Emmy exclaimed, only for Melissa to realize she was joking.

"Hilarious, Emmy." Melissa rolled her eyes.

"I know!" she remarked. "Ya know, it's obvious you look nice for him, so obvious you don't even need to spell it out." She gestured at Melissa's yellow sundress and hefty boots she got for Christmas.

Melissa shrugged her shoulders and said, "I haven't seen my boyfriend for five months. Of course I'm gonna look nice." Her mother raised a brow. "Friend, that's a boy, mom, a friend, that's a boy." She reassured her, using her hands to gesture to calm her down.

Another crowd came out, and Melissa clutched onto the birthday present she was holding.

"He should be here by now," she mumbled.

Once the cluster of people dwindled, she took notice of a head she recognized. His chestnut-colored, scruffy-haired boyfriend wearing a black V-neck, khaki shorts, and an all-black Converse.

Melissa felt her heart palpitating, and she shouted while waving a hand, "Chad!"

His eyes shifted to meet her gaze, and they both sprinted to each other. She jumped on him, expecting him to catch her, but she tackled him to the floor. They both laughed and helped each other to their feet.

"Wow Mel! You've gotten strong." Of course, Melissa had told Chad about the MMA lessons Jacob had been giving her. Still, she didn't expect him to actually notice the changes. Her arms, now toned, taking away their once scrawny appearance.

He brushed his fingers through her hair, acknowledging its new length. Her hair had now reached below her chest. Melissa pushed her hair behind her ear, blushing all the while.

Emmy strolled towards the couple to meet the famous "Chad", with Melissa's mother following behind her. Her mother purposely cleared her throat to get the couple's attention.

Chad and Melissa then let each other go quickly; Chad placed a hand behind his neck, and Melissa looked down at her shuffling feet, holding a snicker.

"Emmy?" Chad asked when he glimpsed her untamed, curly hair.

"No name?" she mocked, and Chad chuckled. "It's so awesome to meet you finally!" Emmy said as she wrapped one arm around his neck and gave him a cheek kiss, to which he stumbled on his words.

"Remember, we Hispanics like to hug *and* kiss on the cheek," Melissa reminded him.

"Oh, right, haha, I forgot about that," he admitted.

"I know," Melissa wore her half-smile and whispered.

Upon seeing her mother, he said, "You must be Mrs. Paz?" Melissa's mother nodded, pursing her lips. Chad embraced her, following with a very awkward cheek kiss. "Thank you for allowing me to come and stay at Rudy's, eres un bobito," Chad said, and Melissa gasped, her hands touching her cheeks, mortified he remembered that comment.

Emmy covered her mouth to keep the laughter from bursting out of her, and Melissa's mother stared at him blankly, her eyes blinking hard.

"I assume you don't know what that means?" her mother said, and Melissa sighed in relief.

"Melissa and Rudy said it's nice to meet you." Chad scratched his head.

"Um, Chad, it means you're…um… dumb." Melissa ended the word in a whisper.

"Oh, my gosh!" he gasped, facepalming himself as his cheeks turned different shades of red. "I am so sorry!" Chad exclaimed, but Melissa's mother laughed it off.

"Melissa, you really have a sense of humor, huh?" She raised a brow at her, and Melissa shrugged her shoulders and sucked air through her teeth. *That's my karma. At least she didn't take it seriously.*

Melissa's mother then motioned the teens to walk to the car.

"Hey," Emmy said. "You promised to let me see your ID. I still don't believe your name is Chad!"

"Oh, you're right." Chad pulled out his learner's permit, which read "Chadwick Lovette." Emmy actually squinted her eyes, checking for any telltale marks of fakery.

"Well, I'll be damned, your name is actually Chad, well, Chadwick, assuming this isn't a forgery."

"What's the big deal that his name is Chad?" Melissa's mother pried.

"Nothing!" all three replied, and Melissa's mother eyed them all, wondering what they were up to.

As they walked, Emmy noticed how Melissa swung the birthday gift. "Girl, you haven't given him your birthday gift?"

Chad's birthday was January 15th, and Melissa's was May 16th. The weight of their long-distance relationship weighed on them on those days and other occasions, too.

Take, for instance, Valentine's Day. Students carried red and pink balloons, oversized teddy bears, and heart-shaped boxes with assorted chocolates. Melissa had gotten an early phone call from Chad before school to wish her a happy Valentine's Day.

Melissa and Emmy hosted the Valentine's Day special, where students paid five dollars to proclaim their crush on live television. Little did Melissa know Chad had promised to pay Emmy back for him to take part.

Melissa's face was tomato-red on live television, and her entire production crew rippled with, "Oohhhhhh." She hated public attention, but it was a rare occasion where she immensely enjoyed it for once.

Mia poked fun at Melissa's long-distance relationship and promised her it would fail. But Melissa and Chad ignored the negative comments because they knew what they had was real.

"Oh, snap!" Melissa facepalmed herself. "I forgot! Happy belated birthday, Chad!" Melissa handed him the black and gray "Happy Birthday" bag, and Chad chuckled. He opened it and saw that it was a military dog tag on which was carved the word 'dream.'

At first, he looked at it puzzled, and Melissa felt her heart drop. *He hated it.* She was already convincing herself. But then a lopsided smile appeared on his face, and he spoke.

"Mel- you didn't have to." He observed the tag. "This is

the nicest thing anyone has ever done for me."

Melissa ensured her mother wasn't looking at them, and she took advantage and pecked his cheek. He cupped her face, pulled it towards his face, and pressed his lips on her forehead.

I can't believe he's finally here. Melissa watched him remove his tungsten chain and put the military tag on it. *Now, his chain has a touch from me.*

"Well, I got you something too for your birthday," he told her once he finished.

"Chad! You didn't have-"

"Shush," he teased, and Melissa scoffed playfully and walked to the car.

Climbing into the car, Melissa's mother told the teens, "Well, we're passing by Rudy's so Chad can drop off his stuff, and then we'll go to the park for a bit. Maybe later we'll watch a movie at the house."

"Yay!" Melissa exclaimed.

"Sounds like fun to me," Chad added.

Uncle Rudy lived just a few blocks away from Melissa's home. Like Melissa, his house was in front of Amelia Earhart Park. Though his home was tiny, he had a huge front and backyard.

Nina had the front of her yard filled with vibrant flowers and bushes. She also had an avocado tree that Uncle Rudy took pride in.

Upon seeing Chad, Uncle Rudy gave him a bear-like hug as if he were family. "Hey! You've grown since I last saw you. Have you been hitting the gym?"

"Yeah," Chad responded, and it was true. Chad had continued wrestling, but he also took it upon himself to take boxing lessons just as he promised to Melissa.

He had grown an inch, and his arms were much more

built and less scrawny than Melissa remembered in December. *Whoaaaa, he really got built with those boxing classes.* Melissa could not help but admire his muscular arms. *His arms are swole!* He caught her staring, and she quickly glanced away. "Thank you for letting me crash at your place, Rudy," Chad mentioned.

"It's no problem. We want you to have fun this summer," he replied with much enthusiasm, which pleased Melissa.

It's like he's part of the fam already! she thought. *He fits right in with us.*

Uncle Rudy showed him the guest room with the flowery wallpaper and pink-colored sheets. "Sorry, Nina decorated this room. At least you'll have a queen-sized bed."

"Hey, I'm not complaining, man," Chad chuckled. "This is perfect and better than a cheap hotel. Not sure how I can ever repay you."

"Noooooo, don't worry," Uncle Rudy assured him. "You're always welcome here. This is your house for the next two weeks."

Melissa and Emmy watched Chad put away his cologne, deodorant, body wash, and shampoo. "Hey, Mel." He put on a sly smile, and Melissa knew he was up to something. "Here's that birthday gift I was talkin' about." Melissa covered her hanging lips with her hand, but Emmy spoke in a mock tone before she could speak.

"You didn't have to." Melissa gave her the stink eye of death. "What? You guys are so predictable," Emmy replied and lifted her hands as if surrendering.

"Anyway, here you go." Chad handed her a little blue box.

"Oh, my lanta, you are not proposing, are you?" Emmy

asked in a half-shocked, half-afraid kind of voice.

"No, Emmy," Melissa scoffed. "You're not?" she asked Chad, her eyes gaping at the little box and then at him.

"Really?" Chad rolled his eyes up.

"Um, yeah, I mean a tiny jewelry box? Hello?" Melissa replied.

"I guess." He shrugged his shoulders.

Melissa opened the little box and stared at a silver ring in the form of a dragon designed to wrap around her finger. Its wings were curled in, and it bore remarkably intricate scales.

"No. Friggin. Way." She stared at it in disbelief.

"Soooooooooooo?" Chad waited for her to say something.

"I love it!" she exclaimed and placed it on her index finger. She flaunted it to Emmy, who commented.

"That ring screams Melissa in every friggin way." Emmy grinned at her best friend. "It looks pretty cool though."

A smile crept onto Melissa's face, and Chad smiled back. "I love it so much, thank you." She pecked his lips with hers, and Emmy's jaw dropped witnessing the smooch.

She added, "Did you just do that in front of me?"

"Sorry." Melissa giggled, forgetting how her friend warned her she did not want any PDA. "I couldn't help it."

"Well," Chad chuckled. "That was my first kiss in Florida." The girls giggled at his comment.

The couple instantly talked about Gemma, and Emmy scoffed upon hearing about the magical world.

"Man, you guys take this whole fantasy stuff seriously," Emmy commented. "Must have been crazy bumping into LARPers in the wild. I hear their BO is horrible."

"Larpers?" Melissa stared at Emmy to elaborate, and she

did.

"Y'know, Live Action Role Players. They go out in costume and have big, fake medieval battles. I can see why someone with an imagination as overactive as yours might think it was real."

Melissa sighed in exasperation. "That doesn't explain the purple sky or the dreams. Or the dragon."

"Well, yeah, that's all clearly drugs," she said in a voice so deadpanned it took a moment for Melissa to process it.

"We didn't do drugs!" Chad exclaimed, but Melissa shushed him. "My bad... Ya know, Emmy, if you went through what we went through, you'd regret not believing Melissa," Chad explained, but Emmy shrugged, and the couple continued chatting about it, adding more fumes to Emmy's annoyance.

Once Chad unpacked everything and felt settled, they entered the dining room and joined Melissa's mother, Uncle Rudy, and Nina. Nina greeted Chad with a warm, welcoming hug and a Cuban-cheek kiss, "It's so nice to see ya, Chad. You've grown so much! How's Alex?"

"Still with Rose," he sneered. "He's good, though. He's annoyed I'm here without him."

"I bet!" Nina responded. "He should come next time!"

Next time, Melissa smirked at the idea. *I sure hope so.*

"Ready to go to the park?" her mother asked, and the three teens nodded.

Chapter Sixteen

They all took a brisk walk to the park; instantly, they were running up and down the small rolling hills while the sun rays peered through the narrow opening of the lazy clouds drifting by.

Elders sat on wooden benches soaking in the sunbeams, toddlers swung high from the colorful swinging chairs, and children played frisbee with their dogs.

Melissa's family found a spot in the grass by the hill and laid out a plaid blanket. Melissa noticed her mother keenly watching how she behaved with Chad.

She turned to Chad and whispered so her family didn't hear. "Hey, let's check out the woods over there! I always want to see it at night, but I'm too scared cause of 'el Coco.'"

"'El Coco?'" Chad's head bounced back, and Emmy snickered before responding.

"Seriously? That's not real, Melissa."

"Listen," Melissa flickered her eyes at Emmy and Chad. "After what we thought in Garnet? I'm pretty sure 'El Coco' is real. C'mon, let's go!" She called her mother. "Mom, we're checking out the woods area!"

"Okay, be back in 15 minutes," her mother warned, and Melissa nodded.

Melissa went ahead, holding Chad's hand, and gestured for Emmy to follow. They walked to the wooded area, only a five-minute walk from where they were sitting.

Sunlight peered through the trees, but Melissa couldn't shake off the feeling of stress it brought. It served as a haunting reminder of her time trapped in the Dark Forest of Garnet.

"Do you hear that?" Chad asked.

"Haha," Emmy mocked. "It's the sound of a werewolf growling, or maybe it's 'El Coco.'" Emmy raised her hand and growled like a bear, but Melissa shook her head.

"No, it's the sound of someone crying…"

The three spun around and saw Mia stumbling towards them with tears spilling from her eyes. Melissa asked, "Whoa, Mia, are you okay?"

"No, I'm not," she hiccupped, and Melissa gagged, inhaling the scent of beer fuming out of Mia's mouth. "I-I went to Josh's house and drank so much beer… and I just crashed my dad's car… he's going to ground me!"

"Um, and that's your concern?" Emmy added. "How about the underage drinking *and* driving?"

"Shut up!" Mia hissed, and Melissa hissed at her back.

"Do *not* tell my best friend to shut up." Chad and Emmy's head bounced back at Melissa's defensive demeanor. "What are you gonna do?"

"Can you please come with me?" Mia begged, her words coming out with a slur. "Take me to my dad's, please?" she hiccupped.

"Ugh, sure," Melissa sighed. "I'll help you."

"Wait," Chad interfered. "Mel, maybe we should take her to your mom," he whispered.

"Who's this cutie?" Mia stretched out her hand, but Melissa slapped it.

"Hey, that's my cutie, okay?" Chad and Emmy glanced at each other with their mouths hanging low. "Mia, let's go to my mom. She'll help," Melissa barked.

"No, no," Mia sobbed. "Because I want you to take the blame, puh-lease." She tripped, her body landing on Melissa, who struggled to help her stand. "Please, Melissa! You're so responsible, and you're sober. You'll barely get in trouble!"

"No, hell no!" Melissa yanked her hand away. "You're not gonna keep using me like this. I'm taking you to my mom. You're gonna drink water, and we'll drive you home and let your dad deal with you." Mia wept and gave a stiff nod.

Melissa, Chad, and Emmy helped Mia to Melissa's family, and she had to explain 'Mia's situation' to her mother.

Her mother drove Mia to her apartment complex on 49th Street, and Uncle Rudy and Nina called the police to report the car crash.

She lives there? Melissa thought while Mia sniffled the entire car ride. *I thought she would live in a massive house. She's always trying to show off designer shoes and all.*

"Thank you, Miss Paz," Mia hiccupped. "I guess I'll see you at my funeral."

Melissa's mother helped walk a wobbly Mia to the front of the house, and the teens remained quiet as they watched.

Once inside the car, her mother said, "If she were my daughter, she'd never leave the house until she turns 18."

"Yeah, she's not going out this summer," Emmy commented.

On the way home, Melissa noticed Jacob's parked car at their house.

Oh snap! They're home. Melissa felt her stomach sink. The idea of Chad meeting her sister made her shudder. "Hey, it's gonna be okay," Chad reassured her.

"How do you know I'm nervous?" she asked.

"You twirl your hair until you make a knot." Melissa looked at her hair, creating a thick knot she had to untangle.

Ugh, she sighed. *Why is she home? I hope she doesn't make me look stupid or say something embarrassing to me.*

Once her mother parked, Melissa sullenly looked down, embarrassed by the outer appearance of her home. "Sorry, Chad, my house is disgusting," she murmured.

"I don't care about that, Mel," he explained.

"Thanks," Melissa muttered, trying to remain hopeful.

Jacob and Victoria sat on the couch, engaging in lively conversation and sharing little laughs, as they often did. Suddenly, an energetic Magic pounced on Chad.

"Magic!" Chad scooped him up out of enthusiasm, and Magic slobbered his face with licks. "Hey there, bud, I missed you so much."

Jacob stood up upon seeing Chad and shook his hand. "Nice to meet you! I hear a lot of great things about you!" Melissa whispered 'Yes' to herself.

"Yeah, I've heard a lot about you too. It's nice to finally meet you," Chad replied, his shoulders tense.

He must be nervous, Melissa wondered. *Otherwise, why would he be so cold like that?* She shook the thought.

"So, this is your invisible boyfriend? Guess he really is real." Victoria curled a smile as she gave him a Cuban-cheek kiss. "How much is my mom paying you to make Snow White think she's special?" Melissa rolled her eyes in annoyance. *Here she goes.*

"You must be Victoria," Chad responded, smiling. "Actually, I'm not on anyone's payroll," he joked, turning to Jacob. "Is that the program you're on?" Jacob rolled his eyes with a light chuckle. "It's nice to meet you," Chad made sure he added.

"How do you like Miami so far?" Jacob asked; he must have felt the tension too.

"I love it! I just hate this humidity. Geez, it's intense." Jacob chuckled, and Chad continued, "But… I'm glad I'm here." He turned to Melissa, and she blushed, growing her half-smile.

Melissa gave Chad a tour of her home. The only room she dared not dare enter was Victoria's, which used to be hers.

When they entered her room, she said, "This is my room. It used to be Pipo's. Victoria and I shared her room before. She painted the walls pink. I *hate* pink, and every time I put something I liked, she'd take it off, or it was 'mysteriously' thrown away. After he left us, I wanted to stay in his room. Victoria didn't give me a hard time about it. I guess because she's always at Jacob's. So, she stayed in the other room, and I kept this one. Plus, it has a bathroom and that awesome window spot." She pointed at the window. "Still," she sighed, "I'd like to change it up a bit. It's kinda boring."

"We can do that," Chad promised her. "We can even draw you a dragon around the cool window spot you like."

"Ughhhh," Emmy grunted, hearing the word dragon. "When will you guys drop the whole act? I opened Melissa's History book once and found a bunch of magical mumbo jumbo words on the margins." Emmy pointed out, facepalming herself.

"Hey, it's not my fault that the king did some boring thing some hundred years ago. Adding lore is how I remember it. Tell our teachers to write better, and I won't have to fix it."

"And then you wonder why I don't believe you when you're making up all that nonsense."

"Emmy." Melissa shot a glare at her this time, and Emmy's head bounced back. "If you don't wanna believe it, fine. But leave us alone. We know what we experienced. We know it's real," she barked. Chad glanced at Melissa, who looked back at him, her eyes pleading with him to follow along.

"Geez, don't gotta get all offended over it," Emmy scoffed.

"It's not that. It's super annoying that we have to prove to you that Chad is real and his *name* is Chad. I showed you the dagger and then told you about Gemma, yet you still don't believe it."

"Melissa... no," Emmy said.

"It's okay. We'll find another way to prove it. We're gonna find Gemma." Chad's voice was firm, and then he switched the tense conversation. "I'm starving. What are we going to eat?" Melissa shrugged her shoulders and went searching for her mother to ask her.

Melissa's mother encouraged Melissa, Chad, and Emmy to take out the dough and make homemade pizza for everyone. They all had fun rolling out the smooth dough, drenched it with the sauce, and then sprinkled loads of mozzarella cheese.

"What are you guys making?" Victoria asked as she stepped out of the room with Jacob.

"Pizza!" Melissa responded.

"Oh God, be careful, babe. You might get food poisoning," Victoria commented.

"Or you'll try the best pizza ever," Chad added to defend Melissa's baking skills.

After eating pizza, Jacob and Victoria offered to play board games. For once, Victoria and Melissa were both giggling together, trying to bring everyone down, and then eventually, when they did, they battled each other.

"Wow, you're both competitive," Chad commented.

"It's the Paz genes," Jacob added.

"It's our nature," Victoria added. "We got it from Pipo, not our dad. So technically, it's the Guerra genes."

"Yep," Melissa agreed, and the sisters continued at it. The adults sat on the couch, watching them all play.

Jacob would throw in a few slick remarks to annoy everyone and throw them off their game, such as "Melissa doesn't know how to do business," or "Look, look, there goes Emmy, pretending she has everything figured out," and even "Pfft, Chad please, don't hurt yourself doing the math."

Emmy and Melissa would playfully laugh, knowing Jacob did not mean it, but she noticed Chad wore a sour expression.

He's not one to take things to heart, Melissa thought. *I wonder why he is now.* He glanced at her, and upon staring into her eyes, his eyes twinkled, and his cheeks turned rosy red.

"Awe," Jacob taunted. "Young love." They continued to play until the game became dull.

"Let's watch a movie!" Melissa suggested, and Chad and Emmy nodded.

Jacob and Victoria joined them since it was an order from Melissa's mother. Even though Victoria rolled her eyes, she seemed to approve of Melissa's choice of genre: horror.

Chad groaned, "Ughhhhhh, I hate scary movies," he admitted.

"Eh, I can watch them," Emmy added. "I don't think I can stomach torture films though."

"I love it all," Melissa stated.

"Scaredy cat much?" Victoria muttered. "Geez, these things aren't even real."

"Yeah, but it's the idea," Chad shuddered.

Melissa snuggled up to Chad as they watched the movie. Meanwhile, Emmy sat on the other side, indulging in a bowl of buttery popcorn.

Chad flinched and yelped at all the jump scares to the point he hid his face behind Melissa's shoulder.

"Chad, the slasher is not real!" Melissa explained, and Chad shuddered.

"Mel," he whispered to her, "now I'm gonna be dreaming about the slasher chasing after me in a colorful sunflower field." Melissa chuckled at that.

"You guys and your dreams," Emmy muttered.

Once the movie ended, her parents picked Emmy up, and Chad departed with Uncle Rudy. He and Melissa said their goodbyes, promising to see each other tomorrow.

Jacob cleared his throat to get Melissa's attention. He said, "Melissa, are you seriously willing to stay with that kid even though you live so far from each other?"

"Yeah, why do you ask? You don't like him or somethin'?" Melissa panicked.

"No, I mean, he's a bit serious-" Jacob explained, but Victoria interrupted him.

"Serious?" she scoffed. "He can't take a joke."

"Well, he's in a new place away from his family." Melissa gave Chad the benefit of the doubt. "He feels a bit off, but he'll open up."

"Still Melissa," Jacob continued, "how are you gonna make it work?"

"I don't know," Melissa shrugged. "I'm going with the flow," she concluded.

Jacob and Victoria disregarded the comment and continued playing board games independently.

Melissa entered her room, showered, and sat by the window. One thought about Emmy clouded her mind. She pulled out her dream journal and wrote:

I might've been too harsh on Emmy earlier today. But it's so frustrating to have been in Gemma and that she finally saw that Chad's name really is Chad. I want her to believe in them. I'd love for her to go to Gemma with us. I know she'll love it and want to learn more about it. The more I learn about the realm, the more I want to figure these dreams out. Maybe I won't feel as empty. What if that's the missing puzzle piece to all this? Or am I just a loony teenage girl losing hope?

She closed her journal, lay in her bed, and ripped out a piece of paper and listed all the ideas she wanted for her room.

She wanted to mimic Gemma with the purplish sky and the stars. She wrote a list until she finally yawned from how tired she was and drifted to sleep.

Chapter Seventeen

Melissa was lying in a familiar tall bed of grass; she sat up and watched the long heads of the sunflowers, this time a vibrant crimson, swaying like waves in a harbor. Their movement and unique color were alluring.

She wore a long, silky ruby gown reaching her ankles. The sky, ever so periwinkle, captivated her attention. A throat cleared behind her, and she scrambled out from the grass and turned around.

Alisha was standing, wearing her iconic white lace dress and her hands behind her back. She tilted her head, waiting for Melissa to speak, and she did.

"He just arrived today."

"Excellent," Alisha's voice hinted at relief. "And the plan, is it solidified?"

"Um, well... I'm hoping my mom will let him stay at my house tomorrow," she replied sheepishly, scratching her head. "Since, you know, he's staying with a family member. That way, we sneak out at night and return in the morning."

"I understand. It would be swifter if you made your life in Gemma permanent. However, I promised your grandfather we would not force you to choose."

"We?"

"Yes, we, the Council of Amethyst. He wanted you to have a life on Earth."

"Oh..." Melissa sighed. "I'd love to trade my Earthly life for Gemma." Alisha's eyes brightened with hope until Melissa said, "But I have a life here. I can't do that to my mom."

Alisha contemplated the situation, her thoughts filling the air. "I understand," she mused. "Once you and Chad arrive, the fairies will break the enchantment between you and him. This will allow you to enter and exit Gemma on your own freely. However, you must commit to coming daily afterward. There is much lost time to make up for."

"But that's going to be difficult," Melissa bit her lower lip. "What am I supposed to tell my mom?"

"You have Earthly responsibilities. Do you not?"

"I guess..." Melissa shrugged. "I can always say I'm hitting the gym."

"Well then, I do not know what gym is, but soon enough, you will be here."

A herd of winged horses neighed above her. She glanced at the sky, and her eyes caught one winged horse with a spiral horn sitting on its head.

"Winged unicorns?" Melissa asked.

"Yes, a hybrid. Sometimes, a winged horse will mate with a unicorn and create the winged unicorn."

"Mh, why can't you show me my dragon?" Melissa quipped at the elf.

"Perhaps I should... perhaps that will encourage you to come quicker." Melissa giggled whole-heartedly, and the elf curled the corner of her lip just slightly. "I hope we meet soon." She sang, and everything surrounding Melissa turned into a mist, and she dissolved along with the dream.

* * *

"Okay, guys, behave yourselves. I won't get out of work till 9ish," her mother instructed as Melissa and Emmy climbed out of the car at Uncle Rudy's house.

"Okay," Melissa kissed her mother goodbye. "Bye mom."

"Bye!" Emmy followed. "So, are we ready to tell Uncle Rudy the plan?"

"Oh, yeah!" Melissa smirked.

Upon entering, Melissa greeted Chad by wrapping her arms around his neck, pecking him on the cheek, and then Emmy fist-bumped him.

"Hey, kiddos!" Uncle Rudy greeted the girls. "What's the plan today? Bayside? Vizcaya? South Beach?"

Melissa sat down, crossed her hands, and elevated her chin. "We've been waiting for all of us to be in the same place without my mom around becaaauusseeee-" She did a quick drumroll on her lap. "We want to clean up the house! I've been saving money for every birthday and Christmas since I was little. I really wanna do this." She smiled, hoping to get a positive reaction from Uncle Rudy and Nina.

Uncle Rudy and Nina exchanged glances, their faces adorned with lopsided smiles. Uncle Rudy replied, "Well, honey, you heard those crazy teens. Let's take charge and fix up the house."

Uncle Rudy and Nina took Melissa, Chad, and Emmy to the store first to buy paint and tools. Then, they drove back to the house, where they worked on it immediately.

Chad assisted with the painting and said, "I'm great at painting." In reality, his paintbrush was making zigzag strokes.

"Chad, why don't you go over by the tree and pick up those piles of mangos," Emmy told him.

"Sure." He dropped the paint, and Emmy took advantage by fixing his artwork. She glanced at Melissa and whispered, "Does this guy think he's Picasso or something? This is not how you paint." Melissa covered her mouth, holding a muffled laugh in.

Instead, Chad raked away all the rotten mangos from the ground, and the girls painted.

Victoria and Jacob stepped outside during their work in progress. Their heads bounced back while watching everyone working on the house. "Whoa, what's going on here?" Victoria inquired.

"Your sister devised this great idea to fix the house," Uncle Rudy responded.

"Why?" Victoria asked, crossing her arms. Melissa noticed her nose flaring.

"I wanted to surprise Mom. She never has time to clean the house, and you always push me away. So, I asked Uncle Rudy and Nina for help," Melissa replied. "Is there a problem?" She knitted her eyebrow and pressed her lips.

"So, you choose to do this right around my graduation?" Victoria muttered.

"No... I had this planned for a while. I was waiting for the right time," Melissa stated.

But Victoria replied sarcastically, "Sure you did. The right time had to be just a few days before my graduation. That way, even though I have my moment to shine, you still gotta have yours, right?"

Melissa stumbled on her words, but Jacob interfered, "Babe, I don't think Melissa had those intentions. How about we just help?"

"No, babe, I need to prepare for my graduation, and anyway, we didn't receive an invitation to help," she retorted. She marched inside the house, with Jacob reluctantly following behind her.

"What's her deal?" Emmy exclaimed. "Seriously, she's always pissy about something."

"She thinks me cleaning the house is taking her 'moment' away," Melissa mocked, quoting her sister.

"What moment?" Emmy asked, puzzled.

"She's graduating with her Bachelor's in psychology this summer; I thought I told ya, Emmy?" Melissa responded, and Emmy thought about it but shook her head.

"You didn't mention anything to me," Chad added.

"Really?" Melissa frowned, recalling if she ever mentioned it. "I could have sworn I did."

The thought stayed in her mind for a while. *Damn... I feel crappy for forgetting.* She shrugged her shoulders and brushed the thought away.

Chad picked up pieces of engine that lay out on the porch when he called Melissa to come over.

"What's up?" she asked, and Chad pointed at four carved gems and a curved letter E on one piston.

"Could it be from," he looked around to ensure they were alone, "Gemma?"

Melissa's heart skipped a beat. Her eyes scanned the curved E, and she visually memorized the way it appeared. She wanted nothing more than to drop the paint can she was holding and scribble it in her journal.

"I don't know…" Melissa mumbled, "It could be nothing… but something."

Melissa cleared the mechanical junk off the porch and grabbed the water hose to wash off all the dirt it had left behind.

Emmy grabbed a fresh bucket of white paint to brush over the swinging chairs, and Nina placed fresh dirt around the edges of the porches to plant the lavender Melissa had purchased.

Magic was sprinting around and playing with his tennis ball, keeping himself entertained. Nina had also bought orchids at her own expense and placed them in random areas on the porch.

Melissa dipped her finger in the white paint and poked Chad in the cheek. "No, you didn't!" Chad gasped, and he went after her and swung her around, to which Emmy fussed.

"Hey, lovebirds! Get to work!"

"Alright, alright, Chadwick," Melissa grunted and flirtatiously pushed Chad.

By evening, they completed everything, transforming the house into something new. They all gazed at it in awe.

"I gotta say, what a difference," Emmy stated, and everyone agreed.

"I know," Uncle Rudy mumbled. "Jane will appreciate this. The house embarrassed her."

"Really?" Melissa asked in disbelief.

"Yeah." Uncle Rudy explained. "Jane is a clean person, Melissa. She just doesn't have time for pretty much anything." They all continued to stare at the house proudly.

They all waited for Melissa's mother out on the porch. Melissa began twirling her hair, creating a thick knot until Chad grabbed her hand to stop her from continuing. "She's gonna love it."

He reassured her, and Melissa sighed but gave him a slight nod. She placed her head on his shoulder and continued to wait for her arrival.

At last, she arrived from work and wore a weary expression. Melissa could tell her mother was ready to drop on the bed and pass out. "Hey, what are you all doing outside?" she asked, confused, not noticing her new home. Everyone looked at one another and snickered. "What's going on?" her mother scoffed. Rudy looked at her dumbfounded. "Jane, take a step back and look at your home." Puzzled, she took a few steps back and analyzed her house.

Melissa observed her mother's nostrils flare, capturing the aroma of her beloved herb. Her mother's eyes widened as she gasped, placing her hands over her mouth. Tears welled in her eyes and flowed down her cheeks as she spoke between sobs. "You all fixed up the house?"

Everyone nodded and watched the tears trickling down her face.

"It was all Melissa's idea." Uncle Rudy flaunted her.

"It might've been my idea," Melissa humbled herself, "but it probably wouldn't have worked out if it wasn't for everyone here." Her mother flung her arms around Melissa. "Thank you, Mija." She then urged Chad and Emmy to join in on the hug, and they did so.

Her mother walked around to inspect and took notice of the orchids and lavender. She sat on the swinging chair and inhaled deeply. "Oh, how I love the smell of lavender." She looked at her new porch. "It looks so different from all that junk Pipo had." Melissa and Emmy agreed.

They spent some time outside, chatting and talking about all the work they did.

Once they were in the house, Jacob and Victoria reminded them of their zoo day tomorrow. "You're lucky we're taking you," Victoria mumbled. "Mom wouldn't stop asking."

"Baby, it's gonna be fun," Jacob glared at Victoria. "It's good for them to go out and a way to get to know Chad," he added.

"Yeah," Melissa agreed. "You guys haven't gotten to know Chad, y'know?"

"Do we have to?" Victoria asked, and Melissa felt her blood boil.

Chad responded, "No, you don't have to; as long as I'm with Mel, I'm cool beans with whatever we do and however we do it."

Damn, Chad's comment took Melissa aback, leaving her surprised. *I like this.*

"Babe that's her first boyfriend. Come on?" Jacob persisted.

"Whatever," Victoria muttered. "Be up early tomorrow, okay?" she warned, and they all nodded.

"Speaking of..." Melissa chimed in. "Can Chad just stay over here? That way, it's easier for him to leave with us in the morning?"

"Ask mom... but it's not a bad idea. He can sleep on the couch," Victoria shrugged her shoulders.

"Mel..." Chad mumbled. He shuffled his feet and placed his hand on his neck. "I didn't bring a change of clothes... and I'm sweaty and gross from today's yard work."

"Chadwick..." Melissa glared at him, and she knew he got the intended message. They were supposed to make their grand escape tonight.

"Sorry..." he shrugged his shoulders, and Melissa smirked.

Uncle Rudy and Nina left with Chad, and the girls took turns showering. Melissa exited the bathroom to see Emmy sitting on the bed reading a romance novel. When Emmy took her turn, Melissa scribbled in her journal.

She meticulously wrote the curved letter E Chad had found earlier. She wrote a giant question mark next to it and wondered, *what does this E means.*

"Wow," Emmy spoke a few minutes later as she returned to the room. "You're literally at the last pages of that journal."

"I know, I gotta buy a new one. This is my third journal."

"Your third?!"

"Yeah," Melissa answered, opening the false bottom in her desk drawer and revealing her two filled-in journals. "See?"

"Is this all from the role-playing game?" Melissa nodded and responded.

"And my experience. Look!" In the first journal, she showed her a drawn-out image of the dagger with the rooster-dragon sigil.

"Wow, what is that?" Emmy pointed at the beast.

"It's called a Cockatrice. It sounds funny, but it's supposed to be a pseudo-dragon. If you look at it in the eyes, it'll blind you, and its breath is venomous. Pretty gnarly, right? I think it's the beast that represents Victor, ya know? While the dragon represents Amethyst."

"You don't know who rules Amethyst?" Emmy asked.

"Actually, no..." Melissa frowned. "It just says the princess is in her castle."

"Okay, not that I'm believing you, but describe what you already know about Gemma."

Seeing her skeptical best friend intrigued by the world of magic made Melissa feel a wind of emotions. Her face glowed with excitement, and she gibbered.

"Gemma would be the realm. It's divided into different countries or continents. If I'm correct, where I need to be is Amethyst, and the Dark Forest of Garnet is where all the bad people live. The game has other lands like Ruby Jungle, The Mountains of Alexandria, Opal Desert, and Sapphire Island. Different monsters live in different areas. As yetis live in the Mountains of Alexandria, you have beasts like the roc living in Ruby Jungle."

"That is pretty cool... ya know, you're destined to be a journalist."

"Thanks?" Melissa shrugged the comment off and continued writing.

"You keep dreaming of your little Gemma world." Emmy snatched the little red dragon from Melissa's bed.

"Ya know I will," Melissa winked, and Emmy scoffed. "Hey, careful with Jake, will ya?"

"Jake? You mean the stuffed toy Chad gave you?" Emmy furrowed a brow.

"Yeah, I named him after my imaginary friend. He was a red dragon, too." Melissa's eyes wandered to the floor. She imagined a red dragon momentarily, and her lips curled into a smile.

"Wow, you really always loved fantasy stuff, huh?"

"Yeah," Melissa uttered in a breath and thought, *it helps me escape.*

Chapter Eighteen

Early in the morning, the alarm blasted, causing the best friends to groan and whine under the bedsheets. Melissa shut it off, and the girls slept longer than expected.

But once Chad arrived, the girls sprang from the bed to change and go to the zoo with Victoria and Jacob.

At the zoo, they strolled around, observing all the animals. Emmy complained about the smell of feces and the monkeys' shrill sound.

Melissa enjoyed watching the vibrant snakes and their scales. She imagined the different dragon species she encountered during her studies. She felt a tingling sensation in her heart and wondered if her dragon knew she was thinking of him.

When Melissa observed how a green anaconda slithered and curled into a ball, Victoria commented, "Checking in on our relatives?"

"I feel bad they're locked up; it's like a prison," Melissa replied, and Chad agreed. Melissa, Chad, and Emmy took silly photos, ate cotton candy and cheap popcorn, and watched all the live performances.

Emmy took a moment to use the restroom, leaving Chad and Melissa to watch a whirlwind of different species of birds fly in an aviary enclosure. Melissa lost herself in her thoughts, watching them fly and chirp.

She observed them soar in an enclosed cage, which pained her heart; she often felt like a bird herself, trapped in her room most days, yearning for adventure.

"Mel, I have to tell you something," Chad let out as if finally releasing a secret, but he hesitated to continue, shifting his eyes to the floor.

"Yeah, what's up?" He paused, but then he responded abruptly.

"I don't like Jacob." Melissa muffled a laugh. "I'm serious, Mel," he added.

"Why?" she clicked her tongue. "Jacob's like a brother to me. Did he say something to you?"

"He picked me up and started asking a bunch of questions, I guess, to get to know me and whatever."

"Maybe he *was* just trying to get to know you?" she emphasized.

"No, Mel, he was interrogating me, and you know what he said?" Melissa gestured her hand for him to continue. "He said we're being idealistic. We think we're fated together and most likely won't last and should take our heads out of the clouds."

"Why would Jacob say that? No, he couldn't have said that. I expect that from Victoria."

"Well, he said it, and sometimes it makes me wonder if I'm only here because you want to go to Gemma."

"How can you say that?" Melissa snapped. "Chadwick, if I didn't want you here, I wouldn't have invited you. I don't use people. People use me." She ended those words sharply.

"You're right," Chad released a sigh. "I shouldn't have

doubted you. It's just Jacob got to my head. I don't like the guy," he blurted out. Melissa could tell the situation had him worked up by his tense shoulders and fidgety fingers.

"Well," Melissa gathered her thoughts and said, "I don't know why he said what he said... maybe he's looking after me? He's been like a brother to me, and I love him like one. Don't listen to him, he doesn't know us." Melissa cupped his cheek in her hand, and Chad made a weak grin.

He held her hand, pulled her closer to him for a hug, and responded with a tender kiss on her lips.

"Alright, Mel," he reluctantly agreed. "All I'm saying is that I get this weird vibe from him."

He let go of her before Emmy pestered them about PDA. His eyes flickered towards her bare hands and widened at the four shiny lines on her palms.

"Wait, what's that?" He looked closer, and Melissa snatched her hand away. "Mel, what was that?"

"It's nothing," her voice squeaked. "Seriously." She ended firmly, but before Chad could question her further, Emmy returned, and the couple dropped the conversation.

As they walked, her thoughts lingered on Jacob.

Jacob had been the only male figure in her life since Pipo passed away. He was also the only one who'd been kind to Melissa and defended her whenever her sister took it too far. He had even been her MMA coach.

Why would he say that? she thought idly. *I bet Victoria told him to say those things to Chad. She needs to stop meddling with my relationship and worry about her own.*

When the park was just under an hour from closing, Melissa dragged Chad and Emmy to see the elephants again. "Ugh, that's so far to walk," Emmy whined. "Do we have to?"

"Come on, Emmy, we're here now. Let's take advantage," Melissa pleaded.

"Come on' Emmy," Chad added.

"Of course, you'll do anything Melissa wants," she bickered.

Melissa, Chad, and Emmy froze as they strolled when they saw Mia dressed in khaki shorts and shirt scooping up animal feces.

"Mia?" Melissa called out, and Mia glanced at her, her face crimson red.

"Hey," she mumbled.

"How come you're picking up animal poop?" Emmy asked, and Melissa nudged her.

"Well, since I took responsibility for crashing my dad's car while drunk, he's now taking me to work with him for the entire summer." Melissa sighed deeply and couldn't help but roll her eyes at how Mia bragged about her responsibility, knowing that Melissa had encouraged her to do so.

She kept her comment to herself, but then Emmy quipped at Mia.

"If it weren't for Melissa, you would have never taken responsibility for anything," Mia scoffed.

"Emmy, just drop it," Melissa mediated. "Mia, I'm glad you're learning your lesson."

"Whatever," Mia murmured and continued to shovel poop.

"Let's just go, guys," Melissa said, and they walked away.

"Mia, you're still not done?" a deep voice scolded, and Melissa glanced back to see a brown-haired man scowling at Mia. "You need to hurry it up."

"Ugh, why do I have to clean the poop, Dad?"

"Because it builds character, and in your case, you need some. Keep shoveling." Her father walked away, and Mia bit her lips and wept.

Emmy giggled, and Melissa shot a dirty look at her. "What?" Emmy asked, dismissing Melissa's glare, "She deserves it."

"I'm gonna go help her," Melissa told them.

"Are you serious?" Emmy scoffed, and Melissa nodded.

"You guys could join me or not, but I'm helping her. She needs to know she's not alone."

Melissa approached a red-eyed Mia, who knitted her brows when Melissa extended her hand. "What are you doing?"

"I'm helping you. Pass the shovel." Mia took a moment to process Melissa's words, and Melissa gestured to her to hurry. She passed the shovel and worked on the disgusting task alongside her. Eventually, Chad joined in, leaving Emmy no option but to assist.

As a team, they finished on time. Mia spoke. "Melissa… I just want to say," she gulped, as if it pained her to finish the sentence. "I'm sorry for always taking credit from you. Thank you for helping me today, all of you, thanks."

"You're welcome, Mia," Melissa half-smiled and departed with Chad and Emmy.

In the car, Victoria complained about the putrid smell emanating from them after scooping animal feces.

"When she was little, I called her smelly Melly, which annoyed her. It was priceless." Victoria continued to irk Melissa.

"And? I used to call you icky Vicky," Melissa retaliated.

"Yeah, but you were actually smelly. You'd come home

from all those stupid classes Pipo put you in, and you smelled awful."

"Whatever, Victoria." Melissa looked away, releasing a deep breath while clawing her nails into her palms.

"It's true. Pipo spoiled you and treated you like a little princess, even though you're not."

"Victoria," Jacob spoke. "Is it really necessary to embarrass your sister like that in front of her friend and boyfriend?" Jacob stated.

"Yeah, she did it to me when I started dating you," she quipped back at him.

"Yeah, but not with the intentions you're doing it with. Melissa was young then. Kids don't know better. So, drop it." How he warned Victoria and scowled at her with his blue eyes shook Melissa. Victoria clicked her tongue, gritted her teeth, and sighed.

Melissa's heart pounded with rage. She felt the urge to scream at her. Not only did her sister make her feel bad about herself, but she humiliated her in front of Emmy and Chad.

She remained quiet throughout the entire car ride. It appeared Chad felt the tension because he held her hand and squeezed it.

Jacob dropped the girls off first at Melissa's home and took Chad back to Uncle Rudy's. Melissa's mother sat inside the house and wrote checks to pay bills. She looked up and said, "Hey, how'd it go?"

"It was nice!" Emmy answered. "We had a blast."

"Nice, Melissa?" she glanced at Melissa, who nodded stiffly. "What's wrong?"

"Nothing," her voice squeaked.

"Ugh, seriously? You're gonna stay pissed? You're such a big baby," Victoria said coolly and innocently. "I told Chad how Melissa used to smell." Victoria then gestured the 'bad smell' sign, waving her hand in front of her nose, and on the spur of the moment, Melissa snatched Victoria's arm and squeezed it.

"Ow!" Victoria snapped and pushed Melissa with such force that Melissa fell on her bottom.

"Did you just try to hit me?" Victoria growled at her while holding onto her arm.

Emmy quickly crouched to Melissa and helped her up. When she did, she yanked her arm away from Emmy and swept Victoria off the ground with a technique Jacob had taught her. Victoria slammed to the ground, and their mother abruptly stood up and shouted, "What is the matter with both of you?"

"She started it!" Melissa barked.

"Can you stop being dramatic and take a joke? Gosh, now you're acting like a baby!" Victoria scoffed as she scrambled off of the floor.

Magic came by and growled at Victoria, baring his teeth.

"A joke?" Melissa scoffed. "You had Jacob interrogate Chad before picking us up at the zoo."

"What? No, I didn't-"

"You're always 'joking' with me," Melissa said, quoting with her fingers. "You call me Casper for being the whitest in the family, and you constantly tell me I smell!"

"Ugh, Melissa, I'm your older sister; it's what we do," Victoria responded with poise.

"WHAT?!" Melissa let out a bellow, and at that moment, she unleashed the dragon wrath of the Guerra. "Chad's older brother doesn't treat him that way! And neither does Rose to

Lily. Yeah, they bicker and all, but- with you, you always tear me down! Rose even taught me to do my make-up, and that's your job, not Rose's!" The words flowing from her mouth seemed to have impacted Victoria since Melissa noticed her eyes shifting to the floor. "You say I'm not as smart as you, so why don't you actually take the time to sit and help me with my homework and projects? Instead, my best friend has to help me because my older sister won't." Melissa's voice cracked, "I mean… Why do you tear me down so much? What did I ever do to you? You're my sister! But you're never there for me." At this, Melissa's lips trembled, and the tears crept down from her eyes. "Sometimes, I just wish you weren't my sister…" She saw Victoria's lips turn downwards and her eyes well up in tiny pools.

"Melissa! Go to your room." Her mother's eyes glared at her.

Hiccupping with tears falling to the ground, Melissa spun around and marched into her room; she heard Emmy following behind her.

Upon entering her room, Melissa collapsed on her bed, grabbed a pillow, placed it on her face, and sobbed. She felt Emmy sit beside her. To comfort the distraught Melissa, Emmy rubbed her back.

The girls could hear Melissa's mother scolding Victoria in the Cuban way that cut off unnecessary syllables, often making it hard for even seasoned Spanish speakers to understand her.

Then, it got quiet, and Melissa sat in bed to prepare for her lecture.

Sure enough, it didn't take long for her mother to barge into the room. Her face poised when she spoke. "Emmy, por favor, wait in the living room." Emmy stepped out, and Melissa's mother stared at Melissa blankly.

"Melissa, that was very aggressive," her mother said, breaking the silence. "I-I've never seen you behave that way. Why?" Before responding, Melissa took a deep breath.

"Mami, I just snapped, I-I, she humiliated me." Melissa recounted the incident and all that led to it. "I'm sorry. She didn't have to embarrass me like that in front of Chad!"

"Melissa..." Her mother placed a hand on her forehead. "You can't keep letting Victoria get to you, okay?"

"You make it seem like I don't try. I'm sorry, Mami," Melissa hunched, "I really am. I just want her to stop being such a douc- I mean, jerk to me." Her mother stared at Melissa and released a long sigh. A sigh dripping with a disappointment that Melissa knew all too well. That disappointment always hurt her more than making her mother angry did.

As Melissa watched her mother ponder the punishment she'd implement, she felt the urge to shout, *I'm lonely.* But the words simply couldn't leave her mouth. *I miss Pipo! I miss my old life.* Her jaw clenched, and her right eye twitched until her mother finally spoke.

"You will not see Chad this week, and that's final. I was going to cancel the camping trip I planned for next weekend with Emmy and Chad, but that wouldn't be fair to anyone. We all asked for the time off to do this, and I haven't had a vacation in years. I already bought all the tents and equipment, so I won't cancel it and worry about returning the stuff. But you need to make amends with your sister." Melissa clicked her tongue, and her mother raised a brow. "Otherwise, I will cancel it with no hesitation if you don't. This time, you went physical, and that is not okay under my roof."

"I'm sorry, Mami, I will never do that again. I didn't mean to."

"I know you didn't, but it still happened, and you need to apologize for it."

"I will," Melissa promised her.

"And you're lucky Emmy's parents are off to Cuba. If not, she wouldn't be sleeping over today," she added.

Melissa nodded, releasing a heavy sigh, and her mother wrapped her arms around Melissa. The love Melissa experienced in her mother's embrace was powerful. As she took it all in for a brief minute, her heart did not weigh heavily in her chest. At that moment, she felt free of the loneliness that had haunted her.

She held onto her for a bit and stepped out, and Emmy stepped in.

Emmy said, "Well… that didn't sound as bad as I thought it'd be, you good?"

"Pfft, yeah," Melissa recapped her conversation with her mother.

"When are you gonna apologize to Victoria?" Emmy probed.

"Ugh, I don't know, but it has to be soon, or my mom will cancel our trip."

"Then you better start practicing your apology speech!" Emmy scolded her.

Melissa could not use the phone but still used her walkie-talkie to reach Chad. Not wanting to explain everything, Emmy had the honor of retelling the showdown between the sisters.

"You and your sister are ten years apart." Chad gave her the benefit of the doubt. "That's hard. Alex and I are only two years off, and we always fight. Plus, you and your sister have been through a lot- it's okay."

"I guess-" Melissa changed the topic. "Can't wait to go camping on Sunday. It kinda sucks I can't see you this week." Chad boasted about how much he loved camping and how knowledgeable he was about it.

Once they hung up, Melissa and Emmy dressed in their PJs and sat by the window.

"Do you feel any better?" Emmy asked.

"Yeah…" she muttered. "Now I just feel bad doing that sweep move on her." Melissa sighed gloomily.

"To be honest," Emmy could not contain her grin. "It was epic!" Melissa finally let out a genuine laugh.

"Yeah, I wonder what Jacob is gonna tell me," Melissa gasped. "Did I tell you what Chad told me today?" Emmy shook her head. "He doesn't like Jacob."

"Whattttt?" Emmy snorted. "He's probably just jealous- Jacob is dreamy and almost perfect."

"Ew Emmy, that's like my brother… I just find it weird he doesn't like Jacob. Everyone loves Jacob. Chad is not really the jealous kind. He's very confident, too confident, actually. I don't know, it's weird."

"I still think it is 'cause he's jealous."

"I guess-"

"Pssh, Chad can definitely be cocky sometimes. Guess the reputation of the name follows." Melissa allowed herself to giggle. "I'm serious. All Chad's are like douchebags."

"Not my Chad." Melissa teased.

"Whatevs, let's go to bed. I'm exhausted."

"Same."

Melissa tossed and turned throughout the night. Her thoughts about the incident weighed heavily on her mind.

I should talk to Victoria now. I feel so bad about the incident. She knew she wouldn't stop thinking about it unless she took some action.

She couldn't sleep, so she stood and quietly walked to Victoria's bedroom. However, she could hear a gentle weeping coming from her mother's room. Melissa walked towards the sound and pressed her ear against the door.

Listening intently, Melissa wasn't sure if she was on the phone talking or praying.

"I hate seeing them fight," her voice cracked. "Victoria feels left out in this family, and she takes out on Melissa. My girls won't stop fighting."

Left out? Why? She has Jacob, and if she feels left out, why does she treat me like crap.

Her mother continued talking. "I can't afford this roof. I can't keep asking Rudy for help. He has his stuff to worry about. I can't even get food stamps because I make too much. I feel so alone. Melissa didn't even get a quince. I couldn't even afford any type of summer camp for her. At least that boy she likes came, but I can't give her the things she wants."

Guilt pressed down on Melissa and she continued to listen. "God, I miss my father so much... Please, God, put your hand over this family, guide me, and show me how to fix this broken family." Melissa had to bite her lip to stop herself from weeping. She tip-toed back to her room and lay in her bed, and a flood of tears poured from her eyes. Frustration overwhelmed her, tears streaming down her face as she drove her nails into her palms, seeking solace in the pain, resulting in blood staining her hand.

She surrendered herself to the embrace of her dreams, allowing them to carry her away from the harsh grasp of reality.

*   *   *

The warm rays from the sun were radiating on Melissa's face. She tried covering her eyes before opening them and saw the lavender sky. She jerked up immediately and noticed she was sitting on snow-like sand.

In front of her was an ocean whose blue was that of a sapphire gem. When she inhaled, she tasted the rich salt on the tip of her tongue. She could feel the magical force in the water, prompting her to want to take a dip.

Melissa's eyes fixated on the tranquil waters, her gaze lost in the mesmerizing sight. She felt a profound sense of peace and tranquility wash over her. A serpent-like beast breached out of the water, and Melissa's mouth hung low. Its bluish-green scales glistened in the moonlight.

"This ocean has always brought a sense of tranquility, does it not?" Alisha's voice spoke behind her.

Melissa turned back and said, "Is it really you?" Alisha took out her moonstone, and Melissa continued talking. "Why are you here? Are you finally telling me when Chad and I will go to Gemma?"

"Yes, but," Alisha paused. "Your dragon sensed an intense sorrow and asked me to check on you. Is everything alright?"

"Yeah," Melissa muttered. "I'm fine-" She was not, and the elf raised a skeptical brow, but Melissa spoke. "The sea calms me."

"Mh," Alisha stepped closer to Melissa. "Your dragon does the same."

"My dragon..." It's all Melissa thought about. He always knew how she was feeling, and she was desperate to meet him already. "Well, you said you're here to tell me how to get to Gemma." Melissa's eyes glared into Alisha's, unnerved.

"We need you both here. Tomorrow, I can meet you in the woods by your home."

"YES!" Melissa squealed but then groaned. "I can't see Chad until next week. I'm grounded."

"Grounded?"

"Not literally, grounded as in... punished. I can't go out now or see Chad," Melissa explained to the elf whose eyebrow arched.

"Dragon rider... we cannot delay this any longer. You must come home." Her tone was assertive, and Melissa sighed glumly.

"I know," Melissa reassured her with a nod. "We have a camping trip coming up this weekend. Tell me where to meet you in the woods when we return, and Chad and I will be there."

Alisha gave one slight nod, and Melissa's eyes continued to gaze at the waters.

*   *   *

Melissa awoke, gasping for air; rubbing her face, she felt a sense of urgency, prompting her to snatch her journal and scribble the details of her dream.

Next weekend, for sure, we'll go to Gemma. The thought of it quickened Melissa's heartbeat.

Her stomach rumbled, and she marched to the kitchen. Sitting at the table was Victoria, surrounded by textbooks and notebooks. She glanced up, and they both locked eyes.

Melissa sullenly looked down and walked to the cabinet to pour herself cereal. The weight of unspoken words hung heavy on her shoulders. It overwhelmed her with anxiety because her conscience was nagging her to apologize.

Mustering up the courage, she said, "I am, um..." She stumbled on her words until she cleared her throat and stared at Victoria straight in the eyes. "I'm sorry for sweeping you to the ground and squeezing your arm. I don't hate you. I didn't mean that."

"Thanks," Victoria said, studying Melissa's body language. "I don't hate you, Melissa. I hope you know that."

"No, I don't know, but thanks."

They studied each other's gaze, and Victoria said, "Um, I'm not going on the camping trip, by the way... but I'll tell Mami we talked so you can still have fun."

The strained sisters locked their eyes, and nothing else had to be said because their silence spoke volumes.

Chapter Nineteen

Anxiety swelled in Melissa as her mother drove to Uncle Rudy's house. She hadn't seen Chad for a few days, and the thought of seeing him made her twirl her hair excessively.

When they finally reached Uncle Rudy's house, Melissa sprinted to the door and tackled Chad with a bear-like hug.

"Are you excited for camping?" Chad asked her.

"Yes!" she exclaimed and whispered, "After we get back, we go to Gemma." Chad pressed his lips on her forehead.

The group first stopped at a breakfast joint to eat a hearty breakfast. Inside, a country-like theme set the relaxing mood, and Melissa noticed checkers pieces to play in the meantime.

"Melissa!" a girl called out, and when Melissa looked up, it was Mia, sitting with her family.

This is the third time I have run into Mia. The thought struck her. She spent so much time avoiding her high school villain, but now she wondered if there was some type of purpose for their paths crossing three times.

Mia gestured to Melissa to join her at her table, and she couldn't help but feel tempted to talk to her and give her a chance. She glanced at her mother and asked permission. Once her mother gave the okay by nodding, Melissa walked towards her, holding hands with Chad while Emmy groaned along the way like a fussy child.

"Hey!" Mia grinned. "Thanks for joining me. What are y'all doing here?"

"Grabbing some breakfast before going camping," Melissa explained, nudging Emmy to speak. Still, Emmy crossed her arms like an upset toddler and refused to talk.

Mia pressed her lips and flickered her eyes to Melissa and Chad, emphasizing her annoyance with Emmy.

"Um, that's nice. I've never gone camping..." Mia replied, and Melissa spoke.

"Neither have I... um, how are things with you? How's Josh?"

"They're good..." Mia glanced at Emmy, who avoided her gaze and pressed her lips. "I'm not with Josh anymore. After that car crash, he said he was too embarrassed to be with me."

"Wow, what a douche. See Emmy? That's a 'Chad.'" Melissa remarked, and Chad gasped.

"Hey! Not cool!" He playfully nudged Melissa, and Emmy finally spoke up.

"Well, Josh didn't seem like a good influence, anyway. You're popular and pretty, so you can do better," Emmy spat.

"Thanks Emmy... Ya know, I think it's cool that you girls do the morning show. A lot of classmates find you guys comical. I signed up to join next year. I hope we can all work together."

"I... would love that," Melissa responded, and Mia's eyes lit up; she shifted her eyes to Emmy, who spoke.

"Sure, you can film us." Melissa nudged Emmy and gestured with her eyes to be more sociable. "Melissa and I want to expand the TV production and do more with it next year. There's always room, ya know."

"I can't be in the spotlight since you guys have TV chemistry, but I'd like to do tech work."

"Tech work is always fun," Chad added. "You can work with the sound system."

"That's true. Chad, how'd you meet Melissa?" Melissa and Chad took turns explaining how they met, excluding all the fantasy and magical parts of it.

"You guys are a cute couple. You're lucky to have a girl like Melissa," Mia smirked. "This doesn't mean I like you now. It means we're even, for you helping me at the zoo." Melissa rolled her eyes up and responded.

"Sure." She used a quotation gesture, and Mia giggled.

They chatted with Mia some more, and it warmed Melissa's heart to know Mia was trying to befriend them despite her 'cool' girl demeanor.

After Mia left with her family, the gang rejoined Melissa's family.

Once in the car, Melissa, Emmy, and Chad were goofing around, annoying the adults who were trying to have a civilized conversation.

Melissa cradled Magic in her arms, snuggling him closely. She brushed her fingers across his fur, occasionally releasing a contented sigh.

At the camping site, everyone set up three large tents. One was for Rudy and Nina, one was for Melissa, Emmy, and her mom, and the last, the tiniest of the three, was for Chad. It took a good hour for everyone, even Chad, the so-called camping expert, to set up the tents.

Once they set up the tents, Melissa, Chad, and Emmy went to the beach, which was only a mile walk, and went for a swim.

All they had to do was follow the tall white lighthouse; Emmy blabbered about the lighthouse and gave facts about them, to which Melissa responded, "And you know this how?"

"I pay attention in class," Emmy quipped back.

They finally made it to the beach. The golden sand felt warm, and the water stretched along the coast. The white-tipped waves crashed onto the shore, filling the sand with foam.

Melissa noticed the way Chad's eyes got lost in the ocean. His nose flared, inhaling the thick, salty breeze, and he closed his eyes to feel the air brushing his hair.

"Are you happy?" Melissa asked him.

"Being on one of the best beaches in the country with you, hell yeah." Melissa blushed and pecked him on the cheek. But Chad grabbed her face and went for a full smooch, to which Emmy yelled.

"EWWW! PDA!!!" The couple laughed it off and chased each other.

This beach was clean, unlike other beaches in Miami that had beer bottles hidden beneath the sand and bombarded with seaweed intertwined with plastic. Even when they saw trash, the three teens would pick it up and throw it out.

Melissa gazed at the seagulls soaring above the water, and Chad grabbed her, placed her on his shoulders, and sprinted to the water.

Emmy laid out a beach towel, sprayed herself with tanning oil, and soaked up the sun rays to get even darker than she already was.

Melissa, Chad, and Emmy walked to the lighthouse with Magic. They climbed the spiral staircase to gaze upon the beautiful beaches of Miami. Emmy took pictures of the couple, and then Melissa turned the camera to take a picture of the three.

"Oh man, hopefully, it came out," Melissa said.

By noon, the trio were all dressed back into their camping gear: khaki shorts, camo t-shirts, caps on, and sat in the sand to watch the waves crash.

"Hey," Melissa whispered. "I heard the further from the city you are, the better you can see the stars. And since we're here, would you like to sneak out and go to the beach?"

"Melissa, are you crazy?" Emmy said sharply. "Your mom would kill us if she found out."

"I know, that's why we won't let her find out! Come on, Emmy, we need some adventure!" Melissa pleaded.

"Chad, are you listening to this?" Emmy looked at him for backup.

"Yeah," Chad scoffed. "I'm down."

"What!? Ugh, I am being eaten alive right now by mosquitoes." Emmy changed the topic, and the couple pouted at her. "Fine, we'll go, but if we get caught, it's your fault."

"Guilty!" Melissa tucked the corner of her mouth into its usual smirk. "And anyway, I'll bring my backpack. I have that dagger from Gemma." Emmy rolled her eyes at the sound of Gemma.

Back at the campsite, Uncle Rudy prepared a warm campfire, and everyone made s'mores, with Magic sleeping peacefully a few feet away from the fire.

Melissa, Chad, and Emmy went to their respective tents. After a while, Melissa whispered, "Emmy, check your watch!"

"It's 12:30," Emmy whispered.

Stiffly, the girls crawled out of the tent. Before she stepped out, Melissa snatched her small backpack containing her dagger, the walkie-talkies, dream journal, and other girlish needs like makeup, perfume, and cream.

They looked out of the tent and ensured Uncle Rudy and Nina were sound asleep. Once the coast was clear, they slipped on their shoes over their Cartoonish pajama pants. The girls dressed in sports bras and oversized T-shirts snuck out of the camping site. Melissa peeped her head in, and Chad was wide awake. "Ready?" she asked, and he nodded excitedly.

Melissa snapped a twig immediately, and Magic came out of her mother's tent with his ears perked. He whimpered, but before he let a small bark out, Melissa snatched him up, and power-walked out of the campsite.

"Go, go, go!" Melissa whispered to them as they rushed out of the woods.

They followed the lighthouse until they made it to the beach they were at earlier.

"At least the mosquitoes aren't as bad," Emmy mentioned.

"I love this adrenaline rush!" Melissa added. "I can't wait to lie down and watch the stars."

"Same," Chad added, saying, " Guys, this has been the best summer I've ever had."

"Totally," Melissa agreed with him and jumped on his back for a piggyback ride. "I will never forget how awesome this summer was."

"You guys are stupidly cute," Emmy said uncharacteristically amiably. "But, I have to agree, this has been one sweet summer."

They took off their shoes and splashed around the shore. Chad would carry Melissa, spin her around, and pretend to throw her in the water. She then hopped on his back for a piggyback ride, and Chad would run around with Melissa giggling and Magic trying to jump on them.

Emmy watched the couple and smiled at them. "You guys won the best couple award!" They then splashed her and chase her around.

They decided to lie down and watch the few stars Miami had. Still, because they were away from the light pollution from the cities, it was enough that it made stargazing worth it.

The pearly moon was visible, not a single cloud in the sky, and they even saw the Little Dipper constellation. Melissa's mind wandered off into her fantasies again.

She imagined soaring in the sky, riding an actual dragon, and visiting the field with the sunflowers that change colors. Soon, I'll be home. The wind carried the sea salt and caressed Melissa's hair, tickling the back of her neck.

"She is always dozing off," Chad whispered to Emmy.

"Oh yeah," Emmys scoffed. "She lives in the clouds. She literally has an apartment rented in cloud nine." He chuckled as he gazed at Melissa, who remained lost in her thoughts. He held her hand and watched the stars alongside her.

Magic whimpered, and Melissa looked at him, confused. The hair on his body rose, and he soon growled. "Magic, what's wrong?" She reached out for him, but Magic dashed off.

"Melissa, go after him!" Emmy exclaimed.

Melissa bolted after her dog, who sped his way down the beach by the lighthouse. He stopped dead in his tracks and jumped as if trying to get the attention of someone or something.

She glanced up and was face-to-face with a shadowy figure wearing a thick, velvet coat with gold linings. Melissa gasped, and as Chad and Emmy caught up with her, she halted them with her hand.

"You both are from Earth." A familiar voice spoke, and Melissa's eyes twitched. "I knew you were not from the Dark Forest of Garnet, but I did not think you were from here either." He pushed back his cloak, revealing himself to be Wesley.

"Wesley?" Melissa took another step back, and her heart sank to her stomach. "How'd you find us?"

"It did not take me long to find you." He crept towards her, and Melissa took another step back. "I caught your scent, and it brought me here. But I am…" his yellowish eyes looked up as if searching for the answer in his mind. "I am perplexed by you."

Melissa gulped, her throat became a thick knot, and her heart hammered against her chest; she circled Wesley and asked, "How'd you even leave Gemma?"

"I have ways of leaving Gemma and coming to Earth. The elves think they are so clever and wise. They think themselves so brilliant that we must be simple, yet they do not have the slightest idea of what we can do." He let out a crazed laugh, revealing two sharp fangs.

"What do you want?" Chad interfered; he was now standing by Melissa.

"You, of course." Wesley licked a fang. "But she intrigues me." He pointed to Melissa with his black dog-like nail.

She raised her hands, balling them into fists, and Wesley cackled.

"Melissa, Chad!" Emmy laughed so hard her face turned crimson. "Wow, now I see why you wanted us to sneak out at night. Do you have your whole family in on this? Haha."

"Hush!" Wesley snarled at her, and Emmy glared at him unamused; Melissa felt her veins pulsing with panic.

"Emmy," Melissa cleared her throat. "Um… right now, it's time for you to trust me. So, do me a favor and shut up." Emmy scoffed, but her pursed lips soured when she saw Melissa's ghost-like appearance.

Wesley then spoke. "There is something about you… it is so strange." His eyes studied Melissa.

"Strange?" Melissa gestured to elaborate.

"Yes." His eyes locked onto hers, and he tilted his head. "You look so much like her."

"Like who?"

"Do you not know anything about Gemma?" Melissa shook her head. "You wear attire with unicorns yet do not know a thing about them. Is your head stuck in senseless dreams?" He touched his chin and scratched his bushy beard. "You look like one of the original dragon riders."

"Like who?" she repeated.

"The female. You have a striking resemblance to her. It is unusual. Who is your father?" They continued to circle each other. Emmy and Chad watched, their heads following each move, unsure how to react.

Melissa stopped and lifted her fist. "Get away from me."

"Foolish girl, you know you cannot battle me alone."

"She's not alone!" Chad growled.

"Now, now," Wesley lifted a hand, and his nails grew into sharp talons. "I am not here to kill your silly girlfriend. I am here to take you to Victor." He pointed at Chad, let out a wolf-like snarl, and just as he was about to slash her, Magic pounced, biting him in the neck.

Wesley snarled, trying to get rabid-acting Magic off of him. "You foolish dog!" he growled, and Melissa yelled.

"Magic!"

Wesley grabbed him and threw him across the ground. Magic thumped to the ground with a yelp.

"No!" she cried, and when Wesley went to slash her, Melissa moved swiftly and hit him with a right hook. The impact turned Wesley's face, and he let out a yelp not too different from Magic as he held his cheek; his yellow eyes squinted at Melissa, and he spoke. "You damn human."

Wesley turned his head, and his piercing black pupils dilated. His neck suddenly snapped to the right, and his left shoulder lifted.

Melissa gasped, and Emmy whimpered with each sound of Wesley's joints snapping and cracking as dark gray fur rose from all over his body. His small fangs grew inches longer, his jaws stretched, and his feet became more dog-like.

Before Melissa witnessed his transformation to a werewolf, she dashed and shouted to Chad and Emmy to run and not look back as she snatched Magic from the ground.

Melissa felt her lungs tighten and her heart slamming against her chest with every step. I have to do something. The knife! Melissa dug inside her book bag, grabbed her pocket knife, and turned around to sprint towards Wesley.

"MEL!" Chad yelled. "Are you crazy?"

"Run!" Melissa shouted back.

"No!" Chad shouted back.

"Chad, you and I have a fighting chance. Emmy doesn't. Protect her. GO!" she urged him, and although Chad hesitated, he snatched Emmy by the hand and bolted off. Melissa stood in a fighting stance with one fist in the air and the other hand holding the silver knife while waiting for Wesley, who was quickly closing the distance.

He was a fully transformed werewolf, but not in the way Melissa envisioned them to be. He didn't appear as a four-legged wolf. No, he still stood upright, but his already wolf-like features tightened, and his body weight and height doubled.

His fangs and nails became thicker and sharper, and his stance became stooped and predatory. His thick fur, animalistic speed, and thirst-like glare shook Melissa.

"Haha," Wesley let out a cackle. "Foolish girl. You think you can fight me?" he snarled and pounced at her.

In a split second, Melissa swiftly evaded, spinning around and unleashing a formidable round kick. The force of her strike jerked Wesley's face to the side, momentarily disorienting him. Undeterred, he lunged at Melissa once more, but she responded with instinctive reflexes and slashed her knife downwards, carving a deep gash across his cheek.

He let out a dog-like yelp, held onto his cheek, growled, and hissed at her. "How dare you?" The wolf was stunned. "A mere human." His head twitched. "You should not have done that."

Saliva dripped from his lips, and he was ready to rip Melissa to shreds, but Magic appeared just then, biting his neck again. The bite pierced Wesley's skin, and he yelped. It distracted him long enough for Melissa to grab and run for Magic.

Chad and Emmy weren't far ahead, and when they turned around, their mouths hung low. Melissa stopped and looked back to watch Wesley retreating into the woods like the cowardly dog that he was.

"What?" Melissa mumbled, confused.

A deafening noise of wings flapping filled the air, increasing intensity and causing her confusion to dissipate. Suddenly, there was a mighty, earth-shaking thud as the legendary creature she loved, a dragon, landed right before her, solidifying its presence.

Not just any dragon, but her dragon. Their connection was undeniable as their eyes met, and a sense of recognition and understanding passed between them.

The thud that shook the ground caused her to wobble and lose her balance.

She toppled backward, but her gaping eyes never lost sight of the dragon. Its elegant yet muscular body revealed its ruby scales that faded into a charcoal black and glistened in the moonlight. It stood on its four slender legs, and from his long yet slim neck, all the way to the tip of his tail were black triangular spikes.

Its onyx arrowhead spike at the tip of the tail looked like it could pierce anything with one swift strike. Its head had two curled black horns, its feet had sharp black talons, on either side of its face were dark, coffee-brown eyes and smaller piercing cat-like black pupils, and between them was a narrow snout. A corner of his lips tugged upwards, and Melissa swore it was a smirk.

It stretched its neck to sniff Melissa, and its elvish ears perked up; it lifted its neck, revealing how enormous it was: it was only inches away from being taller than the lighthouse.

A panic surged through Melissa, and her lungs struggled for air; she clutched onto Magic and whimpered.

"This is a dream, guys." Melissa let out a crazed laugh. The dragon lowered its head to meet her eyes and let out a puff of smoke from its nostrils; Melissa felt the heat from its breath sting her eyes.

She gasped. "Oh… snap…" she muttered.

It spread its bat-like wings, to which Melissa responded with a shrill so loud that it seemed like it pierced his elvish ears since the dragon winced and shook its head. Chad and Emmy followed with a scream after her.

The dragon responded by shooting itself up in the sky, and Melissa dashed away.

But running was useless; the dragon swooped down and picked Melissa up by her backpack with its sharp talons. The initial force caused her to fumble Magic around her hands until she finally could hold a good grip on him.

With its other foot, the dragon flew towards Chad and Emmy, grasped Chad's body, and snatched him up. Emmy had fallen to the ground, shrieking and covering her head with her arms.

The dragon flew high into the sky while the strong winds muffled the sounds of their blood-curdling screams. Melissa felt her bag ripping with every flap of the dragon's wings against the strong winds.

"Chad! I'm falling!" she cried out to him, and Chad reached his hand out, but it was too late. The backpack ripped away, causing Melissa to fall from the sky free with a yelping of Magic. The dragon swooped and caught one of her feet, piercing her with his talons, which made her screech in pain.

He continued to soar, and Melissa felt hot tears streaming down her eyes as she watched Emmy become a tiny figure in the distance. She looked at Chad, but it knocked him unconscious- he possibly fainted from the intense swoop the dragon did to catch Melissa.

As the dragon flew further away, her ears began popping; unable to cover her ears while holding Magic, she cried out in pain and frustration.

Then the dragon took a sharp turn, and when she opened her eyes, the dragon was diving into the water. Melissa shut her eyes tightly, preparing for an immediate death as her mind reeled with memories of Chad, Emmy, and her family.

There was a sudden pop, and Melissa peeked an eye open. She noticed the periwinkle sky turning into an amethyst color with thousands of stars illuminating the sky. The dragon soared, and although Melissa was dangling, she watched the land below with wonder. The air was crisp and rich, and it blew all her tears away.

It swooped down, and the dragon gently placed her and Chad on the ground. It then landed gracefully in a vast field surrounded by ruby-colored sunflowers. Melissa's body trembled, but she was unsure if it was because of fear or the adrenaline rush.

She crawled towards Chad, only to find him knocked out cold. She cupped his face, and her voice quivered. "We're okay... we're okay." Glancing at the dragon; her tongue felt thick and her throat tight.

The dragon lay across the field, studying her with its intense dark eyes; it tilted its head at her like a confused dog, and Melissa studied its gaze.

The sunflowers rippled in indigo, giving off the sweet-scented candle smell she loved. Her hand reached out to touch its soft petals.

"Okay, I'm dreaming," her voice trembled. "I stayed sleeping in the tent, and we never snuck out." Melissa grew a crazed smile and cackled. The dragon rumbled lowly and let out smoke, allowing Melissa to feel the heat again.

Its warmth gave her chills. "Wow! This feels so real. Is this real?" she asked, and to her surprise, the dragon nodded. "You understand me?" The dragon nodded again. "Wow... what else can you do, talk?"

"Yes." The dragon spoke in a deep, masculine voice, and Melissa shrieked.

Her eyes gaped at the dragon, and then she scoffed. "No way, no... no. Hahahaha, you can't be real..." she laughed maniacally.

"Dragons are the only living beast in both Gemma and Earth capable of speaking language. My name is Jakeriah, I am your dragon, and you are my rider. It has been quite some time since I have seen you."

Melissa's vision narrowed into a tunnel as her mind went completely dark, and her body collapsed into the tall bed of grass.

Chapter Twenty

A warm sensation streamed down Melissa's right calf. She lifted her head and winced at the sight of blood oozing out of the two puncture holes.

Magic was lying next to her injury; she attempted to sit up, but sparks of pain shot through her leg, and she whimpered. She took another glimpse at her leg and saw tissue.

"Oh, no- I'm gonna puke," she gagged.

"My deepest apologies," a deep voice rumbled. Melissa yelped and pulled Magic closer to her when she saw the dragon lying on the opposite side of her. "I did not realize your bag was so fragile." Melissa pressed her eyes shut, trying to determine if she was dreaming a dragon was speaking to her. "Oh, my apologies... I did not mean to frighten you. I felt your fear... it was similar to your fear from the Dark Forest of Garnet. I had a hunch Wesley had found you on Earth."

His curled, onyx horn sat in the center of his long, bony head, and he had tendrils scattered throughout his narrow face and angular nostrils.

He watched her with his beady eyes, the tiny black scales slightly expanding with each breath he took. Intimidated, she turned her head away from him.

Her dreams of seeing the legendary animal quickly became a nightmare. Hot tears streamed down her cheeks, and she clenched her fists, with her nails beginning to dig into her palms.

"Stop," the dragon huffed.

Melissa turned to face him and locked her eyes with his. The fear crippling her loosened its grip, and she felt as if the sorrow holding her hostage had slowly lifted just a little.

"How did you know?" Melissa said, glancing at her palms and placing them back down in embarrassment.

"You inflict physical pain to avoid the pain in your heart."

No one knew that, and Melissa's lips parted from the shock. The dragon, sensing her surprise, tilted its head to the side, resembling a puzzled puppy. Intrigued, Melissa observed the creature's scales, admiring the seamless blend of fiery ruby reds and smoky charcoal blacks.

I know now why red is my favorite color. Her mouth hung low. *He's so beautiful.*

They continued gazing at each other, possibly wondering what the other was thinking, until Melissa spoke. "So, um, you're my dragon?"

The dragon remained poised as he lay with his neck stretched when he spoke. "When you were born, I hatched. I am the last dragon egg to hatch in Gemma. My line of dragons has a connection with your bloodline, the Werra bloodline."

"Werra? I don't understand… I'm a Guerra," Melissa stammered, still in shock.

"Yes, there is… a lot more to be explained, but for now, let us wait for the elves."

"What was your name again?"

"Jakeriah."

Jakeriah...Jaker-... That name. The name lingered in her mind; where had I heard that name?

It then clicked for Melissa, and she took a dramatic gasp. "Jake- you were my imaginary dragon... he was red like you." She squealed, and the dragon tilted its head. One side of his mouth curled into a smile with her discovery.

"Your grandfather named me Jakeriah, but you could never say my name. Instead, you would call me Jake until you were three, which is when your grandfather took you away from me." He rolled his eyes, but Melissa thought little of it.

"Do you know my mom?" Melissa asked him.

"No, your grandfather never brought her here. This land is unbeknownst to her, as for most of your family." He stretched his neck forward so his face was closer to Melissa. She saw his cat-like, narrow pupils staring into hers. She took a deep breath, attempting to keep calm.

"I don't understand. Why did Pipo take me away from you?"

"No one knows." Jake avoided Melissa's eyes when he responded. "They say he did it to protect you. He even made you drink a powerful, forgetful potion to make you forget about me and this realm. You almost died."

"Yeah...that's the famous story my mom never lets me forget," Melissa said. "But Pipo almost killed me! That's what Chad and I have been trying to figure out. Why would he risk that?"

"I do not know." Jake sounded sincere, and his voice showed Melissa this was a sensitive topic for him. "I have been so angry at him for taking you away from me. For many years, I have felt nothing but emptiness and loneliness. I have missed your laughter, your innocence. I did not get to watch you grow alongside me as I grew up. Riders before you always grew alongside their dragons. We did not have that chance."

"Empty? Like a piece of you was missing?" The dragon nodded. "You are- a missing piece..." Melissa's eyes welled up in tears.

"Yes." Jake met her eyes, and they both gazed at one another. "And do you know why?" Melissa shrugged her shoulders. "We share an emotional connection because our souls entwined." He stood up and strolled towards her. Melissa felt the hairs on her arms rise and took a big gulp. "Whenever you are sad, happy, or upset, I know. We are one."

"Alisha knew when I was in danger, or sad, because you felt it." Jake nodded. "But... What about all the other times I've been sad... Or-" Melissa stopped. She could not mention her depression.

"You are sad all the time," Jake said. "The elves disregarded it; they claim it is the complexity of human emotions and a rider being away from its dragon, but I know Melissa, your sadness goes beyond my absence." Melissa felt her throat create a knot, but she held back the tears creeping into her eyes. Finally, someone understood exactly what she had been feeling all these years.

So, instead, they continued to observe each other's facial expressions and features. Melissa watched how Jake breathed and how the scales on his face would puff up, and when he exhaled, they would deflate.

"Melissa?" A weak voice called out, and Melissa gasped; she had forgotten about Chad.

"Chad! You're okay!" Melissa cupped his face and pecked him on the lips.

"Where are we?" he mumbled, and Jake answered.

"You are in Gemma,"

"It talks!?" Chad yelped.

"Yes," he snarled and released another puff of smoke that showered Chad, which caused him to whimper. "I have a name." Chad asked his name. Still, before Melissa could explain, there were sounds of footsteps approaching.

"Who's there?" Melissa searched around, her heart pulsing.

"The elves," the dragon said.

Chapter Twenty-One

Alisha appeared in the flesh, holding onto a torch and wearing her notorious white lace dress from Melissa's dreams.

Looking at her brought a cheesy smile to Melissa's face. Behind Alisha was Emmy, whose pale face and sunken eyes disturbed her.

Melissa limped her way to Emmy, wrapped her arms around her neck, and rubbed her back. When she let her go, Emmy wore a crazed smile. "Emmy, are you okay?"

"Pfft, yeah!" Emmy responded, clearly in shock.

"Are you sure?" Melissa asked again and glanced at Chad, who shook his head and mouthed the word no.

"Totally," Emmy laughed, and the couple glanced at one another and back at her. "I'm finally in one of your dreams," Emmy continued. "This is so cool. You were right about the Alisha girl. She's *flawless*! When I wake up, I can't wait to tell you guys about it."

"Emmy, this is not a dream," Melissa explained.

"Sure, it is!" The dragon raised his head to observe her. "Melissa, if this is not a dream, then at some point, we took shrooms or something." Emmy looked at the couple for reassurance, but they stared at her and blinked.

The dragon walked towards Emmy, each step shaking the ground; Chad walked in front of Melissa as if to shield her even while his own legs trembled. Jake peered at Emmy, who stared back at the dragon with a crazed smile.

"You're not real," she muttered. He lowered his head and was face to face with Emmy. He released a puff of smoke through his nostrils, allowing Emmy to feel the way the smoke showered her. Melissa saw droplets of sweat trickle down her cheeks.

"I am real," the dragon spoke. Emmy's eyes rolled up, and she passed out. Jake looked back at Melissa, his eyes widening and filled with concern.

"It's okay," Melissa whispered to him.

"Do you humans normally do that?" He looked at Melissa for an answer, but she had crouched down and held Emmy's head.

Another male voice then spoke. "Jakeriah," he hissed. "You reckless dragon, we had to bring the friend into this realm because she saw you." The man stood next to Alisha.

"Who are you?" Melissa asked, emphasizing the 'you' at the end.

"My name is Ezra." He spoke with poise.

The elves resembled one another. Like Alisha, he had narrow, stormy eyes and similar slim features. He was lean, but his muscular arms hinted to Melissa that he was stronger than he appeared.

His eyes searched her body, and he took notice of Melissa's bleeding legs. "Wesley did this to you?" Ezra asked, alarmed.

"Well..." Melissa's breath quivered, and she glanced at Jake. "The dragon's talons punctured me."

"Jakeriah!" Ezra barked. "First, you are seen on Earth, and then you hurt your rider?"

"My apologies…" He put his head down as if he was ashamed, and Melissa glared at Ezra. "I wanted her safe from the hands of that werewolf," he uttered in a growl.

"It wasn't his fault anyway," Melissa added with spice in her tone. "My bag ripped." She presented the torn strap. "If it wasn't for Jake, I'd be wolf food, „ she added.

Alisha cleared her throat and spoke, her voice soothing a tense Ezra. "We can provide you with new attire if you like."

"Look, it's okay… really, he saved me," Melissa assured them.

"Well, then allow me to help with that." Alisha grabbed a piece of cloth from her wool pouch and cleaned the wound with a silvery liquid that came from a canteen. Then, she pulled out a needle and a bottle of clear liquid from a knitted bag she had over her shoulders.

"What are you doing?" Melissa whimpered, watching Alisha pouring liquid on the wound and needle.

"The silvery liquid aids with the pain, but I need to close this wound, or it can become infected." When the needle pierced her, Melissa winced, thinking she would feel it, but to her surprise, she did not feel a thing.

"Ugh, I can't watch." Chad looked away, repulsed at the way Alisha stitched her up with so much ease.

"My apologies," Jake muttered.

Melissa grinned at him and told him, "You don't have to keep saying sorry. It was an accident." Jake's lips raised into a grateful smirk.

"Alisha," Ezra whispered. "The friend is involved. We must ask the fairies to help erase her memories."

"NO!" Melissa blurted out, and the elves glared at her.

"She cannot get involved..." Alisha explained, and Melissa interrupted her.

"Look, that same potion almost killed me. I'm not letting Emmy drink that potion. She can be involved with-with..." Melissa fidgeted with her hands and looked at Chad for help.

"Planning?" Chad offered.

"Yes!" Melissa snapped her fingers. "She'll be helping to plan and document, um, stuff."

"Oh great," Ezra spoke, crossing his arms. "To my utter shock, another dragon rider has their own ideas of how things we have already done for generations should be done. By all means, do not listen to Ezra. What do I know, anyhow? Only trained four dragon riders and fought in every conflict for over 200 years. But no, do not fret. Just let the mortal girl come and go because she says so. Sounds great, dragon rider. Anything you say, dragon rider, can I get you a cup of tea, dragon rider?"

"Actually, I'm more of a coffee person," Melissa placated, and Ezra scoffed.

"Oh, so you can hear what I said?" Ezra remarked.

"Her ears do more than line her face, Ezra," Alisha spoke, soothing his rough tone.

"Look, it's not like I want her to be a part of this," Melissa explained. "Just let her be my sidekick or something." The elves then ranted in an odd language, which Melissa could surprisingly understand. She then said, "Stop talking about my friend. She's staying, and that's final."

"You understand Elvish?" Ezra stared at her, an eyebrow raised.

"I guess?" Melissa responded, shrugging her shoulders.

"How?" Ezra narrowed his eyes and looked at Alisha for

an answer. "No dragon rider knew our language... well, except Micah..."

Micah? Melissa pondered on the name. *Wesley called me that name.*

Ezra cleared his throat, interrupting her thoughts, and said, "First, we must wake your little friend to explain everything. I will not explain twice," Ezra stated, and Alisha nodded.

Geez, bossy much? Melissa thought, observing Ezra.

Alisha whistled to Magic, who cheerfully dashed towards her. "Can you wake her up?" Magic hopped towards Emmy and licked her until Emmy groaned and fussed.

"Did he just understand you?" Chad asked.

"Yes," Alisha explained. "Elves and animals get along fairly well, more than any other beings."

These people talk like robots, Melissa observed. *No, 'cause Jake talks like them too. They don't speak with contractions! That's why it sounds weird.*

Emmy finally woke up and rubbed her head. "Melissa, I finally had a dream about Alisha."

"Emmy." she helped her best friend up. "It's not a dream." She delivered the news in a gentle tone.

Emmy looked at her surroundings and saw the two elves and Jake all staring at her. "Melissa..." Emmy whimpered. "Please tell me it's a dream."

"Hey," she cupped Emmy's face and assured her. "I'm just as freaked out as you are, but they're not here to hurt us." Melissa glanced at Chad, who nodded in reassurance.

Emmy hesitated but trusted Melissa.

"Let us all have a seat," Ezra spoke to Emmy first. "My name is Ezra. I am one of the Councils representing the Elvish

race. You have already met Alisha." Alisha flashed a smile at
her. "She is one of the few living beings that have mastered the
ability to enter the dream state. Alisha and I will be your
trainers. We trained your grandfather and his father before him.
I am older than I look," he added when everyone looked at him
puzzled. "It is imperative you listen."

The elves urged everyone to sit down; Magic sat on
Alisha.

"Your grandfather, Henry, was born and raised here, in
Gemma, with his two brothers. His real name is Henricus
Werra. His brothers, Pablo and Patricius, who you would know
as Patricio, aided Henry, who was the dragon rider amongst the
three. They all joined Henry on a quest to hunt down a Kraken
that was terrorizing the mermaids in the 1950s. While Henry
rode his ferocious dragon, the brothers sailed on their ship.
However, he ended up stranded on Earth and landed on an
island called Cuba. According to Henry, he attempted
numerous ways to return to Gemma but could not. Henry and
his brothers had to live in Cuba for the time being, thus
adopting the name Henry Guerra. Growing up as a dragon
rider in Gemma, he learned multiple languages, and Spanish
came to him rapidly. He had to speak Spanish during his time
in Cuba, but the customs were different."

"He went from living a life of royalty to a life of poverty.
As he adjusted to his alternative lifestyle, he met your
grandmother, Paloma. She," Melissa noticed how Ezra's tone
shifted, making it clear he disliked Henry's wife, "became his
world. Since he and his brothers had lost all hope of returning
to their royal lives and to his beloved dragon, he settled down
and made a new life in Cuba. However, when a new leader
arose in Cuba in 1959, your grandfather yearned to escape. He

said he knew political turmoil would take over. He had heard of other Cuban natives taking rafts to the United States. Your grandparents wanted to raise a family in a place where the leadership was different."

"In 1960, your grandparents, and Henry's brothers escaped on a raft. On their dangerous boat ride to Florida, Henry, his brothers, and his wife soon realized that in the middle of what you Earth humans call the Bermuda Triangle, unbeknownst to those who inhabit Gemma and Earth, is an entrance to Gemma into which the brothers had accidentally fallen. They also… found the Kraken they were initially searching for. It was dwelling beneath the Atlantic Ocean, entering Earth as it pleased. Your grandfather fought a long battle with the Kraken. It was one of the worst beasts any dragon rider had to face. Krakens are abnormal aquatic creatures. We could not travel by sea for years. Once the merfolk reached out for help, well... your grandfather felt compelled to do something about it."

"See?" Melissa added. "He wasn't so much of a tyrant."

"Realistically," Ezra continued, "if he did not help the menfolk, then he knew he would risk the alliance the Kingdom of Amethyst has with them. Merfolk have assisted us through centuries in wars."

A part of Melissa felt dumbfounded for believing this quest came from the goodness of Pipo's heart. Still, she refused to see it as purely political. Was Pipo the valiant hero she had always viewed him as? Ezra continued talking.

"Once your grandfather landed in Cuba and attempted to flee the land years later, the Kraken found him and his brothers again. While fighting off the Kraken, they all swam beneath and found themselves back in Gemma. This traumatized Paloma for the rest of her life. After that, Henry had to tell her of his prior life, but she never accepted it.

"After he came back, Alisha and I realized Henry had changed drastically. He and his brothers lived in royalty, then lived amongst the poor. We recall a time when he was stubborn, prideful, and even ungrateful. Leaving Gemma changed him for the better, I dare to say."

"Yeah... Pipo was none of those things." Melissa defended him; an inkling of anger rose inside her.

"Well, his life changed during his time on Earth," Ezra continued. "However, he was once again back home but only to find out his dragon died from insanity searching for Henry. She never ate, hardly slept, and in one reckless night of frantic searching, she fell into the ocean and the same Kraken killed her." Melissa felt her heart grow heavy, and she glanced at Jake, who lowered his neck down. "Your grandfather was never the same again after he learned what happened to his dragon. Without his dragon, Henry felt a part of him was missing, similar to how you feel, and that has the potential to drive a person insane. If it was not for your grandmother, Henry, too, would have gone insane like his dragon. We had hoped he would reign again in this land, but your grandmother could not accept the lifestyle- especially after the encounter with the Kraken, and he could not let her go. So, he pleased both sides. He had the fairies create an entrance using the Willow Tree and a tree near Henry's home on Earth. That way, he could live both lives. His wife, however, despied the idea."

"So, Henry had a double life?" Emmy pointed out.

"You could say that. Henry is the only dragon rider to do so. He lived on Earth and ruled in Amethyst, but his absence caused him to lose the respect of many in the Kingdom. Your grandmother," Alisha locked her eyes on Melissa's, "wanted absolutely nothing to do with Gemma. She was relieved when Jakeriah did not hatch for their son Rodolfo nor for your mother, Janessy," Alisha concluded.

"So... There are two entrances? One in Florida and the Bermuda Triangle? Which is where you took me?" Emmy asked.

"There are unknown entrances all around the world." Alisha shifted her stare to Melissa. "Take, for instance, Pegasus. You know him as the pet horse of the Greek hero Hercules... However, Pegasus was a winged horse who merely escaped Gemma."

"Whoa, what?" Emmy scoffed. "What else? Cupid is not really an angel but a dwarf?"

"Actually, Cupid is a fairy obsessed with the notion of love. He assisted the Council of Amethyst with the name of the Tungsten," Alisha added, and Emmy's mouth hung low.

Alisha continued speaking. "That is how your grandfather knew of him, but we are unsure how he actually found him. During your trip in North Carolina, Ezra and I discovered a battle that occurred in the area you were both in, which could explain why it holds a magical energy." Emmy stood up, and everyone jerked their necks towards her.

"Hold up. Melissa, this is insane!" Emmy grunted. "I mean, c'mon, Cupid is an ancient fairy? Pegasus was a pet horse? And the sky here is friggin purple?" Emmy looked up at the purple sky and grunted again.

"We told you," Melissa reminded her.

"How can you expect me to believe this was real!" Emmy spat, her mind still refusing to believe what she was seeing and hearing.

"But I was real," Chad added. "And Melissa has that dagger... that should've been enough proof for you." Emmy rolled her eyes.

Chad bickered at Emmy, and the two went at it, to which Melissa interjected.

"Guys, stop. Let's focus here, please." She looked at Ezra. "So, all that time that Pipo spent in Cuba, who took over here?"

"A lot happened." Alisha's voice shook. "He spent over two decades gone, and the Council of Amethyst protected the kingdom. While Henry was gone, we did our best to take care of this land and decided on his behalf. Many centuries ago, there was a king by the name of Lazarus who ruled over this land on which you are currently standing called Amethyst-"

"Pause," Emmy interrupted. "Gemma? Amethyst? Garnet? Is this place named after jewels?"

"Yes, jewels are... precious to many beasts and beings in this world," Ezra's surprised expression said, impressed with Emmy's quick observation. "Because of the magic of this world, the gems in the ground and in the atmosphere activate and cause humans to develop into other races. For instance, Amethyst and Garnet represent humans because Amethyst represents freedom, as Garnet represents power. Being that humans are the only ones who can ride dragons, it seems fitting. Then, you have Sapphire, which means superior intelligence. That's where elves fall into."

"Shocking," Emmy muttered, and Ezra rolled his eyes.

"We are much like humans, except our physical features underwent a few changes, such as longer ears and taller bodies, also a longer life span. The topaz caused humans to have a horse-like mutation and become Centaurs." Ezra finished and allowed the teens to process the information.

In a fleeting daydream, Melissa imagined Pipo as a dragon rider; with her curiosity sparked, she turned to Ezra and questioned, "What was Pipo like when he was a dragon rider?"

"Well, Henry was… quite ruthless and feared. As a dragon rider, you do not want to be feared. You want to be respected. But Henry never listened to the Council. When he learned a descendant of Lazarus, Victor, was living in the Dark Forest of Garnet amongst the dark beings, he flew with his dragon and rained fire, murdering people." Melissa gawked in disbelief. "His dragon burned his wife and child alive."

Pipo… a murderer? Her hand flew to her mouth.

Ezra continued. "Victor has had a personal vendetta against the Werra's ever since. He has stirred up one battle already during Henry's absence, but we quelled it. Victor's ancestor, Lazarus, used to be the ruler of Gemma five centuries ago. He was not a great king. He often killed those he felt could overpower him, and the beings in Amethyst lived in fear."

"A few of our kind, the centaurs, and the dwarves would search for ways to bring the ruthless king down. The centaurs read the stars for prophecies and hoped to find something about overruling the king. But then, a young centaur named Jinx prophesied humans would learn the way of dragons and become interconnected with them, but to do so, it could not be a fully-grown dragon; it had to be a dragon egg. They kept the details of this prophesy in secret because many elves struggled with whether to remain loyal to King Lazarus or listen to the centaurs. Unfortunately, an elf informed the king who started his own search for dragon eggs.

"Jinx then met Natara, the only dragon who was becoming a mother during that era. Jinx informed her of the prophecy, and he warned her she must give her eggs to someone worthy and not allow the king to find them. Natara, knowing the only hope of ridding Amethyst of Lazarus was listening to Jinx, willingly sacrificed her four eggs to a villager boy named Thomas. Thomas was an ordinary villager, living poorly with his father and mother. Although he was poor, his heart was genuine. He was out hunting for food one day and encountered Natara. Little did he know she was searching for him because she had been observing how he pursued food for his poor family. She chose him to be the first dragon rider and told him to find three other worthy humans and a wizard to cast a spell to connect with the dragons. When the king realized a mere villager had found not one dragon egg but four, he attacked his village. Thomas hid away with his two friends, Gabriel and Simon. He chose his two friends to be dragon riders along with him. Melissa's head swirled, trying to take in the vast history while still in shock from the newly learned information about her Pipo.

"Thomas went on a quest with his friends and the four dragon eggs. They searched for a wizard. After a long and dangerous journey in the forest, they found a powerful wizard. His eyes held deep wisdom, and the creases etched in his skin proved he had withstood the test of time. He trained the boys how to fight. This wizard, unbeknownst to the three young men, was the most powerful wizard to walk in Gemma." Ezra paused and watched Melissa, Chad, and Emmy, who were processing the information, eyes wide and mouths agape.

"The wizard had two daughters. A daughter who was a sorceress named Moonsie, and an adopted daughter, Micah. They chose Micah to be the fourth dragon rider." Melissa interjected after hearing this.

"Wait, Wesley told me I look like a girl named Micah."

"You do," Ezra confirmed.

"How?" Melissa asked, puzzled, and Ezra continued with the story, gesturing to her to be patient.

"Well, when Thomas explained to the wizard what Natara had wished for, he waited for the double moon eclipse to occur, which happens once a year. He then collected a drop of blood from Thomas, his two friends, and Micah, using a dagger designed by the dwarves." Emmy groaned with disgust. "He then procured an ancient white diamond which he had possessed for many decades, knowing he would need it one day. Once the double moon eclipsed, the wizard used the dagger to cast a spell, which caused the moon's light to attach to the blade. He then placed the blade on the white diamond. This diamond, referred to as The Diamond of Dragons, and the dagger successfully interconnected dragons and humans. Now, dragons only hatch when they feel like a genuine leader is born. Each of those four eggs hatched for Thomas, Gabriel, Simon, and Micah. That is how the original dragon riders came to be. As generations of dragon riders came along, dragon eggs only hatched for those worthy to be riders. Jakeriah hatched for you, Melissa." Jake and Melissa both glanced at each other and curled a smile. "Lazarus and the four new dragon riders went to war. Ever since then, there has been war generation after generation. As time went by, wizards and sorcerers became extinct, and the number of dragon riders decreased. Questions?" Ezra concluded with a deep breath.

There was a long silence as the teens attempted to process the information overload.

"Okay, so let me get this straight." Emmy spoke up and gathered her thoughts. "If Melissa looks like Micah, then that means she's her descendant, right?"

"The descendant of two," Ezra added. "Thomas and Micah fell in love, married, and had many children."

"So, they got married, fought a war, blah blah, and I'm assuming they took over the throne and became the new king and queen of this place?"

"That is correct," Alisha nodded.

"And you mentioned Melissa's grandfather is royalty too... So that means..."

"Melissa is a princess," Chad finished with a gasp.

Melissa felt her mind exploding with new information. She simply stared at the elves blankly.

I'm a princess, she felt the words echoed in her mind, I'm a friggin princess. The possibility of being royalty had never occurred to her.

"I'm a princess?" her voice cracked.

"Well, you definitely act like one sometimes," Emmy mumbled.

"Yes," Ezra reassured her. "Welcome back to your Kingdom, your majesty." Ezra and Alisha bowed.

"Thanks?" Melissa shrugged her shoulders and looked at Chad and Emmy; both were beaming at her.

"I can't believe Pipo comes from a line of royalty," Melissa mumbled.

"I can't believe he was douchey once," Emmy remarked, and Melissa agreed and asked the following question.

"What I don't understand... is why Pipo took me away from this place, yet he wanted me to know it through storytelling."

"The prophecy..." Alisha gulped, her eyes avoiding Melissa, "stated that the next rider to be born will end all wars... the last dragon hatched for a female, and the only female rider before you was Micah."

"I don't understand," Melissa said honestly.

"You are the second female dragon rider ever to be born. We-" Alisha searched for the right words. "We are unsure why the eggs have only hatched for males for so long. But we know Micah was powerful, and the people feared her. Some believe she had a connection with-"

"We do not know," Ezra interrupted the teens to raise their eyebrows suspiciously. "We have made assumptions why Micah was powerful, but nothing is concrete." Emmy then prompted a question Melissa was sure had been irking her.

"That doesn't explain why Pipo would wipe her memory clean."

"Henry discovered something but did not consult the Council of Amethyst." Something about Ezra's voice hinted to Melissa that he knew more than what he was saying. "He ripped Melissa away from the kingdom, had her drink a powerful potion that almost took her life, and then created a spell preventing her from coming to Gemma without Chad."

"What did Pipo discover?" Chad inquired.

Ezra's voice contained a slight hesitation. "We do not know. He never told us. It could be to protect her since, without the Tungsten, there will always be war. But because of Henry's action, you lost valuable training time, and he caused Jakeriah to despise him."

"His name is not Jakeriah!" Melissa blurted out, and everyone raised an eyebrow at her. "His name is Jake, and that's final. Pipo might've given him the name Jakeriah, but to me, he's Jake."

"Yes!" Alisha flashed a smile. "You recall?"

"Barely… I remember having an imaginary friend named Jake. The only thing is… is that Jake was a real dragon before I took that stupid potion that almost killed me…" The memories were vague, but just like the realm, she knew she had seen Jake before. "I remember Pipo would get so angry when I mentioned Jake. Now I see why. Pipo took me here before I took the potion, right?"

"Yes, he took you several times, actually," Ezra continued. "We advised Henry, or Pipo, whatever it is you call him, not to take you away from each other, but he did not listen. A rider without its dragon causes the dragon to act…" He searched for the right words. Jake's eyes stayed fixated on Ezra. "…irrational. He knew the consequences of that very well, as it is what led to his own dragon's death. We believe Jake never went insane because he knew you would reunite one day. That same hope kept him sane. You and Jake have a special bond. You feel each other's emotions and share a psychic connection. A connection so strong, many of us envy it."

"We were afraid it would take a few generations for the last egg to find a rider. And he hatched for you, Melissa." Melissa's eyes twinkled; a legendary beast chose her to be its rider. "The Kingdom knows about the prophecy, but the prophecy is still not fully understood. When Jake hatched, we did not inform the Kingdom he hatched for you. Only the Council of Amethyst and two allies from each Council are truly aware of who you are." He paused to let the information sink in, and Melissa spoke.

"So, no one knows I'm Jake's rider?"

"Or a princess," Emmy added.

"If the Kingdom and the Dark Forest of Garnet find out you are the true dragon rider, it may be disastrous. Dragon riders and rulers have ever only been men, and we feared the Dark Forest of Garnet will take advantage and storm Amethyst if they knew the dragon hatched for a girl."

"Ugh," Emmy muttered. "To my utter shock, here comes a country, or 'realm,' demonstrating sexist traditions," she said sarcastically.

Melissa and Chad looked down, holding in their snickers. Still, Ezra glared at Emmy and said, "Henry and the Council of Amethyst protected the kingdom."

"But, if a dragon is flying around the Kingdom, aren't they wondering where the rider is? Or who's the rider?" Emmy prompted, and the elves nodded. "So, who did you tell them the rider was?"

"The rest of the kingdom and the Dark Forest of Garnet believe Chad is the dragon rider." Ezra cleared his throat.

"What?" Chad let out a dramatic "Pfft," and the three teenagers mumbled to one another until Ezra interrupted.

"We must continue to say Chad is the dragon rider. When Melissa was born, the inhabitants of the Kingdom were talking and making connections between Melissa and Jake. But we could convince them the dragon rider was a relative and that one day, he would return. Once you found Chad, we informed the Kingdom we had found the rider."

Melissa breathed heavily, letting all the new profound information and family history sink in. She paused before speaking again. "So, I'm a princess and a dragon rider... destined to fulfill some prophecy- anything else you'd like to add?"

"As a dragon rider, it is your duty to protect Gemma and watch over Amethyst- and ever since your grandfather has gone to Earth, mythological creatures escape from Gemma. It is your responsibility to bring them back here. You and Jake have a duty to protect your land from intruders and prevent magical beings from escaping. We have been doing Henry's and your job for far too long. Also-" He hesitated. "You have to protect The Diamond of Dragons along with the Dagger of Riders."

"I know Victor stole the Diamond of Dragons, but where's the Dagger of Riders?" Melissa asked, but the elves gave each other a sidelong glance. Melissa knew she had brought up a complicated issue.

"The Dagger of Riders is hidden in a cave and only riders can enter it through the help of their dragons. It will be your duty this week to retrieve it. If you were here earlier, then Victor would have stolen the Diamond of Dragons."

"Wow," Melissa hissed. "You say that as if it's my fault. If you needed me here sooooo badly, why didn't you come to me sooner? You had a chance after Pipo disappeared when I was eleven."

Alisha responded. "When your grandfather took you away, he made us vow that if something were to happen to him, to wait for the right moment to reach you. When the enemies took bolder steps into our territory, that is when I appeared in your dreams. And now, war is coming."

"War?" Melissa gulped, her palms turning clammy.

"For Victor to destroy the Diamond of Dragons, he must have the Dagger of Riders and stab the gem on a double moon eclipse, which is occurring this Friday. He will wage war that day."

"This Friday! We only have like a few days to train?" Melissa gasped, and Ezra released a disappointing sigh before speaking.

"We did not have a choice, Melissa. Believe us, we would have trained you earlier if we could have. Your grandfather made certain not to let you into Gemma without Chad. He went to great lengths to prevent you from fulfilling the prophecy, not realizing the dire consequences he has caused and the potential damage that could occur in our Kingdom. We have been desperately attempting to get both of you here, but then Alisha explained your mother banned you from seeing Chad?" Ezra referred to the grounding.

"Yeah, she was. So," Emmy continued to speak, but Ezra rolled his eyes, and she scoffed. "Don't be rollin' them eyes at me, elf! We have questions. This is all new to us. Anyway, this diamond, whatever-"

"The Diamond of Dragons," Ezra spat. "You say it with such simplicity. The Diamond of Dragons is the only one worthy of the name once you have witnessed it. Our land has a fixation on precious stones, and it is the only one that no craftsperson would dare to impersonate with inferior small stones. Regardless of what your heathen, human artisans may design, they will never approach a fraction of the grandeur that is The Diamond of Dragons."

"Geez, didn't mean to burst your bubble, elf," Emmy scoffed. "Let me ask you this: shouldn't you have protected The Diamond of Dragons? How did Victor even get a hold of it?"

"Clever girl. Maybe it was wise to let you in," Ezra complimented.

"Whatever, I still think I'm dreaming. Why couldn't you stop him, or her, or whoever, from stealing this diamond? I mean, you guys look like you can handle it yourselves," Emmy placated Ezra.

"We believe we have a mole amongst us, which is how the enemies realized the rider's absence, and found the hidden location of the gem. We will have to find a new location once we retrieve it," Ezra stated. "We cannot focus on that right now; we have other matters to worry about. Seven days ago, I received a letter." Ezra whispered to Alisha, and she took out a piece of paper and handed it to Melissa so she could read it aloud.

"Ezra, I hear they left you in charge of training the young dragon rider. Like always, the responsibility always falls on you- yet you refuse to betray the dragon riders who have corrupted this land. I have been told a great deal about you and how you train riders. You know, he is a decent individual, I hear. He and his woman escaped my people. At any moment, I can slit his throat in his sleep. But you see, I do not want to do that just yet. I need his dagger, and I need him to give up the throne to give it back to the proper heir, me. I will destroy the Werra's legacy. You have until Friday. If not, I will kill him. I am giving him and you a chance to take your places alongside me. Friday at noon, my people will raid your land unless Chad surrenders the Dagger of Riders. The Diamond of Dragons is with me, and if you wish to protect this realm, I suggest you do as I say.

~Victor"

The letter trembled in Melissa's hand, and she was too afraid to even glance at Chad, who turned as pale as a ghost.

"We cannot prolong this any longer than we already have," Alisha explained.

"Great, so because the kingdom believes Chad is the rider, now he's at risk?" Emmy maintained her composure. "How did you guys convince everyone that he's the rider and not Melissa?"

"Because-" Alisha attempted to speak, but Ezra interfered.

"Since Henry went missing for two decades, and he barely came to Gemma even after his return..." His voice again trailed off. From the corner of Melissa's eyes, she could see Emmy raising a brow out of skepticism. "It was not difficult to hide Melissa being the true rider. You have to trust us; we may not always agree with Henry, but it might have been one of his wisest choices."

"Was wiping her memories clean wise?" Emmy remarked, and Ezra released a sigh and shook his head. "Mhhh." Emmy clicked her tongue and asked, "So what is he planning to do with the 'Diamond of Dragons'?"

"He means to destroy the connection dragons have with the Werra's. His goal is to destroy Henry and his family's legacy and take over Amethyst," Alisha stated. "Without the aid of a tungsten, you cannot end the feud between your family and Victor's."

"That's why Pipo refused to let me come to Gemma without Chad," Melissa suggested, and Emmy spoke up afterward.

"Are prophecies normally that short? I don't know much about fantasy the way Melissa does, but, um, I know prophecies in Greek mythology are very long."

"Yes, they are typically short," Ezra stepped in. "Let us focus on this war before continuing the prophecy. Trust me when I say this is not the war the prophecy refers to."

Oh great, Melissa closed her eyes. *What war could it be if this isn't the war the prophecy refers to?*

"Okay, so back to Chad being the rider... that's what Wesley meant when he said it's the boy he should be after... So, what do we do now?" Melissa asked.

"Do?" Chad scoffed.

He had barely spoken the entire night while listening to the elves explain Melissa's background story. Still, the letter disturbed him. "I'm not the rider, and my life is in danger! I didn't think things would become this complicated! We have to do something about this. This person knows who we are." He was frantic.

"Yes, babe," Melissa said. "But you're not the rider, so you're gonna be okay."

"Mel, seriously? This is not a dream anymore; this is far from a dream. This is a living nightmare!" Chad bickered and snatched his hand from Melissa's. "This is our lives on the line. I'm done."

"You don't think I know that?" she snapped. "How are we going to war, and what are we using? Guns?" She shifted her frantic eyes to Ezra, who responded.

"No," the elf grunted. "Unfortunately, Gemma's latent magic energy negates the explosive nature of gunpowder. We use swords, bows and arrows, and other forged weapons we can make."

"You're kidding, right?" Emmy scoffed. "Like medieval times?" Melissa turned back to Chad.

"Chad, we'll figure it out! Gosh, you're making a big deal. We survived the night in the forest, and we can handle this."

"Seriously, Mel? The night in the forest was child's play. Victor's target is me right now. You can't get upset 'cause I'm upset," he continued, bickering.

"I'm not upset!" Her voice went high-pitched. "You're upset."

"Well, duh, how can I not be upset?"

"Don't duh me," she quipped back.

"You know what-" He looked at her, fuming. "I need air, okay?"

Chad walked away from the group, and Melissa's eyes watered as she watched him storm off. She felt her head thud from consuming so much information in one day. The world around her spun, and she could not focus until she shut her eyes.

He is in danger. She looked down, realizing that her dreams were not fairy tales but a lifelong responsibility. *This is not what I expected this to be. What the hell do I do? No, this is my realm, my life. It's not theirs. I will not let them join in on this, prophecy or not.* Without realizing it, hot tears trickled down her face. It was too much for her to handle.

"Melissa, are you alright?" Alisha attempted to approach her, but Melissa stepped back.

"No!" Melissa croaked. "I thought this was the life I wanted, but I don't. I thought it was all fun and games. Ya know, an escape from my home, but this is serious. I never want to see my best friend or boyfriend get hurt for something that is my fault. I don't want them to be a part of this. They can't just accept this life. I don't even think I'm suited for this." She glanced at Jake, who looked at her back. "I'm-I'm sorry, Jake." Melissa's eyes welled up with tears. "You picked the wrong rider."

Melissa attempted to bolt off, but her injured leg prevented her. She heard Emmy scold the elves. "Don't. Let her be."

Chapter Twenty-Two

Melissa limped away from everyone until she felt her foot sinking with every step.

"What?" She looked down, puzzled, and her foot stood in white, powder-like sand. Her eyes looked forward, and in front of her was an ocean whose sapphire waters unfolded a sense of calmness.

"Wow." Her eyes drifted in the waves, their surface rising and falling with rhythmic ease, soothing the pulsing nerves inside her. The taste of sea salt bounced on Melissa's tongue. She could feel the chaos in her mind quieting.

Glancing behind her, she noticed the grassy plains that led to the vast sunflower field, which eventually led to the evergreen forest. She took a seat, stretching out her right leg that ached, and watched the way the pearly moon reflected off the ocean.

A turquoise, scaly beast jumped the way whales do. Melissa gasped, awestruck; her abuelo told stories of sea serpents breaching the water, but she never thought she'd ever see them.

She stood up for a better glimpse but felt her leg throb in pain. "Ugh!" She placed her hand on her thigh, wincing.

The sound of wings flapping startled her, and she glanced around to see Jake land behind her. The ground shook with a loud thud, and Melissa forgot about her pain for the moment, watching the majestic beast gracefully land.

He walked towards her and sat down in a dog-like manner. She was unsure what to do, but she sat down just inches away from him. They both remained quiet and listened to the soothing sounds of the foamy waters crashing onto the shores.

"Often," he broke the silence, "whenever my rage would consume me, I would come and sit to imagine the day I would meet you."

"Mhh." Melissa managed a soft smile. "At least you knew I'd be coming back. I forgot about you."

"That was not your fault, Melissa. It was Henry, and I do not think I can ever forgive him for bringing this emptiness upon my life."

"I know... I can't help but feel a little, I guess... angry at him," she admitted.

"I spent a decade without you. I am surprised I did not go mad and die like his dragon, my sister."

"In some ways, I was going mad. I wasn't able to talk to anyone about how I feel... No one understands how I feel at home, not even Emmy... not Chad. I'm always... lonely." Her voice cracked. "Ever since Pipo disappeared, I feel like I can't connect with anyone... I can't talk to my mom because she's so focused on keeping a roof above my head, and I can't talk to my sister because she treats me like literal garbage." Melissa hiccupped from all the weeping. "I feel like I'll never amount to anything or find any sort of stability in my life." Jake nudged his head on her cheek.

"I am so sorry I could not be there to relieve some of your loneliness. But, I am here, and perhaps now, the empty void you felt will not be as empty as it used to be." Jake cracked a half smile, and Melissa returned the gesture.

They sat in silence for a moment, and Melissa felt the urge to stand and walk closer to Jake.

She knew she should be terrified that a magical beast such as Jake existed, and she was at first. But something about him brought her a sense of tranquility she never felt before.

He crouched down, his eyes meeting hers, and Melissa caressed his snout.

"Can you ride?" he asked.

"Ride? On you?" She looked at him puzzled and gave a slight nod. "I mean, um, sorta... Pipo used to take me horseback riding back then. I'm guessing it's the same thing?" Jake chuckled. "What's so funny?"

"Henry is a smart man; he has been preparing you, and you were not even aware of it." A series of flashbacks played in Melissa's head.

He'd been preparing her for his departure, which is why he'd imposed all those extracurricular activities. Pipo wanted her ready, and even though Melissa was far from being an actual dragon-riding warrior, she knew she was closer thanks to him.

"So, would you like to take a flight or not?" he persisted, waking her up from the revelation.

"Sure..." Melissa gulped, and Jake bent his neck, allowing her to climb up on his back. She struggled because of her wound, so Jake used his snout to push her up.

Once on top, Melissa felt her heart slump to the pit of her stomach, "Whoa!" She felt queasy. "I didn't think this through…" Compared to a horse, she definitely felt higher off the ground.

"I do not have my saddle, so it may be uncomfortable. Just hold on to my spikes tightly. I will never let anything happen to you. Trust in me." Melissa hesitated, but she felt like she could trust Jake, so she nodded.

Jake positioned himself, and like a bull, he charged. Melissa felt if she didn't hold on tightly, the wind would have caused her to fly off his back. Jake then pounced, and his wings flapped; the impact of the flight caused Melissa to scream at the top of her lungs. She knew they were off the ground, but it paralyzed her with fear.

"Melissa!" Jake called out. "Open your eyes!" She hesitated, but she forced herself to open them.

Jake was soaring high above the sapphire waters, and the amethyst sky and pink clouds surrounded Melissa. The overview of the meadow and fields left her wonderstruck.

A rush of thrill overwhelmed her body, and she slowly let go of Jake's spike and spread her arms wide open. She tightened her thighs on his body and allowed the wind to embrace her.

She shouted, "WHOOOOOOO!"

The dragon took a sharp turn, and Melissa clung to the spike again. Jake chuckled and lowered down to glide above the waters. She dipped her fingers in the chilly water but then remembered the scaly beast and snatched her hand back.

"What if that serpent bites me?" Melissa asked.

"No need to worry about them! They are quite peaceful." Jake swooped back up and continued to soar. "Hold on tight!" he warned and swirled. Melissa felt her stomach twisting as her hair whipped all over the place.

He glided high above the grounds, showing Melissa the beauty of Amethyst: it covered the meadow in a lush green with an endless plethora of ruby sunflowers that rippled all at once to bright emerald.

She then noticed an area that had vibrant, colorful glitter occupying the space.

"What is that?" Melissa asked inquisitively.

"Fairies and pixies flying around," Jake explained, and he swooped down to show her.

He dipped lower and flew slowly; Melissa glimpsed the little human-like being that was the size of her hand. They wore two sets of butterfly-like wings and flew around, letting off colorful glitter.

"Wow!" she gasped, and the fairies giggled as they watched her, looking at them mesmerized. Melissa hadn't even considered the possibility of fairies being involved in the Kingdom, much less part of the Council.

A tiny, scrawny-looking fairy appeared and flew together with Jake. They did not seem human. They each gave off a shimmering dust that was the same color as their sparkling-colored skin, and their eyes reminded Melissa of an alien.

"What are those?" she asked, confused.

"Pixies!" He flew up again. "Better to leave now before they ask for favors," he warned.

Melissa looked down, continuing to watch the glittery space. "Fairies are kind, but it is best not to get too involved with the pixies. They are… well needy." But Melissa disregarded his comment when she spotted a stampede of unicorns galloping just like she remembered in her dreams.

"Look! Unicorns!" she exclaimed, and Jake soared right above them.

On one side of Amethyst was a forest filled with a never-ending cacophony of trees, and just a few miles away was an enormous brick castle.

"That is your home," Jake explained.

Melissa gasped, seeing the castle from afar. To the West of the castle is where the sapphire ocean lies, and just up North of the sea, Melissa noticed an eloquent lighthouse.

East of the castle were mountains that extended high into the sky and set the backdrop to the forests. From high in the skies, Melissa could see wildflowers speckling the base of the mountain.

To the far Southeast was a darkness covering the forest, to which she called out to Jake, "Is that...?" Melissa couldn't say its name.

Every corner exuded a sense of gloom and dreariness that unsettled Melissa. She could hear eerie, dissonant sounds emitting from the depths as if the trees were crying out in anguish.

"The Dark Forest of Garnet," he explained. "We are never to go there, Melissa." Jake turned and flew away, but Melissa's eyes continued to gaze into the dark forest. "That is where all the dark creatures inhabit. If they see us, they will kill us. Somewhere in there dwells Victor, the last descendant of Lazarus." She shuddered.

Jake swirled and twisted around, and Melissa giggled. "I knew it!" Melissa exclaimed. "I knew there was an adventurous world out there!" Jake laughed, and Melissa screamed out and let her arms spread wide once more. "WHOOOO!"

But as he flew high in the sky, her ears popped, and she felt lightheaded. "Jake, I think it's time for us to land." Jake swooped back down and landed gently. With Jake's wing,

Melissa could slide down and land perfectly fine, except her leg still throbbed from the wound. "Jake, that was awesome!" she cried out.

"You did great, Melissa." Jake bent his neck and snuggled his face onto hers. "I cannot wait to do it again."

Melissa allowed herself to pet Jake and slowly wrapped her arms around his neck and embracing him.

An overwhelming emotion of pure joy enveloped Melissa, a joy she hadn't felt since her disappearance. She allowed her finger to feel his rough scales, different from that of a snake.

Tears rushed down her face, and before she could dry them, Jake licked them off with his snake-like tongue, making her laugh.

"I found you," she said, weeping.

"And I found you." He snuggled her once again.

They heard twigs snap, and Melissa whirled around.

"The bond between you," Ezra spoke as he watched them with Emmy, Chad, and Alisha holding Magic, "is powerful, the strongest I have seen in the 317 years I have been living."

"Damnnnnnn!" Emmy blurted. "I knew you said you were old, but not that old! You look better than all of us!" Emmy finally got everyone to laugh and ease up, even Chad.

"So, this war thing, whatever, when do we train?" Melissa sighed, avoiding Chad's gaze.

"Tomorrow morning," Ezra replied. "We are going to train you until Friday. First, Iris and her two allies will come and train you in archery. At noon, we will train with swords, and I will personally train you, Melissa. Meanwhile, Alisha and our elf friend Leon will train Emmy and Chad. Then, after that,

Melissa, you will learn to fly properly as well as fight while riding on Jake."

Melissa's breath caught in her throat, and her heartbeat thundered in her ears. Just the sheer intensity of the training felt brutal. She wondered whether they also put Pipo through this rigorous training. Would her days now comprise swords, archery, and dragon riding?

Yet, the thought of riding Jake from here on out fueled her with excitement. A slight, sly smirk tugged at the corners of her mouth as she secretly reveled in anticipation of the adventures they would have together.

"No, I thought we said Emmy would be a planner or something around that line of duty," Melissa protested.

"You don't get to decide that," Emmy told her. "Who said you were the only one who wanted an adventurous life?"

"But-"

"No buts," Emmy stopped her. "I am in this with you." The two best friends shared lopsided smiles, but then Emmy furrowed a brow. "Wait a minute, what's gonna happen to Melissa's family? They're going to flip once they find out we're missing!"

"They have been searching for you for a while now. Time does not stop here, as you are already aware. Right now, it is five in the morning. I suggest you three come up with a bizarre story of your disappearances for the weeks to come."

"WHAT?" Melissa shouted involuntarily. "Are you crazy?"

"Why?" Alisha responded offensively. "How will all three of you come back every day to train and not make it clear to your family members? I highly doubt you want more people involved with Gemma. Besides, we need you at your best, and that is here, in Gemma. We lost too much time, and we cannot lose anymore."

"Do you know my mom?" Melissa continued her rampage. "She's going to flip! She's gonna tell Emmy's parents and even Chad's parents- oh my god, Chad, if your mom finds out, no, no, no..." Melissa was panicking so badly that she lost the ability to breathe, and she felt the weight of the world coming down on her.

Chad rushed to her aid, with Emmy following. "Hey, hey." Chad gently cupped her face and forced her to gaze into his earthy-brown eyes. "This is all our lives now. We have to do this. We need to protect ourselves and this land now."

"No, you told me I was too selfless. Now, I'm going to be selfish. This is my legacy, my family, my problem, and I don't want you to be a part of it."

"No, Melissa, we're not letting you make that decision," Emmy reminded her. "You need us. This world needs us."

"It needs me, not you guys," Melissa rebutted.

"No, Mel," Chad added, his tone stern. "We're staying here whether or not you like it. You're not doing this alone. The prophecy is not only about you. It's about me, too."

"But Chad, what about my mom?" Melissa attempted to pester, but Chad lifted a finger up and stopped her. She scoffed. "Don't do that again," she warned.

"Sorry... But we shouldn't focus on that right now. We need to learn to fight, or our lives are on the line."

"He's right," Emmy nodded in agreement. "His life depends on it, which is the reason we need to train."

Melissa hesitated, but she gazed at her fatalist friend who once doubted these dreams and said, "Are you sure about this, guys?" They both nodded confidently.

"Okay…" Melissa gazed at them for a moment, and although she hesitated, she said, "Let's do this." Chad kissed her on the lips, followed by a hug that Emmy also joined in on.

Afterward, the elves gestured to the three to follow them into the field along with Jake. They walked for some time, further south of the castle, until a small wooden cabin came into view.

Next to it was the ancient Willow Tree, and Alisha spoke. "This is the Willow Tree. It is also an entrance to Earth. The tree holds a powerful energy force. Moonsie, the sorceress daughter of the wizard who connected dragons and riders, successfully separated Gemma from Earth long after the war between the dragon riders and Lazarus. Her body perished in the process and became a Willow Tree in her memory. It also holds her magical energy. That," Alisha gestured to the cabin, "is my home. You will all stay here for the time being. The castle is not safe at the moment; we want to avoid any danger for your sake. I only have one bed, but we are providing sleeping bags."

The wooden cabin was tiny and instantly reminded Melissa of an efficiency studio in Miami that cost an arm and a leg. To the right of the entrance was a twin-sized bed held together by wood. To the left was a small wooden table with two wooden chairs; at the end of the room was an entrance to a small alcove with a metal bathtub.

"Where do you cook?" Emmy asked the elf, but Jake popped his head into the window and startled Emmy.

"Oh my god! I don't think I can ever accept that you have a pet dragon, Melissa."

"He's not my pet," Melissa scoffed. "He's… my other half, I guess?" Jake gave a half smile.

"Whoa, you make the same cute smile Melissa always does... that's creepy," Chad commented.

"Well, Melissa and I are bound to share similar attributes, traits, and even gestures," Jake grinned, revealing his sharp teeth that only made Chad gasp in shock.

"Wow- that is not scary at all," Emmy replied, and Melissa giggled. "How the hell has no one seen you on Earth?"

"I barely go to Earth. But when I do, I only fly late at night because I appear invisible. My lower body counters the shade with the night sky, and the dark parts of my scales reflect with your Earth's sky, making it seem as if a flock of birds are flying."

"Okay, so I gotta know," Melissa blurted. "How do you blow fire?"

"Dragons carry two separate chemicals in our thorax, a hydrocarbon and a naphthenic acid. When the chemicals combine and I breathe out like this," he blew out a small ball of fire, "I can create fire."

"That's awesome!" Melissa's jaw dropped.

"Alisha," Emmy turned to face her. "That letter, do you think he or she was threatening us about the war? Is it really happening?"

"It is not a threat. Victor's army is attacking at the crack of dawn, with or without the dragon and rider. The mermaids heard the goblins say something along those lines. Those simple monsters cannot keep a secret, but fortunately, that helped us become prepared. Do not worry," Alisha reassured her when she noticed Melissa twirling her hair nervously. "We will have an army, and we will train you three. We will not let anything happen to either of you." Her intense stare shifted to Chad and Emmy. "The elves have always aided dragon riders, and if

Melissa wants you two to be safe, then keeping you safe is a priority." Melissa could tell it was a genuine promise. However, something about the word war made her uneasy and even nauseous.

"Do we have to kill?" Chad asked.

"Of course, you fool," Jake snarled, and Chad was taken aback by the comment. "Goblins and ogres may be stupid, but they will kill in the blink of an eye. Do not forget that."

"Jake, we've never killed anyone," Melissa defended Chad. "We're nervous."

"This would not have happened if Henry had not taken you away. You are a natural-born warrior! You should not be nervous to kill a monster." Melissa took a shaky breath and sighed because Jake was clearly upset.

There was a complete awkward silence in the cabin that followed. "Well, it is time to get some rest," Alisha finally said, and she watched the three all snuggle into their sleeping bags. It was then that Alisha noticed Melissa's dragon ring wrapped around her index finger. "That is a lovely ring."

"Thanks, Chad got it for me." Melissa flaunted it and watched it in amusement. "Oh." Melissa grabbed her ripped backpack. "Here's the dagger." She pulled out the dagger wrapped in one of her ragged T-shirts, and Alisha observed it.

"It belongs to Victor's people. Here, keep it as a memory of that time you escaped. Get some rest," Alisha told them. "Tomorrow, our training begins."

With not much time left until daylight, Melissa, Chad, and Emmy forced themselves to sleep. Alisha warned them they'd be waking up at sunrise, which was in just two hours.

Sleeping proved to challenging since Melissa was tossing and turning. Not only were the sleeping bags annoyingly uncomfortable, but her head felt like it was going to explode from overthinking everything.

Between discovering her true identity and family history, her mother searching for her, the possibility of Chad's or Emmy's life in danger, and a war happening in five days, it felt like her mind would combust.

No longer able to tolerate lying down, she sat up and stared at the wall blankly. On Alisha's bed, she saw Magic sleeping peacefully with the elf.

He always sleeps with me... An inkling of jealousy pulsed through her. To her left was Emmy, drooling in her sleep, and to her right was Chad, snuggled up in his sleeping bag.

She smiled weakly, watching him sleep. "I wish you were awake so I could talk to you..." Melissa mumbled.

Jake popped his head in and whispered, "Unable to sleep?" Melissa jumped in fright. "My apologies. I did not mean to frighten you," he said.

Melissa stood up and stepped out quietly. "I just can't sleep," she admitted. "I'm nervous, I'm afraid, I'm emotional..." she teared up, and Jake lifted his wing.

"Come, it is warm under my wing." He motioned with his head for her to come in.

Hesitating, she walked underneath Jake's outstretched wing and nestled herself within, feeling an immediate sense of comfort and warmth.

Under the shelter of his wing, Melissa felt secure, shielded from the cool night air. The gentle rise and fall of Jake's breath lulled her, easing the tension from today's adventure. Chad and Emmy creeped in her mind, and she felt guilty for leaving them alone in the cabin.

She mustered up the courage to ask Jake, "Do you have a problem with Chad?"

"Mh," Jake growled lowly, making his dislike towards Chad clear.

"What is your problem with Chad?"

"They have stolen time from us, and it infuriates me."

"But it's not Chad's fault, is it?" The dragon grumbled, and Melissa laughed. "We have time now, Jake. I mean, I still gotta get used to the idea I am connected to a dragon, but it won't take long." Melissa snuggled under his wing.

"Not every young lady wakes up and finds out she has a dragon and has to prepare to go to war in five days," Jake responded nonchalantly, to which Melissa let out a genuine laugh and responded.

"You got jokes up your sleeve."

"I do not wear tunics as you do, and so I do not possess sleeves."

"Um, that's not what I meant, but sure."

"Oh." He seemed perplexed. "What did you mean?" Melissa explained the idiom to him, but even then, Jake had a hard time grasping it.

She lay quietly under his wing, forcing herself to go to sleep. "One more thing before I go to sleep." Jake gave a slight nod. "Protect my friends," her voice cracked. "I don't think I could live with myself if something happens to them. I don't even think I could survive if I lost another person I love."

"I promise to protect them. But you must make me a promise."

"Oh, yeah. What's that?" Melissa smirked at him

"You must not harm yourself anymore." Melissa looked down, feeling odd that someone knew about this habit of hers. "You can share your pain with me, rider. You no longer need to feel alone."

His words resonated with her, and he gave her a sweet nudge on the cheek. "I won't do it anymore," she promised.

They looked up to the sky and watched the way it scattered the stars like moon dust. A pearly white rock sparkled through the amethyst sky, and Melissa squeaked, "A shooting star!"

Jake chuckled at her excitement over the soaring rock, but with his snout, he nudged her cheek and said, "Stars have a way of mapping out the future. Only centaurs can piece it together."

"I read about that and always wondered if it was true…" Melissa said. "On Earth, if we see a shooting star, we make a wish."

"And what do you wish for, rider?"

"For many nights, I wished for you." She smirked before proceeding. "And now, I have everything I want."

Jake curled the side of his lip, and Melissa placed her head down and fell asleep.

Chapter Twenty-Three

It was barely dawn when Melissa heard Emmy groaning and mumbling. Melissa, Chad, and Emmy had only slept two hours after their intense night.

"Ya know, if we're gonna be waking up like this, can I just go home?" Melissa heard Emmy whine.

Her body was in the fetal position under Jake's wing.

"Where is Melissa?" Chad asked.

"I was hoping you could tell me if it is possible she ran off?" There was a hint of frustration in Alisha's voice.

"Oh, my god! Jake ate her!" Chad panicked, and then Emmy gasped at the possibility.

"I'm here!" Melissa called out.

"She's inside his stomach!" Chad yelped, but Jake uncurled his wing, and Melissa stretched.

"I spent the night under Jake's wing," she smirked, and Alisha smiled at the sight of them together.

Chad approached Melissa, although he hesitated since Jake narrowed his pupils at him. Once he was close to her, he wrapped his arms around her waist and embraced her.

"You okay?" Melissa asked, barely audible, with her face so tightly against his chest, which she did not mind at all.

"Yeah," Chad said as he relinquished his hold. "I just feel horrible for trippin' yesterday."

"I'm sorry too," she said first, but he pressed his lips on her forehead.

Alisha approached Melissa with her red backpack all fixed.

Melissa gasped and said, "You fixed it?!"

"Yes," Alisha grinned. "You looked so miserable when it broke."

"Geez," she scoffed at the elf's choice of vocabulary. "I was." Melissa mustered her half-smile and then thought, *Victoria got me this.*

She briefly wondered how her family was doing, and her heart hung like the moon, alone in the darkness. Alisha interjected her thoughts.

"Well, Iris should be on her way with some of her friends."

"What being is she?" Melissa asked. "I mean, you and that Leo elf are Ezra's two allies, so who's Iris in the Council?"

At that moment, the floor trembled, and Melissa heard hooves from afar. Three centaurs galloped their way towards the group, and the sight sent shivers down Melissa's body.

Melissa had read and seen countless images of centaurs in books, but to actually see the body of a horse and the torso of a human in real life was an amazing sight, a sight she'd never erase from her mind.

It had four horse-like legs and two human arms protruding from its humanoid chest. The sun danced through their horse-like coats.

"Hello," saluted the female who was wearing a metal breastplate. "I am Iris, the centaur representing the Council of

Amethyst." Her long auburn hair reached her shoulders, and her narrow bronze eyes locked fiercely on Melissa.

Melissa smiled nervously, and Iris continued saying, "This is my brother Nubis, and this is my husband, Nedjem." The males bowed slightly. "They are the two allies I chose to know who you truly are."

All three centaurs had the same narrow bronze eyes, broad nose, thin smile, and perky horse-like ears. Hair was visible on their faces, but Melissa could distinguish their features clearly.

Iris circled Melissa and smelled her. "It's been a very long time since I last saw you, Melissa Paz-Guerra."

"You remember me?" she replied, startled. They stood firm, keeping a composed posture. Melissa couldn't help but stand up straight, just looking at them.

"Of course!" She bowed to Melissa and came face-to-face with her. "Henry brought you here countless times. You used to hop on my back and ride with me."

"Wow," Melissa said gloomily. "I wish I remembered that."

"No worries, dragon rider." Iris beamed at her. "What is important is that you are back where you belong, and we have no time to waste. Alisha, can you give them the proper attire for training? I highly doubt they will fight in... whatever that is." Alisha nodded, and the teens looked down, realizing they were still wearing cartoonish pajamas from the night before.

Alisha hurriedly came back with three sets of chainmail armor.

"Oh, no!" Emmy laughed in a crazed manner. "We have to wear that?"

"It is what you will wear on Friday." Alisha handed each human a set.

Putting on chainmail armor was tedious but also heavy. Each person slipped on a thick shirt first, then placed the chainmail on top with a wide black belt holding it, black pants, and long leather boots.

"We seriously have to fight with this on?" Emmy asked as she struggled to walk with the armor.

"Emmy, would you like to fight on Friday in your PJs instead?" Melissa quipped at her, and Emmy rolled her eyes.

We do not design these for your bodies, but no worries, we have dwarves coming in to help with that on Wednesday," Alisha added.

"Here are your bows and arrows." Iris gave each person a complex bow Melissa had never seen: the wood was thick, and the string felt tight. The point of the bow was so sharp it glared in the sun's light, blinding Melissa.

"We are going to spend the morning practicing shooting the target. But first, let us prepare the training ground," Iris stated.

On the ground, a few feet from Alisha's cabin, they placed grappling mats to cover the dirt, about ten square feet. Iris and the other centaurs set archery targets 150 feet away, standing on the mats.

Everyone placed five wooden dummies on opposite sides of the targets. There were several swords and metal shields on a shelf designed for them to be stored.

Iris strolled on top of the mat, grabbed her bow and arrow swiftly, and shot an arrow, hitting the bullseye. Their jaws slightly dropped, and they simply looked at each other hopelessly.

They spent the morning till noon learning how to hold a bow, how to aim, and how to shoot the target. According to Emmy, it was epic.

Melissa and Emmy got the hang of it within minutes. However, Chad struggled for some time. He could finally get the posture correct, but the arrows would veer off.

"Better than nothing." Iris's intentions were pure; she didn't laugh at their initial failures, nor did she show her frustrations, even though Melissa was sure she was going to rage out at some point.

Chad shot an arrow so hard that the arrow veered off into the willow tree, passing into the regular world. Melissa and Emmy gasped while Ezra sighed and walked out to retrieve the arrow. When he came back through the portal, he glared at Chad and said, "You will have to try harder than that if you want me out of the picture."

Emmy snickered, and Melissa nudged her while shushing her. Emmy gestured, "What?"

Melissa responded in a whisper. "Don't embarrass him. We weren't that great either."

Iris then strolled over to the trio. "Tomorrow will be a better day." It almost seemed like a promise when Iris spoke. "Your arms will hurt tomorrow so be sure you sleep well and rest properly."

"Girl, they already hurt," Emmy mumbled, rubbing her arm. "And it's only the first day, ughhhh."

Melissa watched sweat dripping down from everyone's forehead.

Ezra approached Iris and asked her, "How was archery?"

"Not as bad as I initially thought, given the fact they have never done this, even though they think otherwise," Iris responded.

"What?" Chad scoffed. "It was horrible."

"Chad, it was yours and Emmy's first time. Emmy performed wonderfully." She grinned at them but then glared at Melissa. "However, for Melissa, we expected more."

"Excuse me? Why?" Melissa snapped.

"You are a natural fighter. You should have at least hit on your second try, but you did not."

"Wow," Melissa muttered and rolled her eyes.

"Give her a break!" Chad stepped in. "She just found out she's a princess-slash-dragon-rider and hasn't been in her so-called 'kingdom' for the past decade and has to fulfill some prophecy. Give her a sword. I bet she can fight." Melissa wore her trademark smile as she watched Chad defend her.

However, Iris's words still stung Melissa, who glanced down and shuffled her feet until Ezra spoke.

"Let us continue our training. We will see you tomorrow, Iris, Nubis, and Nedjem. Thank you for your time."

"It is an honor," responded Iris as all three centaurs bowed to Melissa and galloped away towards the castle.

"You okay?" Chad whispered to her.

"I'm fine." Her voice squeaked. "Just fine."

"Alisha," Ezra called out, and Melissa noticed how her cheeks flushed in a faint pink. "You should call in Fabre so he can measure them and forge a proper sword."

"He is coming tomorrow, and on Thursday, when he brings the swords, he will take them to the mines to retrieve the dagger Henry hid." Ezra nodded and shifted his stare to Melissa, who looked down and gulped. "Melissa, come with me."

She sighed, not wanting to depart from Emmy and Chad, and followed Ezra towards the sapphire ocean.

Chapter Twenty-Four

Emmy and Chad watched Melissa following Ezra with her shoulders slumped. "She is soooo not happy to go with him," Emmy remarked.

"Who can blame her, y'know?" Chad responded. "To be honest, she has the most responsibility out of all of us."

"True, but she doesn't have to do it alone. Sometimes, I worry about her. Melissa is always in a state of sadness. She won't talk about it, but she thinks I don't know about it."

"Yeah, I know what you mean. And when you bring it up, she'll change the conversation."

"Haha," Emmy chuckled and said, "I know exactly what you mean."

"I thought reuniting with Jake would help her," Chad mentioned.

"It'll help her," Emmy replied, "but that doesn't mean it'll get rid of her sadness. I think she has severe depression."

"The day of the zoo," Chad was hesitant to share, but he did for the sake of Melissa. "I noticed something strange about her hands."

"What do you mean?"

"On her palms, it looked like cuts."

"You don't think..." Emmy"s voice trailed off, hesitant to even mention the possibility of self-harm. Chad pursed his lips and gave a slight nod. "Nah... she wouldn't, would she?" Emmy's doubt in her friend's well-being was clear.

"She doesn't talk about her feelings," Chad explained. "Not with me, not with you. Not with anyone. If someone holds so much pain, don't they break at some point?"

Emmy"s eyes glistened with tears, and her mind raced with all the ways to confront her best friend, but Chad interrupted her thoughts. "I know you want to talk to her about it, but if you confront her, she will retaliate. We have to be strategic with her. We'll find a way to get her to talk to us about it."

Emmy didn"t want to admit it, but she knew he was right. Melissa was kind, carefree, and free-spirited. Yet, she was not the person to burden others with her emotional baggage.

But that was the issue: Melissa's emotional baggage wasn't a burden, and Emmy wanted her friend to know that. She shoved away the conflict within her, at least for the moment.

Alisha walked towards them, clearing her throat to get their attention. She had two swords, and she handed each of them one and then collected two round metal shields.

When Chad grabbed it, he gasped and said, "Shoot, this is pretty heavy."

"Great," muttered Emmy and grabbed the shield. "Wow, this is heavier than the sword... ugh, I don't want to use it, but I don't wanna get cut." Alisha rolled her eyes at her and spoke.

"First, I will demonstrate blocking techniques while holding a sword. Chad, I would like for you to come and pretend to stab me."

"What?!" Chad exclaimed.

"Come now, do not be afraid. Or are you not man enough to stab me?" Chad frowned and smacked his lips. He lifted the sword in an attempt to stab Alisha, but she lifted her shield quickly and blocked it, swung her shield to knock the sword out of his hand, and then used the shield to push him so hard he fell flat on his back and choked for air.

"You did all that with a friggin shield?!" Emmy rushed to Chad and lifted him up.

"Yes, and you can do even more when you use both a sword and a shield," she remarked.

Coming from the field riding a muscular, striking-black horse was a young man with silky blonde hair like the elves. Emmy gazed at him for so long that Chad cleared his throat.

"My bad." Emmy looked down in embarrassment, her knees buckling.

"Hello Leon," Alisha greeted him. "This is Emmy, the rider's best friend and, well-" She searched for the right words. "Possibly her right hand. And this is Chad, her partner, the tungsten."

Leon's intense, piercing-gray eyes studied each of them. He then spoke in a song-like tone. "Hello, I am an ally of Ezra along with Alisha, and I will be one of your trainers."

"Hi." Chad awkwardly waved at him.

"Um, hi…" Emmy's cheeks flourished with color. "Nice to meet ya."

"Alisha, I will train the boy," he said. "Then we can switch, and I can train with her." One side of his lip curled up, and Emmy grinned, revealing her braces.

"What is that on your teeth?" The elf asked with his head bouncing back.

"Oh, these are braces…" She saw the elves tilt their head and raise a brow. "Right, so um, these are like mechanics from our world to straighten teeth."

"I had them, they suck," Chad added.

"Yep, trust me, I get it," Emmy said. "But, um, yeah, I take them off next year."

"Let us focus," Alisha reminded them.

The elves taught them how to raise a shield and use it to their defense by blocking simple blows. Leon taught Chad how to stand and position himself correctly for battle.

He was incredibly patient, because Chad was a slow learner since he couldn't mimic any of the techniques Leon would show him. He also was an elf with few words.

"You are thinking too much about it," Leon stated. "You must let your mind move freely along with your body."

"How? I'll get stabbed or cut," Chad admitted.

"It is all a learning process," Leon explained. "Take my advice. Let us try again."

Leon went to strike Chad, and he lifted his shield. His eyes widened in fear, and he trembled. Leon struck again, and Chad continued to block. He took a deep breath, erased all thoughts, and blocked Leon with the use of his shield.

"Better!" Leon said, and they continued practicing.

Emmy was using her sword along with her shield. "Good!" Alisha complimented her every time she blocked one of Alisha's blows. But she often swung recklessly, which Alisha used to her advantage to knock her shield out of her hand.

"Now, without a shield, you're vulnerable," Alisha explained. "But don't worry, we will work on multitasking between offense and defense. That is why I wanted to start with the shield first. It is a versatile tool."

"Noted," Emmy muttered.

"Ready to switch?" Leon called out, and Alisha gave a slight nod.

Emmy took a deep breath, preparing herself to train with the handsome Leon. She watched him position himself, and so did she.

"Ready?" he asked, and Emmy hesitated but nodded.

He went for a strike, and Emmy blocked with her shield. She then attempted to swing her shield to knock his sword away, but he proved to be swift when he ducked and went for another strike.

Emmy, however, continued to push him off with her shield and even went for a strike with her own sword, to which Leon commented, "Daring, are we now?"

"A girl's gotta try," she responded to his amusement.

Although Emmy proved to be a faster learner than Chad, fighting with a sword was a challenge for her. Amid their training, she asked Leon, "Can I try to use two swords?"

"Mh, that is difficult, human."

"Name's Emmy," she corrected him. Her comment took him aback, and he arched a brow. "I want to try. Got nothing to lose, right?"

"No, just time," he remarked, but he was smirking, and Emmy interpreted that as okay to do so.

She put down her shield, and Leon handed her another sword and struck her. Emmy could block the first blow, and then she tossed one sword in a high arch, and Leon swiftly batted it away straight up into the air with his sword.

However, Emmy held the second sword in a spear-like manner and attempted to stab Leon in the stomach.

When the second sword made contact, Leon got the wind knocked out of him and fell to his knees. Emmy charged forward, catching the first sword out of the air, and held it up to Leon's chest, claiming victory.

Leon chuckled lightly, and Emmy said, "See, the problem was I wanted to stab you, but you were all the way over here... So... I had to come up with something?"

"Well, in that line of thinking, you will excel in archery. The prospect of stabbing at long distances is precisely the one that led to the invention of the bow."

"She excelled in archery," Alisha commented, "but it was a nice attempt."

They all heard a dragon roaring, and they looked up to watch Jake soar in the sky with Melissa.

"She must be terrified!" Chad said.

"Melissa? Nah," Emmy smiled. "She's too adventurous to be scared."

They then witnessed Jake take a sharp turn, and Melissa plummet downwards. Emmy and Chad dramatically gasped and attempted to scream her name. Still, Leon spoke. "A dragon would never let anything happen to their rider," he reassured them.

Surely, Jake quickly swooped down, diving headfirst, and then used his back for Melissa to grab onto a spike.

"That's so cool!" Chad exclaimed.

"I can't do that," admitted Emmy while holding her stomach. "I hate flying."

"Flying is one of the best feelings anyone can ever experience," Leon said. "I will bring a griffin to you after the war so you may experience it yourself." Emmy stared at him, her expression blank. "Let us continue, Emmy," he added, and Emmy grinned.

They continued to train with Leon and Alisha. Emmy was panting dramatically, droplets of sweat fell from her face, and her cheeks were rosy red.

"You good Emmy?" Chad called out.

"Yeah, I don't think I can do this anymore," she admitted while holding in a gag.

"Can she take a break?" Chad asked Alisha, who was ready to slash Chad. He lifted the shield to block it but fell back from the impact, and the sword flew out of his hand.

"No, we should not," Alisha stated. "However, Emmy has never trained before to be fair, and neither have you."

"Thank you." Chad let out a sigh of relief.

"Do not get accustomed to these kind gestures. Tomorrow, we will not stop, even if it means she passes out." She ended as she turned to look at Emmy with her stormy eyes. Chad picked up his sword and shield to put it away and then did the same for Emmy.

"Thanks, Chad," Emmy mumbled. "I'm sorry, I've never been a 'fit' person, and this is probably way more intense than CrossFit."

"You don't have to say sorry, Emmy. By the third or fourth day, you'll get used to it." Emmy released a deep breath; she looked down at her body and rolled her eyes.

"I've always hated being this fat," she admitted.

"You're not fat-" Chad attempted to disagree, but Emmy glared at him, and Chad interpreted that as don't-even-try-to-make-me-feel-better. But he spoke anyway. "Emmy, you don't look bad even if you don't think so. Stop beating yourself up about it. I used to be friggin scrawny before joining wrestling in High School, and my brother was this tough-looking guy. When people at school would ask me if Alex was my brother, I was kinda embarrassed to say yeah because he was so much stronger than me. But you know what? I joined wrestling, went to the gym after school, and started gaining weight and muscles. And guess what? He still looks stronger than me, but I'm okay with that. So, you're a little thick? And?" Emmy worked up a smile. "Don't compare yourself to others. You have great qualities I don't have, and neither does Mel."

"Awe, thanks Chad... I guess Melissa was right about one thing."

"What's that?"

"Not all Chad's are douchey." They both chuckled and continued chatting while sitting and watching Melissa ride on Jake.

Leon came by, handing the teens a silvery liquid in a canteen. "Drink," he said. Emmy and Chad looked at each other with their eyebrows frowning but drank it.

Chad immediately gagged. "Ew!"

"It tastes so weird! But oddly enough, it's refreshing!" Emmy added.

"It will help relieve your pain and soreness," Leon explained. "How do you know the dragon rider?"

"Well, I met her in third grade when I arrived from Cuba. Her family helped me adjust to America. Her Grandpa, Henry or Henricus, as y'all say, went above and beyond for us when adjusting to our new home."

"That is odd," Leon admitted.

"Why?" Chad asked.

"Henry was... like a tyrant, one would say. His family banished many races and creatures to the Dark Forest of Garnet for supporting King Lazarus in the first war. Henry followed those same traditions. Yet, he helped you, a foreigner, adjust to a new country."

"People change, I guess," Emmy explained. "I mean, when you live in Cuba… it's tough. There is barely any food to eat, lots of wrecked homes, and poverty. But what I loved about Cuba was how united everyone was. I'm sure that gave Henry a new perspective on life."

"Mh, does your friend share the same perspective?" Leon asked.

"Melissa? Oh yeah, I can never picture her being a 'tyrant,'" she scoffed.

"Mhh." Leon continued sitting and watching the sky.

"So, I'm not sure if this is rude to ask because I know it is back in my hometown, but how old are you?" Emmy asked.

"I am 55."

"What?!" Chad exclaimed. "My mom is 45, and you look SO much younger than her. You look as young as us!" Leon cracked a smile.

"Elves do not age the same as humans," he explained. "We take longer. Ezra is aging; you can see a few crinkles in his eyes." Alisha let out a giggle.

"It is true," she added, "and he loathes it when you tell him that." The elves and teens continued their small talk while watching Melissa soar above in the purple sky with her ruby dragon.

Magic clumsily toppled his way towards Chad, sat on his lap, and used his head to push his hand to pet him.

He glanced right back up, smiling as he watched Melissa soar.

Chapter Twenty-Five

Melissa and Ezra walked for some time. *Where is this elf taking me?* she thought *Why did he have to separate me from Chad and Emmy? And Jake?* Her foot sank, causing her to trip. When she looked down, she noticed there was nothing but white, powder-like sand.

"Here?" Melissa asked.

"Yes," he responded bluntly. "You will learn more proficiently without having the tools to make training swift." Melissa rolled her eyes, but the sight of the waves crashing onto the shore soothed her.

He tossed her a sharp sword and metal shield. When she caught the shield, it almost took her down with it. Once she found her balance, she stared at the sword puzzled. "A real sword?" she scoffed.

"Rest assured, we will fashion your very own sword by the end of Thursday. We will then have ample time to practice and sharpen our skills with it before Friday arrives."

"Seriously? I don't think I can fight using a real sword."

"Do not act like you do not know how to fight with a sword," Ezra warned her. "I know you have it in you."

"Yeah, MMA is one thing, but a sword-" Ezra suddenly swirled and knocked her shield out of her hand. "I wasn't ready!" Melissa shrilled.

"In battle, you never will be!" he emphasized, and Melissa took a few steps back to analyze the current situation.

Crippled with anxiety, she took a deep but shaky breath and fixed her eyes on Ezra.

"Position yourself and fight me," he told her, and they circled each other. Melissa's eyes followed Ezra. With each step Ezra took, Melissa would take one back.

"I want you to knock my sword down." Ezra swung his sword at her, and Melissa blocked him with her shield. She attempted to strike him with her sword, but Ezra was too swift. He swung it in a decapitating manner, and Melissa ducked and rolled; she stood up, stumbling, and positioned herself again. "Sloppy, but well done."

There were no breaks in between their fights, and training in the gritty sand proved to be an arduous challenge in its own right. The muscles on Melissa's calves ached, and she trembled.

Ezra taunted her and pointed out her flaws, such as her inability to use her shield to defend herself and dropping her sword whenever she was too nervous. This only infuriated Melissa.

Melissa's thinking got muddled with self-doubt and insecurity because of Ezra's harsh criticism. His brutal remarks just added to her stress, making it impossible for her to think properly or perform well. Her hair became disheveled, adding to her mounting anxiety.

Ezra's swordship skills outshone Melissa's, but when Melissa delivered a backflip to avoid an upper slash, he gawked. Her flexibility proved to be a strength he could work with.

"Wow!" He watched her in admiration. "Of all the riders I have ever trained, your agility is astonishing!" But Ezra quickly swept Melissa, knocking her to the ground, and said, "However, it will take more than some fancy gymnastics to claim victory."

"Gee, thanks-" Melissa replied with a sarcastic tone. She made it highly noticeable that she'd get annoyed by Ezra and his taunting tactics.

Jake flew in, sat in a dog-like manner, and watched Melissa train with Ezra.

"Jake, we still have an hour left," Ezra scolded the dragon.

"I am aware. I would like to see how Melissa fights." Jake blew smoke out of his nostrils, and Melissa assumed that was usually not a good sign. "Is that a problem?"

"No," Melissa interfered before Ezra spoke. "Let's just keep fighting."

Ezra struck her sword, and they both fought again. They clashed their swords to slash each other, rolled over, blocked each other's blows, and danced around each other.

When Ezra went to slash her, Melissa responded by bending down and kicking the shield out of his hand; Ezra retaliated by backing away, and before Melissa could flip her way out, Ezra took advantage and struck her in her back.

Melissa yelped in pain and fell to her knees, holding onto her back as tears rolled down from her eyes, all while the pain intensified with every exhale.

Jake roared and charged towards Ezra, snarling at him with a fierce growl, but Ezra remained poised.

"Jakeriah- you must remain calm," Ezra firmly explained, and Melissa glanced at the two. There was uncertainty in the elf's eyes.

"My name is Jake. Henry named me Jakeriah but because Melissa could not pronounce it, it stayed as Jake. She established this yesterday. And how can I remain calm? She started training today, and you are already abusing her like I knew you would." He let out a puff of smoke through his nostrils.

"There is a war happening in three days. Melissa needs to prepare herself," Ezra stated firmly.

"I sense her pain," Jake growled, "and if you continue to mistreat her, she won't be able to fight effectively."

Before Ezra could respond, Melissa used the little strength she had and stood up, groaning. "Jake, it's okay. It's not that bad." Melissa stood, but the sharp pain in her chest made her whimper. She inhaled, and winced. "Ezra is going easy on me. I need to be ready for Friday. Everyone depends on me."

Jake walked towards her and gave her a nudge with his snout, and Melissa kissed him.

"The connection between the two of you is truly the strongest I have ever seen. Most riders never learn to appreciate their dragon. They treat dragons as a possession or a pet rather than their other half, but you seem to." Melissa and Jake glanced at each other, putting on their trademark smirk. "Melissa, you really are not as bad as you think. In fact, you fought very well on your first day. You still need improvement, however."

"Yeah, but I suck at archery, according to Iris," she grunted.

"You did not 'suck'. You did well on your first day back as a rider. Especially given you have been absent for many years without the proper training," Jake reassured her, and a smirk stained Melissa's face.

"I agree-" Ezra replied, but Melissa spoke.

"Here comes the but..." she murmured. "There is a 'but' isn't there?"

"Yes, unfortunately, you share the same issue as your grandfather. You both have a penchant for allowing other people's words to control you. The Werra lineage carry the dragon's wrath. You fought well every time I battled you without taunting, and you even bested me when you disarmed my shield. However, when I provoked you with my words, you lost control with your dragon rage. I am sure you have heard that words can be more powerful than weapons."

"Yeah," Melissa sighed. "My mom tells me that all the time, that I have the power to avoid things and not make it worse- I guess that's why Pipo told me to kill 'em with kindness..."

"Actually, your grandfather had an axe that had the word 'kindness' carved into it. He loved killing beasties with old 'Kindness.' He might have meant that."

"What?! Wait! Really?!"

"No, not really!" Melissa rolled her eyes.

"Besides that," Melissa sighed gloomily, "he said it because I always let people get the best of me."

"Well," Ezra rested his hand on her shoulder. "Let us hope you are ready by then. Here, drink this." Ezra handed her a canteen with thick, silver syrup that tasted like sugarless chocolate.

"Didn't Alisha put this on my leg?" She looked down to see the two puncture wounds now covered in thick scabs. "Whoa! What is this?" She felt the liquid soothe her throat.

"Unicorn saliva."

Melissa gulped forcefully and gave Ezra the canteen back. "Why the hell am I drinking saliva from a unicorn?"

"It has magical elements to heal you faster. Look at your legs-" Melissa took another glimpse. Her mind could not grasp how her wounds healed so quickly with the saliva of a unicorn. "Yesterday, they were at least a few inches deep. Now, it's healed, but the scar will stay."

"Ooooookay, I believe ya... but let's not tell Chad and Emmy where the magical spit is from 'cause I know they won't drink it."

"How do you feel?" Ezra asked.

Melissa clicked her tongue but soon knitted her brows when she felt her back no longer ached, and the muscles that were sore from archery were back to normal.

"Wow, it is magical!" Melissa gasped dramatically.

"Yes, it is. Hunters target unicorns for the magical element they possess." Ezra dropped his head, and Melissa could tell he had a good heart. The elf cared for the mythical animals and beings in the Kingdom. "The Dark Forest of Garnet has no good-hearted creatures that come from there. They will kill and destroy anything for their benefit, such as gaining power or becoming stronger."

"He is right," sighed Jake.

Melissa twirled her hair and stared blankly at the ground. She thought about Wesley and how he expressed food scarcity in the Dark Forest of Garnet. She wondered if maybe they were mean because her family had wronged them.

Sensing Melissa's unease, Ezra tried to inject positivity into the situation. "But let's not dwell on the past. What is important is that you are here now, returning to your true home and embracing the life you were born to lead. Henry may have robbed you of that, but it is time to leave it all behind. Now, let us focus on the task at hand. Climb Jake's back and begin your proper dragon flight training."

Like yesterday, Melissa was hesitant to climb on Jake's back. This time around, he had a thick leather saddle on him.

"Finally," Melissa commented. "I get to be comfortable!"

"Ready?" Jake asked with a sneer.

"Ummmm, not with that smile. I haven't even settled in."

"Too late." Jake took off, and Melissa began screeching. "When are you going to stop screaming like that? Your friend and lover are laughing at you." Melissa had to muffle a laugh when he said lover with such spite.

She then glanced down and noticed everyone watching her with cheeky smiles. "Okay, I need you to trust me," Jake called out.

"Why?"

"You need to learn to stand on my back. If you fall, I will catch you."

"But I don't wanna fall!" Melissa panicked.

"Well, try not to."

"Jake!" Melissa grunted, and Jake flew higher into the sky. "What do you want me to do?"

"Okay, stand on my back and walk on it as I fly; remember, if you fall, I will catch you." Melissa shakily stood up and took baby steps. Her knees buckled, and she felt queasy.

Hesitating, she looked below, and her feet froze as her stomach took a turn.

"I can't, I'm scared!" she cried.

"Of what? Falling?"

"Yes!" she whimpered.

Jake purposely took a sharp turn, and at first, Melissa hung on to a spike, her body dangling in the air. Jake fussed and snarled, "Let go!"

"No!" Melissa felt the cramping of her fingers from holding so tightly. Just as she pushed her body up, Jake took another sharp turn, and Melissa plummeted down to her death. Her mind went dark.

An ear-piercing scream echoed through the air, filling the silence with terror. Jake reacted, extending his snout to grab hold of Melissa. With a gentle yet firm toss, he carefully placed her back onto his back so they could continue their ride together.

Melissa's hands clenched tightly around the saddle, her knuckles turning white as she desperately pulled herself up. But her efforts were in vain as she felt her breath quicken, her chest tightening with each gasp of air.

Her thoughts swirled in a chaotic flurry, the boundaries between reality and fear blurring. She could feel the panic attack knocking on the door of her consciousness, its presence becoming more pronounced with every passing second.

"Relax!" the dragon said.

"RELAX? I could have died!" she yelled.

"Get used to it! You will fall, but I will always catch you."

"No! I'll never get used to this!" she cried out.

Melissa's heart raced as Jake swerved once again, sending her into a panic. Whimpering, she ducked down, clinging onto Jake's spikes for dear life.

"Did you not want adventure?" he asked. "Is this not the life you craved? All those nights you were alone, you wanted to fly on a dragon. Now you are here. You must trust me, Melissa. Let go!"

Jake's words pierced through the chaos. The days she was trapped in the same four walls that carried her grief, she yearned to be part of her abuelo's world.

Reality struck her as her grip tightened on Jake's spikes, torn between holding on for safety and embracing the adventure she wished for.

She held on longer than she hoped for, and Jake must've lost his patience because he swerved, causing her to topple down. But Jake swooped down to save his rider.

They tried this motion again and again.

She studied the movements of her dragon, memorizing the rhythm and flow of its flight. Gradually, she synced her steps with his body, finding the balance that would allow her to stand and eventually walk.

With her body adapting to the shifting dynamics of the saddle beneath her feet, Melissa discovered she could stand tall on Jake's back. Her body rocked with each movement like a ship at sea. Even when she stumbled and fell on the saddle, she didn't give up.

When she stood and walked on his back without a stumble, her confidence grew. Tempted to feel the thrill of free falling, she asked Jake, "Will you catch me if I jump?"

"Always!" Jake ascended the purplish skies. "Now!"

The wind kissed Melissa's cheeks as she took the leap, and the world around her blurred into an array of colors. Time appeared to stop, and she felt the freedom of a soaring bird, weightless and unfettered.

Throughout her fall, Jake hovered beside her, monitoring Melissa's every move, promising her safety, and offering support while she indulged in the exhilarating experience. When the ground drew near, Jake swooped in to catch Melissa with his powerful wings, gently lowering her back onto his back.

By the end of their training session, Jake landed at their original training site, allowing Melissa to slide down from his wing. When she touched the ground, she landed as if she had suddenly developed dragon legs. This abrupt change left her disoriented and struggling to regain her equilibrium.

"Wow, you look like a warrior already," Ezra complimented.

"Thanks!" Melissa grinned. "I feel I've missed out on so much. This feels like a dream come true, and I'm lovin' it."

"You have missed out on a lot," Ezra reminded her.

They then walked back to Alisa's cabin to reunite with the others.

Chad and Emmy were sitting down, sharing the canteen of unicorn saliva.

If only they knew what they were drinking, Melissa thought idly, *and from the looks on their faces, they did not seem to enjoy the drink, not to mention their painful moans and groans with each sip.*

Near them was a short, blond elf watching them with such intensity that it made Melissa uncomfortable.

His piercing gray eyes shifted to Melissa's glare, and he sneered. "Hello, rider." His voice sang.

"Hi?" Melissa raised a suspicious brow.

"Melissa, this is Leon. He is my second ally. He helped train Chad and Emmy today," Ezra explained.

"Oh!" Melissa smiled at the serious elf.

"Leon, bow to your princess." Leon glared at Ezra, sluggishly stood up, and sarcastically bowed to Melissa.

"That's unnecessary, Leo," Melissa said.

"Leon," he corrected her. "Humble much?"

"Leon is only 55 years old; I intend to have him take my place," Ezra told Melissa.

"Is that like teenage years for elves?" Melissa asked, puzzled.

"You could say so." Ezra shrugged his shoulders.

Melissa sat next to Chad and avoided Leon's intense stare. She was as far as possible from him. Ezra tossed her the canteen, and she drank the silvery liquid apprehensively.

"What is this? It's disgusting!" Chad asked.

"It's uni-" Alisha attempted to answer.

"A unique tea!" Melissa said before Alisha could finish her sentence. "It has a magical element that'll heal you." Ezra stifled a laugh.

"Wow, babe, you're learning a lot already, huh?" Melissa blushed, and she could hear Leon scoffing.

Alisha cleared her throat and declared, "Leon will be back tomorrow to train you. Go wash up. There are fresh clothes for you waiting in the cabin. You might not like the clothes, but it is better than nothing," Alisha explained.

Melissa, Chad, and Emmy took turns washing up in the cold water in Alisha's metal tub. They had to use a strange rose-scented liquid Alisha gave them, which supposedly came from the petals of actual roses.

The elves, the trio, and Jake were sitting around a warm fire that Jake started. They were eating cooked white meat and drinking the 'unique' tea. Magic was eating shredded meat that Alisha cooked for him.

Melissa barely had an appetite and only took a few bites. *I don't even want to know what kind of meat I'm eating.* She pondered on the kind of beast the meat could come from, and her stomach turned. *Ugh, I can't even look at it. What if it's from an animal I don't know about?*

Chad gave her a slight nudge and mouthed, "You okay?"

Melissa shrugged and exclaimed, "What the hell are we eating?"

"Not sure- But... How about we take a walk?" Chad suggested, and Melissa liked the idea.

The couple excused themselves and informed everyone they would take a stroll.

As they walked alongside the ocean, their hands intertwined, they embraced the silence instead of engaging in their usual conversations. The calmness of the sea mirrored the moon above, creating a breathtaking reflection. It adorned the sky with countless stars, filling every inch of the galaxy with their radiant glow.

"How was practice with Emmy and Alisha?" Melissa broke the silence.

"I think I did alright," Chad boasted. "How was your training?"

"It was..." Melissa struggled to find the right words. "Harsh, I guess you could say. The session was intense. But flying on Jake was awesome! Did you see me?"

"Yeah, we freaked out the first time, but then we all laughed."

Appalled that Chad would laugh at her amid danger, Melissa exclaimed, "Laughed?!"

"Like I said, at first, I freaked out, but then it was just funny. Mel, we knew Jake wouldn't let anything happen to you." Melissa's cheeky smile drastically turned into a frown. "Hey, are you alright?" They stopped walking and faced each other.

"Yeah-"

"No." He stopped her. "Mel, you can talk to me... you can tell me anything. You don't have to hide what you're really feeling with me, so I'm gonna ask again. Are you alright?" His words seemed to have resonated with her because Melissa's eyes instantly filled with water.

"Not really," Her voice cracked. "I wanted these dreams to be real, Chad, but now that they're real, I'm flipping out. My abuelo prepared me for this all my life, and I feel the exact opposite. I'm so afraid of losing Emmy and you." Melissa's tears streamed down her face, and Chad hugged her to soothe her.

"Hey, I understand this isn't what you had hoped for... but you were born for this. I am ready to be by your side in this journey, Mel. I believe in you. And let's remember Emmy. You may think you are alone, but you are not."

"I know I'm not." Melissa sighed. "I just know that if something happens to you or Emmy, I won't be able to live with myself. I love you."

The words "I love you" flowed so naturally from Melissa that she had to think twice about the seriousness of what she had just said.

Chad's lips curled into a cheeky smile as his eyes twinkled. He locked his gaze with hers and replied, "I love you too."

He carried her and swirled her around, kissing her romantically out of enthusiasm. They returned to the campsite with wide grins, blushing cheeks, and nonstop giggles.

Alisha stared at them, possibly wondering what they were so happy about. "They most likely kissed and made up," Emmy whispered, and Alisha nodded, understanding now why the couple was so pleased. She quickly darted her eyes at Ezra, who was playing with Magic.

Melissa immediately noticed how Alisha's cheeks turned pink upon watching Ezra. "Are you and Ezra a couple?" Melissa asked in a whisper.

"No!" she blurted, but sighed and explained. "I met Ezra when I was 98. He was 144." The trio looked at her in shock. "I know it may seem like forever, but it is as if no time has passed for us. He recruited me to fight in one of our wars and even trained me personally. He always said I was different from all the other elves he had trained."

"Aw, that must mean something!" Melissa hoped.

"I do not think so." Alisha continued to watch Ezra. "He is my mentor, that is all." Her voice strained to a gloomier tone, and Melissa glanced at Ezra talking to Magic, saying, "Who is a good goblin-eating boy? We are going to eat lots of goblins on Friday."

Melissa shifted her eyes to Chad and stifled a laugh.

"We all should get some rest," Ezra interfered. "We have another long day tomorrow. The dwarves will be here bright and early to measure your arm's length."

Melissa, Chad, and Emmy stood up and sluggishly walked to their sleeping bags.

They whined about how uncomfortable the floor was and then recounted stories of their practices. Emmy and Chad laughed about Melissa's skydiving failure.

"I could've fallen to my death!" Melissa exclaimed.

"Oh Melissa, be real. I don't think Jake would let that happen to you. He's made it clear he loves you," Emmy scoffed.

Upon hearing his name, Jake then peeped his head in through the window and startled everyone, even Alisha. But right after, the teens chuckled at the sight of Jake.

"So, Chad told me he did well at practice," Melissa inquired. Emmy snickered, and so did Alisha silently.

"What? I did good!" Chad said defensively.

"Chad, you can barely shoot an arrow, and you sucked using the sword." Emmy poked fun at him, and Melissa muffled a laugh.

Chad's expression turned sour. "Whatever, it was my first day," he muttered as the girls continued laughing at his hurting ego.

Chapter Twenty-Six

Melissa's ears caught the sound of low grumbling and muffled noises, prompting her to open her eyes. To her surprise, two wrinkly men with the pinkest cheeks she had ever seen surrounded her. Their long gray beards added to their unique appearance.

She yelped, "Who the hell are you?" She scrambled away from the two men from her sleeping bag, only to realize they were only about three feet tall. "Are you the dwarves?" she asked.

"Ye," one of them replied. "Ya a heavy sleeper, we'll wait for ya outside." Melissa watched them exit the cabin and noticed Chad and Emmy were outside. Her armor was waiting for her on Alisha's bed.

Outside, she saw the dwarf and another chunkier dwarf measuring Emmy's body and arms.

"Mh, what jewelz do ya like?" one dwarf asked Chad.

"I don't know... an ocean-colored one?"

"Aquamarine?" Emmy suggested, and the dwarves nodded.

"Sure." Chad shrugged his shoulders and noticed Melissa walking towards them. "Hey! The princess is awake!" Melissa giggled and rolled her eyes playfully at his comment.

"Finally!" Emmy exclaimed. "These guys have been measuring me for an hour and asking us what jewels we like. Uh, hello, can you not touch my butt? Thank you," Emmy scoffed.

"The jewelz are for the handle, me love," said the chunkier dwarf.

The leading dwarf spoke directly to Melissa. "Melissa, follow me."

"Um, okay..." She walked cautiously towards them.

"De namez Fabre, and diz here iz Gar." Gar saluted them with a nod. "Ye may not remember me, but I remember ya."

"Just like everyone else..." she muttered, her eyes rolling upward.

"I'm one of de council members, representing we dwarvez' race. Gar is me ally, me wife as well. Ya de second female rider ever to be born, ya feared in a way."

Upon hearing the word "feared", Melissa displayed a wince, prompting Ezra to clear his throat to divert Fabre from the topic. Letting out a disgruntled grunt, the dwarf tightened his lips and rolled his eyes upwards with an exasperated sigh. Trying to stifle her amusement, Melissa covered her mouth to muffle a giggle.

Fabre took a couple of steps and reached his hand out to Melissa. She hesitated, but she let him take her hand. He stretched her arm out and observed it keenly. Melissa stood awkwardly and fidgeted her hair with her free hand as Fabre continued to scan her arm.

Finally, the dwarf released her hand and spoke. "Seemz like Micah's sword haz de proper length. I just have to sharpen de blade and change de gemz into one of ya liking." He winked at Melissa.

"No, you don't have to," Melissa explained. "It's already enough. You already have to make swords for them and me." Melissa gestured her head to Chad and Emmy. "And anyway, it's not my sword. It belonged to Micah, and I'd feel bad replacing her jewels."

Fabre observed Melissa's eyes glistening in awe and said, "I like dis one." He managed a smile. "She'z different, and it ain't because of de gender."

They approached Jake, who willingly allowed them to measure his body. "Mh, ya seem cheerful diz days," Fabre mentioned.

"Of course, Melissa is back," Jake commented, and Melissa beamed at him.

"Over centuriez, weeve tracked all dragon strikes wee could. Deeze x's dragons dat have made it back show de arez hit. As ya can see, it's very concentrated in da tail, wings, and legs. So weeve planning armor dat will thicken those areas."

Emmy approached Fabre and said, "Wait... these are the dragons that made it safely?"

"Ye... Why?" Fabre tilted his head dumbfoundedly.

"Well, that would imply that they endured those hits, survived, and returned home. I believe the dragons likely received hits in those other areas—the belly and the throat— and did not survive to make it back for you to analyze. So, please provide me with your diagram."

Emmy experimented with the diagram and drew some of her suggestions. She spoke once she finished while demonstrating to the dwarves. "Logically, wouldn't you want to armor these areas and leave the other ones?" She pointed at the belly and neck.

"O'course!" Gar slapped himself on the head. "I cannot believe I did not factor in survival bias! Miss, ya may've just saved dat dragon's life on da field! Ya a clever girl!"

"Pssst, I'm always right," she remarked, and they simply grinned as their red cheeks puffed up.

They finished measuring the group, and Melissa asked Ezra, "So we've met three members of the Council. Will we meet the fairy and her two allies?" Ezra shook his head before responding.

"No, the Fairy race exclude themselves from the castle grounds. They are free-spirited and sometimes even unreliable. However, when we need Sage, she comes through."

"Oh, what about Cupid, though?" Emmy asked.

"Cupid is like a myth himself. He never joins the war. It is not in his beliefs to fight. In all my life, I have seen him only once. That should show you how rare he is."

Melissa and Emmy glanced at each other with their lips slightly parted.

Once the dwarves departed, Iris turned her gaze towards Melissa and asked, "Ready for today?" she groaned. Tuesday was not as dreadful as Monday had been.

Melissa could hit the target on her first try without even trying too hard. "I did it!" she exclaimed confidently.

Iris stood near Emmy and observed her posture and technique. She then commented, "Emmy, I know you can do it on your first try, focus." Iris continued motivating her, and Emmy took one deep breath, aimed, and shot the arrow, hitting the bullseye on her first try.

"No way!" she shrieked. "I did it!" Emmy and Chad cheered while the elves simply watched her, seemingly pleased with her. It impressed Melissa that her once fatalist best friend could shoot the bow and arrow so perfectly.

Sometimes, I think I'm still dreaming. Melissa gleamed at her and turned to look at Chad.

Chad was the only one wearing a sour expression as he applauded. "Are you okay?"

"Not good at the bow and arrow, not the sword. What am I of use here? How can I protect anyone?"

Damn, hurt his ego much? But I guess he's right. She kissed him on the cheek. "You'll find something you're good at."

"Thanks-" he muttered.

"Chad, aren't you good at boxing and wrestling?" Melissa asked.

"I mean, yeah, I guess."

"So then, how about you and I have a session? I'm good at MMA and have a brown belt in judo. Remember? We could train."

"Sounds good," Chad smiled weakly, and Melissa wanted to understand what he was feeling. Chad was defensive of Melissa, and the possibility of him not being able to defend her amid war must have brought him down emotionally and egotistically.

The training session with Ezra by the ocean - isolated from everyone - was much better and swifter. He taught Melissa to block common blows enemies make, to duck and roll when avoiding a slash, to shield herself from arrows, and to use her flexibility as an advantage.

However, Ezra still taunted her, which aggravated Melissa with out-of-control rage in the training session. Ezra simply laughed at her, which only made matters worse. He used his foot to trip her, pointed the sword at her face, and remarked, "You cannot keep letting mere words consume you."

"I'm trying," she snarled in frustration.

She swung her sword, but Ezra swiftly swept her feet to knock her down. He said, "Your anger puts you in a horrific balance despite your great agility skills. You may be the most difficult dragon rider to train with."

"You're such a douche!" Melissa quipped back.

"No, you just are not a fast enough learner," he concluded, but before Melissa could stand up and protest, Jake interfered.

"I will take it from here." Melissa's body quivered from an uncontrollable rage that stirred inside her.

Ezra attempted to help her, but Melissa slapped his hand away and stood up on her own even though she stumbled to find balance. She walked out in a huff, avoiding Ezra's gaze.

"Ready to fly?" Jake asked, and Melissa hopped on his back. The dragon shot through the sky without allowing Melissa to sit down properly. "Hold on tight," Jake said and sped up, swirling in the sky at an incredible speed.

She felt the rush of the wind wash away her rage. Her soul felt free, and she reminisced back to when she rode horses with her.

"Jump," he encouraged her.

For the first time, she did not hesitate to do so. She allowed herself to dive headfirst. Jake caught her with his feet and tossed her to his back. She climbed back smoothly and stood up with no fear. He took a sharp turn like he usually did to take Melissa down, but she crouched, held on tightly to a spike, and stood right back up.

"Wow, you are doing incredibly well today."

"'Cause I trust you!" Melissa called out. "But I don't trust Ezra, and I don't like how he's training me," she frowned angrily.

"I promise you will adjust to it. I had to as well."

"He doesn't need to be mean! He makes me feel bad! He makes me feel I'm not meant for this and that you picked the wrong person."

"I did not. I chose you because of your heart, Melissa. Ezra does not mean those things," Jake reassured her, saying, "He is only trying to make you emotionally stronger." He swirled and glided above the clouds.

"Why? Because I'm a girl? That's sexist."

"No, we have female warriors capable of handling goblins and ogres independently. It is not a matter whether you are female or male." Melissa remained silent, and Jake continued. "Elves are not in touch with their emotional side like humans are. That is why dragons chose humans as riders, for their hearts. It is difficult for Ezra to understand why you become so upset. Whenever he taunts you, remind yourself how Ezra has lived a long, lonely life because he has."

"Lonely?"

"Yes." Jake swirled upward. "The only thing Ezra has ever known about is training dragon riders. His father was a high-ranked elf who trained your ancestors. Ezra learned to fight, defend, and train dragon riders from a young age. Despite being difficult to work with, dealing with dragon riders was a challenging task for him. According to Ezra, Henry was hardheaded and stubborn, making training him a challenge. We know the Werra for their prideful and arrogant attributes, not to mention their rage."

"The Guerra rage, well Werra," Melissa mumbled.

"Exactly." Melissa thought Jake didn't hear her, but he did. "The Werra blood carries a wrath like no other. It is called the dragon's wrath. They say Henry's time in Cuba helped control it."

"Well, maybe Ezra needs a vacation to calm down, and just maybe that'll be my first command." Jake released a chuckle, and Melissa smirked. "Anyway," she laid on his back as he flew and let her eyes wander the periwinkle sky. "I can't picture Pipo being arrogant like that... I know I can be prideful, and maybe it is the Guerra genes, but he was incredibly humble. He always helped people in need. When Emmy's family came from Cuba, he helped them adjust to America." Melissa sighed gloomily. "He must've changed when he landed in Cuba."

Jake remained quiet, and Melissa could feel in her chest that he harbored negative feelings towards her. She didn't know how she knew, but she did.

Chapter Twenty-Seven

Once they landed, they met up with the rest of the crew. Leon was there packing up his weapons. He saluted Melissa briefly and walked away.

"Is he always that quiet?" Melissa whispered to Jake.

"Yes, he is a young elf. It's his first time training with dragon riders."

"I'm assuming elves don't like humans very much?"

"They dislike anyone that is not an elf." Melissa chuckled at the comment, but a thought lingered: *why do elves think they're superior?* It irked her. *Why can't we all get along?*

The trio took turns bathing in the icy water, putting on the spare clothes Alisha brought for them, and speaking briefly with one another.

At night, they ate cooked white meat by the bonfire near Alisha's cabin.

"You know, I don't wanna know what this is because it tastes delicious," Emmy commented as she munched on the meat.

"Honey, it is chicken- like the one you eat from your realm," Alisha giggled. "What did you think it was?"

"Oh, thank God!" Emmy exclaimed.

"Well, you're giving us unicorn saliva. What do you expect?" Melissa blurted out, and Emmy and Chad spit out the drink immediately.

"Really, Melissa?" Emmy grunted. "You said it was a unique tea!"

"If I told you what it was, would you have drunk it?" Melissa quipped back, and Emmy scoffed. "Exactly, and it has magical elements. I mean, look at this bruise." Melissa raised her shirt, revealing the many purplish-blue bruises Ezra had left her. "Doesn't hurt at all."

Chad and Emmy gasped at the sight of it, and even Magic let out a small whimper. That's when Emmy took advantage to ask. "Okay, it makes sense that wild animals from our world would be here. But a chihuahua?" She gestured to Magic.

"Oh, no," Ezra spoke. "That was Henry. He brought two chihuahuas some time ago and wanted the castle to flourish with this breed." Alisha followed his comment.

"If you ask me, it was a wise choice." Alisha caressed Magic softly. "There are bountiful chihuahuas in the castle. Henry always said humans should not be alone. But he particularly loved this breed for their overprotective demeanor."

That's what happened to Pipo's dogs! He brought them to Gemma, Melissa smirked to herself.

"Yeah," Emmy chimed in. "Chihuahuas are like half-dog and half-demon." Melissa and Chad chuckled, and even Alisha giggled.

"Do you have dogs in Gemma?" Chad probed. "Like in POG, I saw dire wolves and even hell hounds."

"Yes," Alisha chimed. "We could train and keep dire wolves as companions, and it appears that humans on Earth continue to choose dogs as their companions. However, Chihuahuas were difficult to train because of their Earthly genes."

"Wait, hellhounds?" Emmy asked. It seemed as if the word hell gave her chills because she turned pale.

"They are not common," Ezra explained. "They have mangled black fur and red eyes, hence why we call them hell hounds. But they are not native to Amethyst nor Garnet." Ezra cleared his throat and said, "Tonight, you three need to rest. Fabre will be here early to give you all your swords. Alisha told me she could not sleep last night." Melissa, Chad, and Emmy snickered to themselves, but when they noticed Ezra's grim look, they all glanced down at their food to avoid his gaze. "It is imperative you get the rest you need. We have a war happening in a matter of days, and you three are not the only ones that need the rest."

With the mood spoiled, Melissa stood up with her unfinished plate, slumped her shoulders, and walked to the cabin. Chad and Emmy followed her.

They all lay in their sleeping bags quietly.

"Ezra, they are just kids." Melissa overheard Alisha say to him. "Do not be so harsh on them. They have been through enough already." Emmy and Chad glanced at Melissa with their eyebrows raised, and Melissa gestured to them to stay quiet and listen.

"She needs to be ready, Alisha. Henry was a warrior before her age."

"I know, but Henry took this life away from her. This is all new for her. On the positive side, she differs from the other dragon riders. She is thoughtful, and incredibly humble. No dragon rider before her had those qualities. Perhaps growing up in a realm different from here did some good for her as a dragon rider." Melissa listened intently but heard nothing but an imminent silence from the two.

"I…" Ezra hesitated, a rare thing for him to do. "Amethyst is counting on her, Alisha."

Melissa bit her lower lip; she felt her eyes sting, and Chad must have known since he grasped her hand and gently squeezed it. When they heard footsteps, all three turned around and snuggled into their bags to pretend they were sleeping.

Alisha entered, and she lay on her bed. Shortly after, Melissa heard Emmy gently snoring. Turning to face Chad, Melissa blushed when she saw his almond eyes. She whispered, "You're still awake?"

"I know you, Mel," he said. "I know those comments hurt." She gazed into his earthly eyes.

"I don't like this pressure… what if I fail?"

"You won't." He intertwined his fingers with hers and pulled her hand towards him to kiss it.

Magic's annoying barking woke up the teens in the morning.

"What are you? An alarm or something?" Emmy groaned. "God, I hate this life already. Melissa, you know I hate waking up early," Emmy fussed, but the couple ignored her. "Um, hello?"

"Emmy, Alisha will bring your food now. It's not long till this is over," Melissa reassured her, and Emmy grunted, to which Chad chuckled.

Melissa went to grab Magic to kiss him hello, but he sprinted outside, making her feel a sense of betrayal.

Alisha said, "Good morning, time to get dressed! They brought the swords." The trio sluggishly woke up and struggled to put on their armor. Not only was chainmail challenging to put on, but they were sore from all the training.

Outside was a crowd of elves, dwarves, centaurs, and regular humans.

"What is going on here?" Melissa asked with an eyebrow arched.

"Today, Chad will obtain the Dagger of Riders." Ezra cleared his throat, and Melissa knew she had to play along.

"Oh, haha, right, 'cause he's the dragon rider," her voice squeaked.

"We are officially training with your crafted swords today." Ezra tossed a sword without a sheath to Chad, and the sword almost took him down with it.

Ezra tossed Emmy her sword, but she let it fall on the ground and glared at the elves. "I ain't getting cut." She picked up the sword.

They had polished the blade into a beautiful silver and custom-designed the handle, mending the jewels they had chosen into it. Melissa marveled at the unique sapphire, unlike any she had seen before, and shifted her gaze to Chad's sword. He had chosen aquamarine, reflecting his love for the ocean.

"Here is yourz," Fabre whispered, shifting his gaze to Melissa and handing her the sword that once belonged to Micah. "It didn't need much sharpenin'. De gem dat's embezzled in it is called Sphalerite, the bright electric yellow on it waz de color of her dragon, and right above, I placed a ruby for ya." He winked, and she noticed the ruby was right above the Sphalerite.

The sword was light and swift. The lustrous handle felt smooth to grasp. Even though it was not custom made, Melissa thought it was perfect for her.

"Why is she getting the dragon rider's ancestral sword?" a woman shouted. "She is not worthy!"

"Excuse me-" Melissa barked, but Ezra interfered.

"Layla, it was a decision made by the dragon rider and prince."

"Oh, your highness, my apologies." The woman bent a knee to Chad, and he looked at Melissa, who was attempting to silence a laugh.

A crowd of female elves and humans gathered around Chad while Emmy approached Melissa. "Um dude, aren't you, like, jealous?"

"Jealous, me?" Melissa shrugged. "No, look how awkward he feels." Melissa pointed out his shuffling feet and how he placed his hand behind his neck.

"Haha, you're right, here he comes," Emmy snickered and walked away.

"Mel," Chad stumbled on his words. "I know this is weird, but I feel-"

"Chad," Melissa placed a finger on his lips. "I'm not worried at all." She kissed him on the lips, and his cheeks turned pink.

"Like my sword?" he asked her, flaunting his sword carelessly. Melissa grasped his hand to hold it still. She studied the sword.

"You would put an ocean-colored stone," she acknowledged, and Chad grinned.

"I am pleased you all like your swords. The dwarves have always done excellent blacksmithing for dragon riders," Ezra commented. Melissa noticed the way Fabre's eyes rolled at his comment.

"Everyone is here to watch Chad go off on his quest to obtain the Dagger of Riders. It is a tradition. Melissa and Emmy, you must accompany him."

"Okay, are you guys-" Melissa was going to say ready until an elf interjected.

"Shush!" the female elf snarled at Melissa. "You must listen to your prince."

"Don't talk to her that way." Chad took advantage of his make-believe royal status. "Respect her as you respect me."

Oh, I like this, Melissa smirked, and Ezra cleared his throat to silence a chuckle and spoke.

"Ready?"

"Yeah, let's go," Chad said, and everyone cheered; he whispered to Melissa. "All I said was let's go." Melissa lifted her hands, unable to give him an explanation.

"Well," Ezra cleared his throat, his voice strong and confident. "Only a dragon can access the cave your grandfather chose."

"Ezra, I believe Henry made the right choice," Alisha commented, and Ezra rolled his eyes.

"He was de king," Fabre sneered. "He didn't need our permission."

"Agreed," Ezra released a sigh. "However, he could have had the decency to inform us of his plan."

"Seems like some people don't enjoy being left out," Emmy muttered, and Melissa snickered.

"Well then, Chad, hop on your dragon," Ezra ordered.

"Um, sure," Chad responded, swallowing a big gulp. "Ya know... Mel, why don't you go first..."

"Wise choice," Jake muttered loud enough for Chad to hear, which made Melissa stifle a chuckle.

"Um, I'm not getting on that dragon," Emmy stated.

"Ye can come on de horse with me," Fabre offered, and although Emmy hesitated, she agreed.

Melissa swung her red backpack over her shoulders and leaped onto her dragon. She gestured to a reluctant Chad to hop on. Hesitating, he carefully climbed his back. Jake released a slight growl, to which Chad whimpered, clutching Melissa's waist.

"Jake," Melissa warned.

"What?" Jake teased, and Melissa giggled.

"Chad, you ready?" she asked.

"Totally!" his voice quivered.

With the strength and determination of a charging bull, Jake thrust his right leg forward and bolted. Chad clutched her waist while Melissa leaned forward in anticipation, awaiting the embrace of the purple skies. The force and velocity of Jake's ascent elicited a startled outcry from Chad.

"Open your eyes, Chad!" Melissa exclaimed, looking at him. Chad had his eyes tightly shut, preventing him from witnessing the events unfolding around them.

"What? Sorry, the wind is bothering me, ahah." Chad's eyes avoided Melissa's skeptical stare and smirk. As Jake swooped down, Melissa felt Chad's hands tightening around her waist.

"Ow! Chad!"

"Sorry, sorry, sorry!" he whimpered.

From above, everyone who watched them cheered and chanted, "Chad, Chad, Chad!"

"Mel, this has to be hard on ya."

"What?"

"The whole 'me being the prince' thing?"

"Oh Chad," Melissa sarcastically responded. "It's so totally okay. I'm not you. I don't like attention."

"Who said I like attention?" Chad asked, but Jake purposely swooped downward, triggering a screech from him.

"Besides, I'm more interested in my dragon than my royal status." She rubbed the side of Jake's neck, and she saw a half-smile forming on his narrow snout.

Jake flew past the castle, and Melissa saw the view of rocky plains. There, Melissa noticed dwarves upon dwarves mining with their tools and digging for materials to the blacksmith. Melissa wondered how they could bear the sun rays beating on their backs as they worked.

Just a few yards away from all the dwarves mining was a large cave. "That's a pretty obvious spot!" Melissa shouted for Jake to hear.

But Jake swirled away from the cave and back into the forest. "Our quest lies here."

When landing, Melissa slid down Jake's wing and assisted Chad, but he slid and fell flat on his behind. There was a small ditch covered in vines, and Melissa felt a magical aura emanating from it. So much so, without realizing it, she was already pushing the vines aside to enter.

"Mel? Aren't you gonna wait for Emmy?" Chad called out, and Melissa snapped out of it.

"Whoa," she said. "I'm sorry... it's just that I can feel the magic pulling me."

"All dragon riders can," Jake added, and Melissa's mouth hung slightly ajar.

Coming in towards them, galloping on the horse, was Fabre with Emmy clinging to him. Based on a pale face and wrinkled forehead, Emmy dreaded the ride. She slumped down to the ground and strolled towards the couple.

"Hey, you okay?" Melissa asked softly, hoping to soothe Emmy.

"Yeah, it wasn't that bad, but still..." Emmy replied, and Chad asked.

"Oh, c'mon, Emmy, you're afraid of planes and horses? What else?"

"Geez, I don't know, Chad." Emmy smacked her lips and pretended to wonder. "How about you spend four days and five nights in a crappy raft with not enough food and water? Oh, and waves as big as that dragon." Chad looked down at his shuffling feet, and Melissa sighed.

"Emmy, he didn't know," Melissa said, but Emmy rolled her eyes.

"Ye ready?" Fabre intervened, interrupting the awkward silence. "De cave, only ye dragon can access it. Once he does, ye are able to enter."

"And why does it have to be me?" Melissa asked. "Couldn't the elves do it? Or dwarves?" Melissa deliberately emphasized her words, fully aware of Fabre's skepticism as he rolled his eyes at the mention of elves.

"It iz only dragon riders who should enter. But the elves still tried anywayz. Dey don't got much rezpect for traditions. But ya grandpaddy set clues in a language only he knew."

"Language? You mean in Spanish?!" Melissa asked, and Fabre confirmed by nodding.

"Mh, pissed off de elves, ya know," Fabre added, but he smirked at the idea. "Smart man if ya ask me. Only dragon riders should enter anywayz." Fabre stepped forward and gestured to the trio to follow him to the cavern before the entrance. "Good luck!" he told them. The three entered the cavern and stood in front of a sheer, unscalable rock face with a white sphere covering the entrance. It reminded Melissa of a giant pearl or a dragon egg.

Jake's head peeked into the cavern, and he told them, "Step aside." Once they did, he blew a fiery flame, and the white sphere rolled away.

Melissa, Chad, and Emmy entered the narrow entrance. Jake, too, attempted to enter. He only realized moments later that only his head fit through the entrance. "I forgot I cannot fit. You three must go alone. Be cautious," Jake warned them. "Read the notes Henry left behind. It will be the only way you will retrieve the dagger and survive."

Melissa took a big gulp and drew a shaky breath; the word survived echoing in her head.

"Wait," Emmy spoke. "Jake, can you grab a branch and light it?" Jake gave a nod and went to retrieve one.

"Nice thinking," Chad murmured. "Sorry about earlier."

"It's fine," Emmy responded dryly, but Melissa tilted her head; she knew Emmy was still bitter about the earlier comment.

Melissa grasped Chad's hand and squeezed it gently. Jake soon popped back in, handing Melissa a piece of a thick branch. She grabbed it, and Jake spit a small ball of fire.

"Thank you, Jake." Melissa kissed his snout, and Jake's ears wiggled.

"Be cautious," he repeated and watched the three disappear into the darkness.

Chapter Twenty-Eight

The chilled darkness engulfed them, and the air was thick with humidity, making it difficult to breathe. Water drops echoed through the cavern, combining with the crackling of the fire and producing flickering shadows that swirled and twisted around the walls.

Melissa's senses heightened, and every sound bounced in her ears. She could hear Chad and Emmy's heavy, almost synchronized breathing against the grim background.

She walked with caution until they approached a stone wall. They pushed it, but it was no use.

"It's blocked!" Melissa grunted. "There has to be some sort of way to open it." She moved the fire around and noticed a rocky stand with a letter on it. Melissa passed the branch to Chad and grabbed the letter to read it aloud.

"Princesa, en una larga abertura tengo yo mi dentadura y luego que empiezo a hablar, todas mis piezas se mueven sin poderlas yo parar." She looked up and noticed Chad lifting a brow. It took her a moment to register that he didn't understand. So she translated. "Princess, in a long opening, I have my teeth, and after I start to speak, all my pieces move without being able to stop them."

"Mh, I've heard this one before," Emmy commented.

"I know!" Melissa said. "The answer is piano... But there's no piano."

"Well, did your grandpa play a song often to you?" Chad asked, and Melissa's mind raced with ideas and possibilities of what the riddle meant.

Think Melissa, think... Oh the lullaby! She approached the stone and, with her knuckles, rhythmically knocked on the rock and mimicked the sound of a Cuban lullaby, her abuelo sang to her. Apart from hitting it, she also hummed it, and Emmy joined in.

When they finished, the stone wall created a rumble and steadily moved on its own. Debris sprinkled down, and the trio all coughed simultaneously.

"No one in Gemma would figure that out," Melissa said.

"Mhm," Emmy responded.

"I wouldn't have figured that out, but I'm a gringo." Melissa and Emmy laughed at Chad's comment.

They entered and approached a wooden bridge. Melissa, Chad, and Emmy remained quiet and looked at one another with wide eyes.

"Do we have to walk the bridge of death?" Emmy asked.

"I guess so," Melissa responded, her voice trembling. She took a hesitant step forward towards the bridge, her foot causing the wood to creak and crunch beneath her weight. The eerie echoes reverberated through the cavern. Her stomach churned as she pressed her eyes and swallowed a thick gulp.

Drawn to the edge of the bridge, she peered down into the seemingly bottomless abyss below. The daunting sight before her made her question whether the risk was worth it. Doubts clouded her mind, but Melissa knew there was no other way. They had to cross the bridge if they wanted to retrieve the Dagger of the Riders.

After walking a few steps, she gestured for Emmy and Chad to follow. As they walked towards the middle, the bridge swung. "I don't like this," Chad said.

"Melissa, I think we should hurry," Emmy added, and Melissa responded.

"Shh, I think we're almost there."

They arrived at another entrance, but this one had a diesel engine with wires attached to the door. "Mel, I think I know why your grandpa had so much mechanical junk on your porch," Chad mentioned.

"Another note." Emmy noticed it pinned to the machine and read it aloud. "I am certain, Melissa, that the elves did not make it past the first riddle. Only you would know the rhythm of the lullaby. This riddle is for you and the tungsten from the prophecy. I know you very well, my little girl, and I know Gemma and Jakeriah are all magical to you, but I also know it will be difficult for you to see beyond the magic. Sometimes, you have to give up on seeing your dreams of magic to make them a reality. May the tungsten hold you up to that reality, mi niña."

Melissa felt her eyes sting as the thought of Pipo writing letters for her to read caused an inkling of sorrow to wash over her. She pressed her lips, scratched her head, and glimpsed at the engine. "Well, I don't know crap about engines." Melissa let out a pfft.

"I've worked on cars with my dad," Chad murmured. "Here, Mel, turn the key, and let's see what's missing."

Melissa turned the key, the engine lights turned on, and the noise of the engine sputtering echoed in the cave.

"Battery!" Chad exclaimed and inspected the battery installed, "Mel, look!" Chad pointed at four carved gems on the machine with the letter E engraved in cursive.

"Again?!" Melissa traced her finger on it.

"What could it mean?" Chad asked, and Melissa shrugged her shoulders.

"Hey, it looks like we have to connect the wires," Emmy interjected, and Chad assisted her with the wires. Melissa continued to ponder on the symbol.

We saw this on the porch when we cleaned the house! Melissa removed her book bag and took out the journal. Skimming through the pages as Chad and Emmy hot-wired the engine, Melissa searched for information on wizards and sorcerers.

Melissa had written that only wizards, and sorcerers have the capability of producing magic. *Pipo had used magic to create the bonding spell with Chad. He couldn't have been the one to cast the spell 'cause he's a dragon rider. Who did he know possessed magic? Could their name start with E?*

"Hey, Mel, mind turning the key?" Melissa snapped out of her deep thinking and placed her journal back in her bag. She turned the key, and the engine rumbled, turning the wires and unlocking the door ahead.

"Yes!" Emmy high-fived Chad, and Melissa smirked, so glad to have them both on board.

They all walked through the entrance and onto a stone bridge. Melissa took one step forward, and she felt a rumbling beneath her foot.

"Oh, snap," Melissa whimpered, and a voice loomed over her.

"Only my blood may cross over and retrieve the dagger."

"Was that Pipo's voice?" Chad asked. "'Cause that's a scary voice."

"Yeah, it's his voice. It sounds deepened," Melissa responded. "I guess I'm on my own."

Just the thought of walking the stone bridge alone sent shivers down her spine. Her jaw clenched shut, and a cold sweat trickled down her spine.

But not this time. Melissa had to do this last part by herself.

"Mel, be careful," Chad said as he held her hand.

"I know." She pecked Chad on the lips and fist-bumped Emmy before she walked on the rocky bridge of death.

Just a few feet away was a stony stand with the Dagger of Riders and a note on top of it. She read it to herself:

"Mi niña, if you are here, it is because I am gone, and you figured out all the riddles I left for you. I know you must be confused and afraid. I am so sorry to have taken this life away from you so early and for nearly killing you. I will forever feel guilty for doing so. But one day, you and Jakeriah will understand why I took this life from you so early. After reading this letter, I need you to go to Iris, the centaur, and tell her, 'dime toda la profecía.' Be sure not to do this in front of the elves. Only Ezra knows the full prophecy, he does not know that I told Iris. It will be one of many things he will hide from you. Elves are always trying to be one step ahead of everyone, but you must be ahead of them. Trust in them for now, but keep your guard up around them, especially with Ezra. You'll find out soon enough why you should take heed of my warning. You are the second female dragon rider ever to be born, and believe me, it may not be a good thing. I never thought my little girl, mi niña de abuelo, would be the girl to fulfill an ancient prophecy. Be safe, mi niña, and know that I have always loved you and searched for a way to protect you. Burn this letter once you have read it."

A teardrop fell on the note, and Melissa sniffled. She reread the note one last time, placed it on her heart, and took a shaky breath. She burned the letter, letting the flames devour the paper.

Melissa grasped on the dagger, and her eyes widened in surprise as she inspected the carved handle of the dagger. The image of the dragon seemed almost alive, its scales and wings etched with remarkable detail. She ran her finger along the edges, tracing the dragon's form.

With a cautious grip, Melissa lifted the dagger, feeling its weight settle into her hand. She noticed the blade was as sharp as the day it was fashioned, and it shimmered in the light, reflecting her dazed stare through the blade.

But when Melissa's finger brushed over the blade, a stinging sensation jolted her back to reality. The dagger's sharpness proved to be as harsh as its appearance.

She took a step back, and a loud rumbling noise of rocks caving in startled her. The unexpected noise filled the air, echoing through the cavern and paralyzing Melissa with fear.

"MEL!" Chad's voice shouted, and Melissa turned around and saw him making his way to her.

"Chad, NO!" Melissa shouted back, but Chad stepped on the bridge, and the cave rumbled even more. Melissa lost her footing, and her mind raced with panic.

"RUN!" Chad shouted.

Feeling the urgency in Chad's voice, Melissa wasted no time and started sprinting. With each hurried step, the ground beneath her seemed to crumble, making her stumble and trip several times. She exerted every ounce of strength to keep the sound of the collapsing bridge echoing in her ears.

"RUN! MEL RUN!" Chad continued to shout.

She was only a few feet away, but the bridge collapsed, and she stretched her arm out to reach Chad. He grasped it, and with Emmy's help, they pulled her up. Chad pulled her to his chest, "I thought you were a goner!"

The ground trembled, and Melissa replied, "We will be if we don't get out of here!"

All three of them sprinted out and back to the wooden bridge. It wobbled and swung as all three darted across.

Then, an arrow shot from above struck the ground right in front of Emmy, and she stopped dead in her tracks. Emmy grabbed it as another arrow came flying right behind Melissa.

"Keep going!" Melissa screeched at Emmy as more arrows rained down on them. Once all three landed on the ground, the wooden bridge tumbled behind them, and they continued to sprint until they each made it out of the cave and back to Jake and Fabre.

Panting, Melissa collapsed on the ground and looked at Jake, who approached them and tilted his head. The dwarf came to them as well and asked, "Ye alright?"

"Phew, we made it out alive," Melissa muttered softly, her voice filled with a mix of relief and exhaustion. "There was so many booby traps!"

She took a deep breath to steady herself before turning her attention to Fabre. Handing him the dagger, she couldn't help but notice the empty sockets in its hilt.

"By the way," she said, pointing at the empty sockets. "Do you have any idea why this dagger's hilt has these empty sockets? It seems like something is missing or meant to go in there."

Fabre tilted the dagger, squinting his eyes and admiring its beauty. Fabre said, "It's been a while since I zeen dis. It had four gems, ya know? No one knows what happened to dem. Da first one to wield it waz Micah. She was de most powerful dragon rider. Den passed it along to de firstborn. Protect it, like all riders before ya have," Fabre explained, and Melissa covered the dagger and clung to it.

"Best place to keep it iz in de thigh, ya grandpappy kept it like dat. I'll make ya a strap for it. It comes in handy." Fabre suggested it and winked at Melissa.

"Mh," Melissa liked the idea of strapping a dagger on her thigh. "Sounds good to me. Let's go back to the training grounds. I don't think I ever want to step in a cave again."

Once Melissa, Chad, and Emmy could catch their breath, they met the elves back in the training grounds.

Chapter Twenty-Nine

Alisha and Ezra were both face to face in a poised stance. Melissa gazed at the way they carefully calculated each other's muscle movements.

Alisha swirled and danced effortlessly, swinging her sword, which clashed with Ezra's sword. Ezra also swung, his feet sliding around the floor.

The sounds of the two metals clashing echoed in Melissa's eardrums, and she wondered if she'd ever reach their level of expertise in sword dueling.

Iris was watching them as well, along with her husband and her brother. Once they landed, Melissa mocked, "Where's all the Chad worshippers?" Chad nudged her playfully for that.

"Oh, they left. Come, we have to focus on training," Ezra responded and then bombarded the teens with questions. The elves listened as Melissa, Chad, and Emmy recounted their quest.

"Yeah, Melissa burned something," Chad blabbered on and Ezra glanced at Melissa, waiting for a response.

"Oh, yeah, it was a riddle I had to solve. Kinda had to burn the paper to release the um," her voice squeaked, and she cleared her throat, "the dagger."

The elves nodded, but Chad and Emmy remained staring at her with blank expressions. Melissa gestured to them with her eyes a look of I'll-explain-later, and they both seemed to have understood since they nodded.

It wasn't the only thing she hid from the elves; she didn't share the knowledge of the strange drawing on the diesel engine, and she was glad Chad had stayed quiet about it, too.

"Hey, Iris," Emmy called out, snapping Melissa out of her thoughts as Iris galloped towards Emmy.

"Yes?" the centaur asked, flicking her ears.

"So, this black arrow came flying down on us, and I was wondering what it was." Emmy handed her the arrowhead, and Iris inspected it.

She then explained, "This is a painkiller arrowhead. One hit will make it seem as if a dozen pierced you. There are different types of arrows used, such as arrows capable of piercing through armor or paralytic arrows. I can teach you if you would like."

"I'd like that." Emmy grinned. "Man, painkillers in our world do the total opposite." Iris tilted her head, and Emmy shrugged her shoulders and pfft.

Watching Emmy talk to Iris tugged at the corners of Melissa's lips. *I need to speak to Iris about the letter and Pipo's drawings. I wonder what else the elves are hiding.* She raised a brow at the elves who were talking to Chad.

They all trained with Iris despite Melissa pleading with Ezra to give them a break. He simply said, "This is the life of a dragon rider. You must continue to train." and so they did.

Chad was finally getting the hang of shooting, but even then, he had a lot of work to do.

"Perhaps archery may not be your forte," Iris commented, trying to be considerate and avoid offending Chad, although her words still held a tinge of implication.

She instructed them on the importance of relying on their senses to stay aware of potential threats approaching from behind.

"Are you sure you never took an archery class or something?" Melissa asked Emmy, who hit bullseye repeatedly.

"No, I've always liked it and read up on it a few times. Never thought I'd actually do it and be good at it. I'm surprised Pipo never put you in classes for it."

"For real," Melissa giggled. "But then again, I'm pretty good with the sword."

For the afternoon session, Melissa begged Ezra to do hand-to-hand combat which, although he contemplated, he agreed to it. Melissa wanted to do it mostly for Chad so he could stop being depressed about being bad at archery and sword fighting.

The first up was Melissa and Alisha. At first, Melissa hesitated to hit her, but Alisha attempted to swing a round kick, and Melissa ducked and rolled. The people watching went, "Ohhh," and Melisa glared at Alisha. "Alright, let's see what you got."

Melissa and Alisha circled each other. A couple of times, Alisha kicked Melissa and even swung a punch. Melissa took advantage and grabbed her arm, swung it over her shoulders, and, with her hip, tossed Alisha.

Her body slammed to the ground, and Melissa grabbed her arm to place her in an arm bar. They tussled on the ground for a while until Melissa held a tight grip.

"Very well done!" Ezra exclaimed. "Who is next?" Chad volunteered, and Melissa sneered.

"Don't go easy on me, Mel," he said confidently.

"Alright, I won't." She winked.

But Melissa didn't have to go easy because finally Chad truly was good at some type of fighting. He knew how to box incredibly well, how to block, and how to avoid a judo toss. When Melissa attempted to judo-toss him, he counter-blocked her and tossed her instead to the ground.

He put her in a wrestling hold until she tapped out. Emmy cheered for Chad, the elves gave an approving nod to him, and even Jake threw a little fireball up in the air for him.

"You see! You were meant for this." Melissa kissed his sweaty cheek, and he beamed at her.

"We were meant for this," he corrected her in a playful tone, brushing her strands of hair out of her face.

"I would like to go against Melissa," Leon said.

"Er-Okay!" Melissa hesitated but agreed to it.

Leon and Melissa glared at one another as they circled each other. His stormy gray eyes read her body language, and Melissa purposely moved forward unexpectedly.

"She is unpredictable," she heard Ezra whisper to Alisha. "That is a plus."

Leon went in for a high kick, which Melissa blocked with her arm, but then, with his left arm, he swung his fist, punching her in the mouth.

Everyone gasped, and Jake snarled. Chad attempted to run to her aid, but Melissa halted him with her hand. She wiped the blood from her lip, and she glared at Leon.

The dragon wrath consumed her: her blood boiled, and her eyes twitched.

With no hint of pity, she allowed herself to show everyone her skills. She took one deep breath, lifted her fists, fixated her intense stare on Leon, and swung first. She swung punches and round kicks, blocked his brutal punches, and whenever he took her down, she'd shrimp out and get back to her feet.

They fought for a while. Everyone watched them nervously until Melissa could wrap her arm around his neck, toss him, and put him in a chokehold, but Leon quickly flipped her instead and put her in a chokehold.

Melissa's face turned violet red, her hand slumped down, and her eyes rolled back.

"Let her go!" Chad pushed Leon off and shook Melissa, "Mel! Mel! Wake up!" Emmy and the elves rushed to Melissa.

"Slap her," Alisha said. "It should do the trick."

"I don't wanna slap my girlfriend!" Chad blurted, and Alisha rolled her eyes and slapped the living life out of Melissa, who woke up gasping for air.

"What happened?!" she asked.

"You passed out," Leon commented, "but you did a decent job, rider."

"You too-" she had dry blood on her chin. Chad attempted to cup her face, but Melissa unintentionally shouted, "Don't touch it!" Melissa winced. "Sorry! It just hurts. I've had popped lips before, but never this bad."

"Mel- it's pretty bad." Her lower lip was still bleeding and became swollen. Ezra crouched and looked at it before speaking.

"Melissa, it will heal. Chad, I am glad you found something you are great at," Ezra complimented, and Melissa could see Chad's ego inflating, but she didn't mind it at all.

Leon continued to train Emmy on how to throw punches, simple judo techniques, and how to block, while Alisha did the same for Chad. Melissa simply drank unicorn saliva while lying beside Jake, whose head rested on her shoulder.

She had ice wrapped in a cloth and placed it on her lips.

"I don't think he likes me," Melissa admitted.

"Leon is simply a serious elf," he commented.

"Too serious…" Melissa watched Emmy laughing around Leon. "I also don't like the way Emmy giggles around him."

"What do you mean?"

"'Cause I know she thinks he is super cute. Just look at the way she laughs and blushes. She does it with my sister's boyfriend all the time."

"It reminds me of Alisha. She acts strange with Ezra sometimes," Jake said, and Melissa giggled at the comment.

For Wednesday night, they all gathered and ate seasoned grilled chicken again. This time, the centaurs joined them as well. They chatted and recounted tales of Henry and his many battles until stranded on Cuba.

Listening to her adventures made her eyes watery. She then said, "Pipo told me about a beast called 'madre de aguas.'"

"Yes," Ezra chuckled. "He told us about that as well, a giant boa with two extrusions on its head, similar to the horns of a dragon."

"Yeah," Melissa smirked. "He said that they live long lives, and if anyone tries to capture or kill it, they'll die."

"It is true, however," Ezra raised his brow. "It belongs to Gemma and he could have easily caught it and taken it back to its rightful home with no dire consequences. We asked him to go back to Cuba and retrieve it, but he did not because your grandfather is deathly afraid of serpents." There was a long silence before Melissa giggled along with Ezra.

"How is he afraid of snakes?" Emmy inquired. "I mean, he rode a giant dragon!" Ezra shrugged his shoulders.

Melissa watched the elf with amusement since he was finally not as tense as he usually was. It painted a smile on her face.

"What about 'El Coco?'" Melissa asked, and the elves each arched a brow and glanced at each other. Alisha shrugged her shoulders at Ezra, and he responded.

"Pardon me?"

"'El Coco' was like this monster a lot of Cubans tell their kids to scare them." Melissa glanced at Emmy, and Emmy elaborated.

"Apparently, they like to eat children."

"So, like the boogeyman?" Chad asked, and the girls nodded.

"We do not know of such a beast," Alisha said. "It could be a shape-shifting monster, as it is common for them to consume human flesh. Perhaps humans witnessed it many ages ago and gave it such a unique name."

"Well," Melissa scratched the top of her head. "I can believe that. Think about it, 'Boogeyman,' and 'El Coco?' It's the same concept, really. Just different cultures refer to it as something different."

"Impressive," Ezra complimented, and Melissa couldn't help but feel a surge of pride. His acknowledgment was a validation of her wittiness. As she glanced at Chad, his amused expression confirmed that her wit had indeed struck a chord.

"See, Chad?" Melissa said with a teasing smile. "I impressed the great Ezra with my insights."

Chad chuckled and shook his head. "I must admit, Mel, you have a knack for making connections others might miss."

He cradled her hand and kissed it, a reminder that he was there for her, to which Melissa responded by kissing his cheek gently, considering her lip still ached.

And for once, she did not hear Emmy groan or fuss. Instead, she was still giggling and blushing near Leon, who paid no mind to her.

I can get used to this. Melissa flickered her eyes at Jake, who was lying next to her. She grew her trademark smile, and he did, too. *I love this world already.*

Chapter Thirty

Melissa's stomach churned, causing her to awaken from her slumber. A mixture of nerves and anticipation flooded her mind as she realized that tomorrow was the day she would head off to war.

Melissa groaned and placed a trembling hand on her stomach, seeking to soothe the churning sensation within. The weight of the impending war left her physically and mentally anxious.

Unable to control the twists and turns of her stomach, she sprang out of her sleeping bag and ran outside, desperate to escape her thoughts. The chilly air caressed her face as she staggered a few steps away before gagging.

"Are you alright?" Jake's voice startled her.

"Yeah!" she responded. She fought hard to regain her composure. "I think I'm just nervous about tomorrow."

Jake nudged her with his snout, reminding her of their countless hours spent together, practicing their skills as a team. "You will do great tomorrow. You are a natural-born rider and warrior. You are ready."

"I hope you're right." She sat next to Jake. The vibrant hues of periwinkle and orange spread on the horizon. Being in her dragon's presence brought her peace. She wished he was there when she needed it the most.

As if reading her thoughts, he said, "I am here now."

Leon and Ezra came riding on Iris and Nubis, with Nedjem behind them without a rider.

"War nerves?" Ezra remarked, and Melissa glared at him. "It will pass," he promised her, but Melissa did not count on it. Chad and Emmy stepped out, groaning at the sight of the sun rising.

"You guys are vampires, ya know?" Melissa said, rolling her eyes.

"Vampires? Why would you compare yourself with such vile beings?" Leon's comment about vampires earned a wry grin from Melissa.

"Well, I'm not sure how vampires are in real life, but on Earth, they hate the sun."

"It is the same here," Ezra added.

"I bet," Chad said. "Wait, will they be at war tomorrow?"

"No, there are certain monsters and beings that do not pay mind to the feud between the Dark Forest and Amethyst. Vampires are amongst them, as well as Wendigos." Leon continued. "There will be goblins, ogres, and minotaurs. Hopefully, no Wyverns."

"What about the Cockatrice?" Melissa asked. "It's Victor Sigil, right?"

"They are extinct," Ezra responded. "It is a good thing they are."

"Not really," Melissa remarked, and the elves arched a brow at her. "C'mon, it's still a species, ya know. Just because they used to be bad doesn't mean they should be permanently gone." Melissa's words seemed to have resonated with Ezra, for he tilted his head and contemplated her words.

"Wyvern?" Emmy interjected, staring at Melissa. "I don't think I've ever heard you talk about that animal." Leon preceded by explaining.

"They are close relatives to dragons, but they only have two legs, no arms, and a reptilian body. They are uncommon here in Amethyst. The Dark Forest of Garnet captures them from Ruby Jungle and trains them." Emmy stared at the young elf, wearing a radiant smile with his answer.

"Let's warm up!" Ezra announced.

Melissa hit the bullseye twice during archery. Even Chad was hitting the target board, to which Iris high-fived him out of enthusiasm. But Emmy was incredibly proficient as an archer, and all the elves were pleased to see her perform so well.

Before the centaurs departed, Iris strolled her way to Melissa and encouraged her. "Dragon rider, I wish you luck for tomorrow. We will do our best like we always have."

"Thanks, Iris. Thank you for training us. We appreciate it."

"Serving dragon riders has always been an honor, especially you."

Melissa beamed; it pleased her that Iris gave her a genuine compliment, and she watched them gallop away.

Melissa and Ezra walked towards their isolated area to train. She gripped her sword tightly, took a deep breath, and blocked out any unnecessary noises.

They circled each other with a flurry of quick moves, their swords clutched in their hands. She calculated every move and motion as they prepared for the conflict. They lunged at one other without hesitation, their swords striking in a cloud of sparks and steel.

Melissa's reflexes kicked in as Ezra swung his blade in a cutting motion. She launched herself into the air with split-second timing, completing an elegant flip that allowed her to avoid a fatal slash. It was a move she had practiced many times, and it had finally paid off.

This pattern continued in their combat, with Ezra trying to deliver a strike only to be dodged by Melissa's acrobatic movements. The repetition of their moves formed a captivating dance packed with tension and excitement.

All the training Melissa poured into was clear, with each bead of sweat that dripped down her forehead and nose. Despite the physical exertion, she remained focused, her mind racing to predict Ezra's next move. Every flip and clash brought her closer to defeating the elf.

That's when Ezra took advantage of her and taunted her. "You are worse than your grandfather. Jake should have hatched for your sister." She gasped, her mouth hanging just a tad. "You are a disappointment to everyone." Melissa felt the urge to attack Ezra, but just as she flinched, she paused.

Breathe in and out. Melissa watched the elf scan her body language. *They are words that mean nothing.* She imagined Pipo speaking to her the way he did when she trained in MMA. They are just words, mija, breath in and out.

Ezra charged at her with incredible speed and slashed his sword, but she avoided his massive blows and countered him, knocking down his shield. He moved away to stab Melissa, but she ducked, and with her foot, she knocked him to the ground.

She kicked the sword out of his hand and pointed her sword to his neck. "You were saying?" She winked, and his eyes studied her determined expression. He finally grinned, and his chin elevated, showing her just how proud he was.

Without Melissa realizing, everyone had gathered in a small crowd and watched her train with Ezra. She heard a faint, slow clap that built into applause, rising from her friends and trainers. Her best friend and boyfriend were cheering her on, and she glanced at Jake, who watched her with his chest puffed and head elevated.

"Very well done," Ezra said, and Melissa helped him stand up. "You are officially ready for war." Those words stirred fear in Melissa. The word war was echoing in her mind. She had always felt destined for more but never thought she'd actually be fighting in a magical war to protect her legacy and kingdom.

All she ever wanted, for the longest, was to fill the void that haunted her since her disappearance. She'd fill it with stories of magic and lore. Her love for dragons and fantasy helped her escape. Now, not only was she still feeling empty even after learning it was all real, but she found herself unable to escape the chaos that came with it all: war, blood, and violence.

She gulped and nodded at him. "Go take a flight with Jake, and this time, enjoy yourself and relax."

Melissa responded by embracing Ezra with a genuine hug - a rare act for Melissa, but something about Ezra's words made her emotional. "Thank you for training me and for everything you've done for my friends and me," she said to him.

Ezra stood there awkwardly, clearly unaccustomed to receiving loving gestures, as Melissa continued to hug him. She expressed her gratitude, saying, "You and Alisha are the best mentors."

With a rare smile, Ezra responded to Melissa, "You are most welcome, dragon rider."

"Ezra, please call me Melissa, it's okay."

"Okay, Melissa." She relinquished her hold, and Melissa sprinted her way onto Jake, hopped on his back with such ease, and he charged forward before taking off into the sky.

She let the wind dance through her hair, and her arms were wide open, taking in the thrill she loved so much. Jake took her to inspect the castle. The castle had a gothic-like architecture with only one tower standing tall.

Melissa noticed a purplish flag with four different-colored dragons circling it. There was a ruby dragon, an aquamarine dragon, an electric yellow dragon, and an ivory dragon.

Other elves were walking around and pointed up in the sky when they saw Jake. "They will be so happy to meet you," Jake told her.

"That flag! Are those the four original dragons?"

"Yes!" he flew over and hovered near the flag.

She noticed each dragon had a tiny human riding on it. The electric yellow dragon was the only dragon with a female rider. "Micah rode the yellow one, right?"

"Yes-" Jake flew off back towards Alisha's cabin. "Funny enough, she was the only dragon out of the four that was female as well. Her name was Brigid."

At dusk, Melissa, Chad, and Emmy washed up and repeated the same nighttime routine. Ezra and Alisha were sitting down, side by side together, laughing with a snuggled up Magic in her arms, and Leon sat a few feet away, pondering deeply, it seemed.

Ugh, I wish Cupid was here so he could tell them how adorably cute they are together. Chad nudged her, and Melissa glanced at him with her classic smirk.

They both kissed, and Emmy scoffed, "Go for a walk. I don't think anyone likes PDA here."

"Are you saying that so you can be alone with Le-"

"Bye!" Emmy glared at her, and Melissa laughed evilly.

Before they walked away, Emmy left to flirt with Leon, but it was short-lived since Ezra announced, "Before you guys go, there are some things we have to discuss." They all groaned. "Relax. It is something minor. Although it has only been four days of training, I am impressed by how you all have been doing. I know you probably have a lot on your mind, like your family." Guilt washed over Melissa since she hadn't been thinking of her family. "They are safe. We keep track of them," Ezra reassured them. "But do not fret over that. What we need to do is focus on taking the Diamond of Dragons back and defeating whoever is behind this. I thought we had finished the Lazarus bloodline. I guess we missed something." He looked at Alisha sorrowfully. "Hopefully, this time, we eliminate the Lazarus bloodline." Melissa's head bounced back at the word eliminate, and she asked.

"Eliminate? You mean like kill?"

"Yes," Ezra responded.

"Couldn't we take him as a prisoner?"

"Mh, I suggest against it," he responded.

"No, we take him as a prisoner," Melissa stated, and Ezra gave a stiff nod. "I wonder if Wesley will be there," Melissa murmured.

"No," Alisha added. "It will not be Wesley. Wesley never comes out for battle. He is strategic and a clever individual, and Victor will not risk his life. Now, it could be an apprentice."

"She is right," Ezra agreed with Alisha. "And whoever the apprentice is must have been going in and out of Earth from the Dark Forest of Garnet. The only two known entrances to Earth they possibly know of are Florida's and the Bermuda Triangle. We would have known who is sneaking out."

"That narrows it down. How about Nina?" Emmy considered.

"Never!" Melissa responded, appalled Emmy would ever think that.

"Rudy?" Emmy suggested. "I know he's family, but you have to think of the possibilities."

"How about your parents, Emmy?" Melissa proposed.

"Um, no," Emmy said defensively. "Why would you even think that?"

"Ah, don't like the feeling, huh?" Melissa quipped back.

"Okay, settle down. Tomorrow, we shall see our options. These are just suggestions. It might just be Victor who will be in the lighthouse." Ezra ended the topic. "I thought Henry finished Victor once and for all shortly before the birth of your sister, Melissa. They had one last confrontation where Victor vowed to make Henry's life a living Hell. I guess-" It was obvious Ezra was holding back vital information. He stopped talking midway through and shook his head as if disagreeing with himself. "I guess we missed something."

"Think we should look into it?" Melissa asked.

"Well… another story for another day. Go for your walk with Chad." He broke off.

"Would you like me to accompany you?" Jake asked.

"Awe, don't worry, Jake. We got it." He gave her a small nod, although he seemed reluctant to stay behind.

The couple walked away from the fire and towards the sapphire ocean. They ran and danced around the shallow part of the water. He swirled her around and pulled her in, kissing her lips.

Melissa's cheeks burned red, and she said, "Chad, once we get back home, you know things will never be the same between us?" Her expression turned gloomy.

"Yeah, I know," Chad paused. "But I'd rather enjoy this moment now, even though tomorrow we're literally going to war."

"You're always trying to focus on me. I'm sorry for not doing the same." Chad smiled and kissed her forehead.

"You're a dragon rider and princess now. Trust me, I get it." Their lips pressed on each other.

The sound of screeching cackles echoed from the dense forest behind them, and the couple whirled around. Melissa's heart pounded against her chest. Her voice trembled as she asked, "Chad, what was that?"

Chad glanced around, his expression mirroring Melissa's confusion. "I don't know," he admitted, his shoulders shrugging. "But we need to get back the elves."

Just as they were about to flee back to camp, a greenish, scrawny figure emerged from the shadows. The figure's Dumbo-like ears and pointy nose startled them, and they froze, paralyzed by their grim features. Soon, three more figures emerged behind what appeared to be the leader.

"Well," he shrilled. "The master wanted us to collect you if there ever came a moment you were alone." He held a sharp dagger.

"What the hell are you?" Melissa asked.

"Tsk, tsk, tsk," the foremost goblin sneered, his voice dripping with malice. "Not very polite, are ya? Goblins don't like rude little girls."

"What? No, leave him alone!" Melissa shouted at them.

"We don't want you, little girl. We want the rider!"

"No! He's not the rider-" Melissa argued, but Chad interrupted her.

"I'll go," Melissa stumbled on her words, but Chad continued. "I'm the rider. It's me they want, Mel." With his eyes, he gestured to her to go back to the cabin.

Melissa shook her head and was ready to protest, but the foremost goblin snatched Chad by the arm, and the other goblin held Melissa back. The goblin held a curvy dagger to Chad's throat. "Do not call on your dragon," the goblin warned him. "Or I will slit your throat in front of her."

"You can't kill me," Chad taunted them. "You need the rider alive." One goblin gave him a disgusted look and kicked him in the ribs. "Fine, I'll kill her in front of you instead."

"No!" Chad yelped. "Leave her and take me." The goblin chortled and kicked Chad again in the ribs. Chad groaned, and Melissa judo tossed the goblin, holding her back and surprising all the goblins.

"Back off," the foremost goblin warned Melissa with a growl and pressed the dagger on Chad's throat. "Do not follow us, and do not call on his dragon, or he's dead." Melissa looked at Chad desperately, but he gave her a slight nod, and she knew she had to comply.

The goblin dragged Chad away, and the other two goblins stayed behind. They glared at Melissa and drifted towards her. "You just said you'd let me go," she whimpered.

"Not after that little stunt," he mocked, and they both cackled. Just as they were about to pounce on Melissa, she swung a kick at the one on the right, knocking him to the ground, and the other goblin stared at her, puzzled. "What, didn't think I could fight?" She delivered a punch to the other goblin, breaking his nose, and he dropped unconscious to the dirt.

Melissa sprinted through the dense forest, her heart pounding in her ears with each step. She strained her eyes, desperately scanning the underbrush for any sign of Chad, but he seemed to have vanished without a trace.

Melissa's mind waged a fierce battle within as she grappled with the decision. *I have to look for him*, she contemplated, feeling the urgency rise within her. But a voice of reason pleaded, *no, Melissa, go back to camp!*

Her heart pounded against her chest, and with every desperate gasp for air, she felt her lungs tightening. Her thoughts became clouded with fear and uncertainty. The unimaginable had become a reality—Chad was in dire danger.

Melissa swallowed back her tears, clenching her fists to steady herself. She forced her trembling legs to move, propelling herself forward towards Alisha's cabin. She held her tears at bay, but they threatened to spill.

The elves and Emmy were laughing and chatting with one another until they saw the frantic look on Melissa's face. "They took Chad!" she cried.

"Who did?" Ezra stood up, ready to fight, with Leon and Alisha following.

"Goblins, there were too many! They took him!!" Melissa wailed.

"Ezra!" Alisha exclaimed. "We have to save him. If Victor finds out he is not the true rider, he will kill him."

"He will not kill him. I assure you of that. He needs the Dagger of Riders, which you have," Ezra reassured them, but Melissa spoke out.

"So now what? We don't even know if he's in the lighthouse!"

"I must go tomorrow and retrieve him," Ezra stated, but Melissa shook her head and responded.

"No! I will go." Ezra attempted to speak, but Melissa stopped him and continued. "I am the true dragon rider. It's time for Amethyst to know that, and you're not stopping me." Her mind wandered to Chad and how she selfishly allowed him and Emmy to take part in Gemma.

Melissa slowly crumpled to the ground and cried, and Emmy rushed to her friend.

Jake snarled, hearing the mention of goblins, walked his way towards Melissa, and snuggled her with his face. "I am sorry. We will save him," he promised her.

"No! We need to do something now," she pleaded.

"No." Ezra said firmly. "I understand your emotions are clouding your judgment, but we have the element of surprise with Victor, okay? He does not know you are the rider." He searched for words to calm her. Still, Melissa continued sobbing. "You will confront him tomorrow. We will take Chad and the Diamond of Dragons back."

"I will get him back," Melissa vowed firmly, and Ezra smiled, impressed, and spoke.

"Jake, fly to the castle, alert the elves, dwarves, and centaurs that we need them here by sunrise. You girls need to get some rest."

"We can't sleep with Chad gone!" Melissa barked. "We have to find him now. If whoever has him captive figures out he's not the rider, they'll kill him!" Melissa continued sobbing, and the elves looked nervously at one another.

"Okay," Alisha finally spoke. "Melissa, we will find him, but we need you to sleep. Chad needs you at your best tomorrow, both of you." Emmy was never much of a crier, but her eyes were teary, and she was clearly distraught.

Melissa faced the reality of her innermost fears—losing someone she loved. The thought of losing him was unbearable; Chad was the love of Melissa's life, a fact even the ancient fairy of love affirmed. The impact he'd made in not just her life, but Emmy's, was too significant.

Ezra rode off while Alisha, and Emmy helped Melissa walk inside the cabin. Magic snuggled next to Melissa to comfort her, and Alisha could not find the words to say to them and only encouraged them to go to sleep. She made a natural tea that soothed them both.

I have to do something now; I need to see him. Make sure he's okay. Maybe I'll sneak out? Ugh, but Jake won't do that for me. It'll put me at risk. Oh, Chad, I should have never let you in on this. You were my dream. Melissa gasped in realization. "Alisha! Your moonstone! Can I use it to find Chad?"

"Melissa..." Alisha shook her head and sighed. "Using the moonstone takes years of practice. It is no simple task, and right now, you are emotional. It can have dangerous consequences. And realities can become entangled in your dreams."

"Please!" Melissa begged. "I need to make sure he is okay."

"Allow me to do it for you, rider," Alisha said.

"No, I want to see him. Please let me do it. I'll contain my emotions," Melissa pleaded, and her eyes watered as she did.

"I am sorry, Melissa, but we do not know how dangerous Victor is at the moment, and he may take advantage of you in the dream state. I will try to locate him for you," Alisha stated firmly, and Melissa inhaled a breath to calm the fury rising in her.

Alisha then prepared the sleeping bags and some more chamomile tea for the girls. Melissa lay in the sleeping bag, her eyes staring at the ceiling.

"Go to sleep," Emmy whispered.

"Emmy, I can't right now."

"Try."

"I need to see Chad," Melissa persisted. "I need to make sure he's okay."

Emmy sighed. "I know. I want to know if he's safe, too."

"Then, help me get that moonstone," Melissa said, and Emmy jerked up.

"Did you not hear Alisha?" Emmy scolded her. "You don't know how to maneuver in the dream state. What if it goes wrong?"

"Please, Emmy, I need to know." Melissa flashed her eyelashes and pouted. "Please."

Emmy groaned silently but nodded. The girls rolled out of their sleeping bags and tip-toed to Alisha. She had the moonstone tucked under her nightgown. Melissa's hand trembled uncontrollably, and she gestured with her eyes for Emmy to grab it.

Emmy took one deep breath and reached her almost-still hand for the moonstone. "I need scissors to cut the cord," Emmy said, and Melissa looked around for something sharp.

"My dagger!" Melissa gasped and snatched the dagger up, handing it to Emmy. Emmy cut the cord, and it separated instantly.

Carefully, Emmy pulled the moonstone out and sighed in relief. The girls tip-toed back to their sleeping bags, and Melissa snatched the moonstone out of Emmy's hand.

"Be careful, Melissa," Emmy scolded her, and Melissa gulped.

"Okay, I guess I'll figure it out in the dream state. Wish me luck."

Emmy gave one stiff nod, and Melissa shut her eyes and forced herself to sleep.

Chapter Thirty-One

Melissa was standing, wearing her treasured combat boots, a pair of blue jeans, and a black tee.

"Weird, but okay," she muttered. She looked around and stood in an empty, white space. The only noise audible was the sound of her pulse hammering in her ears. There were no walls or ceilings.

Melissa wasn't even sure if there was a floor, but she simply stood as if time and space did not exist, just an endless space of blankness. Her moonstone shimmered, and she tucked it away under her black tee.

She took one deep breath and shifted her mind to Chad. She focused on the things that connected her with him, but she found her mind racing with too many things at once.

She shut her eyes tightly and concentrated. When she peeped them open, she was sitting at her kitchen dining table. The rays from the sun peered through the window glass. There was a stack of fliers with a picture of Melissa, Emmy, and Chad together that read "Missing." Melissa's heart fell to the pit of her stomach.

The sounds of someone sniffing turned her head, and by the stove was her mother preparing a mug of cafe con leche.

"Mami?" Melissa called her.

"Melissa?" Her mother whirled around. The white in her eyes was red and puffy. "Are you okay?" She had enormous dark circles around her eyes.

"Melissa, I miss you." She hiccupped. "Are you really here?" Melissa wanted to explain yes and tell her mother everything, but she bit her tongue and pressed her lips together.

"It's a dream... but I miss you too." Melissa held her hand. "I'll be home soon." They both gazed into each other's eyes, and Melissa half-smiled weakly.

"I miss that smile," her mother said, placing her hand under her chin. "It reminds me of Pipo every time."

Melissa sullenly looked down, droplets of tears falling, and her mother said, "I wish you would talk to me. Tell me why you're so sad and cooped up in your room."

"Mami," Melissa sighed, knowing she was in the dream. She let out what her heart had been holding in. "I wish you didn't have to struggle. I wish you were home more, but it's selfish of me to ask for that. I miss -" She couldn't even finish her words, and her mother cupped her cheek.

"I miss you too," she told her, and Melissa wept, her mind spiraling into a darkness of the grief that had held her captive for so long.

As Melissa stood on what felt like a swaying floor, the sterile whiteness around her transformed into a serene landscape. The ground beneath her feet shifted from an empty expanse to soil and lush green grass. A plethora of evergreen trees emerged, encircling her in their towering presence. Above her, a breathtaking sky painted in shades of amethyst stretched out.

A tingling sense of recognition prickled at Melissa's skin, and a wave of realization washed over her. She was standing at the edge of the Dark Forest of Garnet. The murky darkness that lay ahead held an eerie familiarity, stirring fear.

Crap, Messa gulped, *I hate this place.*

She took small steps and felt a tap on her shoulder. Impulsively, she whirled around and held her fists up. But standing in front of her was Jacob, who stared at her, confused.

"Melissa?" he asked.

"Oh Jacob, wait, why are-" she stopped and thought, *Ugh. Alisha said it can tangle reality in dreams. I'll just go with it.* "Pretty cool place, right?"

"Um, yeah," Jacob stumbled on his words. "Melissa..." he sighed and said, "I am so sorry."

"For what?" she asked, but Jacob looked down, shuffling his feet. "Oh Jacob, you don't have to apologize." Melissa wrapped her arms around him "Even though Victoria hasn't always been the best sister... I've been able to find a sibling through you. You always did your best, and that's all I ever needed someone to do for me."

When she let go, she noticed his watery eyes, and Melissa bit her lip, holding back her own tears. She went in for another hug but fell forward. It was all dark, and Melissa felt the unnerving sensation of someone watching her.

Fear took over Melissa, and she attempted to run, but everywhere she ran, she collided into an invisible wall. Melissa hyperventilated. "These aren't dreams... this is a nightmare."

A shadowy figure loomed over Melissa, and she looked up. There was no one physically there, but she could feel a presence. His voice bellowed over her. "You slaughtered my wife, my child. You took everything I love because I share the name of Lazarus. You tyrant, you act as if you are a noble king. But you are worse than my ancestor. I will destroy your legacy first and take away what makes your blood special: the dragons. Then, I will destroy all that matters to you so you can share the same suffering as I have. You do not know it yet, but I have already inflicted suffering upon you."

Melissa attempted to escape, but she crashed into an invisible force and flew back.

"You silly girl. Escaping here is futile, for I am a lucid dreamer, and only I can control dreams. No one but Henricus Werra can defeat me, and he is gone."

The word 'gone' echoed, and Melissa wept, "No, no." She held her head and slumped on her knees. Her world was crashing down on her at that moment, and she felt utterly helpless.

But a warm sensation made Melissa stop weeping, and she looked up; a fiery rain fell upon the dark figure, melting it away into the abyss.

"Jake!" Melissa exclaimed, but it wasn't her red dragon. It was a hunter-green dragon, and on its back was her abuelo, who hadn't aged at all. The darkness once encompassing her was gone, and she was back in the middle of the iconic sunflower field.

Pipo's dragon had gentle topaz eyes; it had a slim neck that flowed down from its head and into a massive torso. Spherical scales covered the top, while it lined the spine with armor plates. This dragon had a feathery body, unlike Jake, who had reptile-like scales. The coarse skin on its underside was slightly lighter than the rest of its body.

The wings were almost angelic in appearance, with thick skin and strange bone formations covering most of the wing and little, pointy ends protruding like enormous spears from either end.

Melissa felt the air escape her lungs as she muttered one word. "Pipo?" Her hand reached out, but then she tucked it back in and said, "It's a dream… you're not real."

Melissa collapsed to the ground and wailed, her hands covering her face as she did.

Pipo slid down the dragon's back with ease and approached Melissa. His familiar voice spoke, "¿Por qué tú lloras?"

"Nada," nothing, Melissa responded. Pipo reached his hand out, and Melissa held it. She knew it was a dream, but she felt it was so real. She admired his grizzly-black hair and the chainmail armor he had on; it made her smirk.

"Mi niña, look how beautiful you are. You really do look like our ancestor Micah, mhh. I am proud of you, Melissa." Melissa bit her lip and did her best to contain the tears, "Don't cry any more mi niña ."

"I'm not crying," her voice squeaked, and Melissa choked back a sob. "I really miss you."

"I miss you too," he sighed and gestured to her to come and sit on his lap. She did so and immediately inhaled a whiff of the fresh scent of cigars on him that she missed so much. She laid her head on his chest, and as the tears streamed down her cheeks, she felt eternally grateful for this blissful moment with him.

But then she fell on her buttocks, and when she looked up, Pipo was back on his dragon. "It's time for your adventure." he told her.

"No!" Melissa cried out. "Please come back," she sobbed. "Don't leave me, Pipo, don't leave me again!" She covered her blotched face with her hands and released a cry.

A hand tapped her shoulder, and Melissa yelped; she spun and saw Chad. They both stared at each other, shocked that either was there. They both flung their arms around each other for a tight hug, and Melissa smooched him.

"I saw that green dragon drop you off! Are you okay?" he asked, his hands cupping her face.

"No," she admitted, gripping his hands. "I kinda stole the moonstone and visited a bunch of dreams to get to you. But that's not important right now, are you okay? Where are you?"

"Mel, the goblins, they took me to the lighthouse and roughed me up a bit. They sent a raven out for Victor, and they said his apprentice would come tomorrow morning to torture me."

"Torture? Apprentice? Could it be Wesley?"

"No, Mel... You won't believe who they said it was," he muttered in disbelief.

"Who!?"

"It's-" Chad's body dissolved in a mist, and Melissa cried out.

"NO! NO! CHAD!" She slumped to the floor and sobbed. "Chad," she hiccupped. "I'm so sorry, I'm so, so, sorry, I failed you."

It was at that moment Melissa felt the empty void surge over her like a wave. Her mind raced with all the things that reminded her of her sorrow: her mother's struggle, her sister's cruel jokes, and finally, how much she missed her abuelo and how she yearned for him to be here to advise her and provide the fatherly comfort Melissa so badly craved.

"WAKE UP!" Melissa's vocal cords shook.

*   *   *

Melissa abruptly sat up shouting, tears streaming down her face, and the image of her abuelo imprinted in her brain.

"Melissa!" Alisha was right in front of her. "You foolish girl." She snatched the moonstone from her neck.

"Melissa? What happened?" Emmy asked, and Melissa found herself unable to breathe.

"Breathe, Melissa," Alisha said. "She is not breathing! Jake!"

Jake popped his head in through the window, "What has happened?"

"I think she's having a panic attack," Emmy explained. "Can you help her?"

"Melissa," Jake spoke. He stretched his neck to her face, his snout touching her nose. "It is alright. I am here. You are here. Take deep breaths in and out."

Somehow, Melissa could hear the slow rhythmic beat of Jake's heart, and she willed herself to match his. After a few minutes, she could inhale a full breath.

"What did you do?" Emmy asked.

"Their souls connect," Alisha explained. "They can calm one another when needed."

"That's amazing!" Emmy watched them and asked, "Melissa, what happened?"

It took a moment for Melissa to gather her thoughts. Her eyes stared at the floor blankly, and she kept imagining her abuelo hopping on his dragon and flying away.

"I saw so much." Melissa described the dreams to everyone. The part of her abuelo was difficult for her to recount. When she finished, Alisha spoke.

"It was foolish of you to take the moonstone." Jake growled at Alisha for the comment, but she continued speaking, unfazed by it. "I could not pull you in the middle of your dreams, even though it was clearly affecting you."

"Well, at least we know where Chad is," Melissa muttered, and Alisha agreed.

"Yes, we must use that as our advantage," the elf added.

"Ugh, you guys and your advantages! It's all you know how to do is take advantage," Melissa mumbled and then regretted it when she saw the way Emmy stared at her with her eyes widened and her jaw slightly ajar. "I'm sorry."

"I understand you are emotional right now; however, you must control your emotions and think logically," Alisha stated.

"She is right," Emmy interfered. "We need to take advantage of what we know and what they don't. Tomorrow, all of us can focus on land, and you can fly to the lighthouse."

Melissa winced at the idea of leaving Emmy in battle alone, so she spoke. "But what about you guys? Jake and I need to join the battle as well."

"Yes, but," Emmy shifted her view to Alisha, "Melissa needs to get Chad. If they find out he is not the rider, they'll kill him. Jake can drop you off by the lighthouse and fly off and join us without you. That way, whoever has Chad captive won't expect you to come. Remember, they don't know you're the true rider. And whoever the apprentice is won't see it coming."

"I agree," Alisha said, and Melissa nodded.

"Go to sleep, Melissa," Jake told her. "You need the rest."

"No, no, I can't sleep," Melissa was breathing rapidly again, and when Emmy stretched her hand to soothe her, she slapped her hand away. Her mind spiraled into a web of darkness. "Don't touch me! Stop looking at me!" Melissa barked and placed both hands on her head.

"Melissa, you need to calm down-" Emmy said, but Melissa shouted.

"No! No! I can't lose anyone. I can't lose him. I can't lose him... not again," Melissa sobbed.

"Melissa-" Emmy's voice cracked, and she cleared her throat. "Please, calm down." But her words were no use.

They let her sob; her hands covered her red, blotchy face, and everyone in the room remained quiet. The sounds of her cries filled the small cabin.

After a while, Emmy grabbed her by the arm and said, "C'mon." Melissa reluctantly stood up, still whimpering with tears.

"Let her sleep in my bed tonight," Alisha suggested.

The ladies laid her down, and Alisha placed the blanket over her. Jake nudged her softly with his snout, and Melissa felt numb to the grief that followed her for years now.

She noticed the way Jake's eyes watered as he whispered, "I wish I could take all your sorrow away, Melissa. Be strong, my rider. You have the dragon's strength in you."

Melissa nodded stiffly, hot tears still rolling down her cheeks, but she closed her eyes, hummed the lullaby her abuelo sang to her as a child, and slept.

Chapter Thirty-Two

Melissa could not recall at what moment she went to sleep, but when she awoke, her head thudded from all the tears that were shed. Her cheeks were puffy, her red eyes could not open fully, and her throat felt parched.

Alisha was up and had placed Melissa's and Emmy's shields on the dinner table. It was polished, and it glimmered in the sunlight, blinding Melissa.

She shut her eyes but then forced them open, grabbed the shield and the sword, and then shook Emmy lightly.

"Huh? What?" Emmy rubbed her eyes and looked at Melissa's face, which wore many emotions ranging from rage distress, and a hint of determination.

"Get dressed, it's time." Emmy shuttered at the sound of those words flowing from Melissa's lips. Beside the bed was a canteen of unicorn saliva and fruits for the girls to eat.

Melissa barely touched the fruits, unlike Emmy, who devoured them.

"What?" Emmy gestured. "If I'm gonna die, it would be with a full belly." Melissa rolled her eyes, but upon seeing Emmy's unfazed look, she cracked a smirk.

They donned their chainmail armor with metal plates on their shoulders, placed their swords in their sheaths, and, instead of tucking away the Dagger of the Riders under her thigh strap which Fabre created, Melissa hid the dagger from the Dark Forest. The polished armor fitted their bodies easily, contouring to their individual figures.

She finished by picking her hair up in a tight bun, which Emmy complimented. "I know, given the circumstances, this is not the right time, ya know, with war and all… But you look really hot with your hair up."

"Pfft, thanks." Melissa shrugged her shoulders.

They walked outside and were stunned to stare at an enormous army.

Hundreds of centaurs, humans, elves, and dwarves covered the field. They gathered the elves who were murmuring amongst themselves; the dwarves were talking more loudly, and Melissa heard the way they boasted about their weapons. The centaurs simply gazed at Melissa, waiting for her to say something.

Each race was significantly different, but it amazed Melissa how they all united for one purpose. The dwarves wore lamella, aegis, and cuirass; the centaurs wore half-plate and leather saddles with metal helmets, and the elves all wore either chainmail or lamellar armor.

"Whoa," Melissa commented. "This is really happening."

Ezra wore chainmail as well and had his bow and arrow at the ready. "There are ogres and goblins surrounding the lighthouse. The fairies and pixies will join later in battle as a surprise attack. There will be elves riding on griffins to fight from above."

Melissa glanced at the tall, eloquent, white body and pyramid black-tip lighthouse north of the ocean side. "I received confirmation from the mermaids that Chad is up there," Ezra added.

"I knew already," Melissa responded dryly.

"How did you know?" Ezra asked, and Melissa briefly told him about last night's dream journey. She instantly knew it displeased Ezra that Melissa had entered the dream state.

"The mermaids witnessed the goblins taking him there last night. Are you ready to face whoever the apprentice is?" Ezra asked. His eyes studied Melissa's expressions.

"Yes," Melissa stated, her lips twitching. "I'm getting Chad back."

"Everyone here wants to hear you speak. Jake has not retrieved Chad, and they are confused." Ezra grinned at her. "It is time they know you are the rider and princess."

"What if they don't accept me?" Melissa gulped.

"Give them a reason to."

"But... what do I say?" Melissa took another big gulp, but Ezra shrugged his shoulders, ignoring Melissa's gaze, and pretended not to know. Melissa rolled her eyes and groaned.

Jake glided in, covered in a set of armor tailored by Emmy and the dwarves for his scaly body. The metal plating covered his belly and throat, shielding his most vulnerable areas. His head had a protective helmet which gleamed, and a sturdy saddle provided both comfort and security for Melissa.

She walked towards him and stared at him in his piercing black eyes.

"We will do well," Jake assured her.

"Ya think so?"

"I know so." Voices and murmurs about why Melissa was approaching Jake flooded her with anxiety.

Before she hopped on his back, she walked towards the crowd that was staring at her. She glanced at Jake, who nudged her to speak, and she felt a lump in her throat.

She always dreaded the spotlight, but here she was, standing in front of a crowd of magical beasts and beings. The ones she'd dreamed of. The ones her abuelo told stories of.

Now, she was here, facing them as their protector and ruler. She inhaled deeply and spoke.

"Hi, everyone," she waved awkwardly, and everyone observed her. "I'm Melissa Paz-Guerra, the granddaughter of Henricus Werra. I am your dragon rider and princess…" The crowd rippled in murmurs, and Melissa, a cold sweat trickled down her back.

She hesitated to speak again and glanced at Emmy, who gestured to her with her hand to continue. "Most of you believed Chad was a relative of Henricus. They did this to protect me and a lifelong prophecy… but also to protect the kingdom. Chad is part of the prophecy, and I am the dragon rider-"

"A human from Earth is part of a prophecy?" one male knight shouted. "He is not from here! Some of us have earned our place here!"

"Um, um, we can't control prophecies!" Melissa replied, her words stumbling out of her lips.

"And if you are the real rider, why have you been hiding all this time when we needed you!" another male knight shouted.

"It was a decision Henricus made," Melissa continued.

"He is a fool!" another shouted, and Melissa felt her ears turn hot. "He put us at risk!" Melissa then barked.

"If you had any respect for Henricus, then you'd respect

his decision!" Jake blew a ball of fire in the air right after she spoke.

"I hatched for Melissa; she is the purest leader to be born. Do you doubt dragons now?" The knights stayed quiet after that.

"Settle down, Jake." She caressed his snout, and the knights took notice of the kind gesture. "Look, I'm here to protect the kingdom! I have come to take up my s-err Grandfather's- long-neglected mantle to be your dragon rider and your leader. As a dragon rider, I will continue the legacy. Today, we fight for Gemma, and we fight to protect the Kingdom of Amethyst and establish a lasting peace in this world! Free from tyranny! Free from oppression! If you will lend me your strength today, I promise to stand by you for the rest of my life! Together, we can... No. Together, we will prevail!"

There was a long silence, and Emmy scoffed. "So what, she's a girl? Y'all don't remember the stories of Micah being the most powerful of the four OG riders? I stand by Melissa." Emmy clapped, and so did members of the Council. Soon, everyone clapped and chanted Melissa's name.

Emmy rushed over to give Melissa a bear hug. "Be safe," she told Emmy. "We are going back home soon with Chad," she promised. Emmy watched her with a radiant smile, her eyes twinkling.

"I'm sorry, by the way," Emmy said.

"For what?" Melissa asked, puzzled as she climbed on Jake.

"For never believing in you when you talked about your dreams. Your head was in the clouds, but I shouldn't have assumed the clouds weren't real." Melissa put on her trademark smirk, and with that, Jake shot into the sky.

He soared high above the clouds and gave one frightening roar. Melissa unsheathed her sword, raised it in the air, and every single magical being below her cheered and marched their way towards the field that led to the Dark Forest of Garnet.

Jake soared above everyone, and goblins and ogres emerged from the Dark Forest of Garnet.

Ogres were much taller and thicker than goblins, and their skin looked almost like that of a rock. Jake blew small fireballs at them to give a strategic edge to their forces on the ground.

Melissa and Jake both heard heavy footsteps storming their way through the forest, and before Melissa knew it, a mob of goblins, ogres, and another dark type of creature Melissa had read about were making their way to fight.

"Minotaurs," Melissa's voice trailed off. "They are way bigger than in pictures."

They all had built chests and arms like professional bodybuilders. Still, their legs and their heads were just like those of angry oxen, ready to demolish anything that came their way. "Jake, are you sure our people got this?"

"I am certain!" And so, it began.

Melissa watched below as her army clashed swords and shot arrows at the enemies. Jake swooped down, and a centaur being overpowered by a Minotaur caught her attention. Standing on Jake's saddle, Melissa took action. Before Jake could stop her, she jumped towards the Minotaur and fought alongside the centaur.

The Minotaur angrily scoured at Melissa and charged

towards her. Still, Jake breathed out a stream of fire, and it engulfed the Minotaur in flames, letting out a primal yell as it beat on its chest to extinguish the fire before he fell to his knees. Melissa was in disbelief that she was willing to kill someone to protect the centaur. The centaur nodded his head, a gesture of thanks.

Jake snatched her up with his mouth, placed her back in his saddle, and yelled at her, "Do not do that again! Your mission is the lighthouse!"

"But Emmy!" Melissa scanned to see if she could find her but couldn't.

"She will be alright. The elves made a vow, and they do not break them!" Jake reassured Melissa. "I know you are worried, but you must focus on your mission."

"I have an idea!" Melissa hurriedly scavenged her backpack, but it proved to be challenging to do so midair. She snatched her walkie-talkie, which fumbled in her hands, and called for Emmy.

At first, it was straight static, and Melissa could feel her gut twisting and turning inside her to the point she wanted to vomit her anxiety. But then a voice cackled, and Melissa gasped sharply.

"Dude!" Emmy's voice broke through, "We need help!"

"Jake! We need to pincer maneuver and order more reinforcements to the weak flanks. We have to minimize the losses! JAKE, watch out!" Melissa screeched as arrows arched through the lavender sky, their sharp heads glistening against the sun as they hurdled toward the two of them.

Jake flew high, twirling around and dodging the arrows. Melissa ducked on his saddle while one hand held the shield over her head.

Flying alongside them were dozens of enormous eagle-lion beasts mounted by armored elves who slung arrows from their backs at the unsuspecting enemy below. They weren't the size of Jake, but they were larger than the unicorns.

"Griffins!" Melissa exclaimed, watching the beast with the body of a lion but the wings and head of an eagle. One elf winked at Melissa and shot below, piercing many of the enemies in the head.

Melissa couldn't bear to watch as some griffins held boulder-like rocks and dropped them on the enemies, crushing them without mercy. She averted her gaze, but the blood-curdling screams of the victims reached her ears from afar, a haunting reminder of the horrific carnage unfolding. The overwhelming weight of guilt and shame draped heavily upon Melissa's shoulders, threatening to consume her entirely.

"It is necessary!" her dragon shouted. He knew her blood froze with a trembling fear she had never experienced before.

As Melissa looked below, the sight of blood spilled by her people and her dragon made her acutely aware of the brutality of war. She realized that all the fiction stories that once resonated deeply in her heart were not merely being cut short but were ending in tragic fashion, leaving behind a void of closure.

Just 'over.'

When a person lives in stories and dreams, it's easy to get spoiled by happily-ever-afters or self-sacrifices that bring peace and happiness to loved ones. Still, there was no poetry, no romance here, no honor or glory, no deathbed speeches, no teleporting healers, and no best friends swearing revenge.

Melissa found herself at the climax of a sad chapter, her

heart heavy with the weight of the events that had unfolded. It lay the fragility of life and the harsh reality of war bare before her, like a torn-out page that ended the story.

"Jake, promise me you'll go back and protect Emmy when you drop me off at the lighthouse."

Her dragon remained quiet, and Melissa could feel his tension growing. Finally, he released a mutter and said, "I promise."

Jake then swerved and flew deep into the forest, away from the war. He landed in the middle of the forest, a few feet away from the lighthouse where the coast was clear. Melissa slid down from his wing gracefully.

Jake lifted his head and narrowed his eyes. "There are three goblins and two ogres guarding the lighthouse," Jake's voice remained firm. Melissa paced back and forth, twirling her hair. "I do not wish to leave you."

"I need you with Emmy. I'll be fine," Melissa reassured him.

"They are approaching."

"Then go!"

Jake released a heavy breath, showering her with his smoke. But he gave her a quick nudge on her cheek. Melissa took a big gulp and hugged Jake's neck; he snuggled his face into hers, and she kissed him.

"If you need me, just yell my name," he reassured her. Jake shot into the sky, and when she heard leaves crunching, she jolted off inside the forest to reach the lighthouse.

Indeed, there were three goblins but only one ogre guarding the entrance to the lighthouse. *Where is the other ogre?* Melissa frantically searched around for the second monster.

Her knees buckled, and her hands suddenly became

sweaty. She noticed they watched Jake fly off.

"Mh, why did the beast leave?" a goblin asked, and another shrugged its shoulders.

Oh my gosh, I can't do this. Yes, I can... No, I can't. I have to do this. Chad's up there. Okay, okay, I got this. Jake said he saw two ogres.

Just as Melissa attempted to sneak around the lighthouse with her sword in her hand, the unaccounted ogre grabbed her from behind and choked her. Both her shield and sword dropped, and Melissa grasped onto him with all her strength, trying to detach the hands that wrapped around her neck.

"Ugh," he looked at her puzzled. "Puny lady." He gripped harder.

Melissa's face turned violet as her lungs burned for oxygen. Desperate to defend herself, she fumbled for the dagger strapped to her thigh, her trembling fingers finding it just in time. With a surge of determination, she lunged forward, slashing at the ogre's face in a swift, calculated motion. Crimson blood sprayed across his cheek, eliciting a growl of pain and fury.

Sensing the need for a more formidable weapon, Melissa quickly assessed the situation, her mind working rapidly. She took a cautious step back, her hand now instinctively reaching for the hilt of her sword. Knowing that the dagger could offer no further protection, she tucked it away in her bag, and prepared herself to attack.

The ogre continued glaring at her and spat, "Who are ya?"

Melissa donned her signature smirk, eluding an air of

confidence as she positioned herself for the impending attack.

"Well," she taunted, her voice laced with a touch of charm. "I am the dragon rider, after all."

The ogre frowned, and Melissa charged at him. He grabbed his club and swung at Melissa, who ducked and rolled away. She slashed his back, cutting him, and the ogre released a cry of pain.

In his moment of weakness, she kicked him with all her strength, which caused her to fall to the ground, but she tipped him over, hitting his head on a tree in the process and knocking him unconscious.

The loud thud drew the attention of the surviving ogre and three goblins, prompting them to investigate the source of the noise. Melissa hurried behind a nearby tree, ensuring she stayed concealed from their prying eyes.

"We should tell him to kill the rider now," a goblin said. "He's useless to us anyway without the dagger."

"It's your fault for not making sure he had it on him," the other goblin whined.

"Quiet," he snapped. "Tell him to kill him now. His dragon has abandoned him."

Melissa gasped and stepped out from the tree. "Not so fast!" she blurted, and they all glared at her.

"She's the one who hit me!" A goblin with a blackened eye grunted when he realized it was the girl who punched him.

"Yeah, yeah, get over it," Melissa chuckled nervously. "Now, you see, haha," she babbled, "you guys keep thinking he's the rider... but what if the rider is a girl?" They all looked at one another and busted out, cackling.

"Seriously? Dragons do not hatch for the weak. What makes you think they'll hatch for a woman?" The comment infuriated Melissa, and she clenched her jaw, but instead of raging, she used that anger to fight.

Her sword clashed with one goblin as the other two followed the other. She could block their heavy blows. The ogre was the quickest to take down; he swung his club carelessly and accidentally knocked out one goblin.

One down, three to go.

Frustration echoed in the ogre's roar after his reckless action. It charged at Melissa with full force, his rigid joints became his downfall. With a simple step to the side, she evaded his attack, leaping onto the ogre's back and covering his eyes.

The ogre grunted and continued to swing his club carelessly until he accidentally hit himself on the head and knocked himself out cold. With two goblins left, they sneered at Melissa. The one with the black eye attacked her and delivered one powerful blow and, knocked her sword away. In a panic, she did a backflip and grabbed her dagger. "Where did ya get that?" He immediately noticed the dagger.

"What is this old thing? It's the Dagger of Riders."

"I know what it is, ya fool! How ya get that?" he snarled.

"Because I'm the rider." With the goblin distracted, observing the dagger, Melissa swung a powerful kick, knocking the goblin down. "You're next."

The remaining goblin dropped his sword, but before he could make a run for it, she whistled, and Jake swooped down and swallowed him whole.

Melissa scoffed, cowardly. She glanced at the entrance that was no longer guarded and took a deep breath. "You got this," Melissa told herself.

Melissa ascended the spiral stairs. It felt like a lifetime to reach the beacon, but the thought of Chad entrapped fueled her to keep climbing despite her calves burning.

She clutched onto the handle of her sword, preparing to meet the apprentice.

"Please, stop! I don't have it!" Chad's voice echoed, and Melissa's stomach took a turn. She dashed upwards and came to a complete stop when she saw Chad's bloodied face.

Someone sliced his scar that lay above his left eyebrow and it oozed blood, drenching his already purple eye.

In the center, where the glazed lantern should have been, was a flawlessly cut gem that glittered effortlessly. It would entrance anyone who glimpsed it.

Whoa… Melissa stared at it, mesmerized. *That has to be the size of Jake's head.*

"Stop trying to protect your dragon and that dagger," a familiar voice snapped her from her daze. "Who are you trying to protect?" Suddenly, she felt queasy.

She moved away from the diamond to see who was clutching Chad by his shirt, and she instantly recognized the broad shoulders and chocolate hair.

"Let him go," Melissa hissed even though her lips quivered as she did. The man stood unwavering, and he slowly turned around, revealing himself to be Jacob.

The metal plate on his chest bore a sigil depicting a demonic rooster-like dragon. His boots and pauldrons fashioned from exotic orange fur.

She took a few more steps and stood next to the Diamond of Dragons; her body turned rigid, and her mind could not absorb the reality that stood in front of her.

"Jacob?" she said almost in a whisper.

"Melissa? You've been in this realm the whole time?" Jacob was wearing chainmail himself and carried a thick, sharp sword with a black leather handle and an emerald embezzled in the sheath. "What the hell are you doing here? Did this idiot get you into this?" Melissa shook her head.

"No," the words barely came out. "I got him into this."

"What are you talking about?" he replied, clearly infuriated.

"He's not the rider Jacob, I am."

Chapter Thirty-Three

Emmy became lost within the crowd of elves who held either swords or bows and arrows. Centaurs ran past her, causing startlement and heightening her existing anxiety. Her hands tightened their grip on her bow, and she consciously took deep breaths to calm her nerves.

I still think this is a dream. Emmy cracked a crazed smile. *No way I'm going to war with a bunch of elves, centaurs, and dwarves to fight off goblins and ogres! Just no freaking way.*

"WATCH OUT!" Leon yelled as an arrow flew right past her cheek, just a few inches away from slicing her. Emmy immediately ducked down as Leon yanked on her arm and snarled.

"We are at war right now. Get to it!" Emmy nodded her head with tears threatening to spill from her eyes.

Her legs were shaking uncontrollably, but she intended to move as swiftly as she was able. Meanwhile, Ezra and Alisha fought side by side, skillfully evading arrows and engaging in sword fights with goblins.

Even in the fog of war, Emmy could not help but think how well they fought together. A Minotaur charged its way toward Emmy, and she dodged him, grabbed her bow and arrow, and shot the Minotaur right in the eye.

She immediately gasped. "Wow, the first time a hamburger tries to eat me. I just killed a freaking bull." Another Minotaur came towards her, and again, she dodged and shot another arrow but missed this time. The bull-like creature glared at her with wrath, and its pitch-black eyes intimidated Emmy.

She glared back at it, taking one big gulp, and readied another arrow. It charged, and she shot it, piercing its head. The momentum of his last charge carried his body forward, crashing into her, bringing her down, and disarming her.

"Seriously?" Emmy was panting. She scrambled to get out from under the bull that almost crushed her to death. She struggled to stand, but with all her efforts, she reached out to retrieve the weapon, only to have it kicked away by an ugly, drooling goblin.

Emmy scrunched her nose in disgust and said, "Ew, need a napkin?"

"ARGHHH!" He pulled out a curved sword. Emmy took out hers, and they clashed swords.

Her hands trembled since her nerves were uncontrollable. The goblin leaped into the air and attempted to decapitate her, and Emmy ducked and rolled away.

As the goblin walked towards her, Ezra stabbed him in the gut and helped Emmy up. "Are you alright?"

"Um, I don't know-"

"It is my duty to protect you." Ezra sounded almost promising, but Emmy did not count on it.

Dwarves scattered all around, either stabbing goblins, climbing on ogres and piercing them, or slicing their heads with a wielding ax or pickaxe. Emmy's lips hung low at how feisty and aggressive the short, stubby beings were.

However, no matter how many they killed, more and more grim creatures appeared from the dark forest. Emmy felt her heart sink to the pit of her stomach as one ogre sped his way towards her.

Emmy shouted, "CRAP!" and rolled away, but there was so much going on that no one heard her, and instead, she caught the attention of another Minotaur.

"You guys sure like me!" It charged its way towards her, and Emmy dodged him, then spun to face the bull. Her bow was just a few feet away, so before he could charge again, she quickly snatched it, aimed directly at his head, and shot an arrow. It pierced the Minotaur right in the forehead, causing it to slump to the blood-soaked battleground.

"And that's what I call ground beef," she chuckled to herself, disappointed that no one was around to hear that perfectly timed pun.

She looked around to find a tree to climb to shoot arrows from above, but she was too far into the vast field. From the corner of her eye, she saw a centaur about to be stabbed by an enormous ogre, and Emmy gasped.

She readied her bow and shot endlessly at every dark creature she saw. She'd aim and shoot without thinking twice about it. Every time an elf, dwarf, or centaur was in trouble, she'd attack.

"Nice!" Alisha called out, and Emmy winked at her. Through her peripheral vision, she caught a goblin charging towards the elf.

"ALISHA! WATCH OUT!" she cried, and Emmy quickly shot an arrow, piercing it right in the throat.

If Emmy was just a bit off in her shooting, she could have instantly killed Alisha, who stared at her, relieved that she did not miss. A large hand gripped Emmy's body and swung her around, squeezing her.

"AHHHHHHH!" Emmy screamed in agony, and she felt like her insides were going to come out through her mouth.

Leon shot a volley of arrows cascading from the woods, turning the beast's arm into a pincushion, piercing its arm until he loosened its grip. Emmy escaped from its hand and jump down.

To her favor, Nedjem galloped by and thrust her onto his back. She struggled to sit but eventually got the hang of it. "You're a lifesaver," she sighed in relief.

"The rider ordered us to protect you at all costs," he explained. "You are dear friends with the rider," he stated. Emmy quickly disembarked from his back, and he galloped away.

Suddenly, Emmy noticed a glittery cloud emerging from the forest. Emmy squinted her eyes and saw the fairies and pixies joining the war alongside the elves, centaurs, and dwarves. They flew, unleashing their magic and using their small size to their advantage.

With agile movements, the fairies and pixies fought by tossing pixie dust to disorient their enemies. Emmy marveled at the unity of this diverse group of mythical beings as they fought side by side, united in their mission to fight alongside Melissa.

The little soldiers hurled pixie dust at their enemies. Unlike confetti or glitter, gravity did not affect it. The pixie dust caused many foul creatures to slump to the ground unconscious.

It mesmerized Emmy, and in the blink of an eye, she shrieked in pain. A goblin shot an arrow into her thigh. She wailed in agony, attracting attention from all over the place.

Nedjem galloped his way towards Emmy to pick her up swiftly and place her on his back. Dwarves all gathered around the centaur, and those little humanoid creatures were bringing down the goblins and ogres that were trying to get Nedjem and Emmy.

He galloped his way toward Ezra, who had finished stabbing a Minotaur. "What happened?" he snarled.

"A goblin…"

"Really? A goblin put that arrow in her thigh?" he asked incredulously. "Get her to safety, now. If we live long enough, you and I are going to have a talk about the meaning of the phrase 'protect at all costs.'" Nedjem bolted off, galloping so fast that Emmy had to grasp his back.

She felt hot tears stream down her face as she wallowed in the excruciating pain she felt in her thigh. Alisha rode on Iris and followed Nedjem. Once they were out of harm's way, Alisha aided Emmy and had her lie down on her bed with blood gushing out from her thigh.

"Emmy, I am sorry, but this is going to sting a bit." Alisha yanked out the arrow, and Emmy shrieked even louder. Alisha forced her to drink unicorn saliva and covered her wound, wrapping it tightly to stop the bleeding. "You will be okay," Alisha promised as Emmy whimpered.

Her head then spun. "You fought so well," Alisha soothed her, and Emmy passed out.

Chapter Thirty-Four

There was complete silence between the three of them. Melissa took a moment to run to Chad's aid and caress his face. He looked up at her and gave a weak grin.

"You're here," he said faintly.

"Of course." Her eyes welled up in tears, and she pressed her forehead against his. "I would never let anything happen to you." She wiped off the blood oozing from his face, and he winced. She clenched her jaw and roared at Jacob. "What did you do to him?"

"Melissa, if you're trying to protect him, stop right now," Jacob replied calmly, demonstrating the contempt in his voice.

"I'm not," Melissa explained. "I'm the rider. I can prove it." She took the dagger from her bag and showed it to him with her hand shaking, but quickly tucked it away before he noticed it was a fake.

Jacob's eyes widened upon seeing the dagger and said, "That means nothing. You're just trying to protect Chad! His grandfather abandoned Gemma many years ago. He returned, but barely! Chad is the dragon rider. I'm sure of it."

"No!" Melissa cried. "I am the rider! Don't you get it? Pipo was the king of Amethyst! He never abandoned it.

Remember POG? The game I love? Pipo and his brothers created it, and Pablo gave it to Chad because-" Jacob cut her off. "You told me Chad introduced you to that game! It's because he is from that world!"

"No! Jacob, my family created that game because we're from this world. I'm the dragon rider. Jacob, why do you think Pipo told me all those tales of magic and dragons? And why do you think he put me in MMA? He knew I'd come back here with Jake, my dragon!"

"Jake? Your imaginary friend?" Jacob recalled and scoffed at the idea.

"Yes, you asshole!" Hearing the word imaginary infuriated her. For Melissa, she knew now all her dreams, all her imagination, and all that magic was real to her. "He wasn't imaginary. He was real before Pipo made me drink a forgetful potion. The one that put me in a coma when I was three!"

For a second, Jacob's eyes hinted at doubt. Still, he shook his head and disregarded what she said. "You cannot be the rider. It's impossible!" he shouted at this point.

"Why?" Melissa shouted back. "'Cause I'm a girl?" He scowled at her. "I know about how dragons have hatched only for men. Just once for a woman." Jacob watched Melissa intently. "Don't ya think if he were the rider, his dragon would've come for him already?" His eyes flickered to the floor. "Jacob, what are you going to do with The Diamond of Dragons? Destroy my connection with my dragon?" She paused, and Jacob scoffed. "How do you even know about Gemma?"

"I'm from here," Jacob explained. "I'm not from Earth, Melissa."

"I don't get it, how? Are you related to Victor?" Melissa prompted.

"How do you know that name?" he spat, his crazed eyes glaring at her.

Chad released a low moan, and she glanced at him; he winced in pain as he held onto his rib. At that moment, Melissa felt guilt wash over her, and she couldn't take her eyes off Chad. "Chad…" her voice whimpered, and she pleaded with Jacob. "Let Chad go, and we'll talk about it." Jacob scoffed and shifted his glare to Chad.

"Melissa, whether you're protecting Chad or you're the rider, I don't care. You're not stopping me from completing the task Victor assigned to me!" His voice dripped with determination.

They continued to stare each other down, and neither of them knew what to do or say. Jacob scanned her, observing her chainmail, her sharp sword, and her hair in a bun.

Melissa gathered her wits and asked, "Does Victoria know about Gemma?"

"No, she doesn't." He read Melissa's body language. "You shouldn't be here; your mother and sister are worried sick about you, and you're here protecting this idiot." He glared at Chad.

"You were in my dream last night; you really were in the Dark Forest of Garnet?"

"Yes," he growled.

"What were you sorry for last night then? Victoria? Or trying to kill Chad?"

"Maybe both," he taunted her. "They've been training you, haven't they? The elves?" They both circled each other, and Melissa observed his every move. "Elves are disgusting beings. That's probably why Chad's family abandoned this place. He disgraced Amethyst when the elves took over."

"It wasn't Chad's grandfather! It was Pipo!" Melissa hissed. "You watch your mouth with my abuelo," she warned.

"Melissa, give me the dagger." He disregarded her comment.

"No," Melissa backed away when he took a step. "I am not giving you my dagger."

"It's not your damn dagger," Jacob snarled, his words now dripping with malice. "Stop protecting Chad. He's not a good person! I know you love dragons, but they're not what you think they are."

"That's not true!"

"It's true! The four original riders took over the throne and exiled my family to the Dark Forest of Garnet."

"Yes, because King Lazarus was unjust!" Melissa explained.

"No!" Jacob exclaimed. "The four original riders took over because they felt superior to my people once they gained their dragons. Chad's grandfather killed my parents in a battle, and Victor helped raise my sister and me to reclaim the throne for him. We will slaughter and eradicate Chad's family once and for all."

"NO!" she wailed.

"Melissa, enough," he warned. "You cannot be the rider."

"I am the rider. And I can prove it." Melissa blew a loud whistle, and there was an utter silence. Jacob lifted his eyebrow at Melissa and then glared at Chad again.

"I'm not wasting any more time if you don't give me the dagger. I will pierce his heart with this sword-"

Interrupting him was the sound of wings flapping heavily, followed by a loud thud that caused the lighthouse to tremble. The unexpected commotion drew Jacob's attention away from Chad, and his eyes flew open to witness the astonishing sight before them. Jake tore off the roof and clutched onto it with a fierce determination in his eyes.

Jake locked his gaze on Jacob and effortlessly flung the roof aside. He sat on the lighthouse's ledge, his murderous teeth bared at Jacob. Jake made it obvious that he meant to defend Melissa. Melissa's faithful imaginary friend appeared to have taken on an important presence, blurring the gap between fantasy and reality.

Even Melissa was so frightened at the sight of Jake snarling and growling that she gulped. "Jake, wait!"

"Why?" he growled. "He has the one thing that connects me to you- and he is threatening you."

"Just wait, please," she begged.

"If he attempts to grab the diamond, Chad is dead," Jacob warned her as he shifted his glance between Melissa and Jake.

"Jake, please," she pleaded, and Jake composed himself reluctantly. "Jacob, please come to your senses. Anyway, without the dagger, you can't do much."

"You just showed me the dagger." Melissa then pulled out the dagger again, demonstrating the Cockatrice sigil.

"You don't think I'm dumb enough to have the actual dagger with me, do ya?" she said. Jacob clenched his jaw.

"No, but maybe your sister was right all along. Your damn head is always in the clouds, and it's time for a reality check." The words struck Melissa.

Jacob had always defended her against her sister's cruel words, but today, he was just like her. She wanted to yell, to cry, to shout at the top of her lungs.

But in that moment, Ezra's words resonated with her: *they are mere words*. She bit her lower lip and said, "Let go of Chad, and we can talk. I'll show you the real dagger, but you need to trust me."

Jacob's blue eyes avoided Melissa's pleading gaze, and he took a glance at Chad, who stared at him pitifully to convince Jacob to trust them.

During the moment of Jacob's doubt, Melissa crept up to the diamond to reach out for it. Jacob pulled out his sword and pointed it at Melissa. She watched him and was appalled. His words dripped with malice once again. "I've lost too much to not take back the throne to its rightful heir."

Jake began inhaling a deep breath of air to create a fireball, but Melissa cried out.

"Jake, no." Melissa dragged out her sword. "Jacob, the rightful heir is not Victor. It's me." She pointed her sword right back at him.

"What are you going to do?" Jacob taunted. "Hurt the one person who's been there for you?"

"If it means protecting my kingdom and dragon, yes." They stared each other down, and although she hesitated, Melissa swung her sword, and Jacob's clashed with hers.

After all the years she had known Jacob, Melissa would have never guessed how incredibly well he could use a sword. He moved with ease and was swift with the sword. Every blow Melissa struck, he would counter-block her.

However, she was not the only one impressed; Jacob's eyes filled with fear since Melissa was so flexible and unpredictable- a skill Ezra pointed out from the very first day they trained. Jake watched the two fight, his head following every movement of the swords.

"You fight well," Jacob admitted, and because of the circumstances, Melissa was unsure how to take this compliment.

Chad watched them with anxiety. "Melissa, you got this!" he shouted while groaning from the painful wounds Jacob inflicted on him.

"Shut it!" Jacob snarled at him as he ducked from one of Melissa's slashes. He then attempted to stab her thigh in one swift, piercing movement, but she swung her blade down, deflecting the blow. Once again she looked at him appalled, and she randomly swung a kick. From the impact, his face turned, and he spit blood out.

At that, Jake released a puff of smoke and gave a pleased look to Melissa, but she gloomily watched Jacob and felt guilty for kicking him so hard. Jacob pushed himself back up, wiped the blood off, and a grimace twisted his mouth.

They both paused in their fighting stance, and sweat dripped down from both their faces. Jacob spit out blood before saying, "This is ridiculous. We're family." He placed his sword on the ground and approached Melissa.

She took a jump back, but he raised his hands as a sign of surrender. She lowered her sword just slightly, and Jake roared, "NO!"

Without hesitation, Jacob kicked the sword out of her hand, depriving her of her weapon. He said, "I'm sorry, but this is the way it's gonna go. You're gonna give me the dagger…" Before he finished his sentence, Melissa swiftly grabbed her dagger, spun with it, and cut Jacob on his chest. The dagger cut right through the chain mail and deeply wounded Jacob, who cried out in agony.

"Jacob!" Melissa contemplated putting her dagger down, but Ezra's voice lingered in her mind to stay guarded at all costs. Blood soaked his chest, and it wracked Melissa with guilt, and she couldn't help but think about all the times Jacob stood up for her against Victoria.

Concentrate Melissa. He's trying to kill Chad.

Jake frantically moved his head to squeeze in and grab the diamond. Still, the battle between Jacob and Melissa prevented him from doing so, and he bellowed.

"TOSS ME THE DIAMOND!" Jacob stumbled in his stance, and a panicked Melissa seized the opportunity to snatch the Diamond of Dragons.

"Whoa!" The weight of it almost took her body to the ground, but she tossed the diamond high enough for Jake to grab it with his talons.

"FLY NOW!" Melissa yelled, and Jake flew off.

"NOOO!" Jacob roared at the sight of Jake soaring away with the gem. Driven by instinct, he recovered his fallen sword and pierced Melissa in her right shoulder blade.

The impact made Melissa gasp in pain, and sparks of pain caused her vision to blur. She turned, and Jacob's eyes met hers. She stared at him in horrifying disbelief as she slumped to her knees.

"NOOOOOOOO!" Chad bellowed and stood up with all the little strength he had left and shoved Jacob to the floor. Jacob, still in complete shock, continued staring at Melissa with tears welling up in his eyes.

Before Melissa collapsed on the floor, Chad used his body for her to fall on, and she whimpered in pain as the wound bled.

"Hey, hey, hey," Chad caressed her face. "It's okay. I'm here." His voice was raspy, and Melissa gasped desperately for air from the unbearable pain.

She glanced at Jacob, whose sorrowful expression clearly stated he regretted his potentially fatal action. But he raised his sword to proceed with another strike, this time towards Chad.

As he swung his sword, Melissa yanked Chad out of the way just in time. But he still took a slice in his forearm. Chad bellowed in pain, and blood gushed from the wound.

Melissa used her last burst of energy to stand and sweep Jacob with the same technique he taught her. Before he had the chance to rise, she snatched her sword and stabbed Jacob in the stomach, driving the blade through him and the floorboards, pinning him firmly down.

Jacob grunted as the sword pierced his gut. He looked at Melissa, puzzled, and his body slumped to the ground as he coughed up blood.

"JACOB!" Melissa cried, realizing what she had just done.

Melissa crouched to Jacob while holding onto her own bleeding wound and wept. "Jacob, I'm so sorry." She held up his head.

"No," he reached his hand up and cupped her face. "I'm... I'm sorry. I love you very much, and Victoria loves you." He was out of breath, and Melissa knew his time was running out.

"Jacob, please don't go...What would Victoria do without you?"

"It's okay...I-I-" He coughed up blood, and Melissa sobbed because she knew his death was inevitable. "Melissa... you-you can't be the rider. Because-" he struggled to breathe one last time, and before Melissa knew it, that was Jacob's last breath. His blue eyes stared blankly at her with a certain emptiness Melissa had never seen before.

She sobbed and attempted to wake him up. Her chest tightened, and she felt she had very little air to breathe. Chad pulled her off of him, and she hugged him, still sobbing.

As Melissa laid her blotchy face on Chad's chest, she suddenly heard approaching footsteps. The couple snapped their heads and looked directly at the entrance of the lighthouse.

Standing tall, a man with a complexion as pale as the moon and sleek, raven hair tied back in a ponytail loomed over Jacob's lifeless body. Melissa's blood ran cold as she locked eyes with him. Without a word spoken, she recognized him.

Victor's eyes, black as inky pools, held an evil glint. He stared at Jacob's lifeless body. His gaunt face and protruding cheekbone turned to face Melissa, and he grew a sinister smile.

"I knew Jacob mustering the Dark Forest armies too early would lead to this failure. Foolish boy." He kicked his body slightly, and Melissa hung her lips low.

"How-how..." Melissa choked on her words. "How can you do that?"

"Granddaughter of Henricus Werra," Victor tilted his head and narrowed his eyes. "A part of me is grateful you are still alive. I want you to live long enough to watch me destroy your grandfather's legacy. I will turn your kingdom against you and your dragon."

Melissa wanted to launch at Victor, but Chad gripped her shoulders to hold her back from snatching her sword and stabbing Victor once and for all.

Victor turned his back to them with ease, and before leaving, he paused and turned his head slowly, sneering, "Let's see how you survive this forsaken lighthouse." He bolted down the stairs.

Melissa and Chad exchanged glances, and just as they stood up an explosion seared the air and a chunk of the roof collapsed, blocking the exit door.

Another piece of the roof fell, smashing Jacob's body, and Chad's hand quickly covered her eyes to prevent her from watching the gruesome scene. Melissa released a gut-wrenching sob, and Chad turned her around and spoke.

"The lighthouse is going to crush us to death. We need to jump!" She looked at him, her face red and blotchy; she noticed blood dripping from his arm.

"Jump? With your arm bleeding like that? Are you insane! We'll die!" she panicked.

"Then what?" he stammered.

"I'll call for Jake!" she said, and they walked towards the edge. Their eyes searched the sky for Jake, but he was nowhere to be found.

"He's too far! What do we do?" Chad exclaimed, his entire arm bloodied.

There was a pause before Melissa said, "The walkie-talkie!" Melissa snatched it from her book bag and called Emmy.

"Emmy? Emmy, are you there? Emmy, if you can hear this, I'm about to do something really stupid. If it doesn't... if I don't... Listen, just... I want you to know that you're the smartest, most loyal person I know, and you're the only one I trust to lead in my place. Please look after Jake. Don't let what happened to Pipo's dragon happen to him. You have been the best friend anyone could dream of. I should know. Over and out."

"Melissa!" Emmy's voice sounded through, and just as Melissa was going to respond, the lighthouse shook, causing her to drop her device, breaking it upon impact.

"Mel," Chad gulped, and Melissa knew what he was thinking.

"We have to jump," he finally said, and Melissa agreed.

Packs of winged horses were flying a few yards away, and Melissa pointed at them, "Chad, winged horses! Alisha once told me they'll let you ride one of them!"

"Melissa, if we jump and don't make it, then we will die."

"It's our only chance." The winged horses were near. "Stand on the ledge and follow me."

As the ivory-winged horses flew right by the lighthouse, Melissa took a leap to one close enough to her. Her body landed sideways on the winged horse's back, and it growled in annoyance.

It took her longer than it should have to pull herself up because of the immense pain in her shoulder blade. Her head spun, and she felt herself wanting to faint. Instead, she weakly turned her head and urged Chad to jump.

Chad hesitated, but he took an enormous leap. He successfully landed on another winged horse but slipped and grasped onto its tail. Enraged, the horse shook his body. It flew away from the pack and kicked with its hind legs, attempting to knock Chad off.

"Mel! I can't!" he cried out in panic. Melissa whistled loudly for Jake, but he was nowhere to be found. The horse continued to kick out of frustration, and Chad was dangling by one arm.

"CHAD!" Melissa panicked as the horse kicked Chad right in the chest, sending him plummeting down toward the ocean. His yelling ceased the moment his body splashed into the watery grave.

Melissa felt her mind go dark as it flooded her memory with all the moments she and Chad spent together: when they met, their first kiss, arriving in Miami, and all of their adventures until now. She watched Chad's body disappear into the ocean. She had just lost the love of her life.

At that moment, she felt everything around her slip into slow motion.

The winged horse took a sharp turn, and Melissa stumbled on the horse. They were no longer over the ocean, and she could see the aftermath of the war below. She attempted to maneuver the horse, but unlike Jake, it disregarded her commands, causing Melissa to panic.

The horse thrust its body violently, and Melissa slipped. She grasped onto its tail, but the winged horse neighed angrily like Chad's and shook. All the muscles in her body felt like they softened, and with the pain and grief she was feeling, she could not force herself to hold on.

It reminded her of her sadness back at home, her depression and loneliness, and now she had just lost the love of her life. She allowed her fingers to slip from the tail, and she went diving. She shut her eyes tightly.

Her mind spiraled, thinking of her mom, Emmy, and Chad. Jake and the elves. All her precious memories with her abuelo illuminated, and she imagined his voice saying, "I love you, mi niñita."

She embraced the fall, but just as her body was going to smash into the vast field now filled with dead enemies and allies, Jake snatched her and crashed to the ground, holding Melissa and using his wings to protect her from the impact. He unfolded his wings and spoke eagerly, "We won! The diamond is safe, and the elves..." He noticed the blood all over her armor, and he gasped. "Melissa, no..." His voice cracked, and Melissa glanced at him, wearing her usual smirk, which was busted and bloodied from the impact of Jake saving her. "No, no! What happened? I should never have left you with him!"

"Jake?" she said weakly.

"Yes?"

"Chad... he's gone." She choked back a sob and continued. "Tell Emmy I love her... tell her to tell my mom I love her and my sister... I love them so much. At least they'll know I'll rest easy." She struggled to breathe, and she felt her body become weaker by the second. "Jake, all I ever wanted was for my dreams to be true...for you to be real. I love you so much, Jake... I wish we had more time."

"No, Melissa, you cannot die! Not like this. I finally have you back." Melissa watched her dragon shed a thick tear, and it fell on her, but Melissa's eyes rolled back in her head as she lost consciousness.

Chapter Thirty-Five

The sounds of birds chirping brought a smile to Melissa's face. She felt a breeze waft by, and she inhaled the smell of fresh wood.

Her eyes fluttered open, and when she slowly sat up, her head throbbed, and she groaned. She scanned her surroundings, and she was in Alisha's cabin, lying on her comfy bed.

When she rolled off the bed, she felt a spark of pain in her shoulder blade, causing her to moan. She took a glance at her shoulder and saw it was all patched up.

Slowly, she peeled back the patch and saw a thick wound stitched up. She winced, looking at its grotesqueness.

"Gosh, my head is killing me," she muttered.

She looked down and wore a white robe that reached her knees, and her hair braided to one side.

"Where is everyone?" Her mind shifted to the last thing she remembered: Jake.

Her dragon ring on her index finger shook, startling Melissa.

"What the?" she muttered. The vibration was soft but enough to catch her attention.

She heard footsteps running, and Emmy burst through the door. It infused Melissa with happiness seeing her frizzy-haired, braces-wearing best friend wearing an olive-green knee-length dress.

"Melissa!" she cried. "You're awake!" She flung her arms around Melissa and hugged her tightly against her chest. She felt full and wonderfully alive under the embrace of Emmy.

"Ouch!" Melissa whined, and Emmy let go of her best friend. Emmy had a minor scratch on her left cheek and a slight cut on the lip, and her eyes drooped as if she hadn't slept in days. A mixture of recuperating after the war and being concerned about the status of Melissa's life.

"I'm sorry! I forgot you got stabbed!" Emmy's eyes welled up with tears. "How do you feel?"

"My head feels like it's gonna explode, I feel disoriented... What's going on? How long have I been asleep?"

"Um..." Emmy hesitated to answer. "You've been out for three days..."

"What?" Melissa gasped, being knocked out cold for so long mortified her.

"Yeah... Melissa, you almost died. You lost more than a pint of blood. Alisha barely brought you back. The goblins, ogres, and ox-looking creatures retreated once the lighthouse tumbled down."

"Bunch of losers, that's what they are," Melissa said bitterly.

"I'm so glad you're okay! If you ever pull another reckless move on me again, I will kill you myself." Confused at what Emmy meant, she arched a brow. "It's one thing to deal with this world, but to deal with your magical mumbo jumbo stuff is a whole different ball game."

Melissa snickered and asked, "How'd you know I woke up?"

"The dragon ring." Emmy pointed at it. "The fairies enchanted it so that you're connected with Jake... Well, you are even more connected than you were before. I guess when you woke up and thought of him, it alerted him, and he told us. He's been worried sick about you."

"The Diamond of Dragons? Is it safe?" Melissa asked.

"Jake took it to an island called Sapphire Island. It's only a few miles from the coast. The fairies placed a magical shield over it so no one could go inside the caves. Only Ezra can enter, given the fact we have a mole we need to worry about. But we're not supposed to tell anyone it's there, anyway. Only the Council and their allies know, which, by the way, I'm considered an ally!" Melissa giggled at Emmy's amusement. "Here." Emmy reached her hand out to Melissa. "Jake wants to see you." Emmy helped Melissa out of the bed.

She looked in the mirror and noticed her lips swelling had gone down but was still in the process of healing, given the fact it was purplish.

Her chest and arms had scratches and bruises from the fall Jake had saved her from, and even the tip of her left ear had a cut. Melissa commented on it.

"I look like I went to hell and came back barely alive."

"We basically did, Melissa," Emmy agreed.

The sun beaming into Melissa" eyes caused her to groan. "It's so bright."

"What are you? A vampire?" Emmy mocked, and Melissa rolled her eyes. "Look."

Once Melissa could clearly open her eyes, she saw Ezra and Alisha. Alisha was holding Magic tightly against her chest.

Their faces instantly lit up upon seeing Melissa, and they each grew a cheerful grin.

They walked towards her, placing Magic on the floor, and he sprinted his way to Melissa excitedly.

"We were told you put up a fight," Ezra commented.

"We are very proud of you," Alisha smiled. "Henry would have been proud."

Melissa pictured her abuelo watching her with pride like he always had before, his chest pushed out with pride, and a cheeky smile pasted on his face. She looked back, her eyes searching for Chad. When she didn't see him, her heart sank.

"Chad," Melissa mumbled, and she looked at the elves as her eyes watered up.

"Melissa, what is wrong?" Alisha asked.

"Chad…" Melissa repeated, and tears streamed down her face. "He fell into the ocean, he's… he's…" She broke down, recalling the image of Chad slipping off a winged horse and disappearing into the sapphire ocean until Jake flew in and caused his usual loud thud.

"Melissa!" he cried, and Melissa ran towards him and wrapped her arms around his neck, still sobbing. "What is wrong?"

"Chad, he's the only one who didn't make it," she wept.

"Are you sure about that?" a familiar voice said, and Melissa desperately looked around, trying to find it. "Right up here, Mel!" Chad was riding on Jake, and he slid down from his wing, tripping in the process. "I think he's starting to like me," he smirked.

"Do not push it," Jake snarled, and Melissa enveloped Chad with a tender hug and kissed him passionately in front of everyone. Bruises marred his face, including a blackened eye, and cuts peppered his face.

"I thought you were gone." He dried up her tears. "How are you alive? I saw you fall!"

"I thought I was gone too," Chad admitted. "But according to Alisha, mermaids came to my rescue. You should've seen them, Mel. They're beautiful!"

Melissa disregarded what he said and gave him another smooch on the lips, to which Emmy groaned, "Here they go, starting with their PDA."

The elves snickered along with Emmy while Melissa and Chad giggled, losing themselves in each other's eyes.

Melissa observed his left eye and its enormous purplish-blue bruise. He also had slight cuts around his body; Melissa tried not to ask questions because he would wince just remembering his time with Jacob in the lighthouse. His arm received stitches to close the gash Jacob inflicted.

She spoke briefly about her encounter with her deceased brother-in-law.

Melissa could only imagine the brutal punches and cuts Jacob had given Chad and the constant torture he had to endure to protect Melissa's identity. Chad suffered through pain to protect Melissa. She knew he loved her without a doubt.

The thought of Jacob's death brought deep sorrow into Melissa's heart. She never imagined that it was Jacob who was trying to overtake the Kingdom of Amethyst and was willing to kill Chad over it. As if Chad meant nothing to her. The Jacob she knew could harm no one.

"You know, Chad," she paused and sighed. "I remember you never trusted him."

"Yeah, I didn't," Chad explained and turned to look at

the elves. "He was a brother to you, Mel, and even to Emmy, but with me… I just felt something off about him."

"Women's intuition?" Emmy mocked, and the couple looked at her, frowning. "Sorry, trying to lighten the mood."

"He was a weird guy. Something was off," he stammered. "I felt the way he'd stare at me and talk to me; it was like he disliked me. At first, I thought it was just out of fatherly protection or the fact that he wouldn't be the only man in the house anymore once I came into the picture." Emmy muffled a laugh, and Melissa elbowed her. "But when he picked me up the day of the zoo, he asked me a lot of weird questions like, 'What's my father like?' or 'If my parents were still together?' It was like he was interrogating me about my family… and then he said we were being idealistic. I think he wanted to put a wedge between us. I don't know, the Jacob you described was not the same guy that picked me up the day of the zoo."

Melissa took a moment to tell the elves about her encounter with Victor, and the elves stood motionless. She explained how unfazed he was watching Jacob's dead body lie in the lighthouse and his promise to destroy Pipo's legacy.

Everyone stayed quiet for a moment, letting all the information sink in. Still, Emmy stood up. "I think Victor intended for Jacob to come to Earth to search for the dragon rider since no one knew it was Melissa. Then, Victor encouraged Jacob to live a normal human life on Earth and encouraged him to fall in love, but not just with anyone," Emmy paused, ensuring everyone listened intently. "With Victoria. That way, he had an insight into Pipo's family because he knew they were the Werras. Oh, and when Melissa mentioned Chad introduced her to POG, it convinced Jacob that Chad was the dragon rider because he knew of Gemma! But little did Jacob know, he was probably being used to keep an eye on Melissa, the true rider." Melissa's mind spun with Emmy's words.

"You're right. It could all be psychological too," Chad added. "Ruin the family from within. Victor didn't care about Jacob; he was merely a pawn in his game."

"Exactly!" Emmy snapped her fingers. "I'm telling ya, if I'm right, then this guy is hella dangerous."

"It's all too much," Chad stated, and everyone looked at one another, confused more than ever before.

"Can we just talk and figure this out another time? My brain can't take it anymore." The back and forth exhausted Melissa. "We all need to go home to our families."

"Um, Melissa..." Emmy shuffled her feet the way she always does when she's hesitant to say something. "I don't even think you wanna know what's going on."

"What is going on?" Melissa glared at the elves and wore a frantic expression.

"We're all over the news." Chad broke it as smoothly as he could. "My mom is in Florida with Alex."

"Oh no." Melissa desperately looked at the elves. "We need to leave now."

"Meli-" Alisha interrupted Ezra before he could even begin speaking.

"Melissa, we just won a war. We have the dragon rider and princess back in Amethyst. You and Jake saved the Diamond of Dragons, and it is back where it belongs. We want to throw a ball for you tonight. To welcome you back home and celebrate your victory."

"Our victory," Melissa corrected her, to which Ezra grinned.

"We also made a brilliant story for all of your families," Alisha said.

"Oh, yeah?" Emmy scoffed. "And what's that brilliant story of yours?"

"Well, you were all kidnapped. Chad was almost beaten to death." Chad rolled his eyes since there was a half-truth to that. "You girls endured some pain. Still, you all managed to escape, and you contact the authorities and come back home to your family."

"Oh my gosh, that is not brilliant! That's mortifying!" Melissa's voice cracked. "Our families, my mom, my sister...They must be distraught."

"Hey," Chad placed his hands on Melissa's face softly. "One last night, and we'll be home. Once we get home, we might not even see each other again for God knows how long."

"Are you sure our families will believe that crazy story? You and I are the only ones that have proof they hurt us." Melissa doubted the plan.

"What do you mean?" Emmy scoffed and lifted the dress she was wearing, revealing the puncture wound on her upper left thigh. "Oh, my gosh!" Melissa exclaimed. "How'd that happen?"

Everyone spent their afternoon recounting the war's events and listening to Emmy, who gave descriptive details. "This goblin came after Alisha, and I shot an arrow, but then this HUGEEE ugly lookin' ogre came out of nowhere and carried me like a doll, shaking me around. I thought he was gonna squeeze my guts out, but Leon came to the rescue." Emmy's cheeks blushed, and Melissa rolled her eyes. "Nedjem killed that ogre, and he let me ride on him, but some goblin shot an arrow in my thigh. That crap hurts!" She kept on and on about the war. Several elves, dwarves, and a few centaurs died in battle, including Nubis, which made Melissa shed a few tears. She promised the elves she would have a moment of silence for those who died fighting for Gemma.

"Ladies and Chad." Ezra put on a sly smile when Chad rolled his eyes. "They are waiting for you in the castle. Shall we fly?"

"Jake can carry you and Chad, but we will have Griffins take us over there." Ezra blew a loud whistle, and three enormous griffins flew towards them. Watching the half-eagle, the half-lion was, according to Emmy, an epic sight.

Melissa felt she was watching an eagle because of its intense white feathers and golden beak. The body, however, was that of a lion with a tail at the end.

Ezra turned towards Emmy and nodded, motioning for her to climb onto the creature. Emmy stood frozen on the ground, and her cheeks flushed away her color. Melissa observed the situation, and her eyes fixated on Alisha as she approached Emmy to lend a helping hand in mounting the beast.

"Emmy, hold tight to their feathery mane. It does not bother them," Alisha explained, but it did not convince Emmy she was safe riding on one. She sat down awkwardly, trying to grip her hand on its feathery mane.

Then Chad and Melissa hopped on Jake, and before Chad settled in, Jake charged like a bull and took off with no warning. Melissa giggled to herself, knowing fully well her dragon did this to frighten Chad.

Chad had his arms wrapped tightly around Melissa's waist and laughed because she knew he was most likely fearing for his life. "I hope you didn't shut your eyes!" Melissa called out teasingly, and Chad chuckled.

"What makes you think they are?"

"A hunch," she giggled. "WHOO!" Jake swooped down, and Chad screeched, piercing Melissa's ears. He playfully swirled and twirled until Chad simply joined Melissa when she shouted, "WHOOOO!"

Melissa experienced pure bliss as she soared atop her dragon, accompanied by the love of her life. Together, they glided through the vast expanse of multi-colored sunflowers, then gracefully traversed the dense forest before finally descending upon the regal grounds of the castle.

Chapter Thirty-Six

Jake dipped down and swirled around the historic brick castle. It was even more magnificent up close and personal than it was from afar.

Ornate windows scattered around the walls and moats in each corner with elves readied with bows and arrows.

Melissa scanned the brick wall. Protecting it from intruders was a great gate with stone doors and two centaurs guarding each side; monitoring who goes in and out.

Inside were lush fields of grass with fawns, gnomes, and brownies running wild. There were a handful of streams flowing, providing water for everyone who lived within the castle walls.

It's not too big, she thought, standing in front of the castle. *I like that.* Melissa was never one to like big and expensive things. She felt simple was more. The castle was rather smaller than those she had seen in movies, but she knew it was well-guarded.

Melissa pointed her finger at the flag right above the peak tower in the center and yelled to Chad, "Look!"

"What?" He looked at it, confused.

"Jake told me those four dragons are the original riders."

"Nice, this castle looks like the one from POG," Chad commented.

Jake circled once more, giving the couple a closer glimpse of the castle that had stood for many decades. Providing a haven for magical creatures and beings in Amethyst.

The griffins landed shortly, and Emmy's face was paler than a ghost.

"You okay?" Melissa asked, holding in her laugh as Emmy threw up, and everyone looked away in disgust.

"Did I ever mention how much I hate flying?" Emmy wiped her chin.

Melissa, Chad, and Emmy stood, mesmerized by the historic grey brick castle.

"This is your home, Melissa," Alisha said. "Generation upon generation of dragon riders have lived here."

The luscious green field held some of the most beautiful and fragrant flowers Melissa had ever seen: a daisy combined with a tulip, roses bigger than her face, and luminilies floating in a crystal-clear pond.

When Melissa approached the pond, the lilies glowed. "Whoa," Melissa commented, "why is it glowing?"

"Those are luminilies," Alisha responded. "They glow when someone's emotion heightens. In this case, your curiosity is rather overwhelming."

"You got that right," Melissa muttered and continued to gaze at the way the flower faded back to its original glow. "Now I know why I love lilies so much."

There was a small splash and Melissa noticed koi fish gracefully swimming in the waters, filling her eyes with twinkles of wonder. The koi fish winked, and Melissa's head bounced back in surprise.

The elves encouraged the teens to walk, leaving Jake outside lying down and Chad grasped onto Melissa's hand, tugging her away from the captivating pond.

They entered the castle through its wooden double doors. Melissa, Chad, and Emmy found themselves captivated by the dark-colored marble floor and the portraits adorning the walls—depicting countless dragon riders alongside their dragons.

At the end of the hallway was a golden double door. The first portrait Melissa stopped to observe was the very first female rider, Micah, and her electric yellow dragon behind her.

Melissa's mouth hung open. "Whoa," she said, "she really does look like me…" The resemblance between the two was quite obvious, leaving no doubt she was her ancestor.

"Mel, that's you, but from another time," Chad muttered in disbelief.

"Seriously," Emmy added, "that's mind-blowing. Is that the rider's dagger she's holding?" Emmy observed, and they all squint their eyes for a better look.

Indeed, it was the dragger. It only had the four missing gems ranging from the stone's ruby, opal, aquamarine, and sphalerite-like the one on Micah's sword.

"Whoa," Melissa gasped. "Same colors as each dragon, right?" The elves nodded.

"Yes," Alisha replied. "The dagger is as old as they are. Those gems are meaningless, hence why we do not focus on the empty sockets." She changed the subject. "They say Micah was a reserved person, and she preferred to keep things to herself. She did not trust anyone. But Thomas was different, he was a dreamer."

"Sounds like someone we know," Emmy elbowed Melissa with a smile pasted on her face.

"That's him over there." Alisha pointed at a portrait with Thomas and his ivory dragon, "His dragon's name was Thor, and Micah's dragon was Bree." Thomas' scruffy brown hair, round light brown eyes, and thin lips gave him a boyish appearance.

"Who's that?" Chad asked, pointing at a man with long, midnight black hair that reached to his shoulders, narrow green eyes, and a petite nose.

"That is Simon," Ezra explained. "He's one of Thomas's friends. He was a very serious and rather dull person. His dragon's name was Oceanus."

"Oceanus? That's one odd name," Emmy commented.

"Well, his dragon was obsessed with water." Oceanus' intense royal blue color was beautiful, observing it through the portrait. Melissa could only imagine how it would look in person. "Lastly, we have Gabriel." Alisha pointed at a young man with dirty, long blonde hair picked up in a ponytail and small hazel eyes. "Ruby was his dragon. They say Ruby was obsessed with the actual gem... Gabriel sacrificed his life for Thomas. They were the best of friends." The trio continued walking along the halls, observing different colored dragons and riders.

Melissa knew she would see her abuelo in a portrait, and seeing him warmed her heart.

Pipo was young, around 18 at the time of the portrait. His olive-colored skin was not as wrinkled, his narrow, hazel eyes were not as sunken, and his silky black hair reached to his shoulders. Pipo had Melissa's trademark smirk painted on his face.

"I had no idea Pipo had long hair." Melissa pressed her lips, observing her young, handsome grandfather. He looked like a warrior with his metal plate, thick sword, and round metal shield.

Behind him stood his hunter-green dragon, and Melissa recalled seeing her in the dream state.

"What was his dragon's name?" Melissa asked.

"Genesis," Ezra answered. "Jake's sister." Melissa felt her heartache, not just for Pipo but for Jake because he lost his sister to insanity. His dragon's mind derailed because she thought Pipo was gone.

But all along, he was just on the other side of the world, living on an island filled with poverty. She felt thankful Jake held on to hope. Otherwise, he would've lost his mind, too.

She recalled moments Pipo would sit down on the swinging chair, gloomily watching the sunset on their porch.

Her tiny self would climb on his lap and ask, "What's wrong?" He'd inhale a deep breath, exhaling the smell of fresh cigars, responding, "Sometimes, I wish I was on a green dragon, riding the skies."

Now Melissa understood it wasn't a metaphor for freedom, but it was him literally missing his own dragon. The idea of losing her dragon gave her an empty feeling.

Ezra said, "It broke your grandfather for a long time, and he never spoke about Genesis after that. When he left," he sighed, shifting the topic, "he said he had to discuss something privately with Patricio, and then they both set off on some adventure, not telling us where. Once he left- he never came back."

"I know," Melissa's voice shuttered. "He left for Alaska…"

"No," Ezra said. "He left for the Mountains of Alexandrite and never came back."

"Could he be... alive?" Melissa's heart pulsed faster.

"No," Ezra said with such assurance. Melissa felt dumbfounded for hoping such a thing. "No one ever comes back alive from the Mountains of Alexandrite."

"Does Uncle Ozzy know about Gemma?" Melissa asked.

"No. Pablo did not want to involve his family with Gemma after living on Earth for so long. Even after he married, his family never knew of his true identity. Yet, he still assisted Henry with his crazy schemes." Ezra meant Pablo's involvement with Chad and collecting his blood. He continued to speak.

"Patricio had his family and even grandchild involved but still lived on Earth instead of here. However, he moved from Florida, and we have not seen him or his family since."

"So, Ethan knows about this realm?" Melissa gasped.

"Who's Ethan?" Emmy asked.

"My favorite cousin; I know we're not supposed to have faves, but I love Ethan. We were close when we were young."

"Yes, you were," Alisha added with a soft giggle. "Inseparable, actually. You both caused mayhem in the castle." Melissa laughed, imagining her and Ethan running around. "But yes, he knows, and he knows not to tell you anything. It was a wish Henry asked Patricio and his son, Eduardo, to keep."

"Wow, so Uncle Eduardo and Ethan know about this realm? I am soooooo calling him back home," Melissa mumbled. *But why move from Florida?* Melissa pondered for a moment. *Why take Patricio's family away from Gemma?*

"Ethan's mother is from Gemma," Alisha added, and Melissa responded with wide eyes.

"Aunt Luna is from Gemma?" The elves nodded in unison.

They all continued admiring the portrait of Pipo until Melissa gathered her wits and asked, "Ezra, do you know why Pipo didn't trust you?"

"No," Ezra said bluntly, but Melissa had a gut feeling that Ezra was not being completely honest. "Maybe one day we will have the answer to it all."

Melissa took one last glance at the portrait of Pipo and sighed. I miss you, Pipo, so much.

In the center of the castle were six large pillars holding the castle up with carvings of dragons. There was an exquisite candle holder in the center, and at the end of it was a golden throne.

Dusting the chair was a furry little cat-like being cursing under his breath.

"Who's that?" Melissa asked, hardly realizing her own voice set off an echo in the room.

The little brown-orange furry being glanced at Melissa, Chad, and Emmy and squinted his cat-like green eyes. "Who are ya?" he asked grumpily. The color of his fur gave Melissa a flashback to when she was at the Inn with Wesley.

"Roofus, this is Melissa, Henry's granddaughter and the true dragon rider." Upon hearing the dragon rider, Roofus gasped and rushed his way to get a closer look at Melissa.

"I remember ya," he muttered. "Ya made a mess in here all the time, and I always had to clean up after you. I have to clean up after everyone, including ya brainy elves."

"I did?" Melissa looked at everyone, confused. "I'm sorry, what are you?"

"What am I?" Roofus said, offended Melissa would ask such a question. "I'm a brownie. How do ya not know this?" Melissa felt her head get dizzy and her heart slump to her stomach. She felt a certain guilt, and her eyes watered instantly as she remembered the Brownie rug during her encounter in the Dark Forest of Garnet.

"Roofus," Ezra spat. "Respect your princess. She has to learn since Henry wiped her memory." Ezra sighed, and turned to Melissa, "Roofus has been in this castle for a long time and always kept it nice and clean for dragon riders."

"Mh, ya bet I do, and no one ever appreciates it." Roofus glared at Chad and Emmy, who looked at the brownie oddly. "What are ya staring at?" Chad and Emmy looked at each other nervously, unable to respond.

"Roofus," Melissa bent down to reach his level of height, her voice soft and her tone full of sorrow. "Does anyone tell you thank you for cleaning?"

"No," he frowned, pouting his lips with one fang sticking out.

"Well, thank you. Why don't you take a break today and join us for the party." Roofus stared at her, appalled, and Melissa could not register if it was a good or bad thing.

"Really?" he asked as his eyes lit up and his little tail swung back and forth like a happy cat. Melissa nodded. "Th-tha-" He struggled to say thank you. "Let me go get dressed then." He rushed off.

Ezra waited no time to tell Melissa his thoughts on the kind gesture. "Melissa, you cannot always be nice to them; they can be ungrateful. Someone has to keep the place in moral order, and the food served if we are to maintain a good diplomatic standing. Inviting them is kind, but it will not always be prudent." The way he sighed made it clear he was unhappy.

"I totally get that, but have you considered they may be ungrateful because we don't show our appreciation enough? A ruler should also be kind to their people. That way, I am respected, not feared. And in the Inn where Chad and I were hostages, there was a rug made of his kind. I want those little beings protected," Melissa replied, and Ezra shrugged his shoulders and continued giving a tour of the castle.

Ezra and Alisha walked to the right of the castle, revealing an enormous two-story library with a velvet red carpet; the scent of old pages like that of a newspaper filled the room, and there were wooden tables with wooden chairs to sit on to study.

"Whoa," Emmy commented, "this is awesome."

"Of course, it's awesome to you," Melissa said sarcastically. "You can learn here."

"Nothing wrong with learning Melissa," Alisha added. "You might actually come here often." Emmy's curiosity led her to crack open a few books, which let off dust.

"These are about how to make potions," her friend mentioned. "Melissa's abuelo made her drink a forgetful potion. Maybe we can make a remembrance potion so we can bring back any type of memory she may have from when she was three? I mean, I know it's not much, but something is something, right?"

"Not a bad idea," Melissa agreed. "I have no memories anyway from when I was three... I guess we already have a quest of our own to do," she mocked, and the girls giggled.

Chapter Thirty-Seven

A lisha and Melissa had to drag Emmy out of the library or else they would have stayed there all night long and missed out on the ball. Chad left with Ezra to the other side of the castle while Alisha ushered the girls to the master bedroom to change.

Inside the master bedroom, was a bed wider than a California king bed on which the girls allowed themselves to lay, soaking in the mattress's softness.

"Wow, I can sleep in here forever," Emmy said dramatically. "Ugh, can we move here?"

"We can... technically, this is my castle. It feels so weird saying that aloud. I'm a princess," Melissa admitted, and Emmy nodded.

"For real, dude! Who would've thought, huh?"

"Ladies," Alisha pulled out a long ruby red dress with silver lining and an emerald dress with gold linings. "Here are your dresses for tonight. Fabre's wife, Belinda, made them for you. Be sure to give her thanks. The red one is for you, Melissa, to match with your dragon."

Melissa's eyes gleamed as she recognized the dress. She wore it many times in her dreams. She giggled to herself and lifted the dress. Delicate silk embroidered the sleeveless dress; it was floor-length and had a V-shaped cut in the back.

Melissa glared at Emmy and giggled. "Why are you laughing like that, weirdo?"

"I am soooooo doing your hair and makeup."

"No," Emmy said bluntly, and Melissa continued to glare at her. "I said no. There is no makeup here in this realm." Melissa pulled out her backpack and took out her makeup bag, which made Emmy grunt in annoyance.

"Pretty please, with a cherry on top?" Melissa pouted, and Emmy sighed.

"Fine," she said bluntly. "Just please don't make me look like a clown."

"Girl, by the end of the night, you'll have all types of men going after you."

"Melissa, that sounds so disturbing."

"Yeah, you're right, haha." They laughed.

Melissa spent an hour brushing Emmy's mane to pick it up into a tight bun revealing Emmy's beautiful complexion. She then helped put on the asymmetrical strapless dress. "Wow, you look so hot," Melissa complimented, watching the way the dress hugged her hips, revealing her thick figure.

"Wow," Emmy blinked her eyes several times to make sure it was her in the mirror. "Melissa, you killed it!"

"Why, thank you." Melissa half-smiled and did her own hair. She let her hair hang down, wearing a thin diamond headband she found.

"You know," Emmy watched Melissa do the finishing touches on herself. "You really look like a princess right now."

"Haha, stop it." Melissa laughed.

"I'm serious," Emmy said, and Melissa looked at her seriously. "You're so beautiful and natural. You don't try to be anyone else but yourself, and you don't have to try to be pretty 'cause you're already beautiful. I look up to you, Melissa."

Melissa wasn't sure why she was feeling the urge to show physical affection to her friend, but she did; she wrapped her arms around Emmy's neck and they both hugged each other. Alisha walked in on the girls, sharing their moment. "Ladies, are you ready?"

Alisha herself was wearing a long ivory lace dress, to which the girls said, "Ohhhhhh…"

The elf's pale cheeks turned slightly pink. "Stop it," she said modestly. "You both look gorgeous. We have guests from Amethyst coming in already, and a handsome man is waiting to see you, Melissa." Melissa blushed, and her stomach twisted inside her.

They followed Alisha down the double stairs and there was Chad, wearing a red tunic and shuffling along in high leather boots and carrying his sword.

He glanced at Melissa, and he watched her in awestruck. "Wow," he mouthed, and Melissa felt her cheeks turn almost the same color as her dress. He reached his hand out to her, and they both smiled. "You look beautiful."

"Thank you, you don't look so bad yourself," she smirked.

"Ugh, I beg to differ."

Emmy came down afterward, and Melissa elbowed Chad to say something. "Whoa, Emmy! You look gorgeous!"

"I know," Emmy agreed as she put a finger on her butt and mimicked the sound of steam. "Gosh, Melissa, how do you walk in heels?"

"You get used to it," Melissa promised.

As they walked through the last set of double doors that led to the throne room, the teens gasped as they noticed it filled with many mythological creatures, some that they had not even seen yet. Iris and all of her centaur's friends were in a corner chatting.

Dwarves and gnomes mingled by the long-stretched table filled with different meat they had never seen before and were laughing obnoxiously.

Roofus was scampering around all over the room with a few other mischievous brownies, and it warmed Melissa's heart to see him enjoying himself. Mostly because they were picking on the snobby elves and annoying them. Elves scattered around the room, either observing everyone else or chatting privately with each other.

Bunch of snobs, Melissa thought. She half-smiled watching a brownie poke at an elf. That's what you get.

The only elves Melissa liked were Alisha, Ezra, and Leon, and even then, she only tolerated the lattermost. Not to mention that she couldn't bring herself to trust Ezra. She then saw a few humans here and there with gowns and tunics on.

"Is that a fawn?" Chad asked, looking at a hairy half-goat, half-man dancing and prancing around.

"They are fawns!" Melissa exclaimed.

"Yes," Alisha added. "They can be a handful."

"Why?" Emmy asked.

"They escape to Earth all the time, and catching them can be tedious," Alisha explained, and Melissa, Chad, and Emmy laughed it off.

How hard can it be to catch a fawn? She shook the thought.

Ezra climbed the stairs holding Magic, who was wearing

a floral crown. She watched as Alisha grinned, snatched Magic from Ezra's hands, and snuggled him close to her face.

Melissa saw the chemistry between the two and thought, she takes way better care of him than I do.

"Chihuahuas really are everywhere!" Emmy gasped, and Melissa saw Chihuahuas scattered on the dance floor following their owners.

"Wow, Pipo really brought chihuahuas to a world of magic." Melissa was in complete disbelief.

"Melissa, are you ready for me to introduce you?" Ezra asked, interrupting her from her thoughts.

"Not really," she admitted, "but do I have a choice?"

"No," Ezra sneered and faced everyone.

He cleared his throat loudly, and everyone quieted down. "Behold! I am beyond ecstatic to give you Gemma's dragon rider and princess! Melissa Paz-Guerra!"

Melissa walked slowly and watched as everyone gave her a round of applause. Her mind drifted for a moment. *Damn, I'm a princess!* She gulped and walked steadily beside Ezra.

Once more, she was in the spotlight with dozens of beings waiting for her to speak. She swallowed a big gulp. The acid rising from her stomach stung her throat as the taste of bile ascended to her mouth. Even her vision became cloudy while a cold sweat covered her body. She cleared her throat before beginning.

"Hi everyone!" she squeaked. "It's-it's..." Melissa helplessly looked at Chad and Emmy, but they urged her to keep speaking. "I know for many years, you thought Chad was the dragon rider. But it is actually me. And just like you, I am getting used to all of this. I have always dreamt of Gemma, and for most of my life, I believed this place existed. That all of you existed. For a while, I thought maybe I was a little crazy or just a hopeless dreamer. I am so… shocked and beyond happy to see that my dreams were real after all. It wasn't just a dream. It was my memories," she giggled and continued.

"I know some of you expect me to just take this honor and glory all for myself, but it'd be selfish of me to do that since I had others to help me." The crowd stared at her, puzzled as if it was an uncommon thing for a dragon rider to say. "I want to say thank you to Alisha and Ezra for always training dragon riders, including myself." The elves looked at one another and grew a grin. "To Leon, Iris, and Fabre for also aiding us. To my best friend, for being loyal to me even if it meant it'd change her life forever. To the love of my life," she glanced at Chad and grew her half smile, "for believing in me and being willing to sacrifice his life for me. To my abuelo," Melissa took a deep, shaky breath, "for keeping my dreams alive and preparing me beforehand. Lastly, to Jake." Jake popped his head in through a window, and his eyes sparkled. "For filling the empty void I've had my whole life. This is the first time I have felt this complete. I love you."

"I love you too," Jake replied.

"I'd like to take a moment of silence to honor those who died in battle." She counted thirty seconds and concluded her speech. "Thank you to all of you for always fighting alongside the dragon riders. I promise, as the princess of Amethyst, that I will protect our realm." With that being said, everyone cheered.

Before walking towards Chad, Ezra approached her. He placed a hand on her shoulder to whisper, "You really are unique among all the other riders I have ever met. You are the most humble and selfless rider, Melissa, and I look forward to training you. You still have a lot to learn." Melissa gave him a small nod and reached her hand out to Chad, who grabbed it, and they walked down together.

Everyone wanted to meet Melissa, and she felt uneasy being called 'princess' and being bowed to. She eventually asked them not to because of how uncomfortable she felt.

I don't like this attention. Melissa fidgeted with her fingers, and Chad held her hand, a gesture to stop.

Some of the female knights, like Layla, approached Melissa and apologized for flirting with Chad and being snarky to her.

"It's okay, you didn't know," Melissa assured them.

"You are such a young dragon rider," Layla mentioned. "I want you to know I support you, and I am here for you." Melissa gave her a hug, to which Layla responded by hugging her back. For a moment, Melissa felt she had a sisterhood with the knights. They supported her and embraced her as the Amethyst dragon rider and princess. She briefly wondered if Victoria would support her the way they did.

Some of the male knights bowed to Chad. "Whoa, I'm not your prince!" Chad said.

"Yes, but we were wrong to believe you are not the Tungsten from the prophecy." Chad shook their hands and glanced at Melissa, whose radiant smile made him crimson red.

By the time Melissa, Chad, and Emmy went to eat, there was barely any food left.

"Sorry." Gar, the dwarf, approached them and burped loudly. The three teens groaned, smelling his meaty breath. "There's still some dessert and wine left."

"No, thank you." She referred to the wine, but Melissa looked over at the dessert and said, "I guess we can have some desserts." Some desserts they gazed upon were obscure. Unfamiliar fruits and exotic spices hinted at a culinary adventure waiting to unfold in Gemma.

Melissa filled a plate with blue strawberries, filled with a sweet cream, and chocolate-covered pink cherries that danced on your taste buds with a sweetness beyond the usual cherry.

"Wow, this tastes friggin' amazing!" Emmy exclaimed, stuffing the blue strawberries in her mouth until Leon came by and asked her to dance. Emmy looked at Melissa and Chad, turning scarlet, and they encouraged her to dance with him.

The couple savored their desserts, sipping on a thick blue liquid that tantalized their taste buds with a blend of blueberry and kiwi.

Iris trotted towards them and expressed her gratitude to Melissa. "I heard you fought well, rider."

"Thanks." Melissa shrugged her shoulders. "I am so sorry about your brother."

"He died with honor."

"Thank you for training all of us, by the way," Melissa repeated.

"It has always been an honor to train dragon riders." The couple smiled and spoke briefly with Iris.

"I've heard in many stories back in my world that centaurs can see the future. Is it true that your kind can make prophecies by reading the stars?" Melissa asked, choosing her words carefully. Iris may be kind-hearted, but she still intimidated Melissa.

"Yes," she replied with poise. "It can be rather difficult. I am sure Ezra informed you about Jinx, mh?"

"Yes, and the prophecy, um," Melissa looked over her shoulder, making sure the elves were far. "Dime toda la profecia."

The Spanish words seemed to not have phased Iris, but her ears flickered, and she spoke in a whisper, "Very well, as your grandfather wished.

Upon the day the last pearl breaks,
And the aid of a Tungsten ring,
It shall be then the final war wakes,
And the Ruby shall confront the false king,
As the enchanter awakens the soul,
But without the four stones,

The Ruby shall lose control. Dragon riders will be no more."

Melissa paused, allowing the words of the complete prophecy to penetrate her thoughts and understand their implications.

"What?" Melissa felt like she hit a brick wall. "An enchanter? Lose control?"

"Dragon riders will be no more?" Chad added.

"We do not know," Iris's voice was sincere, unlike Ezra's. "But I have faith you will complete the next part of the prophecy, and you will find that wizard."

"Wizards? Don't they extinct?" Chad asked.

"Seems not. Your grandfather knew who it was, otherwise, he would not have been able to create that spell preventing you from coming without Chad. But do not fret. I have faith You will find the answers." The couple gave each other unnerving glances. "However, you must not repeat the prophecy. There are ears and eyes everywhere. I know you will want to inform your dragon but do so wisely. The same with your dear friend, Emmy." Melissa nodded, and Iris then said, "Thankfully, this battle was swift. However, the next one will not come or go so easily."

"The next one?" Melissa's dread washed away her sense of accomplishment.

"There will be another battle dragon rider, and it will not be swift."

"How did the stars tell you that?" Chad asked.

"I do not need to read the stars for that love." She gave them a gloomy smile. "The life of a dragon rider is never an easy one. Some have had minor disputes; others have had long-lasting wars. You will soon wish your dreams of this realm were never real- and that your grandfather made the right choice by keeping you away, especially since you are the Ruby fated to end all wars." With that being said, she galloped her way back to Nedjem.

Chad looked at Melissa uneasily. "Mel, promise me when I leave Florida, you will stay safe."

"I will, Chad." He kissed her.

A band of elves played wooden instruments mimicking those from Earth, like a wooden flute, a guitar, and even a harp. They played a soft tune everyone danced to. Melissa enjoyed the evening and would address Iris's bad news in the coming days.

Chad offered his hand to Melissa. "Shall we dance, my lady?" he said in a British accent.

"We shall!" she replied, continuing along.

From the corner of her eye, she noticed Alisha and Ezra dancing and giggling. "Oh my gosh, they're dancing together."

"Who?" Chad looked around.

"Alisha and Ezra! They are so cute!!"

"Yeah," he agreed. "Not as cute as us though." He swirled her, and Melissa giggled.

"I can't believe this is all real," Melissa exclaimed as she wrapped her hands around his neck. "The dreams."

"Mel, you are more than just a dream to me. You are everything I ever wanted." It all felt surreal, and Melissa couldn't grasp the idea that she was a princess of Amethyst now, that she was a dragon rider dancing with the love of her life.

Fabre danced his way over with his wife, Belinda, and said, "Enjoying de dance, eh dragon rider?"

"Yes," Melissa answered cheerfully. "Is that your wife?" The pink-cheeked, chunky dwarf nodded shyly. "Thank you so much for the rad dresses you made."

"Rad?" Fabre tilted his head in confusion.

"It means awesome," Melissa explained, but the dwarves just raised their eyebrows and danced along.

"Will we ever get used to anything here?" Melissa asked.

"Mh," Chad swirled her around. "Probably not." Dancing a few feet away from them were Emmy and Leon.

After dancing to a few upbeat songs, Melissa saw Jake laying his head through the window, watching everyone dance. He let out a puff of smoke through his nostrils, clearly bored out of his mind.

"Hey, before the night ends, I'd like to spend some time with Jake," Melissa told Chad.

"Yeah," he said, "go for it." Melissa pecked his cheek and was off to be with her dragon. Melissa felt her heels click-clack the rounded cobblestones of the outer courtyard as she click-clacked the clumsy shoes toward the double wooden doors.

"Melissa?" he lifted his head up upon seeing her. "Why are you not dancing inside?"

"I wanted to spend some time with you, maybe even take a quick flight around the castle."

Jake's face lit up with excitement as he crouched down, offering his back as a platform for Melissa to jump onto. Melissa leaped onto Jake's back with her signature smile beaming from ear to ear. As he straightened up, they soared into the sky, ascending high above the towering castle.

Chapter Thirty-Eight

Within the castle grounds, Jake flew across the forest, showing Melissa all the small villages and wooden cabins throughout the evergreen trees.

Centaurs lived in the forests with the griffins, the elves occupied wooden cabins, and the dwarves stayed in small villages near the caves.

They could see griffins through the forest and even a similar beast Melissa could not recognize. It had the body of a horse, like a centaur, but the head of an eagle.

"That's a hippogriff," Jake explained. "They are strictly wild, unlike Griffins." He crossed the forest and glided above the waters.

Melissa inhaled the sea air's salinity. The beach in Miami offered golden sand, and the sun glistened on it like a thousand tiny gems. Waves of white-tip foam crashed on the coastline; the waters were typically a soft turquoise. Without a doubt, the beaches were pristine. It's a shame someone frequently littered it with glass beer bottles and empty potato chip bags.

However, the ocean in Gemma was a rich blue, like a sapphire gem. Melissa's tongue tingled with the flavor of sea salt as the water stood still. Something was intimidating about Gemma's waters. It was dark but captivating. The sea's palpitating pulse was placid, and its sound enchanted Melissa. The beach in Miami had nothing on Gemma.

A sea serpent jumped, startling Melissa, and kept jumping out of the water to look at Jake. She grew a grin and observed the teal color of its glistening scales. A few miles off, she could make out a few islands covered in mist, and she asked Jake, "Is that Sapphire Island?"

"Yes," he turned around. "The new location where the Diamond of Dragons is kept." Jake twisted in the air and dipped below, where Melissa saw the ruins of the former lighthouse.

"Jake, take me there!" she blurted.

He flew above the ruins and landed a few feet from them. "The elves are still recovering bodies," Jake mentioned. "They already disposed of Jacob's, if that is what you are wondering."

"Why?" Melissa asked.

"They are going to make Jacob the man who kidnapped you." The thought made her wither.

The dragon landed near the ruins, and Melissa stood, observing the crumbling debris beneath her. A river of anger, sadness, and frustration flowed through her. Melissa closed her eyes and remembered every detail from her confrontation with Jacob. Her mind shifted to Victoria, how her sister, despite her tough demeanor and hardened personality, was in love with Jacob, and how they had planned a future together.

Was his love for her even real? Melissa wondered. *How did he not know who Pipo truly was?*

Her emotions erupted; she felt her tears stream down her cheeks, and she allowed her guilt to overtake her like a wave.

"I am sorry." Jake's snout touched Melissa's cheek. "I did not know how much he meant to you."

"How am I supposed to look at my sister in the face, knowing that it's my fault he's dead?"

"I am sure if she knew the circumstances, she would understand. After all, she is part of Thomas and Micah's heritage, just like you."

Jake was right, but it didn't matter at that moment to Melissa. Because Jacob was a brother to her when Victoria wasn't a sister.

At that moment, she realized she had once again lost someone she loved and felt as if a sword had pierced her heart.

She dropped to her knees and sobbed. Jake placed his head down near her and shut his eyes to allow his rider to grieve.

When Melissa finished mourning, she pulled herself together and explained to Jake why Jacob was so important to her.

"He was almost a father figure to you," Jake sighed. "I am sorry Melissa, really, I am."

"It's okay…" She dried her tears. "No, it's not okay actually, but it's going to be okay." Melissa hopped on his back, and Jake took a last look at the lighthouse before he flew off to the castle.

When they landed, Melissa slid off his wing and turned to Jake to ask him, "Does it look like I've been crying?"

"Based on your swollen, red eyes and cheeks, yes," Jake said honestly. "Why do you ask?"

"Because I don't want Chad or Emmy to know I've been crying."

"Why is that?" Melissa shrugged her shoulders.

"Melissa, dragons chose humans as riders because humans are the most emotionally complex beings in all the land. They have hearts. It is important to take care of your heart. You must learn to communicate your feelings with others, or it will destroy yours."

Melissa listened to her dragon, and she knew deep down inside he was right. She inhaled a shaky breath before responding.

"I will talk to Chad and Emmy tonight," she promised. Jake seemed pleased with the idea because he curled a smile and nudged her cheek.

"Go to sleep," he then said, "it is rather late."

"I know, but I kind of don't want to go to bed," she admitted.

"Why?"

"Because tomorrow I go home, and I'm afraid to go home. I mean, pfft, the only reason I want to go home now is because I want some café con leche." Melissa thought of the warm milk with the fresh smell of coffee brewing from it. "And hug my family," she added.

"I know tomorrow will be difficult," Jake said. "But you do need the rest." Melissa nodded and then suddenly remembered the prophecy.

"Um, when you can, come to Earth... I know it's risky, but I have to tell you something." Jake nodded, and with that being said, she wrapped her arms around Jake's neck and whispered, "I meant what I said, Jake. I love you."

"And I love you too." She pecked the tip of his snout and walked back inside the castle. She glanced at Jake before entering, and his chest elevated with pride.

Melissa lifted her chin and felt her dragon's love resonate deeply in her heart. It reminded her that her dragon chose her to be his rider when he could've chosen anyone else. She had never been the kind of girl to believe in herself. But she did at that moment.

The castle at night was eerie and darker than it was during the daytime. She strolled along the halls, observing each portrait of riders and their dragons.

Micah's portrait fascinated Melissa, not just because of their striking resemblance but because, supposedly, Micah was the most powerful being in all of Gemma. Now, Melissa was second to that.

Melissa looked at the rider's dagger she was holding and observed the four vibrant gems in the portrait that were now missing. She took the dagger from under her thigh and compared them.

With the four stones, she covered her mouth. What if this is it?

"What are you doing?" Emmy popped out and startled Melissa. "Jumpy much?"

"A little," Melissa sighed. "Is the party over yet?"

"Eh, there's still a lot of people talking and celebrating. Half of the dwarves are drunk. It's hilarious."

"How do the humans act here?" Melissa wondered.

"Dudette? We've been in Gemma for a week and a half! Please don't start talking like Alisha and the elves," Emmy said, and Melissa laughed. "They are a little off, though."

"I bet," Melissa said as they both walked back to the party. "You and Leon got it going on, girl."

"I know!" Emmy exclaimed. "Is it weird to have a boyfriend that's an elf?"

"Oh God." Melissa facepalmed herself. "Yes, it's weird!"

Emmy was right. A bunch of dwarves were still drinking their liver away and laughing loudly the way they did. Melissa searched for Chad and found him sitting down with dwarflings, telling them fairytale stories.

One girl blushed every time Chad smiled at her, and Melissa found the sight admirable. She walked towards him, and the dwarflings all gasped and muttered to one another.

Melissa smiled at them, and Chad told them, "Go ahead, ask her."

The blushing dwarf shuffled her feet and spoke low. "Is it true you fell from the sky and let the dragon catch you?"

"Yep!"

"How does it feel falling from the sky?"

"It's- it's…" Melissa searched for the right words. "It's scary but fun!" The dwarflings all chuckled and gave Melissa a hug out of enthusiasm. Melissa wasn't sure how to respond, but she embraced them with one big hug.

They ran off back to their parents, and Chad stood up, placed his hand around Melissa's waist, and said, "Back to reality tomorrow."

"Don't even talk to me about that," Melissa grunted, rolling her eyes at just the mere thought of returning home.

"Melissa, we have to," Emmy added. "We can't avoid this."

"Ugh," Melissa sighed, "I know."

"Let's go somewhere private," Emmy suggested. The couple agreed, and they walked up the stairs and into the master bedroom, where Chad immediately took advantage of the heaven-like bed.

Melissa scanned the room and gestured Emmy to come closer, cupped her ear, and whispered the entire prophecy to her. Then she told both Emmy and Chad about the gem-like image on the diesel engine, Pipo's letter, and her thoughts on the four stones.

"Why would Ezra hide the whole-?" Emmy was about to say the prophecy, but Melissa raised an index finger in a shushing manner.

"I don't know," Melissa shook her head. "We just gotta be careful around him. I think Pipo knew the wizard. Otherwise, that letter and four stones wouldn't have been on that engine," Melissa expressed. "I just wish I knew what he discovered that spooked him out so much that he had to wipe my memory clean."

"I know, it's irking me too," Emmy agreed. "But I think it had to do with the prophecy. You are the key to saving this realm." Melissa shuddered at that. "It's true, and he doesn't trust Ezra or the elves. I don't think Pipo handled the situation right, but we also have to trust him. What if his disappearance has to do with that?"

"I didn't think about that," Melissa admitted.

"I know," Emmy agreed. "Gosh, talking about Pipo is making me miss my family. We're gonna have to lie, y'know?" Emmy told the couple. "I'll be the one to talk. I'll tell them Jacob kidnapped us because he knew where we would be and he used that to his advantage and that they took us to some weird motel in Miami. They beat the crap out of Chad, they cut me and you. When Jacob left, one person stood guard, Chad beat the crap out of him, and we were able to escape."

"Why can't I believe this insane story? Jake told me we're using Jacob as the one who kidnapped us." Emmy covered her mouth with a hand and responded.

"Oh, my gosh... Now I can't believe the story!"

"Because it's not what happened, guys," Chad explained. "But we have to pull through with this story."

"Melissa, even though we all know what happened to Jacob...this is going to destroy Victoria." Melissa pressed her lips and looked down to hide her already teary eyes.

Emmy gently grabbed Melissa's hand. "I miss him too," her voice cracked, and Melissa glanced at her. "Melissa, I am so glad you didn't die from that fall. I don't think my heart could have taken losing you, too," Emmy said.

"Oh, yeah..." Melissa murmured. She felt her heart beat faster because she wanted to fulfill her promise to Jake: talk about her feelings.

"What fall?" Chad asked, and Emmy explained.

"Mel, I didn't know that happened; whoa, you're strong enough to survive that fall."

"Actually," Melissa bit her lip and finally said, "I was weak." Emmy and Chad looked at her perplexed, and she continued. "I let myself fall..."

"What do you mean you let yourself fall? Why would you do that?" Emmy questioned her; her eyebrows creased.

"Because..." Melissa's eyes watered, and her lips trembled, but the words could not break free from her lips.

"Mel," Chad held her hand and said, "talk to us."

"I..." She hesitated, took a deep breath, and croaked, "Ever since Pipo's disappearance, I have felt like I have a massive hole-" Her voice cracked. She cleared her throat before continuing, "-Hole in my heart... and I hate how empty I feel because I know I should be grateful... but I just hate the way things are in my life."

In a moment of vulnerability, Melissa extended her trembling hands, showing the visible scars that marred her palms from countless instances of digging her nails into her skin during moments of overwhelming grief and anger. Chad and Emmy gasped, their mouths dropping open in stunned silence as they stared at the raw evidence of her pain.

Melissa tucked her hands away, avoiding their worried looks, and continued talking. "I hate seeing my mom working like a slave. I hate I didn't get to have a quinces. I hate that I always get hand-me-downs. I hate I can't call Victoria a sister, and the one person I felt close to a family turned out to be the villain." She paused before finishing. "I have an amazing friend, an amazing boyfriend... and now a dragon, haha. But I still feel empty and-and lonely, and I don't know why."

As her hands shielded her face, tears streamed down her cheeks like a child feeling lost in the world. Chad wrapped his arms around her, bringing her close to his chest, as Emmy spoke through sniffs. "Melissa, hear me out. Your life is valuable, not because you're a princess or a dragon rider, but because you persist and strive for your dreams despite the hardships life has thrown at you."

"And you're always looking for the good in everyone, Mel," Chad added, and Emmy continued.

"But you're only seeing the bad in yourself. Stop being so hard on yourself. It's okay to still cry about Pipo. He was basically your dad. He wouldn't want you to feel this way. I wish you could use that love you have for others and love yourself like we love you," Emmy whimpered.

"It's true, Mel," Chad added. "You bring out the good in all of us." He opened her palms and pressed his lips on each one, and Melissa managed a weak smile.

"Thank you, guys." Melissa wiped her tears and said, "It actually felt great letting it all out."

"Of course! You were suffocating..." Emmy told her. "You're not alone. Everyone has their demons, some more than others, but that doesn't mean you can't talk to us or that it makes you less special. Bottling all of that is dangerous "

"You're right. This is the first time I've ever talked about the 'hole'." Melissa referred to the empty void.

"Maybe it's time to consider talking to your mom about it and getting some therapy," Emmy suggested.

"Therapy?" Melissa's eyes gaped.

"Yeah?" Emmy scoffed at Melissa's crazed look. "Nothing wrong with therapy."

"It's true, I went to a psychologist," Chad added, and the girls looked at him, amused by his comment. "When my parents divorced, Alex and I went to therapy to cope... you need to find healthier ways to cope with your loss."

"You're right," Melissa smiled weakly. "Ya know, I love you guys."

"Us too," Emmy reassured her.

For a moment, Melissa felt their love resonate with her, and the immovable weight of her grief didn't feel as heavy.

Her mind raced, thinking of her blissful moments with Pipo, then shifted to Emmy, Chad, Jake, and all of Gemma.

But when she thought of her mother and sister, her heart sank, and she quickly sat up. "Oh man, our parents... what's going to happen tomorrow?"

Chad shrugged, and the couple shifted their worried eyes to Emmy for a response.

"Well, let's be real here," Emmy stated. "They will not yell at us or punish us for being kidnapped."

"Emmy, you forgot that Chad's mom is in Miami... and how we lied to her and my mom."

"Oh snap," Emmy grunted. "We're screwed."

"Yeah," Chad sighed, his voice filled with weariness.

"We are." The room grew quiet as they settled in, unknowingly slipping into a deep and much-needed slumber.

Chapter Thirty-Nine

Magic woke the trio by licking them, his tail wagging energetically. "Magic, stop!" Emmy groaned, feeling exasperated at their inability to get a good night's sleep. Melissa heard Alisha giggle in response to Emmy's whining.

"Wake up, loves! It is time to go home."

Home. Melissa felt anxiety flood her body, and without realizing it, she huffed.

"Mel," Chad mumbled. "Relax."

Wide awake, he reached over and gripped her hand. Melissa interpreted that as a gesture that together, they'd get through it.

They wearily got to their feet, their party attire from the night before still clinging to their exhausted bodies. Alisha tossed them the tattered pajamas they had worn when they first left the camping site.

The once cozy sleepwear now bore evidence of the wild night they had endured, with torn fabric, bloodstains, and the unmistakable odor of sweat and body odor. Chad excused himself to find a separate room to change into his pajamas, allowing the girls to change into theirs in privacy.

Once the girls dressed, they walked outside, met with

Chad, and followed Alisha outside the castle. Jake was rolling around in the grass the way dogs do.

"Jake? Why are you doing that?" Melissa asked.

"My back itches." He sat right back up. "And it feels good." She giggled at that, and they embraced.

"Good morning," he beamed at her, Emmy, and Chad. "Ready to go home today?" They all shook their heads without thinking twice about it.

"You guys should practice your stories before anything," Alisha told them, and they all nodded.

Melissa, Chad, and Emmy diligently rehearsed their lines, attempting to piece together the narrative of their supposed abduction. Practicing the fabricated story proved to be an emotional ordeal for Melissa. Deep down, she recognized the devastating impact it would have on her mom once she learned of their alleged disappearance.

Melissa couldn't quell her curiosity about the thoughts and emotions running through her mother and sister's minds, as well as Emmy's parents and even Chad's mother. The uncertainty of their perspectives weighed heavily on her, adding to the already tangled web of emotions swirling within her.

She had forgotten how racist his mother was. Melissa felt Diana would most likely never forgive her and would hate Latinos more than ever.

"Hey," Emmy pointed at Magic. "What do we say about your dog?" Magic was walking, trying to play with Jake, who stared at the pup with his head tilted.

"We can just say they tied him up?" Chad suggested.

At that moment, Melissa knew in her heart what was the right thing to do: to leave Magic where he belonged. Her heart ached, but she spoke.

"No." Her voice trailed off. "Magic is gonna stay here with Alisha. It's where he belongs anyway."

"What?" Alisha overheard and gasped. "What are you saying?"

"Alisha, I want you to have Magic. He's happy with you, and I know you'll take good care of him." She looked at Magic while her heart shattered, but she knew she'd see him again, and he'd be in good hands with Alisha.

"I-I- I do not know what to say," she stammered.

"Thank you?" Melissa shrugged her shoulders.

"Right," Alisha was still stuck on her words. "Thank you so much."

"Well, now we can say the guys who kidnapped us killed Magic," Emmy stated, and everyone looked at her with their jaws open. "What? We gotta make the story sound real."

"We could've said he ran away?" Melissa said.

"Nah," Emmy disagreed. "Killing is better, more realistic."

By mid-afternoon, Ezra had arrived with Leon and, together with Alisha, covered Melissa, Chad, and Emmy with twigs and dirt, making them look extremely filthy.

"Alright," Ezra announced. "You officially look like someone kidnapped and tortured you."

The unicorn saliva had somewhat healed Emmy and Melissa's wounds. Still, they painfully ripped off the scab, making it look fresh. Alisha helped by cutting away Melissa's stitches from her right shoulder blade, and when she did, warm blood oozed from it.

"Ew," Emmy scoffed. "That must've hurt."

"Oh, you have no idea," Melissa replied.

"Yeah, right, this is gonna hurt more." Chad held out his arm with the stitched wound Jacob had inflicted. Alisha then preceded by cutting the stitches in it. Even with the amount of unicorn saliva Chad had consumed, the gash was still deep.

Melissa and Chad hopped on Jake, and everyone else rode on griffins and flew back to Alisha's cabin. They all stood in front of the willow tree and stared at it blankly.

"So, how do we break the spell?" Chad asked.

"Hands out, Chad and Melissa, this will sting," Alisha warned as she pulled out a small dagger. She sliced the palm of each of their hands. Chad winced, as did Melissa, while the warm blood oozed out of their palms. Alisha then encouraged Chad and Melissa to touch the tree at the same time.

At first, nothing happened, and the couple wrinkled their foreheads at each other. But then, a magical wave of energy pulsed from the tree, and Melissa felt its power. She stumbled from the impact but steadied herself and clutched onto Chad, who held her.

Alisha gasped and said, "It worked."

"You're saying that with relief," Emmy added. "Did you doubt?"

"For a moment, yes," Alisha admitted. "Through the hole in the center, it will lead you to the park, and Melissa will know the way home," Alisha explained.

"Um, what if someone sees us go through?" Emmy asked.

"They will not," Ezra promised. "Your grandfather made certain he found a tree no one would find or enter. The fairies enchanted it many years ago." Emmy watched Ezra in disbelief, and he then assured her, "Even if someone were to accidentally enter this world, we would make sure they would not remember."

They all three looked at each other uneasily until Melissa spoke. "You said there are very few portals around Earth that lead you to Gemma, right?" The elves nodded at Melissa. "Is there a possibility to build one in North Carolina for Chad to enter?"

"I am afraid not," Alisha answered. "They take years to build, and finding the ingredients is tedious since they are uncommon and often rare. I highly advise you not to go find that portal again back in your home, Chad. The Dark Forest of Garnet is a place you should never go alone. You are both very fortunate to still have your heads attached."

"It'll be okay," Chad promised, shifting his gaze to Melissa. "I'll be back and living here permanently before you know it."

Yeah, in about three years, Melissa sighed.

"Chad, it was an honor working for you. Soon, we will meet again." Ezra shook his hand, and Alisha gave him a warm hug. Jake even gave him a slight nod of approval.

He was the first one to enter the hole, and he disappeared; Emmy followed him right after.

Melissa looked back at the elves and smiled. "I'll see you guys soon," she promised and blew a kiss to Jake, who looked proudly at her like he always did.

Melissa entered the hole to find herself coming out from a tree at the park. She knew she was back on Earth just by looking at the blue skies.

"I already miss Gemma," Melissa muttered. She walked around and realized she was emerging from the hidden woods that always called to her when she sat by the lake.

She searched for Chad and Emmy, who were staring at Melissa's house. There was Emmy's parent's car and a random car Melissa assumed was Chad's mom's since it had a North Carolina plate.

They all looked at one another, hands trembling, and with much hesitation, walked to the house. People who were at the park stared at the trio strangely, and even whispered amongst each other, making Melissa awfully uncomfortable.

Do they know we're missing? Is that why they're eyeballing us so much?

They were about to cross the street when she felt her heart race, and she twirled her hair.

"Are you guys ready?" Chad asked, his voice thick with fear. "'Cause I'm not."

'Me neither," Melissa replied shakily. 'We just faced a war. Why is this so hard?"

As they crossed the street, Melissa felt the weight of her emotions pressing down on her. Her eyes burned with tears, and she could hear Emmy's steady breaths next to her. Chad, sensing the hesitation, stepped forward and offered to be the one to knock on the door. Taking a deep breath, he hesitated briefly before finally rapping on the door twice.

Chapter Forty

As the door creaked open, Melissa's mother, whose eyes appeared sunken and heavy with the weight of exhaustion, released a deafening sob. The enormous bags under her eyes spoke volumes, revealing the struggles their family faced during their disappearance.

Melissa's mother, overcome with emotion, flung her arms around Melissa, holding her in a tight embrace. The hug was so tight that Melissa felt her breath catch in her throat. It was a hug filled with love and relief.

Everyone inside rushed to see what all the commotion was about, and when they saw the teens, they all either gasped, shrieked, or wailed.

Victoria made her way through for a closer look at Melissa; she looked like she'd been to Hell and back. The sisters stared at each other. "So you're back, huh?"

"Yeah... I..." Melissa said, and Victoria wrapped her arms around Melissa's shoulders and ruffled her already messy hair.

Melissa hugged her back awkwardly and said, "Ummm... You know you're... hugging me, right?"

"Shut up, and don't get used to it. No one gets to mess with you but me," Victoria replied, hiding the tears forming in her eyes.

Emmy's parents cried upon seeing their daughter and embraced her with a hug. They spoke in Spanish and peppered her with questions.

Alex ran to his little brother and enveloped him in a hug, with Diana following. They both gasped upon seeing his bruised face.

There was a moment where everyone just hugged and shed tears together.

Melissa, Chad, and Emmy glanced at one another, and Melissa knew their minds were racing. But at that moment, being in the embrace of her tiny family gave her peace.

They had just fought a war, and staring death in the eye made them appreciate this moment.

The families took Melissa, Chad, and Emmy inside, sat them down, and prepared them warm food.

"Where have you guys been?" her mother's voice cracked, and Melissa continued to cry, unwilling to speak.

"Someone kidnapped us," Melissa hiccupped. "It-it," she sobbed, and Chad picked up where she left off.

"It was Jacob," he finished, and Victoria let out a wail.

"That's why Jacob has been missing Victoria..." Melissa's mother gasped, shifting her focus to a crying Victoria, and then gestured to Chad to continue.

"Jacob was the one who suggested we sneak out at night; he said it was time for us to live a little..." He could not look his mother directly in the face, much less her eyes. "We just wanted to see the beach at night."

"Why didn't you wake us?" Melissa's mother asked. "We would've gone with you."

"We thought you would not let us, plus we wanted it to be an adventure," Emmy replied and continued to speak. "But then we saw Jacob... and he was with some guy who pointed a gun at all of us in the middle of the beach and forced us in his car. He killed Magic in front of us as a warning." Everyone gasped, horrified at that part. "He wanted to use us for human trafficking. They had a buyer lined up for Melissa and me on a private island in the Caribbeans, and they were hoping the buyer would put them in touch with someone who wanted Chad. They cut me and Melissa, and they beat Chad up every time we tried to escape."

"Oh my god," Emmy's dad bickered in Spanish. "I will kill Jacob if I ever see him again."

"Mi amor, we need to take them to a hospital now. Look at their cuts, what if it's infected?" Emmy's mom persisted.

"We have bruises all over our bodies," Melissa revealed her back, showing them the bruises she received from all her fighting with Ezra. "We don't even know how long we've been gone. "

"How did you guys escape?" Victoria asked, hiccupping, and Chad responded.

"When Jacob stepped out, it was just that one guy keeping guard. I don't know how Melissa got her hands out of the duct tape, but she did, and she took off ours. Once we were all untied, we all ganged up on him, took some money he had on him, and took a cab here." Inside Melissa's head, she facepalmed herself.

Wow, this story sounds ridiculous.

"I am..." Melissa's mother held back her tears, "so thankful you're all alive."

Melissa sighed in relief; they bought it.

The police and paramedics arrived, and it was time to make a false report about Jacob and the imaginary suspect who kidnapped Melissa, Chad, and Emmy.

They pulled off a second white male. A bald man in his late forties claimed Jacob owed him money, possibly a drug deal of some sort since that was common in Miami.

The police asked for in-depth details that Emmy gave explicitly, and they wrote every little detail down in their notepads. They left promising that they'd find Jacob and the man, but the trio knew they would never find those men.

Melissa's mother cooked them warm soup before preparing to leave for the hospital. Chad's mother kept a serious expression that intimidated Melissa until Alex broke the silence. "Mom, let's be happy he's alive, alright?" She scoffed.

"I am beyond happy that my son is alive, but I am infuriated by how he and your father lied to me." Her voice cracked as she yelled. "Your father let you go on a trip without my consent. I told him I was taking his custody away. You've only been here less than a month, and already bad things happened! That is what happens when you go out with a filthy Latin girl. You get kidnapped as a result!"

"Don't ever call Melissa filthy," Chad stood up from his chair. "Maybe if you weren't such a racist, I wouldn't have to be lying."

Diana stared at her son, appalled. Her lips trembled, and her eyes turned manic; she slapped Chad so hard that the impact turned his face.

Everyone in the room gasped, and Melissa's mother marched towards her. "You may speak to your son that way, but not my daughter. I never want to see you or your family in my daughter's life. Get out!"

Chad's mother snatched her purse and was ready to barge out of the room. "You are never allowed to speak to her," Diana threatened Chad, and she eyed Melissa "again."

Chad glanced at Melissa, who was ready to burst into tears, and he ran to her, wrapping his arms around Melissa and kissing her goodbye.

They held onto each other, both muffling in a sob until Diana yanked Chad by the arm. Melissa attempted to reach out to him, but her mother stood between Chad and her.

"I will be back!" he yelled to her. "I am coming back for you!"

"Chad…" Melissa choked, and she broke down crying.

In the car ride to the hospital, Melissa's thoughts became a whirlwind of emotions. The image of Chad's departure replayed over and over in her mind. She found solace when she rested her head on her mother's shoulder.

Melissa's heart sank as she noticed her mother's glistening tears flowing down her cheeks in the rearview mirror. The image struck her with guilt and amplified her anxiety. It was a cruel reminder that her time in Gemma had caused her loved ones as well as herself suffering.

She imagined her sister discovering the truth about Jacob's death and played the scenario in her mind. A combination of devastation and betrayal would consume Victoria if she knew Melissa was responsible for his death.

Melissa felt the weight of these imagined scenarios bear down on her, adding fuel to her shame and regret. She carried it alone, knowing that the truth would only deepen the wounds that had already scarred their family. The fear of worsening the already broken relationship between the two sisters fueled the turmoil within her.

When Melissa arrived at the hospital, a team of doctors met her and checked her injuries. Taken aback by what they discovered—or rather, what they didn't discover: no broken ribs or symptoms of infection, and her wounds appeared to be healing despite the many bruises she wore.

Afraid of her medical case escalating, when the doctor felt her back, she feigned it hurt, even though there was no evidence of anything amiss.

Confusion flashed in their eyes as they sought to understand the remarkable speed of her recovery. They exchanged looks, murmuring questions amongst themselves, unable to find a broken bone or infected wound.

After some time, a psychiatrist approached Melissa and bombarded her with a series of questions and discussions. The medical professionals sent her home with a prescription for antibiotics to aid in the healing of her wounds, as well as anxiety medications to address any distress.

Back home, Melissa stepped into her room and noticed the missing fliers and posters scattered across her bed. Uneasiness washed over her as her eyes caught the bulletin board on one of the dull walls; someone pinned a map of the camping site with various scattered pins. She turned pale at the sight.

"What the?" she muttered, and Victoria commented behind her, causing Melissa to jump in fright.

"Sorry, haha...I um... We set up a board to figure out where you guys were at."

"Oh..."

"I'll help you clean." Melissa knitted her brows. Her sister's kindness perplexed her but she didn't protest. Together, they took down the bulletin and threw away the fliers and posters.

When they finished, Victoria spoke. "So, I um...saw your ideas listed on a piece of paper of how you wanted to decorate your room." Victoria placed her hand behind her neck. "You've always been very imaginative, like Pipo. I was thinking maybe we can buy supplies now that you're home safe again."

"I..." Melissa's lips hung low and then closed several times. She couldn't believe how kind Victoria was being. "I'd love that." Victoria gave a stiff nod and a weak smile.

Melissa walked inside her bathroom and took a much-needed long, hot shower, only to turn the heater off and let the cold water hit her instead.

She dried herself, put on a fresh set of pajamas, and stepped out. Victoria was still in her room and sitting down at the foot of Melissa's bed with puffy eyes and pink cheeks. She asked her how the shower was.

"It was nice," Melissa replied dryly and sat by the window seat to isolate herself from her sister. "Nice and cold."

"Cold?" Victoria walked to her. "After what happened, I thought you'd take a long, warm shower." She gave a soft laugh, but Melissa continued staring outside. "Pipo used to take cold showers too. He used to say it was so he wouldn't wrinkle so fast." Melissa cracked a weak smile. "Hey, I'm glad you're okay. Things weren't so good when you left, and it could've been the last time I ever saw you. I'm so tired of pushing the people I love away. First Dad, then Pipo, now Jacob." Victoria sobbed after his name flowed out of her mouth.

Guilt surged over her as the images of her stabbing Jacob played in her head. Melissa gulped; her eyes created little pools, but she rushed to her sister, wrapping her arms around her, and they both wept together.

I should tell her the truth. Melissa debated doing so and thought of all the scenarios that could happen if she did. *Would she forgive me and believe me? Would she say I'm delusional? Maybe it'll just push her away from me more... It's best if I don't say anything.*

Victoria let her go, and Melissa saw the sorrow and grief holding over her head that consumed her eyes, which Melissa knew so well, and that was what convinced her it was best not to tell her.

Melissa's mother then walked in and saw the girls, and Melissa knew it warmed her mom to see her daughters embrace.

But then she cleared her throat and said, "Victoria, can you give me a moment with Melissa?" Victoria nodded and walked out of the room.

"How do you feel?" her mother asked.

"Okay," she replied as her mother sat on the edge of the bed. Then she remembered the words of her friend and boyfriend about therapy. "Mommy, I'm not okay."

"I know, honey. Did you drink the medications?"

"Yes," Melissa sighed gloomily, "but that's not why I'm not okay." Her mother tilted her head, confused, and Melissa spoke.

It was difficult at first. The words stumbled and bounced on her tongue as she told her mother about her ongoing depression and grief. But she said all she had to say.

Even though Melissa was anxious about what her mom had to say, she definitely didn't expect her to say what she said.

"Mija... I am so sorry. I didn't know you were feeling this much pain." Her mother released a stream of tears from her eyes as she spoke. "I failed you as a mother," she covered her face with a hand.

Melissa quickly placed her hand on her mother's free hand and spoke, her voice cracking. "I don't blame you. I didn't want to burden you."

"You and Victoria are never a burden to me, mi niña linda." My beautiful girl. "No matter the cost, I will take you to therapy, and together, we will heal as a family. All of us. I miss Pipo too... every day."

"I do, too," Melissa cracked a smile. The mother and daughter embraced in a tight hug. For the first time in a long time, the empty void that had conquered Melissa for the past three years no longer felt as empty. She knew healing was coming, which gave her a sense of relief.

When her mother relinquished her hold, she took a deep breath and said, "Mijita, I didn't want to do this, but you lied about Chad being here. You lied this entire time to me." Her mother choked back a sob. "You realize his father can lose his visitation and custody privileges now?" Melissa bit her lip and held her tears back. "This is serious! What if he killed you guys?"

"I know!" Melissa popped and let her tears stream down. "I didn't mean for this to happen. You think I knew Jacob would do that? I'm so sorry for sneaking out... I'm so, so sorry," she repeated.

"I know," her mother sighed. "I guess you really don't know a person... You do not know how it's been this last week and a half. Your Uncle and Aunt had to pour all the savings they had for an in vitro to a private PI."

The mere thought of Uncle Rudy and Aunt Nina pouring their money into a PI felt like a goblin stabbing her heart. *No, that money was for a potential pregnancy.* Her eyes brimmed with tears, and her mother continued speaking.

"I never want to hear from that stupid boy again."

"Wait, what?" Melissa's head bounced back. "What did Chad do? It was my idea to sneak out..."

"Yes, but you would not have done something stupid like that if it wasn't for the influence of a boy," her mother said bluntly. "Look, I get he's your first boy crush, and you guys got away with murder and had fun together, but he's a reckless teenage boy, and I can never forget what happened. I'm warning you now; I never want to see or hear from him again." Her mother gave Melissa a forced kiss on the forehead. "You're grounded for a very, very, long time. No computer, no phone usage, no more sleepovers with Emmy until I say so, and absolutely no Chad. I don't even want to hear his name in this house."

"Home sweet home," Melissa muttered.

Her mother walked out of the room, and Melissa continued looking out of the window. Her eyes searched the dark skies, and her mind flickered with memories of the lighthouse tumbling down. She blinked hard and then looked at her nightstand, avoiding the outside.

She immediately noticed a new walkie-talkie with a sticky note on it. She stood up from her spot and grabbed the walkie-talkie.

The note read, "Hey Melissa, I hope you come back home soon. I need someone to do my homework when we start high school. I miss you. If you come back, don't tell anyone I wrote this and got you a new walkie-talkie. Over and out."

A smile crept onto Melissa's face, and she pressed the button and said, "Melissa here, over and out." The static noise rang, and Melissa placed her hand over the speaker to mute it out. She sighed, disappointed no one answered, and then placed the walkie-talkie back.

But then a voice spoke. "Melissa? Is it really you?"

Melissa snatched the walkie-talkie again and replied. "Mia, yeah, it's me."

"Oh my gosh! Are you okay?"

"Yeah." Melissa recapped the entire story to Mia in a hushed voice.

"That is such an insane story... everyone will remember you as the girls that were kidnapped!" Mia commented and then continued. "Whatever, I'm glad you're okay."

"Thank you... and thanks for the walkie-talkie," Melissa told her. "I actually needed a new one."

"Yeah, yeah... We'll talk more tomorrow; I'm sure you need the rest. Maybe Emmy can join in on the call since I got her a walkie-talkie, too." The idea of Mia being part of her friendship with Emmy warmed her.

"Sounds like a plan, bye Mia. Melissa, over and out."

"Over and out," Mia said.

Melissa smiled to herself and yawned deeply; she stood up, sleepily shuffled to her bed, and laid down, allowing her eyes to become heavy and sleep to overtake her.

Her dragon ring vibrated, waking Melissa up from her deep sleep at four in the morning. Confused why Jake was calling her, she rolled out of bed and looked out the window. To her astonishment, she could see Jake's long neck and head from behind the little hills at the park.

She snuck out through her window and strolled towards the park to meet Jake. Seeing him brought her pure joy, and she wrapped her arms around his neck, and he gave her a cute nudge with his snout.

Suddenly, all that drama that had happened washed away when she met his piercing black eyes.

"Jake, someone could see you!" she hissed at him.

"Well, you said you wanted to tell me something outside of Gemma. And I wanted to see you. I can feel your sorrow amplified, and I was worried. How was your first day back on Earth?" he asked, and Melissa recounted the entire story dreadfully. "I am sorry about Chad."

"Me too," she said. "I know we'll be together again."

"Well, at least for the next few years, you are all mine."

Melissa chuckled and responded, "Jelly much?"

"Jelly?" he tilted his head in confusion.

"It's kind of supposed to mean jealous-err it won't make sense to you. Anyway, Jake, I know you're mad at Pipo." Jake grumbled. "But Emmy mentioned something worth noting. I think Pipo's disappearance has to do with the prophecy and whatever he discovered. I know we lost time that we'll never get back, but Ezra is also hiding something from us, Jake." Melissa recapped the entire prophecy to her dragon.

Jake stood motionless and even avoided her gaze until he spat out. "Why wouldn't he disclose the entire prophecy to us? We are the dragon and rider destined to fulfill the prophecy; we should know about it."

"I agree, and right now, our next quest should be to find the wizard and not tell the elves about it."

"Agreed." Jake nudged her cheek softly with his snout. "As of right now, I trust no one but you, Melissa. We will find the wizard together. Maybe he or she will have the answers to your grandfather's disappearance."

With that being said, Jake and Melissa quietly sat and gazed upon the stars.

"Ugh, the stars in Gemma are so much better," Melissa groaned

"Let us take a flight there," he curled a sly smile. "Come on, you will be back on time." Melissa giggled and hopped on him.

He shot into the sky and sped his way towards the beach of Miami and to the Bermuda Triangle, where he dived into the waters, only to come back up into the realm where thousands upon thousands of stars peppered the amethyst color sky.

Melissa stretched her arms wide open and let the wind brush her hair. Jake swooped down and made a massive loop as Melissa shouted, "WHOO!"

Together, they rode on, ready to face whatever challenges the future lay ahead.

Acknowledgements

The story of *Dream into Amethyst* would not have been possible without the unwavering love and support I've received throughout this journey. I'm deeply grateful to God for inspiring this dream and for giving me the strength to bring it to life.

The first person I want to thank is Noah Jenkins, along with his wife, Casey. Noah, for being the first individuals to read *Dream into Amethyst*. You both gave me constructive criticism, which, at the time, I didn't fully appreciate. Now, looking back, I see that without your honest feedback, my story wouldn't have been able to stand. Melissa Paz-Guerra came to life because of you. Your support means everything to me. I will forever be indebted to you for reading the earliest draft of *Dream into Amethyst* and for enduring countless re-reads of several drafts. Your feedback and ideas helped me blossom in my journey. You and Casey played a significant role in making me the writer I am today, and I wish there were more words I could write to express my eternal gratitude.

To my mom, you will always be my inspiring hero. I am who I am today because I watched you survive and thrive for your daughters. You learned to stand on your own two feet despite the adversities you faced. Thank you for believing in me and for never discouraging my creative mind.

To my best friend, Debora Flores, you believed in me even when I didn't believe in myself. Your drive, passion, and energy fueled me to keep going, even during moments when I was ready to throw in the towel. This story and this dream would not have come true without you cheering me on.

To my best friend, Natalie Perez, you, too, believed in me. You always encouraged me to live wildly and freely.

Nothing ever stopped you from doing what you wanted, so I will do the same.

To my best friend, Jennifer Matus, thank you for cheering me on and providing unwavering support. You always knew I was a writer and that I'd become an author someday.

To my family, though tiny but mighty, my uncle and aunt, Rolando and Nelly De Armas; my uncle Jesus De Armas; and my cousin, Jasiel De Armas—thank you for believing in me and supporting me throughout my life.

To my Mima, who didn't get the chance to see me become the author I am now, you saw me typing endlessly and hoped my dreams would come true.

To my friends—Crystal, Bryanna, Aileen, and Becky—thank you for always asking me questions about the book and making me feel my dreams were within reach.

To the #Unbreakable—Stacey, Shelley, and Michele—thank you for being inspiring and powerful women in my life.

To Michael Stephens, thank you for manifesting that I'd be an author one day and truly believing it.

To Ernesto Sanabria, one of my earliest beta readers, without your feedback, I might have given up.

To Giselle Flores, thank you for always listening to my ideas and asking questions that filled me with excitement and curiosity.

To Vanessa Solis, thank you for helping me with the final touches of *Dream into Amethyst*.

To my students who read my book as beta readers, thank you for reading *Dream into Amethyst* and providing me with honest feedback.

To my publisher, Line by Lion Publications, thank you

for changing my life with a phone call. I'm honored to work with you.

Finally, to you, reader, thank you for reading *Dream into Amethyst*. I am beyond blessed to have you as fans.